Cassandra Parkin grew up in Hull, and now lives in East Yorkshire. Her debut novel *The Summer We All Ran Away* was published by Legend Press in 2013 and was shortlisted for the Amazon Rising Star Award. Her short story collection, *New World Fairy Tales* (Salt Publishing, 2011) was the winner of the 2011 Scott Prize for Short Stories. *The Beach Hut* was published in 2015, *Lily's House* in 2016 and *The Winter's Child* in 2017. Cassandra's work has been published in numerous magazines and anthologies.

Visit Cassandra at
cassandraparkin.wordpress.com
or follow her
@cassandrajaneuk

For my husband, Tony
Who took me to the right place at the right time,
and gave me the space to do the right thing

Cassandra
Parkin

Underwater Breathing

Legend Press Ltd, 107-111 Fleet Street, London EC4A 2AB
info@legend-paperbooks.co.uk | www.legendpress.co.uk

Contents © Cassandra Parkin 2018

Print ISBN 978-1-7871984-0-1
Ebook ISBN 978-17871983-9-5
Set in Times. Printing managed by Jellyfish Solutions Ltd
Cover design by Anna Green | www.siulendesign.com

Chapter One
2008

Jacob floated still and suspended beneath the surface of the water, his ears filled with the slow hissing swirl of blood and water spiralling on either side of his eardrums. If he opened his eyes, he would look up through warm water to the roses and cherubs that clung sightlessly to the ceiling above his head, occasionally dropping crumbs onto his hair and shoulders as he and Ella shivered in the draught from the badly-fitting window; but Jacob found it easier to concentrate with his eyes closed, his focus turned inwards.

His toes were clenched tight. He forced them to relax. His fingers were claws. He let them unfold. The dripping tap made the water tremble. He told himself not to think about it. His ears were filled with water, but the sounds of the house still came to him in waves. The rattle of the window as the wind kissed it. The sound of their parents' voices, their mother's piercing descant rising over the angry bass mutter of their father as they argued in the never-used morning-room, which he'd privately re-christened The Arguing Room because of his parents' persistent delusion that they couldn't be heard while they were in there. His little sister Ella, steadily counting. How was he doing? What number had she reached? Was she distracted enough from the chaos unfolding in the room below? And had he beaten the record yet?

As soon as he thought of the record, he knew he'd made a mistake. The idea of winning ignited in his brain a great surge of hope and excitement, racing down his spinal cord and out into his limbs, waking up nerves and muscles, burning through his reserves, and then he heard something that sounded like smashing, either in the house or out of it, and he knew it was all over and he couldn't stay under any more. With a gigantic whoosh he flung himself upright, grabbing onto the sides of the bath as he gulped down air like water.

"How did I do?" he asked, between breaths.

Ella was tightly cocooned in the towel he'd wrapped around her, to cover the places her swimming costume left exposed to the cold air. When they'd first played this game, she'd been happy enough to hop into the bath naked, but since her seventh birthday she'd insisted on a costume. ("You always wear one," she told him, "so now I should wear one too.") Her feet – once so pudgy and squeezable, now slender and vulnerable – were lifted onto the toilet seat to save them from the chill of the cracked black-and-white tiles. "Four minutes and forty-nine seconds."

"Really? I thought I'd managed at least five minutes."

"Maybe I counted wrong."

Now he was free of the warm imprisonment of the bathwater, the air laid a cold mouth against his skin, sucking away the warmth. Earlier that day he had fantasised about getting into a cold bath of water and never getting out again, soaking the humid stickiness from his skin for ever, but the storm had stolen all the heat from the air. ("That bathroom's too big for the house," their mother frequently said, a mysterious phrase which was sometimes followed up with "and this whole house is too big for us.") Jacob could see what she meant about the house – surely no modern family could possibly need six bedrooms, two large bathrooms, two staircases and all the half-empty rooms downstairs – but the too-big bathroom still baffled him. Perhaps what she meant was "it's too big to keep warm and dry," which was definitely true. Especially when the storms blew in like raiders across the North Sea, driving salty rain against the windows and taking giant bites out of the crumbling mud cliffs that crept closer to their house with each assault. He wrapped a towel around his shoulders and dropped another onto the floor to stand on.

"We'll be in trouble for using all the towels," said Ella.

"I'll be in trouble. They won't shout at you. Maybe we can dry them before they notice."

"And I'm sorry about your phone. Now we can't time ourselves properly any more."

He was sorry about his phone too, but there was no point telling her off again. The noises below were growing louder. Despite the distance of three rooms separating them, some mysterious confluence of pipes and walls and conductivity meant that whole sentences occasionally flung themselves into the room like stones. Ella seemed oblivious, but how long could that last?

("You can keep me shut up here, I can't stop you doing that, but I'm allowed to bloody well *write*, you unutterable bastard!")

("Then write about something that doesn't upset you so much!")

"Forget about my phone," he told her.

"I can ask for one for Christmas and give it to you."

"Stop going on, it's annoying. Are you getting in or what?"

Still clutching her towel around her, Ella shuffled over to the bath.

"Maybe we should lie face down? That's how the world record holders do it?"

"Don't you dare."

"You did it once."

"Yes, and it made you cry because you thought I was dead."

"But I'm older now, I know better. And I never last as long as you do, I need something to make it more fair."

7

"Not a chance. What if you start drowning and I don't realise?"

"But –"

"Not happening. Or I'll pick you up and carry you out and we'll never do it again, you hear me?"

He could see Ella wanted to press her point further – even at seven years old, there was a streak of stubbornness in her that would soon be a match for his sixteen-year-old strength – but his approval still meant a lot to her. Or maybe there was just enough anger in their house already. Ella shed her towel; he lifted her into the bath. She hurried beneath the surface to escape the tendrils of cold air creeping around the window-frame.

"Are you ready?"

"Ready."

Shrouded in towels, his feet already aching with cold, Jacob watched his little sister's face sink below the water. He began the count.

One. Two. Three. Four. Five.

Which storm was it most important to shield Ella from? The one raging in the morning-room below, where their mother and father tore into each other with the weary expertise of seasoned gladiators? Or the one driving the sea into a frenzy, raising towering cliffs of water that threw themselves against the soft mud and raced back to the ocean bed with chunks of land clutched tight within the heart of the waves? (*Fifteen. Sixteen. Seventeen. Eighteen. Nineteen.*) That dream she'd described to him when they first came here, their house falling and the water taking them. And his ridiculous promise, *we'll learn to hold our breaths underwater and then we'll be fine even if the sea does come.*

("You're a bastard. Do you hear me? An absolute bastard…")

Twenty-three. Twenty-four. Twenty-five. Getting the pitch and tone of the count right was tricky. Count too loudly and the echo-chamber effect working in reverse would summon their parents upstairs. Count too quietly and he risked losing his thread among the strangeness of sitting in this cold, badly-lit tower-room, looking out to a boiling sea that edged closer with every storm. Living in this house was like making a wager with the water. *Bet we can grow up and escape before you can eat your way through the cliffs. Bet you we'll be gone before you get here. Bet you're not strong enough.*

("He's still looking, Richard, he'll always be bloody looking! And the amount you drink, you'd never see him coming…")

Ella's face was still and blank like a mannequin, the planes of her face just beginning to sculpt into the beauty that belonged to their mother, and that would one day surely be hers. When Ella was smaller, they'd climb in together and lie down at opposite ends of the bath, her small body crammed into the triangle of space beside his legs. Now, despite the giant-sized bath left behind by the madman who built this house, they could only fit one at a time. But that was okay. He was happier when he could watch over her as she lay beneath the water. *Forty-eight. Forty-nine. Fifty.*

("Of course I bloody well drink, who wouldn't drink if they had to live with someone like you?")

One and seven. One and eight. One and nine. One and –

The rumble that shuddered up through the house's bones was strong and lasting enough to be mistaken for an earthquake. Ella bolted upright, brushing frantically at her hair and face as the cherubs sent down a shower of white dust and spider webs. The window jumped and juddered in its frame, and Jacob held his breath, waiting to see if the glass would break. If the pane gave way, that would be the end of the game. The bath at the other end of the house, which they were supposed to use, was too small for even Ella to lie full-length in. But the glass held, and the frantic panicky movements of wood against wood subsided into the usual fretful rattling, and they both let go the breaths they'd been holding.

"That was loud," he said, forcing himself to smile. Ella's answering smile was small and careful.

9

"How long did I manage? That wasn't a proper go, was it? Can I get my breath back and try again?"

"Maybe, but it's getting late –"

"Kids! Kids!" Their father's voice, booming up the thin steep staircase that had felt like luxury when they first moved there. ("It's a servants' staircase," their mother had laughed, "we're going to live in a house with a servants' staircase! How about that?") "Kids! Are you okay?"

"We're fine!" Ella shouted back, before Jacob could shush her. "What? What's the matter?"

"Now he'll know where we are – oh, never *mind*, there's no point getting upset now."

"Are you up in that bathroom again? How many more times do I have to tell you, use the *other* one. How about you, Jacob? Are you up there with Ella?"

"Yes. We're fine, everything's fine, Ella's not scared or anything, don't worry, we're fine –"

They could hear their father's tread in the corridor now, and the creak of floorboards as he grew nearer. His breathing was heavy. Was their mother there too? "Come out here where I can talk to you."

Because there was no point doing anything else, Jacob lifted Ella out of the bath, wrapped a towel around her shoulders, took a deep breath, and opened the door. He knew the underwater-breathing ritual made their parents angry and upset. He still didn't understand why – any more than his parents could understand why they both felt so compelled, in the face of all the ferocious tellings-off and punishments they'd received, to keep doing it – but he knew what was coming next. Their parents, united for once. Their father, red-faced and powerful, his breath sprayed with whiskey. Their mother like a one-woman Greek chorus, joining in with the most important parts. He felt Ella's little hand slip inside his and squeeze his thumb.

"Right," their father said, and Jacob felt the first stirrings of uneasy surprise, because their father was alone. "There's a chunk of cliff gone again. Your mother's gone out for a bit, to look at the damage from the storm, so I need to go after her and… and look after her, make sure she's… make sure –" His breathing was heavy, as if he'd run up the stairs, as if he'd run for miles. "So you both stay inside, you hear me? Stay inside. Do not go out of the house. It's pissing with rain –"

The word shot through Jacob like electricity. Their father never, ever, ever cursed in front of them.

" – and you'll catch your death of cold. Understand?"

Did he understand? There was something mysterious here, something in the look on his father's face and the sound of his breathing, and the air that was chilled with more than Nordic winds and driving rain. He was glad for the feeling of Ella's hand still tucked inside his like a nut in a shell. His father shook his head in despair.

"God almighty, the pair of you… Get to your rooms, you hear me? And not another peep out of you tonight, or you'll know about it. Right, I'm going to find my boots, I might be out for a while."

Baffled and breathless, Jacob watched his father's lumbering shape disappear down the narrow staircase.

"Did we not get in trouble?" Ella whispered at last.

"Maybe. Or maybe he's just saving it up for later."

"Or maybe he didn't notice we were wearing our costumes." Ella nibbled at her thumbnail and grimaced. Their mother was forever painting her nails with aloe to try and stop her, but her fingers remained gnawed and raggedy. "Where's Mum? Why wasn't she with him?"

"She's gone out to look at the storm."

"But where is she? Should we look out of the window?"

"We can look out of the window if you like, but don't be surprised if you can't see anything, it's pitch-black out there."

Ella hopped back into the bathroom to press her nose against the window. Outside was no more than a wall of driving raindrops in an ocean of black. Jacob sighed.

"Wait a minute, I'll put the light out."

"No, don't, I don't like it in here when the light's out!"

"You can't be scared, I'll be here."

The darkness flooded in. Ella squeaked, but waited by the window for him to join her so she could grab onto his hand again. After a minute, the night began to resolve itself into a murky series of shadows, in which shapes moved that could be their mother and father, or the bushes and trees bending before the power of the wind.

"Where are they? I can't see them, I can't see anyone." He could feel Ella shivering. "Where are they? What if they've gone over the cliff?"

"Of course they haven't gone over the bloody –" he forced his voice lower and softer. "They're fine, you dipstick. They'll be out there somewhere, don't worry." His gaze snagged on a long finger of light that stretched briefly back towards them before turning outwards across the garden. "Look over there. That's a torch. That must be them."

"Where? Where?" Ella's fingers on his hand were tight enough to be painful. "Is that both of them? I can only see Dad. What's he doing? Why's he going so slowly?"

Their father's huge wavering shape was bent double as he strove against the weight of wind pushing him back. Was their mother with him? It was impossible to say. Ella's teeth had begun to chatter. "I think Mum's there too. Yes, I can see her. There beside him, look. See?"

"I can't see her. What if she's not there? What if she's lost?"

"She's not lost, she's right there with him." Their father's progress was painfully slow, but he was almost sure now he could see a second shape with him. They were close together, leaning on each other for support. He was surprised by how happy that sight made him. "Come on, it's time for bed."

"Just another few minutes. Oh!" She grabbed his arm. "Is that another light? Is it? Is it Mrs Armitage's house? Has she put the light on for us?"

The rain made everything uncertain. He cupped his hands around his eyes to form a tunnel to peer into the night. For a moment he saw another brief gleam, wavering as if the person holding it was struggling to stay upright.

"No, it can't be her house, it's moving around. Maybe it's Mum with her own torch."

"But you said you could see her with Dad, isn't she with Dad?"

"Well, then it must be Mrs Armitage then. She might be out looking at the damage as well."

"Or maybe she's gone diving."

"She'd never get the boat out in this weather."

"She goes diving when it's rough sometimes," Ella said, pressing her cold little nose against the window. "She says when you get below the surface everything turns quiet and calm."

Jacob thought of Mrs Armitage, slick in her black scuba suit, striding out across the cliffs as if they belonged only to her. The first time they'd met her, Ella had been terrified.

"Or maybe," said Ella through shivering lips, "maybe that was her house. That noise, I mean. Maybe it was her house falling into the sea."

"No, of course it wasn't."

"But it might have been. It's closer to the edge than ours."

"Look, it wasn't Mrs Armitage's house. Mrs Armitage is fine, Mum and Dad are fine, we're fine. Now it's time to go to bed."

"But should we wait and see –"

"Stop arguing. Bed."

"Will you carry me?"

"No! You're too heavy." Ella's face crumpled. "Oh all *right* then, but no more messing around, okay?"

When he lifted her, her towel unravelled and fell to the floor, shortly followed by the one around his own shoulders. The draught from the rattling window was like a cold mouth moving over his bare skin. With his sister in his arms, he staggered awkwardly down the corridor to the relative warmth of her bedroom, where a plug-in oil-filled radiator created a small unmoving patch of dry air and her discarded pyjamas lay like a shucked pink skin at the end of her bed.

"Come on then. Cossie off. Pyjamas on."

"I don't want to, I'll sleep in my costume…"

"No you won't, it's soaking wet. You can't get into bed in wet clothes. Hurry up."

She looked up at him hopefully. "Can you take it off for me?"

At moments like this, when she tried to take them both back into the years when she was small enough to pick up and put down at will like a downy little pet and he was her hero, he both loved and resented her. Resented her because he was a boy of sixteen and he was cold too and he didn't want to be responsible for her, he only wanted to go back to his own room and shut the door and pretend everything was fine in his family, and their house wasn't too big and too old and their parents were downstairs watching a box-set and the storm wasn't bringing the North Sea ever closer to their back doorstep and when he woke the next morning it would be to a bright and ordinary day. Loved her because he couldn't help but love her. He sighed, knelt down and peeled the costume from her shoulders and torso in a single brutal movement like tearing off a plaster.

"There. Now get your pyjamas on. And your socks and dressing gown. And then get into bed."

"Can you read me a story?"

"God, can you let me go and get warm first, please! Okay, yes, I'll read you a story, but only if you're in bed when I come back."

He closed the door on her quivering lip and retreated to his own room to shiver into his nightwear. He'd thought he wouldn't need this again until winter, but the storm had stolen all the heat from the air. Long-sleeved pyjamas, thick dressing gowns, socks and slippers, clothes for children from old-fashioned storybooks to go with their old-fashioned storybook house. He thought again of Mrs Armitage in her scuba suit, of her body disappearing beneath the waves to find the quiet places beneath the churning brown water. When the waters closed over her head, did it feel warmer than the air?

Somewhere downstairs, a door banged in the wind – once, twice, three times. Was that his parents coming home? Was it really possible his father hadn't noticed that he and Ella were dressed in their swimming costumes? Perhaps if he was quick enough he might get the bathroom cleared up before they saw any evidence. Or were his parents already on their way upstairs? He listened hard, but the house remained silent. His feet slithery because of the slippers, he hurried down the corridor to the bathroom.

A few minutes of frantic effort, and the evidence of their crime was as gone as it was going to be that night. The bath was drained and empty, the pools of water mopped from the floor, except for the one by the window which was not bathwater but rainwater, and which he left as a small reproach to his parents for complaining about the water they spilled from the bath when the house itself was so far from weatherproof. (As he thought this, the downstairs door began banging again.) He stole the clothes-horse from the junk-room, set it up in his room by the radiator and hung the towels out to dry. He hid their wet costumes at the back of the airing cupboard behind the boiler, then opened Ella's door a cautious half-inch. Perhaps she'd have drifted off to sleep and he would be free? He peered in. Ella was cocooned in the heavy duvet, but her eyes were wide open and her gaze was fixed on the door.

"Do you want some hot milk?" he asked her, to make up for being cross earlier.

"Yes please."

"Hang on then."

The kitchen was like a freezer with a gale blowing through it and the back door threw itself back and forth as if it was trying to beat its own brains out against the wall. After a few attempts, he caught it and forced it to shut. Their father must have left it open when he went out. How long had their parents been out there now? He poured milk into two mugs and put them in the microwave. He despised the taste of hot milk, but it would give him something warm to hold while he read to Ella. Please let her not pick one of the Rainbow Fairy books. The back door rattled and tried to break free. He gave it a kick as punishment.

Back up the stairs to Ella's room, where Ella was growing sleepy beneath the duvet. When she saw him she reached out a warm little hand and took hold of his arm, trying to draw it under her chin.

"Hang on, let me put the milk down first." He balanced the mugs on the drawers by her bedside, orange pine and as ugly as sin. They were supposed to contain her socks and knickers, but she'd filled them with an assortment of dried-up felt-tip pens, empty Kinder Eggs and plastic giveaway gifts from the fronts of magazines. "Right, what am I reading you?"

"Can you sleep here with me tonight?"

"No I can't, there's no room. Am I reading you a story or what?" Ella held up something thin and mauve and glittery, watching his face to see if she was pushing her luck too far. "Oh come on, no, I'm not reading that, forget it. Right, I'm picking." Rummaging through the pile of books, he found the Ladybird *King Arthur* he'd inherited from his father and loved fiercely for years. "We'll have this one."

"I don't like that one, it's silly."

"It is not silly. Why is it silly?"

"Because the sister, the one who can do magic I mean. What's she called again?"

"Morgan le Fay?"

"Yes, Morgan le Fay. She says her son is the King's son. But he can't be, because the king's her brother. So why does she even say it?"

"Never mind that. Look, it's this one or nothing, so which is it going to be?"

"Can I hold your arm while you read?"

"As long as you let me have it back when we've finished."

Crammed awkwardly into the spaces where his little sister wasn't, Jacob propped himself up with the pillow and began to read. Ella yawned widely, exposing the clean pink of her mouth and tongue, and snuggled against his arm. He could smell the cooling milk on the bedside table. Ella began to twitch and fidget, a sure sign she was about to fall asleep. He made his voice as low and boring as he could. Ella's eyelids fluttered shut, then open, then shut again. Her breathing grew slow and heavy. He shut the book, watching her carefully to see if she would wake when his voice stopped. She sighed, muttered something and squeezed his arm tight. He waited a minute longer, then slid off the bed and pulled his arm out from Ella's sleeping grip. His little sister was asleep. He was free.

The storm was beginning to blow itself out at last. The rattle of the windows was gentler, and the rain on the glass no longer sounded like handfuls of flung gravel. His room was foggy from the drying towels and his bed was cold, but at least he was alone now, his responsibilities over for another day.

Just another two years and he would be entirely free. What would happen when he left home? Did Ella have any idea how close he was to escape? Did she even realise yet that such a thing was possible? Her whole universe was contained in the brown sea, the frowning sky, the flat fertile fields, the sunshine that lit up the landscape like a torch and turned everything briefly beautiful. When he left, would it be enough for her?

Never mind. As much as he loved Ella, she was his mother and father's responsibility, not his, and they'd surely be back soon. It was strange that they weren't back already. Perhaps he should go out and look for them. But that would mean leaving Ella in the house on her own, and besides, he was finally growing warm now, the heat from his body spreading out in the bed so that he no longer had to lie rigid and unmoving for fear of touching a chilly patch. He'd done enough for today. He was allowed to go to sleep and let his parents take over.

And as he had this thought, he heard the kitchen door opening and closing, and footsteps clattering into the house. So they were safe and well, and not at the bottom of a cliff. It was a good thing he hadn't gone out to look for them, they'd have killed him if they found he'd left Ella alone…

Later, his sleep was dimly broken by small sounds that told him his parents had not yet found their own rest. Footsteps in the corridor outside. A door opening; a small whimper of protest from Ella. *They must be checking she's asleep,* he thought blearily, and then, as Ella's voice, made young and soft with sleep, came to him through the wall, he thought, *just let her sleep, will you? I've done all the hard part for you.* The sound of footsteps retreating again, heavier and slower this time. Silence. And the peace that came from being in one of the few warm spots in a cold world.

I should go and make sure she's okay, he thought. *Sometimes they wake her up and she doesn't go back to sleep because she's scared.* But he was finally warm, and Ella was seven years old and it was time she learned to settle herself, and in the end he closed his eyes and let sleep reclaim him.

In the years that came after, he wondered what might have happened if he'd done everything differently that night. If he'd gone out into the storm to search for his parents. If he had given in to Ella's request and slept in her bed instead of his own. If he'd got up to check she wasn't lying awake and petrified, staring into the dark. But when he woke the next morning to the sight of his father looming over him, pale and gaunt and reeking of alcohol, a dreadful artificial smile stretched out across his face like scar tissue, his first thought was simple resentment. *I wish you wouldn't come into my room when I'm sleeping,* he thought. *I wish you'd stop coming into our rooms and frightening us like that.*

I've been thinking lately about becoming someone else. I haven't decided quite who I might become yet, but whoever she turns out to be, she will be someone quite different from me. She will be small where I am tall. She will be sturdy. Not fat, but stocky like a farmer's wife, where I am waify and lanky and underfed, like a weed grown in the dark. Apparently, I am beautiful. So, when I become whoever it is that I am going to turn into, I will have to stop being beautiful.

The woman I am going to become will be cold and strong where I am warm and feeble. It's too easy for someone to charm their way into my bed. I like it too much when they're there. But when I put on my new skin, no one will ever come near me in that way again, and I will no longer crave it because I will have learned at last how dangerous love is. I will love nobody and nobody will love me. I think perhaps that will be better for everyone.

The hardest part, I think: she will be someone who can leave behind people who she cares for, and who care for her. She will be completely free.

Chapter Two
2007

On the third morning in their house at the end of the world, Jacob woke to sunshine and silence and a sky that stretched out and out like a flat blue sheet.

He lay in bed for a few minutes, listening to the small sounds of the house as it moved and settled. He was still learning the personality of this new home. The warm places and the draughty ones. The spots where you could walk freely and the ones where the boards would shriek like mandrakes. The welcoming rooms and the ones that brimmed with darkness. After so many years of smallness and making do, the emptiness and light made him feel as if the top of his head might come off.

So far, this house seemed worn but welcoming, the way he imagined it would feel to visit grandparents. He wondered if the house knew it was destined to fall into the sea eventually, or if it believed it would stand for ever, as solid and permanent as the day it was first built. In the corridor outside, a small sound like a mouse told him Ella was there. After a minute, the door moved slightly and half of her face peered cautiously in.

"It's too early," he told her, not because it was too early but because he wanted her to start learning that it wasn't okay to come into his room without being asked. Then, because her face looked so resigned and sad as she turned away, he added, "but you can come in anyway. As long as you don't fidget."

A scurry of feet and a glad little hop and his bed was full of Ella, smelling of clean childish sweat and strawberry shampoo. At six, she was getting too big to do this; her sharp little toes scratched against his leg as she wriggled beneath the covers. He'd been exactly the right temperature when he woke up, but with Ella beside him the bed was like a superheated prison. He'd have to get up soon.

"Do you like our new house?" he asked. To his surprise, she immediately shook her head. "You don't? Seriously? Why not?" She whispered something, but he couldn't make it out. "Don't whisper, I can't understand you. Talk to me properly." She looked at him silently. "Fine, don't talk to me properly, that's up to you. Come on. It's breakfast time."

His room and Ella's were at one end of a short corridor that terminated in a rounded turret. When they first looked at the house, he'd seen the turret from the outside and hoped it might be his bedroom. As it turned out, the turret room was a cavernous bathroom that his parents had instantly told them both they were never to use – a rule Jacob took great secret pleasure in ignoring. He shut the bathroom door on Ella's hopeful face. He wasn't going to have her watching him pee. When he opened the door again, her expression reminded him of a dog waiting for its owner.

"I waited for you," she said, and took his hand confidingly.

"You did."

"Are we going downstairs now?"

"We are."

"Shall we have breakfast now?"

"Yes."

"And Mummy and Daddy aren't awake yet?"

"I don't know." It was still strange to find himself in a space where every action of every person in the household wasn't instantly telegraphed, not just to everyone in their own home, but to everyone in the homes on either side and on top of them as well. "We'll go past their bedroom and listen."

"Did they argue last night?"

The sudden question pierced him. He'd wanted to believe that, with this new home, the shouting would stop.

"No, I don't think so." Lying to his little sister felt wrong, even when it was for her own good. "You didn't hear anything, did you?"

"Yes."

"You can't have done, you were asleep. You must have dreamed it."

"I woke up and I couldn't sleep again because I was frightened. I don't like it here. The sea's too close. It's going to come and take our house away."

"Don't be silly, the sea's not going to take our house away."

"Yes it is, that's what the man said. It's going to come in the night when it's raining and take our house away and we'll all go floating in the water and never see each other again."

"Stop it. That won't happen. Well, it might happen *in the end*, but not for years. Now come on, we're going to find some breakfast."

The door to their parents' bedroom was closed as they passed it. He paused a moment in case he could hear anything, get a measure of the emotional temperature of the household, but there was nothing. The acoustics here were another mystery he was still exploring. Sometimes you could stand by a half-opened door and hear almost nothing of what was being said on the other side. Sometimes you could be three rooms away and a voice would come to him with startling clarity. ("My head's like a beehive," his mother had said yesterday as he stood in the tiled room by the front door, idly contemplating the patches of damp that bloomed across the bare walls, and he was so convinced that she was behind him and speaking to him that he turned to ask her what she meant. "And you're like a beekeeper. You keep the bees in order and stop them from

22

swarming too far." And it was only when his father replied, "So do the bees like it here?" that he realised he was standing beneath their bedroom and eavesdropping on their private conversation.)

They left their parents' room and went downstairs. The flowing wooden curve of the bannister beneath his hand felt like an old friend. He had to stop himself from laughing out loud as the hallway came up to meet him.

The kitchen smelled of last night's dinner – a chicken curry that had been delicious at the time, but now just smelled gross. He wrestled with the back door for a while, until finally a gust of warm clean air rushed in. Another glorious thing about their new home: the garden that came with it. He still couldn't quite believe it was all theirs.

"Do you want a picnic?" he asked Ella.

She was rummaging in the cupboard where she'd insisted on stashing her own special plastic cups and plates. Her face looked at him doubtfully over the top of the door.

"Come on, let's go outside and eat. It's warmer outside than in here." The breeze tugged at his hair and the legs of his pyjamas.

"My feet will get cold."

"Put your wellies on."

"It'll be all wet."

"No it won't."

"I don't like it outside, I'd rather eat inside –"

"I'll get your wellies for you. Don't try and make breakfast, I'll do it." He crammed the toaster with bread, then sprinted to the tiled room by the front door, which his mother had now declared to be the cloakroom. If he wasn't quick enough, Ella would think he wasn't coming back at all and would start assembling her own breakfast, which was unlikely to end well. Ella's wellies – purple and white with a unicorn face moulded into the toes, a magical charity-shop discovery – lay at rest between his father's muddy work boots. As he picked them up, he heard his parents speaking in the room above,

23

and paused a moment, holding his breath so he could hear more clearly.

"We shouldn't have come here." His mother, her voice low and full of conviction. "It's too quiet."

We belong here, Jacob thought furiously, trying to send his thoughts up through the ceiling and into his parents' brains. *Don't argue. Please don't argue. This is our home, we've finally got one. Don't ruin it.*

"And that's exactly why we bought it! Because it's quiet. We'll be safe here. End of the world and turn right, remember?"

"But if the world ends and we turn right, do you know where we'll be?" A little frightened laugh. "The sea wants the house too."

"We've got time. We've got at least twenty years, that's what they said. Isn't that enough for now?"

"And you're drinking again. Don't tell me you're not because I know you are, I could smell it on you last night."

"We were celebrating! Last of the unpacked boxes? You had some too."

"I saw you drink three glasses of wine and a glass of whiskey with me, and I saw you down three fingers of whiskey in the pantry and then refill your glass and bring it out again."

No, thought Jacob, *don't do this, stop it. Don't ruin this house.*

"Are you spying on me?"

"No. Yes. Yes, I was. I spied with my little eye. I'm good at watching you, I have to be."

"For God's sake! Look, that's all in the past, isn't it? It was a hard life for both of us and we both had our ways of coping, didn't we? And sometimes – *sometimes* – I *used* to drink a bit more than I ought to. But now we're here and we're safe, so you can stop looking over your shoulder all the time, and I –"

"Can stop drinking in secret?"

24

"It wasn't a secret, it was an impulse. I had one extra mouthful of the good stuff because I was happy and then I came out. It wasn't three fingers, it wasn't even three millimetres, it was just a little mouthful. You're exaggerating again. And I wasn't drunk, I'm never drunk." A brief silence. "Now why don't you come here?"

The sound of feet moving above him, and then a single murmur of pleasure with two notes to it that sent him scurrying to the doorway, Ella's boots clutched tightly in his fingers. He'd been listening at doors since his father's first hesitant question ("Jacob, would it be all right if I brought a girlfriend home one time?") – but his parents doing *that* wasn't something he wanted to listen to ever.

In the kitchen, he found imminent disaster. Ella, industriously busy as she always was when left to herself, had used a chair to climb the worktops, opened all the cupboards until she found the Cheerios, filled her bowl and the surrounding floor with crunchy cereal hoops, climbed another chair to reach the fridge and taken out the milk. Now she was struggling with the screw-top, her mouth open with concentration and her hair tousled and fluffy in the sunlight. He yelped in panic, took the milk from her and put it out of reach.

"I told you not to try and get your own breakfast," he said, unsure whether to tell her off or admire her persistence. "Never mind. Put your wellies on."

That garden! His heart lifted every time he caught a glimpse of its wild neglected tangle. ("It used to be bigger," the vendor said ruefully as he showed them around a lawn bursting with dandelions, bounded with rose bushes at the sides and with a scrub of brambles and gorse marking the spot where the garden spilled onto the cliffs.) Jacob didn't care about how big it had once been; what they had now was astounding. In the middle of the lawn, a crabbed old apple-tree crouched over a patch of barren earth made briefly lovely with fallen blossom. Ella made a beeline for the spot beneath the tree, milk and cereal slopping out of the sides of the bowl as she went.

"Come on," he coaxed Ella. "Let's go closer to the sea." She shook her head. "We might see a seal. Like in your animal book?"

"I want to sit under the tree."

"No, we'll sit where we can see the water at least." She shut her eyes and turned away. "There's a beach down there. We could paddle maybe. Look for shells. Come on Ella, don't be a pain. I've done everything you want so far, I spent ages yesterday helping you get your room sorted, now it's time to do something I want."

"No. I don't want to see the sea, I want to stay here and play in the garden."

"Well, if you won't come with me then I'm going on my own," he declared, and marched off with his toast, knowing he'd just invoked the nuclear option and she would follow him, because she worshipped him. He wasn't being fair, but then it wasn't fair that he'd spent most of yesterday unpacking clothes into drawers and books into bookshelves while she endlessly rearranged six plastic unicorns along her window ledge, so now he got to cancel out that unfairness with a bit of his own. He heard Ella scurrying behind him. She had discarded her cereal bowl somewhere in the garden. After a minute he took her hand in his and gave it a squeeze.

Sharing Jacob's toast between them, they pushed through the grudging gap in the tangle of gorse and brambles that marked what Jacob presumed was the end of their garden. The spines of the gorse glinted with the raindrops it had captured last night. ("Now everything will grow," his mother had said dreamily, looking out of the window. "Like having a gardener come for free. Free rain. And tomorrow you kids can have free rein…") Beyond the thin thread of pathway, the cliff-edge rushed downwards.

"Is this still our garden?" Ella whispered. "Are we still in our garden?"

"I don't know. Maybe."

"There's a path, though. Are people allowed to make a path in our garden?"

"I don't think anyone really comes here anyway. It's too –" he stopped before the word *dangerous* could get away from him – "too quiet."

"So who made the path then? Jacob, what if people can come in our garden?"

At the foot of the cliff, an empty, shingly beach had rolled itself out. Sunlight washed over the pebbles and struck sparks off the water. A rowboat bobbed a few feet from the shore, oars resting on the cross-struts that braced its wide-bellied shape. There was no sign of the boat's owner.

"We could maybe get a boat," he said. Ella shook her head. "Come on, it could be fun."

"I don't want to go in a boat, they're dangerous."

"No, they're not. Shall we go down there?"

"Please can we go back to the house now?"

"No, let's explore." A crumbly brown pathway led like a slipway onto the pebbles below. It looked steep but doable. "Hey, this might even be our own private beach. How cool would that be?"

"I don't want to go on the beach, please Jacob, I don't want to go on the beach." He picked her up and slung her across his hip. "No, please put me down, put me down, please, Jacob, please –"

"Shush. You'll like it when we get there. And stop wriggling or I'll drop you."

He scrabbled down the slope. Ella was a dead weight in his arms, fingers hooked into him like claws. He would have bruises later. The sand was as deserted as it had looked from above. They might be the only people left alive in the world. Against his chest, Ella was like a vibrating drum.

"Come on," he said coaxingly, half-ashamed now he'd got his way. "It's lovely down here. Do you want to paddle?" She shook her head. "We can play some games if you like, or just collect stones and stuff. What's the matter now?"

Ella pointed to the slick black shape that lay, basking in the sunshine, a few feet from the base of the cliff.

"Is it a monster?" she whispered. "Is it? Will it get us?"

"Oh, wow." Jacob's heart swelled with gladness. "Oh, wow, that's a seal. Ella, that's a seal."

"It looks like a monster." Her fingers were slackening their death-grip on his arms. He put her down before she could grab on again. "Is it really a seal? An alive one? Not a toy one?"

"Of course an alive one, who'd make a toy seal that big? Do you want to go closer?"

"Should we stroke it?"

"Definitely not, but we can look."

"Would it be soft?"

"I don't know, it might be, I know they're furry but I don't know what they feel like." There was something odd about the seal's shape; it was thinner than he'd thought at first, lacking the acute upward curve of insulating fat, and while its tail-flippers looked right, there was something odd about the fore-flippers. Perhaps it was dead; perhaps that was what it was doing all by itself. "Actually, maybe we shouldn't get too close, we don't want to frighten it."

"It's waking up," Ella breathed. "Is it going to come and see us?"

"No, don't go any closer, it might not be safe, Ella please, no, don't –"

And then the seal turned its head and he saw that they were stalking a woman, small and round and sturdy, lying in the sunlight in a thick black wetsuit that covered her from cap to toe, and now was sitting up and looking at them.

"Sorry," he muttered, trying to take Ella's hand so they could get away. The woman shaded her eyes with her hand so she could see them better.

"We thought you were a seal," Ella said.

"There are seals around here," the woman said. "But you shouldn't go near them. They're hunters, not cuddly toys."

"I'm called Ella. And he's called Jacob. And my mum's called Maggie and my dad's called Richard and we live –"

"Shush, Ella." Jacob felt as if his face might burn right off his bones with embarrassment.

"And I'm Mrs Armitage." She got to her feet, taking her time about it. Her face was brown, her gaze piercing. "Do you know there's no way off this beach?"

Jacob looked at her blankly. "We got down here."

Mrs Armitage nodded towards the steep slope of earth. "That's not a path, that's a cliff-fall. Coming down is one thing. But if you try and climb back up it, it's liable to come down on you."

"Oh. Okay. We'll find another path then."

"You won't find any. There are no safe paths down here. And you can't climb the cliffs, they'll come down on you."

"Jacob," said Ella, her eyes widening.

"Shush," said Jacob. "It'll be fine."

"But how are we going to get home?"

"We'll be all right, Ella! Stop fussing!"

"You'd better come with me," said Mrs Armitage. "In my boat, I mean. I'll row you round to the next cove. You can pick up the path and walk back."

"We'll be fine," said Jacob.

"You'll drown if you don't," said Mrs Armitage, her voice as flat and calm as a millpond.

There was no way off the beach. Or was there? What if this strange woman was simply telling them this so she could lure them out onto the water?

"Have we got to go near the sea? Jacob, have we got to go on the *boat?*"

Mrs Armitage was older and smaller, he could probably fight her off if he had to, but what if he couldn't? And what if she was right about the beach? What was the right thing to do? "Ella, will you just shut up, please!"

"I don't want to go on the boat, I don't want to go on the boat, please don't make me go on the boat, the sea will get

29

me!" Ella clung to his leg like a bramble. Her face was white. Jacob realised for the first time the scale of her terror. And he'd made her come down here…

"Ella?" Mrs Armitage knelt down at Jacob's feet. "Ella? Listen to me. I need to tell you something."

"She doesn't like strangers," said Jacob wretchedly. "Don't, you'll frighten her."

Mrs Armitage took no notice. Instead she smoothed Ella's hair back to expose the tender pink shell of her ear. She put her mouth against it and whispered. And to Jacob's apprehensive surprise, Ella's grip on his leg began to loosen and she turned her face towards Mrs Armitage.

"Shall we get on my boat now?" Ella's face was white, but she nodded and held out her arms. "No, I'm not going to carry you, you can walk."

As if Mrs Armitage had cast a spell on both of them, they trailed in her wake towards the waiting water.

"Take your trainers off and roll your jeans up. No, don't carry them, tie the laces together and hang them round your neck. And the little one needs carrying." She scooped Ella up under one arm, not the way a woman would normally lift a child but like a farmer lifting a lamb, and held her out to Jacob.

The water was so cold it felt as if it hated them. Jacob gritted his teeth and kept wading. Ella's foot slipped briefly below the surface, and she whimpered and drew herself up against his chest.

"The boat's going to be heavy," said Mrs Armitage. "So I need you to get in when I say and sit where I say and *sit still,* you understand me? And don't put your feet on my scuba gear."

Stacked beneath the seat was a pile of equipment – a tank, a mask, some sort of thing like a thick sleeveless jacket. Mrs Armitage pointed at Jacob.

"Pass your sister to me, then get in. Slowly, don't tip the boat. Now sit right in the middle of that thwart."

"I don't know what the –"

"The thing like a seat that's clearly the only place you can sit and that I'm pointing at," said Mrs Armitage, with no particular emphasis. "And then keep still."

Jacob climbed obediently in. He'd thought the point of boats was to keep the water out, but there was a good inch of sea water sloshing around. He tried not to cringe as it washed over his naked feet.

"Now I'm going to pass Ella to you. Sit her on your knee so the boat stays balanced." Ella's teeth were chattering with fear and her fingers clung like twigs to the thick black material of Mrs Armitage's wetsuit. "No, none of that, thank you. Let go. That's right." She dropped Ella onto Jacob's lap. "There you are." Then there was a quick slither too fast to follow, and Mrs Armitage was effortlessly balanced in the centre of the boat, which – just as she'd said – now rode alarmingly low in the water, with what seemed like only a few inches of woodwork separating them from the waves. Mrs Armitage took the oars and began to pull. This was it. They were officially out at sea with a total stranger. He held Ella as tightly as he dared.

Getting the boat moving through the water took a lot of effort. He could see the strain in Mrs Armitage's face as she wrenched at the oars. After the first few strokes, she paused to push the black cap from her head, revealing cropped brown hair turned tufty and wild by its confinement.

"Can I help?" Jacob asked after a while.

"I don't know. Can you row?"

"I've never tried."

"Then no, you probably can't help."

She kept rowing. The beach was growing more distant. The silence settled around them like mist.

"Our house is going to fall into the sea," said Ella suddenly.

"Ah." Mrs Armitage nodded. "So you're the ones. And that's your house."

He glanced over his shoulder. They were far enough out now that their house was visible. Did this mean his parents, looking out of a window, might be able to see their children afloat on the North Sea with a stranger? He wondered if they were looking for them yet, and how much trouble he'd be in when they finally got home.

"It's not going to fall into the sea," Jacob told Ella.

"Yes it is." Mrs Armitage's voice was so flat and calm that it took him a minute to realise he'd been contradicted. "This whole coast is going to disappear in the end."

"Could you stop frightening my sister, please, she's only six."

"But the good news is," Mrs Armitage continued as if he hadn't spoken, "you're a good twenty feet further from the edge than I am, so mine will go first. So as long as you can still see my house, you'll know you don't need to worry. I leave a light on in my bedroom window all night. You'll be able to see it from your turret window." She paused for a moment to catch her breath. The boat hopped up one side of a wave and down the other. Ella grabbed onto Jacob's t-shirt. "I live in the white cottage just along the cliff. My husband chose it. He always liked to be near the sea." They both looked where Mrs Armitage was pointing. "Then, of course, he ended up drowning in it."

On Jacob's lap, Ella shuddered. He wondered what would happen if he stood up and pushed Mrs Armitage into the water.

"But when your house falls into the sea, you'll be in the sea too," said Ella. "And then you'll drown."

"No, I won't."

"Yes you will."

"No, I won't. I told you. I can breathe underwater."

"How? How can you breathe underwater?"

"That's my secret," said Mrs Armitage.

"But I can learn to do it too?"

"She's a scuba diver," said Jacob crossly. "See those tanks? They're full of air. She puts them on her back and she can breathe the air through the pipes."

"A lot of people don't rate the North Sea as a dive-site. I like it here because you're not surrounded by holidaymakers making a nuisance of themselves. The water looks muddy but it's clearer further down. Worse after a storm, of course."

"What is there to see?"

"Some good wrecks. Most from the Second World War. A few fishing boats." When her gaze fell on Ella's terrified face, her expression softened. "Wrecks are good for the ocean. Fish like them. They make good habitats."

Jacob looked dubiously round at the little boat and wondered how Mrs Armitage could possibly row out far enough to find a shipwreck.

"I have another boat," she said, as if she could read his thoughts. "Bigger than this one. I just use this for pottering around the coast where the water's shallow."

"Where's your other boat?" Ella looked around as if it might be hidden under the thwarts.

"At the marina, just along the coast from the beach where I'm taking you. You can ask your parents to take you there if you want."

"No, thank you," Ella whispered.

"Ella's scared of the water," said Jacob.

"No she isn't. She's scared of drowning. That's only common sense. That's why you have to learn not to drown." She rested the oars on the rowlocks to catch her breath again. The boat slowed to a rocking, unstable halt. When he looked behind him, Jacob saw the shoreline of another cove, close enough to make out the dogs and people roaming around on it, but too far to swim. Was Mrs Armitage strong enough to get them back to the shore? Was she willing to? Was she even sane?

"How about I row for a bit and you –"

"No!" Mrs Armitage's bark shocked him into instant stillness, frozen foolishly in the act of rising from his seat. "Sit still. I told you, we're too low in the water. If you start wandering around you'll tip it. Sit back down. Slowly." Jacob

33

sat back down. "That's better. So. Why did your parents buy a house that gets more worthless with every year that passes?"

"I think it's what they could afford," said Jacob, shocked into honesty. Mrs Armitage laughed.

"It's not a bad place to live. Quiet in the winter, but some people prefer that. Not so good for teenagers, of course." She rested the oars once more. "The tide will carry us in now."

"See, Ella?" Jacob smiled encouragingly. Ella rewarded him with a small stretching of her rosebud mouth. "Nearly there."

Another few strokes. Another break. How deep was the water now? Jacob willed himself to sit still and wait. Mrs Armitage peered down into the water, frowned, rowed another few strokes.

"Right, that'll have to do. Sit tight. Don't try to get out until I say." In a slither of neoprene, she slipped over the side and stood thigh-deep in water. "There's a shelf in the bottom just here, so be careful." She held Ella as Jacob clambered awkwardly over the side. The water came well above his knees, but when he took a step towards the shore it was just as Mrs Armitage said: a sudden shelf that dropped the water level from his thighs to his calves.

"There's a path at the top of the beach," Mrs Armitage told him. "It takes you along the cliff to the end of your garden." She turned her gaze towards Ella. "It goes right past my house, so you could use it to visit me, if you liked. Or you can walk back through the village if you prefer. That takes longer."

"Thanks."

"I'm sorry your house is going to fall into the sea," said Ella.

"Why?"

"Because then you won't have your house any more."

"Then I'll live in the sea where I belong," said Mrs Armitage.

"Thanks," Jacob said again, unsure of what else to say. With Ella in his arms, he began the slow wade back to shore.

34

When Ella's feet touched the sand, he felt her let out a long breath of relief.

"She can turn into a seal," Ella said to Jacob.

"No, she can't."

"I wish I could turn into a seal." And then, all in a rush, "Last night I was asleep and I thought the house was falling into the sea and we were falling through the water, and there was an old broken boat and some fish were going to eat our eyes and a crab was going to walk over our skulls."

"Is that why you were so scared? Oh, Ella."

"Is that going to happen one day?"

"No, of course it isn't, that was just a nightmare. Why didn't you go and get Mum?"

"It's dark on the way to their room."

He sighed. "I tell you what. If you have that dream again, then come and get me. Don't wake me up or anything," he added hastily. "But if you're really scared, you can get in bed with me for a bit. As long as you lie still and don't wriggle. And you won't need to be afraid, ever, because we'll be together."

"Even if the sea comes?"

"Even if the sea comes. I promise. Do you want to wave goodbye?"

They turned to face the sea and saw that Mrs Armitage was still standing in the water, one hand on her boat, watching them.

Chapter Three
Now

Objectively, there was nothing to distinguish Jacob's class-room from the others along the corridor, and certainly nothing worth loving. But over the years, its quirks and individualities had grown on him. On the wall behind the radiator there was a vast, grotesque tumour built of discarded chewing gum. He checked on it from time to time, but it never seemed to grow or – thank goodness – shrink. The door to the stationery cupboard swelled in the winter and shrank in the summer, the change in effort needed to get it open marking the change of seasons as surely as the slimy glut of leaves in the playground. When he sat at his desk, the small crack in the bottom-most pane of glass sent in a liquid thread of air to chill his neck and stiffen his shoulders. The slow growth of his affection for these small details reminded him that time was moving forward, not simply around the same loop.

The bell rang. When he'd been a pupil here, this signalled a riotous scraping of chairs on the floor, an instant rise in the noise level, the resigned shout of the teacher – "*Wait*, please, until I say you can go…" Today, pupils were called students, and despite what he heard from others, they seemed more civilised in a lot of ways than his own generation had been. They waited for his nod before putting their books away, and sat politely through his recommendations for holiday reading. Whether that would translate into actual reading was another thing, but nonetheless, it was satisfying. He held the door open for them as they left. He enjoyed the chorus of "Bye sir" that fluttered around his ears, but savoured even more the silence that fell like dust in the wake of their feet on the stairs.

"Jacob, mate. I know it's the last day but you're not allowed to leave the building yet. One final meeting at four before we're all free. Soz." Donna popped her head around the doorway, sleekly pretty and still fizzing with energy even though it was the end of a long school year.

"That thing about the new progress reports? Yeah, I know. See you there."

"I know it's all bollocks but we've got to do it so we might as well do a decent job of it." Her gaze fell on the open laptop. "You got much to do before you finish?"

"A few bits."

"You got to get straight off after?"

He nodded.

"Thought so. Pity, I was just about to ask you to come out with the rest of us for a drink then. Good thing I remembered in time you don't *do* fun. Can you believe they made us come in on a Monday? Who plans these things? See you at the meeting."

"See you," he said to the back of her head. She was already gone, whirling away to the next task that required her ferocious energy, her endless commitment. She was a far better teacher than he was, and a far better member of the profession, too. When he sighed and knuckled under to the endless assessment, the endless paperwork, she did all that was asked of her to an impeccable standard, then fought back and challenged and wrote letters and was active in the union. Perhaps Donna and Ella might have –

As if he'd been stung by a small insect, he took in a sharp breath, rubbed the back of his neck, let his breath go slowly. The pain was always waiting. It would never go away. But he could manage it by approaching it cautiously, by not letting it ever fully wake.

He sat down at his desk and opened his file. They'd spent the term ineptly dissecting *Romeo and Juliet*, and now he wasn't sure he could ever stand to look at it again. Next year it would be *Hamlet*. Would that be better, or worse? At least there was a skull in it.

If he brought a skull in for them to look at, would they be willing to engage with it, to probe the delicate architecture with their fingers and marvel at the articulation of the jawbone? Would it help them understand how Hamlet must have felt in that moment, holding the clean bones of a man he had known in life? Or would they just declare the whole thing to be gross and refuse to touch or look at it? He could picture it going either way. Maybe he could borrow one from a museum.

The meeting about the new progress reports was just under half an hour away. He had to have some thoughts to share; it wasn't fair to leave all the burden of this hopelessly dull and thankless task to Donna. He opened a spreadsheet that he'd begun to half-heartedly populate with blocks of colour. The only part that caught his attention was the names he'd invented for his pupils. Scattered in among the Amber Stathers and George Rileys were Bruce Wayne, Peter Parker, Jean Grey, Ororo Munroe. He wondered if Donna would notice. Heather Violet. Was that a made-up name, or a real one? Where had he –

("Please, Jacob." Ella's hopeful little face, and the glittery book clutched in her hand. "Just once, and I promise I'll choose something different next time.")

He shook his head and stared up at the ceiling, muttering under his breath *don't think about it don't think about it don't think about it*. When he looked back at the screen, the words blurred before his eyes. His heart galloped like a frightened cat.

"It's okay," he said, into the empty silence of the class-room. "It's okay. You're okay."

("Or you can choose next time. Or you don't even have to read to me, you can just sit with me for a little bit.")

"Come on, come on, it's okay, don't think about it. You're okay. That's it. You're okay."

He took a breath in and held it, and began the count. *One. Two. Three. Four. Five.* She'd dropped his phone in the bath that time, and he had been so angry with her – he couldn't think about it. Keep counting. *Thirteen. Fourteen. Fifteen.*

She was still with him, still hovering at his elbow and whispering in his ear. He had to get out of here. He closed the lid of his laptop with a shaking hand. Sometimes movement helped, nothing too fast or panicky but a slow controlled orderly sequence of motion that would take him away from the past. *Thirty-one. Thirty-two. Thirty-three.* His hand scrabbled at the power-cable, trying to free it from the socket. After a minute he managed it. He forced his hands to move smoothly. He was not going to drop his laptop. He was not going to drop anything. He was going to be fine. The door of the classroom seemed oddly far away, then suddenly the handle was jabbing into his stomach and he almost hit his head against the frame. He closed his eyes, then opened them. His lungs were burning, but he was free, the empty corridor before him a long reach of possibilities. *Forty-five. Forty-six. Forty-seven.*

He deliberately chose the longest possible route to the staffroom to let both time and distance do their work on him, pushing his way through the grease-scented dimness of the dining hall, finally letting himself take deep sweet breaths of dusty, diesely air as he crossed from the new building to the old.

The pain was leaving him now, ebbing away from his head and his heart. Eyes closed, hand on his stomach, he pictured a fast-running tide, racing down the beach to leave behind smooth pebbles and shining mud, and in the shelter of a clutch of stones, a lone crab hunkered down inside its shell. When he opened his eyes again, he saw that someone had stuck a jam sandwich to the roof of the canopy.

In the staffroom, Donna was connecting her laptop to the whiteboard, swearing fluently and continuously under her breath as she did so. In a different life he might have dared to ask her out some time. In a different life he might have been a little bit less out of his league in doing so. But this was the life he had. There was nothing he could do to change it.

"They're doing that thing with the sandwiches again," he said, to let her know he was there.

"Oh for fuck's sake, not the sandwich game back a-fucking-gain. I thought we'd seen the last of that bastard load of nonsense. What's wrong with our kids? None of the other schools – come on, you bastard –" she jabbed a cable viciously into its port – "have the twatting sandwich game. Why have we got stuck with it? Pissing well right you're searching for connections, you motherfucker. Aren't we all?"

In his secret heart, Jacob rather enjoyed the pointless disgusting anarchy of the sandwich game, whose sole and only goal was to stick a slice of bread to the underside of the canopy between the two buildings, and have it remain there for the longest possible time before it fell to earth again. Where had it come from? As far as anyone could tell, the sandwich game was an original invention, belonging to their school only. How long had it been going on for? Impossible to say. It was only discovered when a festering slice of Warburtons peeled itself off a canopy and landed at the astounded feet of the Head of History. When he looked up, a vast colony of sandwiches clung like anemones to the underside of the roof. How had the headmaster kept a straight face while telling a hall full of enthralled students that sticking food of any sort to any ceilings anywhere in the school would be regarded as an S3-level offence? No one knew, but that announcement had gone down in history as the finest moment of his career.

"At least they're original," he risked, and was rewarded with an answering smile that told him Donna rather enjoyed the sandwich game too.

"Yeah. At least there's that. Maybe we can include it in their evaluations. Evidence of original thinking. Not that anyone values original thinking these days. Another term like this one and I swear I'll quit."

"Don't say that."

"You're not the boss of me."

"But if you're not here to swear at the projector it'll never work again."

Donna laughed. "You could be as sweary as me if you had to be."

"I'd miss you."

"Well, maybe I'd miss you too. I bet I'd get over it though." The door opened and a thin trickle of people began to arrive, shoulders heavy with end-of-term tiredness and the knowledge of a mountain of work still to come before they could claim a small slice of the six-week break for their own. "I've got the projector working so you can all come in now. Just the meeting left to get through and we're free."

In another life, perhaps he could have been like Donna. He could have thrown himself at the rough bright surface of the world, exposing his whole self to the unwelcoming forces waiting to bruise and pummel him. He could have taken the blows on the chin and kept on fighting, determined to face down the storm. In another life, he might still have been driven on by the glorious, show-off urge to be someone's hero.

No, he thought. *Not here. You're not going to do this here. Not now. When you get home. That's the place where you can think about this. But not here.*

He took his place on the uncomfortable plastic chair, and let the meeting close over his head.

It was always a relief to get back home to the village and find there actually was still a village. The original estimate of fifty years until Doomsday was proving wildly inaccurate. Last autumn, the final remnants of the coast-road had been taken by the ocean. How long until the first houses began to disappear? Ella was plucking insistently at his elbow now, but he didn't dare give in to her, not while he was still behind the wheel of the car. He drove slowly along the high street, raising a hand to the people he recognised. A dog sat patiently at the side of the road, waiting for permission from its owner to cross. A slim little cat streaked over the tarmac like a weasel, and the dog's disapproving gaze reminded him of the way his students could look sometimes at a misbehaving classmate.

Some days the rough track that led up to his home could look charming, especially when the sun shone and the clouds scudded across the sky and dappled your eyes with shadows. Today was not one of those days. Nonetheless, he felt his shoulders sag a little with relief.

"It's just me," he called to the empty hallway. As always, he was filled with the superstitious fear that there would be no answer. But almost immediately he heard movement, and then Mrs Armitage appeared.

"You're late," she said.

"I'm sorry. I had a meeting that ran over."

"I'm not asking you to apologise, you fool."

"Who's there?" His father's voice, stretched tight and anxious. Jacob felt his heart drop towards his stomach. "Who is it?"

He followed Mrs Armitage into the living-room, where his father stood at the window. He'd been watching the apple tree – dripping with half-grown fruit and oblivious to its peril – that now marked the last outpost between their house and the waiting water, but Jacob's arrival had jolted him.

"It's just me, Dad."

"Thank God for that." His father looked him up and down. "You're late, aren't you?"

"I didn't mean to be."

"I was starting to worry."

"I didn't think." His father raised his eyebrows and looked at him sternly, but Jacob was well-practised at deflecting these moments and knew he didn't need to panic, not yet. "How about you? Have you been busy?"

"Not so bad. You look tired, though."

"It's just been a long day."

"They work you too bloody hard up at that school. It's a disgrace." His father's hand came up towards him and he tried not to flinch, but it came to rest against his cheek. "Don't you let them do it to you, you hear me? You've got to find time to relax as well."

He put his own hand over his father's, feeling the papery warmth of his skin. Mrs Armitage must be in the kitchen. He could hear the small sounds of someone moving around. His father heard them too. Instantly he was on the alert.

"Is there someone in the house? Can you hear someone?"

"Dad, it's fine, I promise. It's just Mrs Armitage."

"Who?"

"You remember, Dad. Mrs Armitage. She comes in to help look after –" he caught himself in time – "you know, to look after us."

His father shook his head impatiently. "No, she's gone, she left earlier, she always goes when you get home. Listen!" He held up a hand. "That was footsteps – there's someone coming to the door – get back."

"Mr Winter?" Mrs Armitage's voice was very clear, very calm. "It's Mrs Armitage. I'm outside the living-room door and I'm going to come in now. There's no one with me."

"Are you sure?"

Mrs Armitage opened the door, slowly and carefully, and as wide as it would go.

"Very sure. Do you see? It's just me. I'm leaving now. It's the summer holidays so you won't see me for a while."

"Fair enough." His father rubbed at his hair distractedly. "So, will you send me the invoice, or – ?"

"I'll see you out," said Jacob hastily. "Back in a minute, Dad. Okay? I won't be long. If you hear someone moving around, it's just me or Mrs Armitage."

"You don't need to treat me like I'm ninety, you know," said his father.

"I know, I'm sorry. So I'll just be a minute, yes?"

He followed Mrs Armitage into the kitchen and towards the back door. The cliff-edge had crept closer over the years, but she still insisted on taking the cliff-path back home. *I'm not afraid of the sea,* she always said on the few occasions he'd brought this up. *When the time comes, I'll be ready.* The smell of something savoury came from the oven.

"I put dinner on for you," Mrs Armitage said.

"Oh! Thank you, but you didn't need to –"

"No, I know that."

"So how has he been?" he asked, desperate to hold onto this small amount of adult company.

"The same as he always is." She took her rucksack from the kitchen chair where she always left it. "As long as he knows it's me, he's perfectly pleasant to be around."

"So he hasn't been violent or anything?"

"Of course he hasn't."

Jacob waited, as he always waited, to see if she would ask him anything more about this, but she simply adjusted her rucksack on her shoulders. She'd long ago made clear the limits of what she would and would not do to help him, and of precisely how much care she had for his welfare.

"I'll see you tomorrow morning, then," he said.

"Yes. But it'll be the last time until September."

"No, I know that, I haven't forgotten." As if he could have thought of anything else for days and days; the dreadful weight of these six weeks of aloneness with his father, with no one to share the burden.

"You don't have to keep doing this," said Mrs Armitage. It was the closest she would ever come to sympathy.

"Yes I do."

"No, you don't. You're perfectly entitled to have him put into some sort of –"

"He's my dad," said Jacob, firmly.

He wanted her to argue some more, not because she had any chance of persuading him but because the arguing would prolong the time until she left him. But she simply shrugged.

"As long as you remember it's your choice to live this way." She turned away and reached for the door handle, as if they'd been discussing nothing more important than whether Jacob needed milk, or could last till the morning. He reminded himself that this was only fair. Mrs Armitage owed him nothing.

"See you tomorrow morning, then," he said. "If you still want to, I mean."

"It's what we agreed," she said, and closed the door behind her.

In the kitchen, he opened the oven door and found crusted chicken breasts baking in a foil tray alongside two plump jacket potatoes. He decanted two portions of frozen peas into a bowl, started the microwave, laid out the knives and forks and glasses of water. Then he went back to the living-room door.

"Dad? Dad, it's just me."

They ate in a silence that Jacob supposed could be described as companionable. The food provided both focus and distraction. Fully occupied and with his senses engaged, his father seemed, for once, rooted in the present. Jacob left the table for a moment to get another glass of water. When he returned, his father was holding a piece of the chicken breast up to the light so he could examine it more closely.

"This coating's pretty good," he said. "Some sort of herbs, is it? And breadcrumbs?"

"That's right."

"It's lovely. We should have it again some time. What? What are you laughing about?"

"I'm not laughing, Dad, I'm smiling. I'm really glad you like it." They had this dish at least twice a week. It was one of his father's favourites, and while the memory of what he'd eaten would soon slip away from him, the glow of satisfaction would help his mood for the rest of the evening. "We'll have it again soon, shall we?"

"Sounds like a plan." His father glanced down at his plate. "D'you know, I can't think, just remind me, Jacob, what day is it again?"

"It's Monday."

"Shit! Is it? Christ, Jacob, did I go to work this morning? Oh my God, I didn't –"

"Are you ready for some pudding, Dad? We've got some cakes, really nice ones."

"Don't interrupt me. I won't have rudeness out of you, do you hear?"

"No, Dad, you're right. I shouldn't have interrupted."

"I won't have it. Not now. Not ever. Bad behaviour is never acceptable."

"I know. I'm sorry." He had the physical strength to manage his father but not the will, and he was too tired to think of a way to distract him from what he honestly thought was his parental duty. That was the hardest part. The knowledge that his father was only doing his best. "I won't do it again, I promise." He glanced wildly around the kitchen for inspiration. "Why don't I do the washing-up to apologise? And you can sit in the living-room and have a break."

His father's gaze flickered for a minute.

"Oh, Jacob. You're a good lad. But you have to learn, we all have to learn…"

"I know. So why don't I do the washing-up by myself? Make myself useful."

His dad sighed. "Okay. You do the washing-up and we'll call it quits." He looked uneasily around the room. "Just remind me, mate, what day is it again?"

"I got some cakes for pudding." Feeling like an inept magician trying to stop his audience from glimpsing the assistant behind the curtain, Jacob fumbled on the worktop for the box containing the toffee Danishes.

"Those look good. You shouldn't be spending your money on stuff like this, though, son. It's my job to look after the bills, not yours."

"I don't mind, I wanted to. Shall we eat them in the living-room?"

"Why not?"

"So why don't you sit down and eat yours while I wash up?"

He saw his father safely through the door, pulled it closed so he'd know if he started wandering. Then he filled the sink with hot water and piled in the plates.

He took his time over the washing-up, putting off the moment for as long as possible. He'd heard only silence from the living-room, but he checked to make sure the door was shut anyway. Then he went to the fridge and filled a mug with milk. He stood still for one moment more, trying to tell himself he still had a choice. What was it he was always telling his students? *It's never too late to change your mind.* But of course that wasn't true. He had already made his decision.

With quick, furtive movements, he took down the box of herbal teabags from the top shelf. Beneath the brownish paper packets of powdered liquorice was a long white box of with a pharmacist's label on it.

He popped two tablets from the blister into a spoon, hesitated, then popped a third. It had been a long week. Then he put another spoon on top of the first, and pressed down hard. The tablets yielded beneath the pressure, crumbling with a satisfying little pop and creating three perfect starbursts of powder. He tipped them into the milk and stirred rapidly until they dissolved. Then he took the bottle of whiskey hidden in the Weetabix box and added a furtive slug. *Do not drink alcohol*, the label on the pill packet shrieked. He put it back in its place behind the teabags without looking at it, and took the mug to the microwave.

In the living-room, his father had once again stationed

47

himself by the window, staring out at the long orange fingers of light that reached blindly towards him through the branches of the apple tree. When Jacob opened the door, he steeled himself for the clenched fists, the look of fear; but when his father looked at him, he saw only tenderness.

"Hey," he said. "Come and look at this view."

Jacob joined his father at the window. The light was so low and bright that he had to squint to see anything at all.

"Isn't that beautiful?" his father said. "All ours."

Did his father see the garden as it was now? Or did he still see it as it had been when time stopped for him?

"Not much chance of anyone coming in that way," his father said with satisfaction. "Not unless they're bloody Vikings, anyway."

"And there's no Vikings round here as far as I know."

"We're lucky."

Jacob clenched his fingers tight around the mug and made a fierce wish for this moment to last for ever. Somewhere in the house, a floorboard creaked.

"Did you hear that?"

"It's nothing, Dad, just the floorboards moving. They do it all the time."

"There's someone in the house."

"Dad. Shush."

"I'll check upstairs, you check downstairs and give me a shout if you find –"

"Look, how about I check and you sit down and drink this?" He held the mug out where his father could see it. The cheap, sweet, smoky scent drifted into the space between them.

His father looked at the mug suspiciously.

"Is there whiskey in this? It smells like it's got whiskey in it."

"Just a bit. I thought you might like it."

"You're not supposed to touch my – oh, well, never mind," his father said wearily. "You meant well. Can't make a habit of it, though." He looked around the room. "What was I going to do? I was going to do something, I'm sure I was…"

"You were going to lock the front door. I'll do it. Don't worry."

"Getting a bit forgetful," he muttered with a sheepish smile. "First sign of old age." He looked again at the mug, then sat down in the chair that faced the garden and took a large gulp.

Jacob lingered over the locking of the door, wanting his father to finish his drink with no distractions. Soon it would be time to start chivvying him upstairs to bed before the diazepam turned him into a shambling zombie.

But for now, let his father enjoy his drink in peace.

An hour later and their unequal skirmish was complete. His father, unbathed but with his teeth clean and in some approximation of pyjamas, lay in a drugged slumber in the bed he once shared with his wife. Jacob had a new tender spot on his shoulder where his father, bewildered and frightened, had landed a brutal punch as he flailed and struggled to escape the bathroom, but at least there was nothing that would show above his clothes, and no blood. Downstairs, he got out his laptop. Checked the living-room door was closed. Took out the photograph that never left him. His little sister, her face serious as she stared warily up at the camera, and behind her, her arms around Ella's waist, her chin on Ella's shoulder, the woman he'd once called *mother*, laughing as she knelt to fit herself into the picture. He would have liked to cut the woman out and throw her away, but she and Ella were intertwined.

He began, as always, with Facebook. He typed her name into the search box. *Ella Murray.*

He already recognised many of the results, but clicked on them anyway, just in case. What would Ella look like now? She'd been blonde as a child; it was likely she would be blonde still, but you never knew –

But none of the girls whose profiles he studied looked back at him with the face of his sister.

He tried again with his mother's name. *Maggie Murray* yielded nothing that looked possible. *Margaret Murray. Daisy Murray. Meg Murray.* An abundance of women, mostly on the wrong side of the Atlantic. Would she have left the country? She'd destroyed their family and broken his father, who knew what she might do next?

But if he let himself consider the idea that Ella was living under another name or in another country, he'd go mad. Better to simply try his less likely search terms, *Ella Winter* and *Meg Winter*. She'd never used her married name before, and after leaving her husband would be a strange time to start, but he always had to try.

He knew many of these faces too – had begun to feel as if some of them were even friends of his, whose lives he'd dropped out of for a while – but he went through them carefully anyway. Then, the sudden shock of novelty: a woman whose profile picture showed her sitting on a park bench, a teenage girl beside her. For a moment, he thought he saw something familiar in their faces.

Forcing himself to stay calm, he clicked onto the profile photo and studied it intently. The shot had been taken from a distance, the colours of the grass and the huge rhododendron bush behind them dominating the shot, and it was hard to see their faces clearly. Nonetheless, he zoomed in as far as he could, dwelling for slow intense minutes over the curves of their cheeks, the shading of their hair. When he looked more closely, the likeness that had briefly caught at his heart dissolved and disappeared; the woman's figure was too heavy, the girl beside her too young. But if he looked away from the screen to the photograph and then back again, flicking his eyes casually over the image rather than staring directly at it, he thought he glimpsed something.

Both the girl and the woman wore sunglasses that hid half of their faces. The girl's were large and tinted pinky-brown, almost wider than her face; the woman's were hearts with thick white plastic rims. They must have swapped for the photo. Of course the girl was too young, but it might be an old picture, perhaps uploaded when she first joined and never amended. He clicked onto her profile to see what else he could discover, but the page was empty. No workplaces to show. No schools or universities. No places. No relationship status. A small clutch of friends whose profiles revealed nothing he could use.

His heart thumped in his chest. That might be about right. It really might be about right. That was exactly what he might expect.

Except, a cold voice whispered to him, *it's not. She wouldn't join Facebook. You know she wouldn't. And she wouldn't let Ella join either.*

But Ella was seventeen years old now, old enough to rebel. Ella might be out there looking for him right now. He went back to the photo of the woman with her daughter on the park bench. The more he stared, the less the two people on the bench looked like the ones he sought. It was no good. Another false alarm.

His phone vibrated against his leg, the alarm a stern reminder that he couldn't lose his entire night to his search. He'd learned the hard way that the shockwaves of sleeplessness would make the next few days almost unbearable. He had only another ten minutes to check his other sources, not because he thought he'd find anything but because he knew he wouldn't sleep without it. Working quickly and efficiently now, he scrolled through his bookmarked selection of databases, checking the names and likely locations with the automatic efficiency of a skilled office worker. Nothing; nothing; nothing. Another night of not knowing. Or, perhaps, another night gone before the one when he would finally find them.

Wearily, he began his pre-bed routine: checking the doors and windows were locked, checking his photograph was back in his pocket, checking he'd hidden his laptop. Before he went to bed, he peeked in at his father, deep in the arms of chemical sleep. He thought the other man was too far gone to be aware of the door opening, but his dad stirred and sighed, then lifted his head from the pillow.

"That you, Jacob? Had a nightmare? Get in w'me if you want."

"I'm fine, Dad."

"You sound upset. You're not crying, are you?" His dad was half-awake now, fighting the downward pull of the sleeping tablets. "You lie down here w'me, I don't mind. C'm'ere, love."

The sheets smelled of sweat and fabric conditioner, their usual midweek scent. Thank God his father hadn't yet started pissing the bed. Thank God they were stuck on the plateau and not sliding down the slope towards disaster. One day there would be another crisis, another chunk out of his father's crumbling defences, but until then, they would endure.

His father patted sleepily at Jacob's shoulder. Jacob turned obediently onto his side and let his father lay a protective arm over his arm and chest. He wondered how old he was in his father's mind at this moment. His father's breathing began to slow again, his breath warm against the back of Jacob's neck.

He lay quietly, listening to his father's breathing, counting in his head. When he reached five hundred, he slipped out of his father's embrace and crept next door to his own room.

Chapter Four
2007

Mrs Armitage heard them before she saw them – a family party whose voices stirred a faint sense of recognition.

The salt and wind had taken their toll on her fence, and there were several places where the knots had fallen out of the wood. Lowering herself slowly to her knees, she took a careful slantwise peek through the knothole.

She could see mostly legs and plastic carrier bags crammed with towels and tinfoil parcels. She watched the feet for clues. A man; a woman; a younger man. Then, at just the right height for her to make eye contact, a face. The girl she'd rescued from the beach. Ella. The identities of the other three fell into place. A small mystery solved.

Enjoying her new role as a spy, she sat back on her heels and listened as they passed, to a casual chatter so inane it could hardly be called conversation. Exclamations over the thick brown sea ("It's probably the mud"). A dispute about how long they'd been walking ("We left at six minutes past, so it's seven minutes." "Yes but we don't know *where* in the minute, so there are some seconds as well." "Ella, does it matter that much? Really?"). And the parents, inevitable as a Greek chorus; "Kids, come on, keep up, stop dawdling!" Nothing to draw her back to the knothole for a second stealthy glance. She looked anyway, and found herself staring straight into Ella's face.

"Jacob, look." Without the fence, Ella would be close enough to touch. "There's an eye in the fence." A little finger burrowed curiously through the knothole.

"That's a knothole, Ella." His voice took on the artificially enthusiastic tone of an older child explaining something to a younger one. "You know when a tree grows a branch? When they cut the tree into logs, the branches leave a sort of circle behind, and that's called a knot. Only sometimes they fall out."

Ella's finger probed at the edge of the hole, then withdrew. "It looked like an eye, though. An eye looking at me."

"That's your brain making things up. There wasn't really an eye."

"Oh. Like there aren't really burglars?"

"Yes. No. Well, I mean, there are burglars, but probably not here."

"But there are. Because, that's why Mummy can't go out. In case some burglars get all our things."

"Nobody's going to come and get our things."

"Yes, they are. Because, that's why we have to stay in all the time. And keep the doors locked."

"We don't stay in all the time." Mrs Armitage could hear his impatience, the way his attention had already wandered away from his sister. "We're out right now, aren't we? Going to the beach. Come on, we're getting left behind."

"There was an eye, Jacob, I saw it –"

"I've finished listening to you now. Stop talking and start walking."

"That's what Dad says." The voices were receding now. One more peek through the knothole showed her Ella's backpack, the plastic pink head of a creature that could have been meant for a horse protruding from its gaping mouth.

"I said no talking."

"Ella and Jacob!" That must be their father, Richard. What did he do for a living? Something far enough away to need a car. Around here, that meant practically every job imaginable. "Keep up!"

The children scurried after their parents.

This brief sighting of her new neighbours had been interesting, but unimportant. Nothing to get excited about or to spend time mulling over. She was a busy woman with plenty to occupy her day: a house to tend, a garden to care for, a difficult and absorbing hobby. Books to read. Places to go. An absence of people to see, but that was her choice and she'd never regretted it. The family was nothing to do with her.

Besides, she thought as she went to the shed and took down her wetsuit from its hanger, small children were given to odd remarks about their parents and hair-raising details about their apparent home lives. Jacob himself had dismissed it. *There was an eye in the fence. We're not allowed to go out. There was a unicorn in my cornflakes.* (Of course, there really had been an eye in the fence. But still.) Her skin felt tight and uncomfortable, her scalp itchy with irritation. She was missing the hushing silence of water filling her ears, the thin stream of bubbles rising above her. She needed to clear her head.

She packed her rucksack and set out. Her wetsuit would be hot and uncomfortable on the boat, making the water more welcoming. Her head buzzed unpleasantly, as if her innocent act of espionage had let a wasp into her brain and now it was banging its head against the windows, trying and trying to escape. The sooner she was in the water, the better. She climbed down the headland to the tiny concrete mooring where her boat waited for her.

As she pushed the rowboat away from the rocks (*water not too cold, waves not too choppy, the diving will be good today*), she recalled Ella's face the day she rescued them. The look of pure terror, barely mastered. A strange thing to see on such a young child.

"Forget about it," she said out loud. Normally talking

to herself was forbidden, but today she would give herself permission. "Keep rowing. And forget it."

She climbed onto her motorboat and tied her rowboat up behind it and thought that the family would have been going to the beach where she'd taken the children – or rather, the beach where she'd left the children to wade through the water to. They'd build an enclave there, with their plastic bags and their plastic toys and their plastic cheerfulness. Probably they'd have a picnic. Sandwiches turned greasy in their foil cocoons, diluted juice made warm by the sun, the bottle-rim crusted with sand. A picnic with children was supposed to be one of the greatest pleasures the world held, but she couldn't imagine why.

The way out to her favourite diving site was a straight steady course to sea, and then around to port and in towards the coast where the rocks gathered like sharks. But for some reason her boat wasn't co-operating today. No matter how many times she corrected her course, still it stubbornly pulled around to starboard, towards the sand that was now as crowded as it would be all summer (which meant not very crowded at all, but nonetheless meant more people than she wanted to see *ever*, never mind stripped to their white-and-scarlet skins, awkwardly cavorting with frisbees and footballs). The place where Ella would be.

I'm going diving. That's why I've got my wetsuit ready and my boat loaded with gear. I'm going beneath the water where it's cool and dark and nobody will speak to me or even look at me or even know I exist. That's where I'm going. She thought this as severely as she could, but still the beach grew closer.

"Oh, have it your way," she said crossly, and let the boat take her where it wanted. Sometimes you had to accept the will of the universe.

She moored her motorboat as close to shore as she dared, and dropped the anchor. She packed her wetsuit and flippers behind the diving gear. She clambered into the little rowing boat that followed her like a straggling child. She took hold of the oars.

After all, they might not even be here. Or she might be unable to find them. Or they might recognise her and welcome her over, in which case she would – well, what would she do? How rude was she willing to be? Could she simply ignore them and go back to her boat? How much did she care what they thought of her? Normally the sea cleared her head of anything she didn't want to dwell on, but today, the silence refused to come. *We have to have the doors locked all the time. Mummy can't go out.*

She reached the beach, grimly accepting the faint flicker of interest from the children whose parents pointed her out (*see those long pieces of wood those are called oars see how she's pulling her boat right up the beach that's because of the tide no you can't play in her boat no you can't ask her for a ride no we can't afford a boat shall we go and get an ice-cream?*). The children all looked bored. The beach looked golden enough, but the sand ran out a couple of centimetres below the surface, replaced with a thick layer of cold wet shale that was useless for digging, useless for building. Some had tried anyway, harvesting sand in long careful scrapes to build castles that were already drying and crumbling in the sunshine. Wandering as slowly and aimlessly as she could, she scanned the beach with long careful glances.

They were sitting apart from the thin crowd, tucked into a sandy gully between two long fingers of muddy cliff. Jacob was making a careful meditative ring of tiny stones, all gathered from beneath the sand he could reach with his fingertips. As she watched, Ella trotted into his line of vision and held out a bucket. He shook his head and sent her away. She began scraping at the sand, slowly filling the bucket and packing it down after each spadeful. The woman, Maggie, sat with her hands wrapped around her knees, her face turned towards the water; her man sat with his back against the rocks, watching his wife. It was hard to blame him. Even from this distance, Mrs Armitage could see the long slim pale shape of her, the halo of flaxen hair.

The cliff-path dipped down to the sand and then back up again, rising with the swell of the land. At the point where the family were sitting, she would be no more than twenty feet above their heads. If they looked up, they might see her; but people rarely looked up. She allowed her feet to turn slightly to the right, taking her towards the spot where a brief slope of concrete provided the illusion of permanence and led up to the coastal path. Today was a day for water, not land. A patch of sweat bloomed between her shoulder blades and her face felt too big for the bones beneath it. She wished she'd brought supplies with her, water and food and a hat, instead of leaving everything on the boat.

Hot and uncomfortable, she climbed the slope and trod gingerly along the path, conscious that the land was not her natural element and she'd formed no accommodation with this particular patch of it through long years of occupation. She settled as close to the edge as she dared, alert for the hiss and rattle of falling earth. It took her several moments to pick out the rising sound of conversation.

"Don't talk to me like I'm a child." Paradoxically, Maggie sounded like the child she said she wasn't: her voice petulant and pleading, the voice of someone without power who was used to being told what to do. "I hate it when you patronise me."

"I'm not patronising you. Don't be prickly."

A brief silence. Were they sulking? Sleeping? Kissing? People often said they could "hear" the quality of a particular silence, but what they were really hearing was the language of the body. Bereft of sight, a silence was just empty space. She considered wriggling closer, trying for a glance, looked at the raw edge where no green shoots grew, decided against it.

"You taste of whiskey," said the woman at last. (*Kissing, then,* thought Mrs Armitage.)

"It's the weekend. I'm allowed."

"I don't know how you can stand it before lunch. Did you bring a hipflask?"

"I did actually. Do you want some?"

"Not right now. If I was prickly all over would you still love me?"

"Of course I would."

"Are you sure?" There was laughter bubbling in her throat. "I'd be so sharp and dangerous you'd never get near me."

"Yes I would. Hedgehogs manage. And porcupines."

"How do they do it? Do they do it in the missionary position?"

"I don't know. Maybe."

"Hedgehog missionaries." Maggie laughed. "I wonder how good their conversion rates are. Maybe they wear suits and give out magazines. Porcupines are American, aren't they? So they'd be more like the ones who shout about Hell. I wonder which kind God prefers?"

"You're talking rubbish again," said Richard, unwittingly earning Mrs Armitage's approval.

"Well, what do you expect? I don't get any conversation while you're at work, when you come home you're tired. And of course I've got nothing to talk about except bloody hedgehogs and porcupines. I'm in that house all day, every day…"

"That's what we agreed. Remember? I go to work. You look after Ella."

"She could go to school. Then I could get a job too."

"And who'd take her and collect her? And there aren't any jobs round here."

"How do you know there aren't any jobs? It wouldn't have to be anything amazing, I could work in the shop during school hours. Or I could work at the school."

"Maggie." He must have used the pause to calm himself, because his voice when he spoke again was softer. "That's not what we agreed."

"We could change what we agreed."

"No we couldn't."

"Why?" That little-girl pleading note again, as if she knew she couldn't win. Had Maggie always been so spineless? Or was it a skill she'd had to learn?

"You know why."

"Did Jacob's mum go out to work? Or was she a burden?"

"You're not a burden, please don't say that, you've never been a burden. I love you more than anything."

"But did she?"

"Well, for a while she – look, why does it matter what she did? It was years before I met you."

So Jacob and Ella were half-siblings. Another silence below. On the cliff-top, the cool breeze lifted the sweaty t-shirt from Mrs Armitage's back, caressing her spine with gentle fingers.

"It's just I get bored sometimes," Maggie said, all in a rush as if she was afraid of being interrupted, or as if she was breaking a taboo.

"How can you be bored? You've got Ella, you've got your writing. We chose this place because it's quiet. End of the world and turn right, remember?"

"I know, I know! Here I am, all shut away safely where no one can get to me. I feel like Rapunzel sometimes. She was shut away in a tower, wasn't she? But the man found her in the end."

"Give it a chance. We'll be happy here, I promise."

"How can you promise, Richard? You don't control the world. Only me."

"Don't say that. Please don't say that. I don't control you, I *protect* you."

"That's what Rapunzel was about. Keeping women under control. She wasn't allowed to go out, or to talk to anybody, the witch brought her food every day. I wonder if she used to drug her? The witch, I mean. Drugged Rapunzel. Otherwise she'd have gone mad, wouldn't she? All on her own with nothing to do and no one to talk to."

"Maggie." There was, Mrs Armitage thought, such tenderness in his voice. "I'm sorry I can't make your life perfect. But it's good, isn't it? We've got the sea. We've got the garden. No noisy neighbours to worry about. And you've been sleeping much better. Haven't you? Maggie? Have you been dreaming again?"

"No. Well, not really."

"Maggie."

"Why do you care anyway? Everyone dreams."

"Just tell me."

"Dreams are private."

"I need to know what's going on in your head. We can't keep secrets from each other."

"It was about the sea. We were swimming naked together."

"Don't lie to me, love."

"I'm not lying, why would I lie? We were swimming naked. It was lovely. I'd love to make that dream come true. If we were selkies, we could turn into seals and nobody would ever find us. Only we'd have to hide our skins really well when we came to shore or we'd be stuck in our human form for always. Do you think the kids know about selkies? Let's tell them and then take them paddling."

"But I need you to tell me –"

"Later!" Maggie's voice was on the move now, and a moment later she came into view, half-dancing backwards across the thin sand, beckoning. "Come on! Let's have some fun. Kids!" She waved impatiently. "Come on! Let's have some fun!" Mrs Armitage couldn't see the children or Richard, but perhaps they were resisting, because she beckoned again. "Fun! In the sun! Time to run!"

She looked powerful now, Mrs Armitage thought, powerful and confident and in control, her husband and children dragged helplessly after her towards the water. And yet a moment ago she had been pleading with her husband to leave her the minimal privacy of her dreams. Which was the real Maggie? Which was the real Richard?

They made their way down to the sea: Maggie in the lead, Jacob and Ella at the back, Richard a bridge connecting the two halves of his family. Once she was sure they weren't watching, Mrs Armitage came down from the cliff and inspected their belongings. The greasy remains of the picnic she'd expected, and a tangle of shed clothes, with a gleam of silver peeking coyly from Richard's jeans. She thought about stealing the hipflask as a trophy, but Maggie had mentioned whiskey and she herself preferred rum. In the spot where Ella had solemnly played under Jacob's fitful instruction, a single sand pie sat in a ring of white stones.

The family were wading through the shallows, two and two, both holding hands. Maggie fair and lovely in her sheer white shirt and frayed cut-off jeans. Richard in her wake, not nearly so good-looking but providing a necessary balance for his wife's effortless beauty. Jacob and Ella like unformed echoes of their parents, Jacob holding Ella's small hand with a reluctant tenderness. They looked like a family from a holiday brochure. So beautiful that you were compelled to imagine dark secrets, a counterbalance to their seeming perfection.

Perhaps that was it. Perhaps she'd simply willed the dark undertones to their conversation into existence. Perhaps they really were as happy as they looked.

Her rowboat waited, a patient old friend. A man with two children was pointing out the eyes painted on the prow. It would be polite to let him finish speaking before she took the boat away, perhaps exchange a friendly word. There was a distinct pleasure in being rude instead, dragging the boat down the beach in fierce silence. She was aware of the twitch and mutter of the father, the bewildered fluting of the two children. Their discomfort was sharp and good in her mouth.

Making her way past the breakers, she saw the family strung out in a line across the water. They were jumping each wave as it came in, leaping in unison like puppets. She climbed into her boat and took up the oars and wondered what pleasure they took from it.

As she began the swift steady pull back to her motorboat, aware of the tide tugging against her, her eyes dwelled on Ella, watching the movements of her expressive little face. Startled recognition. The thought that she could tell her mother who she'd seen: an equally quick decision to keep it to herself. She glanced towards her mother and father to be sure they weren't looking, then gave Mrs Armitage a very small wave.

Unable to stop herself, Mrs Armitage waved back.

Chapter Five
Now

In the exhausted dreamless stillness of the third hour after midnight, Jacob was woken by the sound of shuffling footsteps in the corridor outside his door.

He was awake instantly, lurching out of bed and halfway across the room before he'd consciously processed what it was that had woken him. He opened the door cautiously, not wanting to frighten his father. His dad had a habit of filling his empty days with the collection of household objects that could be used as improvised weapons, and stashing them around the house. Jacob did his best to keep on top of them, but it was impossible to find them all, or to deduce that this time his father had stashed the garden spade, not beneath his bed as he usually did, but in the corner of the airing cupboard.

"Dad?" Jacob knocked on the inside of his door, feeling absurd but knowing this was necessary for his own safety. "Dad? It's just me."

"Jacob." His father sounded grimly determined. Jacob's heart sank. "Jacob, get back into bed. Nothing for you to worry about."

"But what's wrong?"

"Nothing. Back to bed."

Jacob risked opening his door a fraction anyway. In the

dim light, left on all night so no one would break their necks as they roamed the house, his father stood his ground with hair on end and a long shard of fence-post clutched tightly in both hands like a sword.

"I said," he hissed to Jacob through gritted teeth, "get back into your room. There's someone in the house."

"Dad." He knew it was futile and arguing would only turn his father's distrust towards himself, but he couldn't keep quiet. "There's no one in the house, there's no way they could get in. I locked everything up when we went to bed, I promise."

"You didn't do a good enough job then, did you?" His father stared wildly around. "There! Did you hear that? Someone's trying the front door, I can hear them –"

"How about we go and look together?"

"You're not coming with me, my lad. It's my job to look after you."

"But Dad, I'm –" he stopped himself. There was no point in trying to explain to his father the growing gulf of years that yawned between Jacob as he was now, and the teenager his father still remembered. He needed a different approach. He was so damn tired, that was the problem. Couldn't his father have waited just one night, just until the worst of the exhaustion had left his body?

"But what if you're not here? I need to learn what to do." He could see his father half-liked this idea; the spar of fence-post wavered in his hand. "Let me come with you, Dad, please."

"You keep behind me and do what I say."

"All right."

"Come on, then."

Like a pair of cartoon robbers, they crept along the corridor, peering behind doors and checking corners. Only the door to Ella's room, still sheltering the clothes she'd once fitted into and the bed she'd once climbed out of and the toys that waited in rows for her return, was left unsearched and untouched. What did his father see when his blank eager gaze strayed over that sealed-off space? Did he remember, somewhere in the long corridors of his memory, that he'd once had a daughter? Did he understand how she'd been taken from him?

"There's no one up here," Jacob said when they had finally, painfully, crept over every part of the upstairs floor. "Maybe we should go back to bed –"

His father's sudden blow caught the tender edge of his ear, sending up a blaze of red sparks that made his eyes water. While he was still recovering from that, another blow, smashing against his ribs. He fought back a whimper and made himself breathe slowly and steadily.

"Be quiet!" His father hissed. "He'll hear you! He's downstairs. I can hear him moving around. Listen."

In spite of himself, Jacob found himself holding his breath and straining his hearing. But the only sounds that came to him were the creak and murmur of the house settling on its unstable clay foundations.

"I'll check downstairs," his dad said. "Go back to bed, son. I'll handle it."

Jacob's whole body ached for sleep. He wanted nothing more than to go back to his room and fall onto the sheets and let his exhaustion take him.

"No, I'll come too."

His father's smile was warm and real and almost worth it. "You're a good lad."

Together they crept down the narrow back staircase, his father wincing and freezing with every creak and crack of the ancient wood. His father eased open the door to the kitchen, his back and shoulders rigid. The sudden click and buzz of the fridge sent his father surging into the room, his wooden post held high and triumphant; but there was nothing, nothing, nothing at all no matter how hard he stared into the pantry, and eventually he came back out again and began to creep towards the living-room, his face scared but determined. Jacob, watching, thought he could feel his heart coming apart in his chest.

"Ha!" The sudden syllable made Jacob grunt with fright. "I've got you! Got you, you utter bastard!"

"Dad! Dad, don't, please, don't – !" He was through the door in a moment, staring wildly around. What had his father seen this time? Was it even possible that there might actually be...

"Keep back, Jacob!" His father pushed at Jacob with one arm. "He's got a baseball bat! Now come on, mate, you know I'm going to win this one, just tell me how you got in and –"

And for a single wild moment Jacob saw what his father saw: a threatening man, eyes blazing with fathomless rage, weapon held ready to strike. It was only when his father took a step towards their attacker and he saw the movement reflected that he understood.

"Dad, it's your reflection. See? It's just you, in the window." He patted gently at his father's shoulder. "Can you see my hand on your shoulder?"

"Is that really – ?" His father held up a hand, waved at his attacker. The stranger in the window waved back. "But, my God, Jacob, what happened to me? I look so old. That can't be me, can it? Jacob, what the fuck's happening?"

"Let's shut the curtains. Keep the warmth in." *Make sure all the curtains are shut. Another job for the never-ending list of bloody jobs.* He took the stick from his father's hand and hid it as well as he could behind the sofa. "Shall we get some hot milk or something?"

"But I look so old... Have I been ill? I can't remember... I wish I could..." his father stared at him in bewilderment. "What was I talking about? I can't quite remember what I was talking about... Were we looking for someone?"

He had to distract his father as quickly as he could, give him something to think about besides the adrenaline that told his body there was something to fear, even as the memory of what had frightened him slipped from his grasp. "Let's go and get something to drink, shall we? Warm ourselves up. I'm cold, Dad, aren't you cold?" He was sweating and exhausted and standing in the kitchen watching the microwave warm a mug of milk was the last thing he wanted. Almost the last thing he wanted. His father was glancing around the room again, and he fumbled for a way to get him moving, onto the next task. "Or I could make cocoa? Would you like some cocoa?"

"Too much sugar in cocoa," his dad said, looking austere. "Bad for your teeth."

"Just some hot milk, then. Come on, I'll make it."

"You be careful."

"I will, I promise. D'you want to sit in the kitchen while the milk warms?"

It took him a few more tries, but eventually he got his father away from the living-room, looking old and exhausted as he sat at the table and waited for his son to bring him a mug of warm milk. The clock on the wall above the cooker read *4:07am*. Had he ever been this tired in his life before? How was he going to get his dad back to sleep? He couldn't risk more tablets, but perhaps –

"Would you like a couple of biscuits to go with this, Dad?"

"D'you mean, *Dad, can I have a couple of biscuits*? You know it's the middle of the night, don't you?"

"I know, Dad. I just thought –"

"Teenage boys. Can't ever get you filled up." His father smiled indulgently. "Oh well, why not? Get some for both of us. Only make sure you brush your teeth afterwards."

"I will."

In the pantry, he fumbled for the whiskey bottle, adding a generous slug to his father's milk. *Do not consume alcohol. Do not drive or operate heavy machinery.* But what did it matter if his father drank? The damage had been done years ago. If it helped them both cope, where was the harm? Sunlight was sneaking past the edges of the kitchen blind. His father was yawning and rubbing his eyes. He took the milk from Jacob's hand and, ignoring the packet of biscuits, drained it in a single long swallow.

"Shall we get off to bed, then?" he said to Jacob, then smiled. "You're getting so grown up. Used to be I'd put you to bed and then have a good three hours or so to myself before I went up. Funny how things change."

"I know. I'm growing up."

"You'll be leaving me one day soon."

"No, Dad. I won't. I promise I won't leave you."

His father put an arm around his shoulders. "You're my boy."

With his father finally returned to his bed, Jacob had hoped for another hour or so of sleep. But the singing of the birds and the merciless jabs of sunlight were too much for him. He was awake, and another day had dawned, and he had to face it with the few scraps of sleep he'd managed to scavenge already. It was the first day of the holidays. How were they going to make it through?

He rolled over and reached for his phone. It was half-past six and Donna had sent him a text message.

What do you get when you cross
a teacher with a vampire?
Lots of blood tests :-D :-D :-D
Okay it's a bit crap but it's only the first
day. See you in September. D

He smiled to himself and texted back:

Very good. Why aren't you on the telly? - J

She would send him one joke a day, shortly before midnight, on each day of the holidays, and each time he would ration himself to a single reply. It was the only way any of his colleagues would know he was still alive. Some days he thought it was the only way he himself knew he was still alive.

Trying not to feel the exhaustion that made him feel as though he was walking along the bottom of the ocean, he crawled out of bed and opened the curtains. The day was postcard-beautiful, all green plants and golden light and milky brown water. Perhaps some fresh air might fill him with the strength he needed to make it through another day. He pulled a jumper over his t-shirt and pyjama bottoms. In the corridor, the door of the tower-room bathroom had come open again in the night. Trying to move without thinking, he padded down the corridor in his bare feet and pulled it closed.

("Is it the sea coming in?" Ella whispered in his ear. "Is it the water pushing the door open?"

("No, of course it's not. Water spreads out, if the sea came in through the window the whole corridor would be wet. But it wouldn't come this high up anyway."

("Can we hold our breath for long enough to escape yet? Can we practice again tonight?")

He held his breath as he crept past his father's room, on the alert in case the other man was waiting behind the door. Several times he'd had to fight his father off as he exploded out from the doorway, convinced their household was under threat and he was the only one who could save them. He could have avoided this by going down the back staircase instead, but he couldn't face the eternal spectre of Ella, her hair flying as she hopped down the stairs just ahead of him, breathlessly singing as she went. That inane little song she used to adore, about cutting up pieces of fruit –

The thing he had to remember, he thought, as he made it safely to the top of the stairs and allowed himself to breathe again, was that at least this way, Ella had escaped. He was the only one strong enough to cope with his father now. At least Ella had been saved. The words were the mantra that got him past the bitterness that filled his heart each morning.

In the kitchen, he unlocked the door and let the outside burst in over the doorstep. The dew was on the grass and the world smelled fresh and good. The scent of crushed greenery beneath his wellies spiralled up to tickle his nostrils. He drowned it out with a swill of black coffee, liking the way the caffeine jangled along his nerves.

("I don't want to see the sea. Can we sit under that tree there and have a tea-party?"

("Come on. We're going to see the beach. You'll like it when we get there.")

Over half of their garden had vanished now, although if his childhood self had first looked out onto the expanse that still remained, he would have marvelled at the extravagance of space. Once, they'd been told the cliffs would last another fifty years at least, and he'd thought with satisfaction that fifty years was a lifetime, and the house only needed to last until he and Ella were grown. Now the sea had eaten half of the land they'd imagined was theirs, and the time he needed was now measured in the likely span of his father's life, which could be... well, what? Decades, perhaps. His father was a strong man, not yet sixty. Was the house going to last? It had to. He was too tired to contemplate a future where it didn't. On the edge of the cliff, a familiar figure stood like a sentry.

"You're up early," he said, so he wouldn't startle her with his approach. The look Mrs Armitage turned on him was severe – she had no time for small talk – but he took his place beside her anyway, pressing his mug of coffee against his chest as a defence against the breeze that riffled across his hair and crept beneath the cocoon of his jumper and stole the warmth from his skin.

"You should have put a coat on," she told him.

"I'm wearing a jumper."

"So I see. And are you warm enough? Or are you wishing you'd put a coat on?"

The words were on the tip of his tongue. *I'm twenty-seven years old, I don't need you to tell me what to wear.* He kept silent. He didn't want her to know how much he craved even this small sharp approximation of being mothered.

"Look." Mrs Armitage pointed.

The light coming off the water was so bright it was painful.

He had to shade his eyes and squint. After a minute, he made out a smooth slick ball-shape bobbing in the water.

"Seal," she said. "Keep watching. It's hunting."

Jacob watched obediently. After a minute, the seal dived, its body a thick smooth curve of flesh that appeared briefly above the surface.

"I should get back to Dad," he said, hoping for an escape.

"No. Wait." Mrs Armitage's hand on his arm was commanding. "Wait until it comes back up again."

"But –"

"He'll be fine."

He stared perseveringly at the surface of the water. How long could seals hold their breath? He and Ella had known once, but –

("Did you know seals can hold their breath for two hours?" Ella's eyes, wide in disbelief and bright with hope. "That's like four episodes of Scooby Doo. If we practice hard enough we'll be able to do that too.")

"He used to say one day I'd turn into a seal and go back to the sea," said Mrs Armitage, as if she could read his thoughts.

He could feel her looking at him, but stubbornly held off making eye contact for as long as he could.

"Who did?" he asked, when he couldn't avoid her gaze any longer.

"You know perfectly well. Once, we had an argument, and I said I was going out to think about things. When I got down to the boat, he'd taken my scuba gear and hidden it. I was so angry I took the boat out anyway and didn't come back for ten hours. When I got home, he was crying."

"Don't." He had to fight the urge to press his hand over her mouth. "Don't talk about him. I don't want to talk about him."

"You're not talking about him, I am. I asked him if he'd thought I'd drowned, and he said no, he thought I'd left him and gone to live in the ocean instead. It was such a strange thing to hear a grown man say, I wondered if there was something wrong with him. Now it's your turn, Jacob."

"Please stop. It hurts too much to think about. I can't stand it –"

"I can't stand it either, but we both have to stand it. This is the price you pay me. If you don't want to pay it any more, feel free to pay a nurse instead. One thing you remember about Ella."

"Why do you have to keep doing this to me?"

"It's how we keep her alive. Oh, look at that. The seal's come back up."

Out in the water, the seal twirled calmly on its axis, its huge liquid eyes fringed with impossibly long lashes. Jacob wished desperately he could be there with it. Better yet, he wished he could dive below the surface of the water and stay there, quiet and secret, invisible –

"She used to collect stones," he said desperately. "Not just from the beach. Anywhere we went. Off the drive, sometimes. In the road. And when she had too many to hold in her hand, she'd take one of her socks off and carry them home in that. She never did anything with them though. She just left her socks lying around with the toes all full of stones, and I used to find them and empty the stones out and put the socks in the wash so she wouldn't get into trouble. There, is that enough for you? You made me cry, you made me bloody well cry, and now I've got to go back to my house and look after my father and if he sees I'm upset he'll be upset too and I'll never be able to explain why. Are you happy now?"

"Of course I'm not happy. And neither are you. But it's important to remember them, the ones we loved and lost. How else do we keep them alive? You can go now. I'll see you on the first day of term. Be careful."

He could hardly see the ground beneath his feet for the tears that danced in his eyes. He had to force himself to concentrate, aware – as they both always were – of the greedy mouth that gnawed wetly at the land that held them up. Back in the garden, he stopped beneath the apple tree to compose himself, wetting his hands in the dew that clung to the long grass and rubbing them over his cheeks. He couldn't let his father see him with tear-marks on his face.

When he got back inside, he could already hear the fitful panicky stumbling that told him his father had awoken to an empty house and was roaming around upstairs, trying to orient himself.

"Dad!" he called up the stairs. "It's me."

"Jacob!" His father appeared at the top of the stairs, leaning precariously on the bannister to catch his breath. "I've checked upstairs and there's no one, but we need to check downstairs too, they might have got in during the night."

His heart sank. It was going to be one of the days when his father's anxiety clutched him from the moment he opened his eyes, tearing at him throughout the whole weary length of the day. He'd done his best to fathom what might trigger these days, kept a diary of what they had done and said and eaten, noted down the brief glimpses of television they managed to share, but he found no pattern, and after a while the effort became too much. And it was only the first day of the holidays...

"I've checked downstairs. Right round everywhere. There's no one, I promise."

"What did you do that for?" His dad's eyes were wild with horror. "You stupid boy, I've told you – if you think there's someone in the house you come and get me, do you hear?"

He couldn't stand this. He simply couldn't. Not for a whole six weeks. If only he could get his father to go back to sleep for a few hours.

"I'll remember next time." He needed a distraction, but what could he conjure with this little sleep and at this early hour? "Do you want a shower? I can give you a hand if you like."

His dad looked baffled. "Why would I want you to give me a hand in the shower?"

"Never mind. How about you go for a shower and I'll make you a coffee for afterwards?"

Somewhere in the house, a door blew shut. His father's head snapped up.

"What was that?"

"Just a door in the breeze."

"Don't be stupid. We can't afford to be stupid." His dad was already hurrying down the stairs, gesturing imperiously to Jacob to get out of the way. "Go to your room and shut your door. And don't come out until I call you."

"Dad, there's no one... Let me come with you."

"No. It's not safe."

"I can help. I'll help you look. Please, Dad. I need to learn what to do."

"Then stay behind me, and do exactly what I say."

And they were off, a fruitless tour of the house that ended with his father, almost in tears with frustration and terror, slapping Jacob brutally around the face. The blow hurt, but Jacob almost welcomed the release of tension that it brought. Afterwards his father sobbed for a while, until Jacob managed to persuade him upstairs to the shower. When he came down again, subdued and frail-looking in his dressing gown, he accepted the toast Jacob offered him with a smile.

The day trundled along in its familiar groove. They spent the morning checking the doors and the windows, the afternoon sitting quietly in the living-room while his father dozed and grunted and occasionally startled himself awake. Jacob normally fought the temptation to let his dad sleep during the day and knew he'd regret it later, but the early start had eroded his good intentions. Perhaps he could give him one extra tablet this evening, just this once, or perhaps go back to the doctor and ask for something slow-release to keep him under for longer... He was falling into sleep himself, he knew he was, and he ought to fight it, but he couldn't. It was easier to give in to the slow pull and drag of exhaustion and let the waters close over his head.

In the border country between sleeping and waking, he

heard his sister singing to herself. As a baby, she'd always woken before him, and he would open his eyes to the sound of her singing or babbling to herself in her cot. As soon as she could climb out, she'd seek out his company above their parents', pushing open the door a fraction so she could peer in and see if he was still asleep. As long as he kept his eyes closed, she'd occupy herself with whatever she'd brought with her, tucked under her arm like a talisman to shield her on the perilous journey from her room to his. When they'd moved here, his day always began with the distinctive creak of the floorboard outside his bedroom. If he'd known then how few of those mornings there would be –

Coming back to full wakefulness with a start, he saw for a startling heart-stopping moment a face looking in at the window. A couple of rapid blinks, and the face was only the brief conjunction of two wild rose blossoms and a shadow from a cloud passing overhead. His father slumbered on, oblivious and innocent. Jacob's face throbbed. Was it swelling? Would his father notice? And what could he say to him that would satisfy the anxiety this would raise? Perhaps if he got a cold compress? Was that a thing that really worked, or just a parenting fiction to get Ella to calm down and stop crying? The memory drove him from his chair in a kind of frenzy. Why couldn't he get her out of his head today?

In the kitchen, he ran cold water over a clean tea towel and held it to his face. His parents used to use kitchen roll, but of course they had none in the house. The pantry door was ajar, and when he went to close it he saw that another whiskey bottle had materialised, like a confession, among the baked beans and tinned tomatoes. This one was new, the bottle plastic, the label fresh; the brand was the one they stocked in the village shop. Had his father slipped his moorings, crept away from Mrs Armitage's supervision, walked into the village and bought it? The man who ran the shop would probably have noticed nothing unusual. His father could seem quite normal and lucid as long as he kept off the subject of the people who were coming to his house to find them, and as long as the person he was talking to didn't realise everything he said about himself and his family was hopelessly out of date.

Or had he himself bought it and forgotten about it? He hid it beside its identical twin in the Weetabix box.

("Can I tell you a secret?" Ella, smiling and patting at his arm as he put down her breakfast in front of her, the house so silent they might as well have been alone in it. "I don't actually like Weetabricks." She took a huge, heaping spoonful and put it in her mouth, her gaze fixed on his. "But I tell Mummy I do, because she likes me to eat them, and I'm so good at pretending I can even make myself think I like them. So my secret really is, I actually *do* like Weetabricks." A typical Ella-statement, absurd and contradictory and impossible to get to the bottom of.)

He came back out of the pantry, slamming the door to dislodge the thoughts in his head. One of the great puzzles of his father's illness was the way Ella had slipped between the cracks of his memory. It was only Jacob whose days were haunted by the little girl who lived in terror of the lurking sea, but overcame that fear to seek out the things she craved. Daisies and dandelions, stuck in cups of water and left around the house for people to knock over. Pebbles for her socks. Time with her older brother. Ella was with him every day, even as he tried to deny her. Why else was he still living in this house with his father, if not so he could suffer the sweetness of her haunting?

The kitchen was dank and stuffy. The whole house was dank and stuffy, smelling of old food and old man and old memories. He clambered onto the worktop and wrestled with the half-rotten sash window over the sink. The wood had swollen and shrunk over so many winters that it rattled and shook in the breeze that was sometimes the only ventilation the room got, but the window itself stubbornly refused to open. He swore and climbed back down again, unlocked the back door and threw it wide instead. After a minute, he walked out into the garden. Perhaps the fresh air would help the swelling in his cheek. The world was so bright and lovely, surely he could make himself enjoy it.

The shape beneath the apple tree was so still his eyes barely snagged on it at first. It wasn't until the third time that he came back to study the newly-thickened outline of the trunk (*apple tree must have had a growth spurt don't be stupid it's a tree they don't grow that fast there must be something wrong with it no hang on that looks like who the bloody hell*) that he understood what he was looking at.

Someone had come into their garden. Not to the front door, not crunching over the gravel and ringing the doorbell, not someone legitimate he could explain to his terrified and disbelieving father. Someone had crept past his defences, and now they were in his garden. His heart, angry and sore with a too-long effort of patience, swelled with rage. He strode down towards the apple tree, aware that some sort of bellow was coming out of him like steam from a kettle, accompanied by words that came out of his mouth without any intervention at all from his brain ("get the fuck out of here you little bastard this is private fucking land now get moving or I'll fucking kill you right now and throw your body over the cliff –")

"Jacob? Is that you?"

The light was behind the tree and he couldn't make out the face, but the voice was straight out of his dreams.

"I'm sorry, I didn't mean to sneak around – Jacob, it is you, isn't it? I've got the right person?"

His mouth was dry with shock. He could hardly move for hope and fear. He wanted to hurt himself to make sure this was real.

"I – I don't know if you remember me. I didn't know where else to come."

When she moved away from the tree, he could see her in silhouette. Small and slight, long hair streaming down her back, her shoulders sagging under the weight of a rucksack that looked too heavy for her. Jeans and trainers. He shaded his eyes with his hand and blinked, and the colours and details began to come into focus. Fair hair. Blue eyes. All the prettiness he'd known she'd grow into, finally come into being. Her face, grimy and anxious. Her lower lip, chapped and dry, caught beneath the white of her front teeth. She was waiting for him to say something, but he couldn't think of anything to say.

"Jacob, please." She was trying not to cry now. "It's Ella."

And as if her name was a spell, his legs unlocked and he could move again, and he threw himself across the few feet of grass between them and held his little sister in his arms.

Today I realised that the man who hunts me often comes to me in disguises. I think perhaps he must put them on and off like suits. Skin-suits. Flesh-suits. Flesh-and-bone suits. I wonder where he keeps the ones he isn't wearing? Does he hang them in a closet? And what on earth can he look like in the moments when he's naked? If I could catch him in the moments when he changes his suit, perhaps I might begin to understand him.

He was wearing a particularly lovely one the first time we met. We undressed each other as soon as we decently could, or perhaps as soon as we indecently could, and I thought then that I was seeing the core of him, his true self beneath the clothes, but I should have known it was just another disguise. There is nothing more deceptive than the sight of a beautiful face and body. And I deceived him too. I want to forget that part but I can't. I fooled him as well. I showed him my skin-envelope, no scars or inky lines on it yet to tell my story, and he thought he could read everything about me from the touch of his fingers on my flesh. But really I was full of secrets. And over time he began to discover them, just as I began to discover his.

He used to tell me I was his goddess and he wanted to worship me. We both thought he meant it. It took me longer than it should have to realise it was simply the spirits inside him, speaking with his mouth and tongue.

Only by then he was too much in love with me to let me

go, so I had to run away. And now he's found me again, and the only way I can escape from him is to tear off my skin and grow a new one and never, ever let him see it.

It would be easier if I didn't secretly like the suits he wears. He looks good in all of them. It was the suits that first attracted me to him. All of this would be so much easier if a part of me wasn't secretly in love with him.

Chapter Six
2007

The high fence gave Mrs Armitage the comforting illusion that her world was static and secure. The North Sea could continue its campaign to tear down the cliff, but she would know nothing of it. Pressed close against her fence, her fingers grubbing in the clay-heavy soil as she prepared the pit where her new viburnum would sink its roots, she could imagine everything was unchanged from the first time she came here. But wilful blindness was for children and fools, so she opened her eyes and stood up and opened the gate, forcing herself to confront reality.

The land had already begun to settle into its latest shape. Within weeks of a fall, plants would begin re-colonising the edge, making it seem as if this was how it had always been. It was only in her memory that the past would live on.

There was a very small person coming along the cliff towards her. She'd normally describe this person as a child – the person was child-sized, child-shaped, wearing purple wellies with unicorns on them and carrying a small tatty plastic object clutched tight in one small paw. But there was something so utterly un-childlike about the way she walked; very slowly and carefully, shoulders tense, head bowed. As Mrs Armitage watched, the small person stopped, glanced towards the sea, and shuddered. Then she squared her shoulders, took a deep breath, and recommenced her slow careful tread across the scarcely worn grass.

I should go back to the garden, Mrs Armitage thought, *and finish planting that viburnum.*

The soil was beginning to shrink and dry on her hands. She rubbed them against her jeans, knowing she would regret the muddy streaks later when they crumbled onto her carpet. She should wait and wash them properly under the tap. She should go back into her garden, right now, and shut the gate behind her and shoot the bolt home and finish planting the viburnum and go into the house and wash her hands and then decide what to have for lunch. It was ridiculous to stand here, watching the slow agonised approach of this small tousle-haired girl. If she didn't move soon, the child would arrive, and since they already knew each other, they'd have to speak. How did she know her, though? She made a point of not getting to know anyone new.

After a moment's intense thought, the answer came to her. Of course, it was Ella – that frightened little scrap who had thought she was a seal and had to be rescued from the beach where her older brother had stranded them both. The little scrap who she had told to come and visit her some time, if she wanted. Why had she said that? She didn't like people in general, and children were among the least appealing ones on offer. In the moments when she berated herself for her stupidity, she saw that Ella was now far too close for her to make an escape without seeming rude, and she would have to go through with whatever encounter was coming her way.

She was not pleased about this. The treacherous little leap of her heart was nervous anticipation, not pleasure. She wiped her hands again, as if Ella might want to shake hands, and waited for Ella's resolute steps to bring her within speaking distance.

"Hello," she said at last, since Ella didn't seem to be going to say anything.

"I've come to visit," said Ella.

"Yes, you have."

"You said I could visit?"

"Aren't you supposed to be at school?"

"I don't go to school, my mum teaches me at home."

"So why isn't she teaching you now?"

"She's asleep. And so, this is my free time. I'm allowed to go out and play."

"I don't have anything for you to play with here."

"That's all right." Ella held up the plastic thing she was clutching. Mrs Armitage could see now that it was an improbable blue-tinted doe-eyed rainbow-maned creature, about as far from an actual horse as it was possible to get while still somehow looking recognisably like one. "I brought Rainbow Dash." She glanced towards the sea again, giving it the kind of glance one might give to a snake coiled behind glass or an alligator lounging in a concrete pool twenty feet below. "Should we maybe go into your garden?"

"But it's so nice and sunny out here," said Mrs Armitage, with a sudden impulse of cruelty. "I could bring you a drink and a biscuit and we could sit out here and enjoy the sunshine?"

She saw Ella's eyes darken with fear, saw the little fingers clutch tighter around the neck of the plastic horse-thing, and realised she was going to have to let her in before Ella crushed her toy to death. Not that she was concerned with the fate of a piece of vacuum-formed tat, but Ella would be upset; and not that she cared if Ella was upset, but an upset child would be harder to send back along the cliff to her own house when Mrs Armitage's small store of good-will was exhausted.

"Or we could go into the garden and you can help me finish planting something," she suggested, and stood aside from the gate. Ella scurried inside as if the hounds of Hell were snapping at her heels.

Once behind the apparent security of the fence, Ella blossomed. Her death grip on the pony-creature (*Rainbow Dash,* Mrs Armitage thought scornfully, *who thought of these names?*) relaxed, and the tight, frightened concentration on her face dissolved into a smile. When she turned to Mrs Armitage, she seemed three inches taller.

"What shall we do first?" she asked. "Are we planting that plant over there?"

"That's all we're doing. And I've nearly finished. But you can help if you want."

"What do I do to help?" Ella reached out a curious finger, then winced.

"Don't touch it," said Mrs Armitage, too late. "It's spiny. Here, give me your hand." She took Ella's finger and squeezed it until Ella squeaked in protest and a fat bead of blood grew and swelled, then lost its shape and spilled off the end of her finger.

"That hurt." Ella put her finger in her mouth.

"The blood will wash away any germs. You don't want an infection."

"It's a horrible plant. Why did you choose a horrible plant?"

"I like things that know how to defend themselves. Do you still want to help?"

Ella sucked her finger, trapped in the dangerously wobbly moment between tears and stoicism. Then she peered into the shallow pit Mrs Armitage had dug.

"Did you dig that?"

"Yes, of course I did. Who else would do it?"

Ella knelt down and measured the depth with her hand. Then she reached for the trowel and began to scrape away at the base of the hole.

"I think this needs to be a bit deeper," she said, with the total confidence of the very young.

Mrs Armitage opened her mouth to tell her it was already the perfect depth, then closed it again. She had no idea how long the child was planning on staying, but it would be easier to get through it if she was busy with a project outside, while Mrs Armitage hid safely in the kitchen and boiled the kettle for a mug of tea.

What was she going to give Ella to drink, though? A child

that age wouldn't drink tea. She had milk, of course, but some children disliked milk. Other than that, there was water. Rummaging in her cupboards, she was surprised to find a vivid orange bottle of dilutable squash.

As she took it down to examine, she uncovered a vague memory of dropping it into her basket on her way around the village shop. The basket already held a packet of biscuits, shaped like rings and painted in the colours apparently favoured by the people who had designed Ella's dreadful plastic pony. Another moment's investigation revealed the biscuits cowering towards the back behind a can of baked beans.

Of course, she hadn't been hoping Ella would visit. She didn't like visitors. But when you found yourself accidentally inviting them anyway, it was best to be prepared. She studied the instructions on the bottle, then took down a glass. On the counter-top beside her, the kettle shuddered and steamed and clicked itself off.

Out in the garden, Ella was peering into the hole with great concentration.

"I've made you some squash," Mrs Armitage said to Ella's back. The hole had grown at a rather alarming rate. If she put the plant in now, the soil would cover up the first three or four inches of its leaves. "You'll need to wash your hands before you drink it."

"It's not really deep enough yet," Ella said. "I'll just dig a little bit longer first."

"It looks quite deep enough to me," said Mrs Armitage.

Ella reached for the trowel. The light of fanaticism gleamed in her eyes.

"Fine," said Mrs Armitage. "Another few minutes. And then you can come and wash your hands and have something to drink and a biscuit."

Ella blinked. "I'm having juice *and* biscuits?"

"Or you can stop now. It's up to you."

"Just a little bit more," said Ella, and bent over the pit.

Just a little bit more turned into another twenty-eight

minutes of solid effort. After the first five minutes, Mrs Armitage wondered whether she should simply insist Ella stopped digging; after ten, she wondered if she should help her. But it was pleasant sitting in the patio chair with the sun warming her shoulders, and Ella seemed happy enough. And besides, it was her trowel and her garden and if she wanted to let a small child dig a pointlessly large pit in one part of it, who was going to stop her? One of the great advantages of living alone was that no one would know anything about your life unless you chose to tell them. She drank her tea and ate one of the biscuits. A small black fly crawled around the rim of Ella's glass of squash, then fell in. For a moment it was safe, then the surface-tension broke and its legs wriggled in panic as it began to drown. She wondered if Ella's mother had missed her child yet, and if she minded.

"There." Ella straightened up and dropped the trowel onto the grass. Her face, behind the streaks of mud, was rosy and triumphant. "I think it's deep enough now." Her hands were thickly crusted with muddy soil and the knees of her jeans were filthy. "Now I can have my juice and biscuit."

"Not before we clean you up first," said Mrs Armitage sternly.

"Do you want to see how deep the hole is now?"

"We'll look in a little while."

"It's really, really deep. It took me ages."

"It won't get any less deep for not being looked at for ten minutes. Come along."

At the door of the kitchen, she encountered a new problem; Ella's jeans and boots were so thickly plastered in mud that there was no way of getting her to the sink without ruining the kitchen floor. She pondered the dilemma for a moment, Ella waiting trustfully at her side, then took off Ella's wellies and jeans, leaving her standing in mismatched socks that were far too big for her and a pair of tiny white pants.

"Why do the heels of your socks come all the way up the back of your leg?"

"I borrowed some of Jacob's," said Ella. "I like his socks more than mine."

"Does your mother know?"

"She lets me get myself dressed."

"I see. And how about Jacob?"

Ella shrugged. "I'll put them back before he gets home."

None of this seemed satisfactory, but it was hardly her problem how other people chose to raise their children. So she shooed Ella towards the kitchen sink, fetched a chair for her to stand on, and worked grimly away with a nail brush until Ella's hands, a little pink from their scrubbing, emerged once more. There was a small scratch on her finger where the viburnum had jabbed at her, and another small ooze of blood.

As a child, Mrs Armitage had been to a zoo once and watched two chimpanzees as they sat under a dripping wet wooden platform in the rain and groomed each other, one sitting tranced and blissful as the other combed through its fur and occasionally extracted a tick, which it put in its mouth and ate. Her friends had cooed and sighed over the sight, then confessed how much they loved having their hair played with, as if they were the first humans who had ever discovered this. Mrs Armitage had wondered how it felt to eat a bug that had grown fat on the blood of your best friend, and if the burst of red iron in your mouth would spark darker wonderings about how the rest of their body might taste.

The girl's hands were fit to be seen now, which made the contrast with her streaky face more distressing. There was no flannel here but there was a clean dishcloth, so she soaked that in warm water and dabbed and rubbed at Ella's face until the sink was filled with fine gritty fragments and the elfin face was clean. Ella stood obedient and patient as a well-trained dog, letting this strange woman groom and neaten her as if they'd been friends all their lives. Her hair was beginning to unravel from its plait. Leaving Ella standing on the chair, Mrs Armitage took a comb from her rucksack, tugged the bobble from the end of the plait and began work. Ella's whole body radiated the satisfaction of a cat being stroked. She finished the plait and lifted Ella down from the chair. Ella hesitated between the biscuits, chose a lilac one, and drank her juice in a long, industrious swallow.

"Shall we go and look at the hole for the plant now?" Ella asked.

"What do you say first?"

"Oh. Thank you."

"Thank you for – ?"

Ella looked confused. "The biscuits?"

"And…"

"And… the juice…"

"And…"

"And…" Ella waited for a clue.

"And washing your hands and face and brushing your hair."

"Oh yes. And washing my hands and face and brushing my hair. And for letting me dig the hole for the plant."

"You don't need to thank me for that, that's the thing you did for me. So, thank you. Now shall we go and have a look at it?"

In the doorway, Ella leaned against her as she put her feet back into her wellies, ignoring her jeans. The warmth of Ella's body against hers was disturbing. She had to fight the urge to move away. She wondered what it would feel like if Ella tried to hold her hand. She could see the mound of soil from the kitchen doorway.

Side by side, they stood and inspected the pit Ella had dug.

"I think it's deep enough now," said Ella, flushed and modest.

Mrs Armitage wondered how a child as small as Ella had dug such a thing, and if a few more trowelfuls of earth might disclose molten lava.

"I wanted to make sure the whole plant can get buried," said Ella. Mrs Armitage blinked.

"I take it your parents don't do much gardening," she said after a moment.

"We plant bulbs, I've planted lots of bulbs, that was really fun. And seeds, one time I grew sunflowers. Anyway, I made the hole really, really deep. That way it can be nice and warm while it's growing."

The laughter was bubbling up in her throat like champagne, as if she was a bottle and someone had uncorked her and the slightest movement would send golden bubbles pluming up into the sky. Mrs Armitage kept herself very still.

"Did I do it right?" Ella asked, like a skilled actor covering for a friend who had blanked on their lines.

"It's an excellent hole," said Mrs Armitage briskly. "You did a splendid job. It looks exactly the right depth. And very strong sides as well. We don't want it to cave in."

"It was hard work, but I wanted to make it a really, really good one."

"It's possibly the best planting pit I've ever seen," said Mrs Armitage, wondering where this effortless facility for lies had suddenly come from. "If I had a camera I'd take a photograph."

"I could draw a picture of it for you. Only it might not be until tomorrow, because I'm a bit tired now."

"I should think you are a bit tired. Anyone would be tired after digging a hole that big. I don't know if I could have dug a hole that big." Was she doing this right? Laying it on too thick? Ella's eyes were shining with pleasure. "Now, shall we get this thing planted?"

Her gardening gloves were made of tough golden leather and fastened tightly around her wrists. The viburnum protested when she lifted it, but its thorns were no match for the cured skin of a dead animal. She pulled it free of its black plastic pot and lowered it carefully into its grave. Ella watched, quivering with excitement and tension, as the plant's spiny tips disappeared below the surface of the soil.

"It was just right," she breathed, obviously relieved.

"It was. Well done."

"So, now do we fill all the soil in?"

"You can do that part, you've got the trowel. I'll keep an eye on you and make sure you're doing it right."

The viburnum had been a strong healthy plant, chosen with care from the garden centre and carried perilously home on the bus. It had cost her eighteen pounds and ninety-nine pence (actually, nineteen pounds, since she'd put the penny in the charity box on the counter). She'd been looking forward to seeing if it would have time to grow and thrive and blossom before the sea came for it. Nonetheless, there was a certain fierce satisfaction in seeing the flat smooth circlet of earth that Ella had patted down with her trowel and watered carefully. It was a strong plant, chosen with care. Perhaps it would break through the surface and survive despite being buried alive. If not, at least she'd had this afternoon. Ella was leaning on her again, but this time she did not move away. There was something warm and silky beneath her fingers. When she looked down, she found that she'd removed her glove and placed her hand on top of Ella's head.

"Now it'll grow beautiful and strong," said Ella, with great satisfaction, and yawned. "I like gardening."

"You can come and help me another time, if you like." Her voice, like the treacherous hand that stroked the smooth dome of Ella's newly-plaited hair, seemed to have found a will of its own. "Or come for some juice and a biscuit. Unless you're busy. I'm sure you've got plenty of other friends to play with."

"No, not really. I do work with Mummy in the mornings, and then when Jacob comes home from school I play with Jacob."

"Why don't you go to school?" What she really wanted to know was *is there something wrong with you that means you can't go to school like a normal child?* Why was she hesitating? "Is there something wrong with you that means you can't go to school like a normal child?"

"Mummy says she likes to teach me herself," said Ella, her voice calm and easy. "But I don't think that's the real reason. There's a very bad man looking for my mummy and daddy, and they have to keep moving house to hide from him. Only now they've bought this house, so we can't keep moving, so they have to try and stay hidden as much as possible."

Mrs Armitage considered this for a moment.

"So your father doesn't have a job?" she asked. "And what about your brother? Doesn't he go to school either?"

"Oh, it's safe for Daddy and Jacob. I think the bad man's only looking for Mummy." She said these words so easily, as if what she was describing was as mundane as *and on Saturday mornings we go to the supermarket and then for lunch at a café*, that Mrs Armitage wondered if she was understanding correctly. "So Daddy goes to work and Jacob goes to school, and Mummy stays at home and I stay with her so she's not lonely."

"And how do you know all this? Have they told you about it?"

"I hear them arguing sometimes," said Ella, with a shrug. "Can I go to the toilet, please?"

"But what about – yes, I suppose so. Take your wellies off at the door and don't touch anything on the way upstairs. I don't want to find mud on my walls."

Alone in her garden, she stared at the spot where her new plant was buried and reminded herself that she didn't want to get involved. She had her own life to live and her own demons to face. As she said these words, out loud and very firmly, to the buried viburnum, she remembered that she hadn't told Ella which door led to the bathroom, had not even checked if Ella was capable of using the toilet without supervision. The child ought to be old enough by now, but she was home-schooled and her parents both sounded entirely mad, so it was best to be sure. She hurried inside, stumbling over Ella's discarded wellies. There were a few crumbs of mud on the stairs, but the walls were clean of fingerprints. She could hear Ella singing to herself. There was a muddy streak on the bathroom door, and another one on the door to her bedroom. She tapped sharply on the bathroom door and the singing stopped.

"I forgot to ask if you need any help," she said into the silence.

"No, I'm fine." The toilet flushed, and then there was the sound of running water as Ella began washing her hands. She was only little; the chances were she'd give them a quick rinse and then smear the rest of the soil off onto the hand towel. Mrs Armitage pushed the door open and came in.

"Use plenty of soap," she instructed. "That's it. Now rinse, and wash them again. I don't want my towels ruined." Ella reached for the nailbrush and looked at Mrs Armitage questioningly. "That's right, give them a good scrub if you like."

"I didn't know you could get brushes for your hands."

"Well, now you've learned something worth knowing. Another rinse. That's it. Now dry them."

"I got some mud on the door," Ella confessed.

Mrs Armitage held the cloth out to her. "You can wipe it off, then."

"And I got some on the other door too. I didn't know which was your bathroom so I went in your bedroom for a minute. Then I came straight out again and went in here."

"Then you'd better wipe that door too."

"I saw a photograph by your bed."

"If you saw the photograph then you certainly didn't just go in for a minute and come straight out again."

"Is it your husband? The one who drowned?"

"Why do you want to know?"

"I just wondered."

"Yes, it is. Go and wipe the door."

"How did he drown?"

"I told you. He went out in his boat when he shouldn't have."

"All by himself?"

"No, with a friend. His friend drowned too."

"Do you miss him?"

"I loved him, of course I miss him. But these things happen. And just so you know, you shouldn't ask people questions like that. Now go and wipe the door."

"And didn't you have any children before he died?"

"No. No, I didn't. I live entirely on my own and I have no husband and no family and no friends or gentleman callers. And I am completely happy with all of that. Do you have any more questions, or are you going home now?"

"What's a gentleman caller?"

"If you need to ask, you don't need to know. Go home now."

"Should I come again?"

"Did I say you could come again?"

"Yes."

"Then that's the answer, isn't it? Now put your jeans on and off you go."

Standing beside the gate that led to the cliff outside, Ella paused for a moment. Mrs Armitage felt her shudder.

"You don't have to go back along the cliff," said Mrs Armitage. "There's a perfectly good road. It's even got a footpath."

"I'm not allowed on the road."

"You're allowed to walk along the cliff-top on your own, but not on the road on your own?" Ella looked guilty. "Does anyone even know you're here?"

Ella stuck out her lip. "Mummy said I was allowed to go out and play so I went out and played."

"Well, all righty then." If this strange girl's even stranger mother was wandering the garden or roaming the cliff-edge, or even on the phone to the police or the coastguard, that wasn't Mrs Armitage's problem. "Off you go." Ella hesitated. "What's the matter?"

"I don't like the sea being so close," Ella whispered, then took another deep breath and climbed out through the gate.

Mrs Armitage watched as she picked her way home, as slowly and carefully as if the path was littered with broken glass. It must have taken some courage for her to come here. Or perhaps it was simply the desperation of the lonely. She herself had never minded being alone, but she wasn't much like other people.

She thought about going after the girl, about taking her hand in hers and putting her strong stocky body between the girl and the edge of the cliff. She could imagine exactly how Ella's hand would feel in hers, the softness of her palm, the slight but growing strength of the muscles beginning to form beneath the remnants of the childish pudge. Ella's legs were shorter than hers, and the child would have to take three or four paces to every two of hers, bobbing alongside her like a puppy on a lead. Of course, she could always slow her pace to the child's, but she imagined that she would choose not to. She was done making compromises to please other people. Instead, other people would have to fit in with her, or not.

She watched Ella as far down the cliff as she could. When she returned to her house, she found Rainbow Dash standing on the kitchen table.

She put the toy on her bookshelf, turning its face to the wall so she wouldn't have to see it staring at her. Then she took down a gardening book. Before Ella came again, she would have to dig up enough of the viburnum to take some cuttings, so she could deceive Ella into believing the plant had begun to put out strong green shoots above the ground.

Chapter Seven
Now

Afterwards he had no clear recollection of the time that took them from the fierce tight embrace beneath the apple tree to the two chairs in the kitchen and the glass of water and the single brimming bowl of cereal that she tore into with the shameless concentration of the truly hungry. He could remember only a series of small distinct moments that pricked at his skin. The sobbing hitch in her breath as she waited for him to recognise her. The thundering of blood in his ears. The flashes of light that came through the leaves of the apple tree and jabbed him in the eyes before he closed them. The way she smelled, warm denim and warm human and a blue-scented deodorant.

Now they were in the house, and his heart was beating at a near-normal speed once more, and his most prominent feeling was a sharp pang of loss. The sister he'd lost had been small enough to carry, downy hair and peach-fuzz skin, her body straight and true like a stick of rock, her face plump and childish. The sister who had come back to him was almost a woman, older than the students in his class. Her hair had darkened a few shades, no longer cornsilk but a golden sand colour, the colour he'd once imagined the beach would be, before the day they first climbed down to the sea's edge and found pebbles and seaweed and brown, and it was clumsily plaited into a thick braid that hung over her shoulder. Her ears were pierced and her bitten fingernails were polished a bright aqua that had begun to chip at the edges.

If they'd been allowed to grow up together, these changes would have passed almost unnoticed, and he would have felt the shock of her transformation only when he happened across an old photograph. As it was, his heart careered around his chest as if it was trapped in a pinball machine. Joy. Sadness. Elation. Heartache. Joy. Confusion. Sadness. Confusion. Elation. Fifty thousand points ratcheted up in the space of time it took him to make a sandwich and put it on the table. His sister had come back to him, and she was a complete stranger. A stranger who he didn't yet dare to get to know, a stranger who he was terrified might disappear again at any moment, driven away by the wrong question asked in the wrong tone of voice.

Nonetheless, when she saw the sandwich he had made for her, cut into triangles because she always preferred it that way, and when they saw into each other's eyes and knew they were both remembering the same moment in their shared past, the girl was unmistakeably Ella.

("I like it best when they're in triangles," she whispered, leaning against him as she wobbled on the chair she stood on, her breath hot and tickly in his ear. "Only, if I ask for triangles that makes them taste like squares. But the bread can't hear me when I whisper, so it doesn't matter if you make them into triangles this time even though I told you, because they won't taste like squares." And he'd thought about telling her not to be ridiculous, but then some softer instinct had prevailed and from then on he'd always cut her sandwiches into triangles, and each time she'd waited until their parents weren't looking and then rewarded him with a secret smile.)

"Is ham all right?" he asked. "You're not a vegetarian or anything?"

"No, it's fine, I'm not vegetarian. Are you – um –"

"No, I still eat meat too. Couldn't give up bacon, I'm afraid."

She smiled at him shyly, as if she too was afraid that one or both of them might suddenly vanish. "Bacon's good."

"I could make you a bacon one if you prefer? I just automatically made you a ham one because –" on the precipice of the past, he teetered, hesitated, pulled himself back from the edge. "I mean, it's like, the default sandwich, isn't it, and –"

"Is this your dinner I'm eating? I don't want to eat all your food."

"I've got plenty." His heart ached. Where and how had she been living that she thought she might need to worry about eating more food than he could spare?

"I know you weren't expecting me."

"Ella, for God's sake stop it! You're my sister!" The words made the moment real for him at last, and he felt tears gather in a solid lump somewhere in his chest. "You're my sister, of course you can have – look, where have you *been*, anyway, what *happened* to you?" A ridiculous question, as if Ella had simply slipped out of the house to visit a friend and been a couple of hours longer than he had expected. His voice sounded familiar in some unwelcome way, as if he had heard the same phrase before from someone else, not once but many times, and he realised with a kind of sinking horror that he'd entirely forgotten about his father.

"Wait here," he said, hurrying from the kitchen. How was he going to explain Ella's presence? Could he hide her in the house somewhere, conceal her behind the door his father passed by as if it did not even exist? But then, what would happen if his father heard something and chose to finally open it? What if he was armed with the spade or the garden fork or some huge spar of wood stolen from a fence somewhere? There would be nowhere for Ella to run. He couldn't hide a whole extra person in the house, that was ridiculous. He would have to come clean. But then, what could he tell his father?

"Is there somebody there?" His father's voice, rising with the panic that often took him when he woke suddenly from afternoon slumber. "Who's there? I've got a gun, so don't try anything."

"It's me, Dad." He tried to make his voice simultaneously loud and reassuring. "Don't worry. There's no one else here." He'd said it so many times the words came out automatically, but now they were a lie. There was someone else here, and soon he'd have to find a way to explain her. Would his father remember Ella? And would her presence bring back the memories of the woman who had taken her away? As if frantic movement could somehow drive away the problems, he flung open the door of the living-room.

"Jacob!" His father stood behind the door, holding – where on earth had he found it? – a blackened iron poker over his head, ready to strike. When he saw it was Jacob, he lowered the poker but did not let go. "I heard someone moving around and you sounded like you were scared so I thought –"

"There's nobody." He swallowed the lie. "There's nothing to worry about, I promise." He reached out a hand for the poker. "Shall I put that away?"

His father shook his head stubbornly. "You don't know where it goes."

Neither do you, thought Jacob wearily. The poker was nothing he recognised, but his father had a gift for rummaging out improvised weapons from long-neglected corners of the house.

"You can make us both a cup of tea, though," his dad said. "Time you learned how."

"Dad, I – okay, yes. I'll go and make a cup of tea." He tried hard not to mind these moments, knowing his dad couldn't help it, but sometimes he felt the frustration might split him in half. He reached again for the poker, but his father moved it firmly away from him. "Why don't you sit down?"

"No, I'll come with you," his father contradicted him. "I'm not leaving you on your own with a kettle yet."

What was his dad seeing when he looked at him? He'd been allowed to use the kettle since he was ten years old. Surely his dad couldn't believe he was looking at a pre-teen boy?

"I can manage, I promise."

"I tell you what, if you do well this time then I'll let you do it by yourself next time – what the hell was that?"

"What was what?"

"There's someone in the kitchen."

"Dad, wait. Wait a minute."

"Keep back." He gripped the poker with both hands. "I'll sort it."

"Dad, listen to me, there is someone in the kitchen but it's someone you know, I promise, you mustn't –"

His father wasn't listening. He was completely lost in his own head now, and nothing Jacob could say would reach him. His hand was on the kitchen door. Jacob took in a deep breath, ready to yell to Ella to run and not come back.

"Hello." His father sounded bewildered but welcoming, unexpectedly gentle, as if he'd discovered an unexpected small animal waiting by the door. "I didn't know we had a visitor."

Ella sat mouse-still at the table. She looked from Jacob to their father, then back again. Her face was white.

"It's all right, I won't bite." The poker clattered to the floor, just missing his sock-clad foot. "Are you a friend of Jacob's? I'm his father. Nice to meet you."

"Dad," said Jacob. "This is Ella. You remember Ella?"

"Ella." Their father frowned. "I don't think I know an Ella. But you know what Jacob's like. He likes to keep his cards close to his chest. Have you known each other long?"

"Dad, it's *Ella*," Jacob repeated, wretched and miserable. "Your – um – you remember? She used to – I mean, she – um – you know her, Dad, you do know her, I promise. She's your –" the word clung to the end of his tongue, and it took him several tries to dislodge it – "your daughter. Remember? Your daughter."

"My daughter?" His father looked baffled. "Ignore my son, he says ridiculous things sometimes. It's nice to meet you. Has Jacob been looking after you properly? He's never brought a girl home before."

"Oh God," said Jacob. "Ella, I'm so sorry –"

"Let me make a cup of tea." His father's smile was terrifying in its twinkly indulgence. "Then I'll leave you both in peace."

"Dad, she's not my *girlfriend*, she's my... she's your daughter, don't you remember? Please try and remember."

"Good God, Jacob, you're allowed to bring a girl home."

"Dad." Jacob knew it was useless, that there was no way he could bring back the parts of his father's memory that had been lost for years, but he had to try. "Dad. Please listen. This is Ella. Don't you remember? Ella." His father frowned and Jacob knew he was on dangerous ground, but he had to keep trying, if not to make his father remember, then at least to show Ella that he was doing his best for her. "She was born when I was ten. You took me to meet her in the hospital. Remember the hospital? And when I held her, you said –"

"Be quiet!" His father's sudden roar of rage came out of nowhere, as did the flailing arm that struck Jacob heavily on the shoulder. "Be quiet, you stupid boy! I won't have this, do you hear me? I won't! Stop it, just shut the fuck up with all your stupid fucking – stupid – fucking –"

"Dad, please, I'm sorry."

"So you should be. Talking rubbish like that. I won't have it. I won't."

"I know, I shouldn't have said anything, forget I said anything. Would you like a cup of tea?"

"Don't think you can get round me by being nice to me. You're in trouble, do you hear me?"

"I know Dad, and I'm not trying to get round you. I just think I ought to make you a cup of tea. Would you like that?"

"I'll make one," said Ella. Her eyes were fixed on their father. She looked as if she was thinking furiously. "If you don't mind me going through the cupboards?"

"Someone's brought you up properly. Jacob, you could take a few lessons from this one." His father looked beadily around the kitchen. "I see he made you some lunch, at least. Jacob, make sure you clear that lot up later, don't leave it for me to do, and don't be getting your friend here to clear up after you. I'm so sorry, love, I've forgotten your name."

Her hands fumbled in the cupboard. A mug fell out and she caught it with shaking hands. "It's Ella."

"That's pretty. Like the girl it belongs to."

"Let's go into the living-room," said Jacob. "Dad, shall I get you some biscuits as well? Would you like a biscuit?"

Sweating with embarrassment, he shepherded his father back into the living-room, got him installed with his cup of tea and his biscuit, praying he wouldn't hear anything strange, say anything strange, start ranting about people breaking into the house or begin another endless fruitless hunt for intruders. *Please, Ella,* he thought, *please don't leave while I'm not there to keep an eye on you, please stay and let me explain.*

"I'm sorry," he said as soon as he was back in the kitchen. "I should have warned you." He wanted to touch her, to make sure she was real, but he wasn't sure how. How could this be the little sister who had once crawled all over him and blown raspberries down his ear? She looked as shy as he felt.

She raised her hand to her mouth, nipped at the skin at the edge of her finger and peeled off a thin little strip. "Does he think it's still before I was born? Does he think you're still little?"

"I don't know how old he thinks I am, to be honest. Sometimes he sounds almost normal, asks me how school was and what the kids are like. Only then he says something about homework or the queues in the dinner-hall or something, and I realise he's remembering me being a student, not a teacher."

"So you did it? You became a teacher?"

"Yep."

"That's brilliant."

"How about you? I mean, do you have any plans right now or –"

"I don't really know. I'm not clever like you. I mean, I'm doing A-levels but I'm not doing very well. My teachers are really nice about it but I'm pretty sure I'm going to fail."

He'd never pictured her at school. But then he'd never pictured her growing up, either.

"Your finger's bleeding," he said.

"Oh." She sucked at the bead of blood. "That's what I get for biting my nails."

"Let me get you a plaster – oh, for God's sake, was that Dad calling?"

"It's all right, I know he needs you."

"We'll talk properly later, he'll go to sleep after dinner – hi, Dad," he called back, as his father's voice grew louder and more anxious. "I'm here. Everything's safe."

It was the best evening of his life. Everything he said and did and thought felt different because Ella was here once more, recalling that magical year when their house had been a happy one. Three places laid at the kitchen table: three plates in the washing-up bowl. Such a small token of such a huge change. Outside the door to the living-room where he'd risked leaving his father alone with Ella for a few minutes, he found himself breathless, and realised this was because he was holding his breath, as if even exhaling might shatter the reality that his sister had come back to him and was here in the house, waiting for him, in the shadowy half-light of the tightly curtained living-room. But she was still there, still real, and when she turned to look at him and smiled, he thought his chest might burst with the complicated joy that bloomed behind his breastbone.

In his chair, his mug of milk and whiskey drained, his father was already nodding where he sat. Jacob patted at his father's shoulder (*be extra sure to be gentle because Ella's watching*), helped the older man from his chair (*Ella's here now so make sure you don't complain when he falls against you*) and herded him upstairs, into the bathroom and then into his bed (*please don't ask me to lie down with you tonight I want to talk to Ella*). When he came downstairs again, his face was split wide with a smile he simply couldn't keep in check (*you have someone to smile at now because Ella's come home*). The whole house felt different, lighter, warmer, fresher, more welcoming. For the first time since he was sixteen, he was glad for the holidays.

Ella had half-opened the curtains and was standing at the window. With her back to the room and the sunlight turning her shape to shadow, she looked almost terrifyingly like their mother. This must be how the world was for his father all the time – half-remembered ghosts and memories lurching out of corners, and a home where nothing quite made sense any more. Not wanting to frighten her, he waited until she turned away from the window and saw him, then realised that discovering he'd been watching her for an unknown length of time was probably worse.

"I didn't mean to make you jump," he said, wishing he dared give her a hug, the way he would have done when she was small. How much did normal brothers and sisters touch each other when they were out of childhood? How would they ever learn the rules after so long apart?

"The sea's so much closer."

He reached past her to pull the curtains shut again.

"No, I'd rather see it. That way it can't creep up on me while I'm not looking."

Even on the coldest night, she'd always slept with the curtains open. When the howl of the sea became too much for her and she crept into his bed instead, she would open his curtains first. If he got up in the night to close them, she'd wait until he was asleep once more, then open them again.

"It's not that," he said. "It's just my dad – our dad, I mean – he wanders sometimes. If he sees his reflection he thinks there's someone in the house with us."

"Okay. I'll remember."

"I wish he'd remember who you are. He might do better tomorrow but I doubt it."

"Was Dad – I mean, how long has he been – ?"

"He was never right after you and – " he still couldn't quite bring himself to say the word. "I mean, after you – when you –" his throat was tight and full of mucus and he could hear his voice cracking in the way it did when he was thirteen.

"Shall we not talk about this tonight?" Ella whispered.

"Okay, good idea. Let's not." He cast desperately around for something normal they could talk about instead. "Um – would you like a snack or something? Or would you like to, um, see your room?" What was wrong with him? That made it sound as if she was a hotel guest rather than the daughter of the house and his beloved sister. "You are staying, aren't you?" She hesitated. "Come on, Ella, you've got to stay. Where are you going at this time of night?"

"If you're sure you don't mind."

"Don't be daft, you live here!" The words sounded stupid as soon as he'd spoken them. "I mean, this is your home." Better? Worse? "You know what I mean," he finished, and led the way out of the living-room.

He'd grown used to the half-furnished state of their house, the few rooms they lived in vastly outnumbered by those they didn't, but with Ella by his side he was once more conscious of the strangeness of the place he called home. But of course it was Ella's home too, and she seemed to know it as well as she ever had, avoiding the creaky floorboards and the places where the nails would snag your socks with the same instinctive movements he made himself. She knew as well as he did that her room was next to his, that the door creaked if you let it open too wide, and that the rattle of the window in its frame meant dry weather and a fine day tomorrow…

"Oh my God," Ella whispered.

"I didn't like to get rid of anything," he said. "I know

105

the clothes won't be any good to you any more, but I didn't like to…"

She wasn't listening; she was down on her knees in front of the doll's house, tugging open the door and peering inside as if the only space she could cope with in this moment was the tiny ordered domesticity of the imaginary people who lived there. The house had come with people made of wood and bendy pipe-cleaners, their spherical smiling heads beaming blandly up from beneath their woollen hair, but Ella had replaced them on the first day with the plastic ponies she adored, and now every room in the house was filled with doe-eyed horses with rainbow manes.

"I thought I'd dreamed this," she said. "I used to dream sometimes I had this doll's house, and I loved it so much. There was so much I thought I could remember, but I was never sure… Do you ever have that feeling?"

Looking at his little sister, he thought he might be having that feeling right now.

"Is it too creepy in here for you?" he asked. "You can have my room if you like, and I'll sleep in here. The room I'm in now, I mean. I moved next to Dad so I can hear him."

"No, it's fine. It's not creepy at all."

"I know it's really early but I don't stay up late because Dad often gets up in the night. But you don't have to –"

"It's fine. I'm tired too."

It sounded like a polite fiction but he could see she really meant it. From his perspective, Ella had simply materialised under the apple tree, but of course she'd had to travel to get here. Would he ever dare to ask her about that? Would he ever dare ask her about where their –

"Um, do you need anything? Toothbrush or toothpaste or anything?"

"I've got everything with me."

"You'll have to shut the door," he blurted out clumsily. "Dad wanders sometimes but if I leave this door shut he seems to sort of –" he managed to stop himself from saying *forget about what's in here*, but she must have known what he was going to say. How must it feel to her, to know her father had retained no memory of her?

"I'll be fine." She smiled. "I promise. I'm not seven any more, remember?"

He didn't want to leave her here alone, in a room she'd been frightened of as a child, with all the emptiness of the house and the sea echoing in her ears. But he couldn't think of anything else to say.

"I'll see you in the morning, then."

He woke shortly after midnight to an eerie silence, and the paradoxical conviction that he was needed. *Dad,* he thought blearily, and stumbled out of bed to peer in to his dad's room. But his father was still mercifully asleep, starfished across the bed with his mouth slightly open, his heavy breath verging on a snore. The sight was too vulnerable and intimate to be endearing, but he lingered anyway. Did his father still dream? Or was sleep now a blessed relief from memory?

The need for sleep dragged at him like water, but still there was a lightness in his body, a sense-memory of something good that had happened and was still happening, even as he struggled to think what it might be. When he remembered, he knew at once what it was that had woken him. She'd never liked to sleep in her own room. She'd always been afraid of the sea.

Thank God his father was still asleep. Perhaps he, too, felt the joy of Ella's return, even if his conscious mind couldn't connect the young woman who had come back to them with the small daughter he never mentioned. He inched along the corridor, wincing with every crack and murmur of wood, looking over his shoulder to check that his father was not creeping up on him, determined and terrified.

The door to Ella's room was open.

But the room itself was as empty and desolate as if he'd dreamed her.

His first thought was that this was exactly what had

happened: he'd dreamed his sister's return, and was only now waking to the truth. But no; there was Ella's rucksack, the bedclothes were disturbed, and there was a faint warmth in the room. She was here, he hadn't dreamed her. So where – ?

He opened the door to the room next to Ella's that had once been his, trying not to see how desolate and dreadful it looked with the gaping space where his bed had been, and the un-treasured possessions of his childhood littered where he'd thrown them. Had she come in here, half-asleep and looking for comfort? If so, she must have been so frightened –

"Hey." Ella's voice, ghostly, came to him from low down and beside the door, and he almost swallowed his tongue. "I'm here. I know I shouldn't be."

She was crouched on the floor, with her back against the wall. When he sat down beside her, he could feel the tension radiating from her skin.

"I moved into the room next to Dad's," he said. "It's easier to look after him. Can't you sleep?"

"I'm fine, I can hear the sea, that's all. I know it's stupid. I forgot you'd moved rooms and I wondered if you were still awake, and when you weren't here I thought I'd stay for a bit."

He wished he had something to wrap her in. He'd forgotten how much she truly hated this house.

"Ella, did you ever try to find me?" Here in the dark he could finally ask the question that had haunted him all day. "I mean, I'm so glad you have now, I'm so glad you're here, but – I looked and looked for you, I always hoped you'd write to me or come back, but you never did. I thought I'd never see you again, and then you came out of nowhere."

"I wanted to. Mum wouldn't give me the address."

He wasn't sure he was ready to talk about their mother at all yet, let alone to hear her mentioned with such casualness.

"But the internet? I'm on Facebook, I've got an open profile. You know my name, you know Dad's name, you knew what the house looked like and roughly where we lived. There aren't that many villages that are –" he stopped himself from saying the words *falling into the sea* – "along this bit of coast."

"I know, when you say it like that it sounds so pathetic. But Mum – well, she didn't want me looking for you, and I didn't want to –"

It wasn't her fault she loved a monster. She'd been left with no one else to love.

"I'm so glad you came here."

"Please don't be angry with her. I know she left you behind but she was doing her best."

"Of course I'm not angry with her," Jacob lied. Was he convincing Ella? The little sister he remembered took her older brother's opinions as gospel. He would have to get used to the idea that she might have her own opinions.

She was looking again at the shell of his childhood room, made ghostly by the night and the vanished furniture and the posters that peeled from the walls. It was, if possible, even more creepy than her own. "You didn't take your stuff when you moved rooms."

"I was in a bit of a rush."

"And you never came back for it?"

"I didn't, no." He'd come back just once, for the photo of Ella and his mother that he'd used as a bookmark for a while. Their family had never been much for photos. He'd been lucky to find that one. "I didn't seem to need it." Before he could stop himself, his face split wide with a yawn.

"I'm keeping you up." Ella was on her feet instantly.

"No, it's fine, I don't mind. It's nice to wake up and chat to someone lucid."

"Does he wander?"

"Sometimes. If you hear him, it's best to stay put."

"Okay. I'll remember."

He wanted to keep Ella here with him for longer, the two of them surrounded by the ghosts of their discarded childhoods, but the morning was already rushing towards them and he needed to be ready for the day. He wanted to kiss her goodnight, but she was still half a stranger to him. So he stood in his old room and watched her leave it, heard the hesitation of her feet outside her own doorway as she gathered herself for what lay on the other side, then went back to the room next to his father's and let sleep take him.

Chapter Eight
2007

In her dream, Mrs Armitage was in her rowboat, pulling hard against an incoming tide. The sea was thick and opaque like soup and the air around her was warm; she had the feeling that if she chose, she could walk across the water. Her boat was low in the water, perhaps because of the stack of equipment at her feet – newly-filled air-tanks, the spare gas-can, her wetsuit – or perhaps because her husband was with her, watching with grave, attentive eyes as she bent forward and pulled back, bent forward and pulled back, dipping the oars again and again.

"I know this is a dream," she told him. "You're dead. I wish you weren't, but you are. So whatever happens next is just my brain amusing itself while I sleep."

Her husband smiled and reached out a hand towards her. For a moment she didn't dare look for fear it would be grey and swollen, the flesh nibbled by the delicate mouths of fish as it soaked off the bones, but then she remembered that she was dreaming and she could control whatever happened next. So she told herself that his hand would be as she remembered, and when it came to rest on her knee, it was warm and strong and smooth and brown, long fingers and knotty knuckles, the way she remembered it. He was wearing the clothes that belonged in the photograph that sat by her bed, and she realised with a sinking feeling around her heart that she had lost the memory of how he'd looked outside of that photograph, his entire complex physical self reduced to a single frozen image.

"I can't remember what you used to look like any more," she told him. "And there's something wrong with the sea. I can't get the boat to move. This is my dream, so why can't I get the boat to move?"

He didn't speak; he never spoke to her in her dreams any more. Instead he looked very earnestly into her face, as if he could convey his message simply by staring. The sea had turned to cloudy glass. Her boat was trapped, her oars wedged in place. If it wasn't for the warmth of the air, which she knew was the warmth generated by her own sleeping body, she would have said it was frozen.

"What do you want?" she demanded. "What do you *want*?"

Over his shoulder, she could see her own house, and also the house where the child Ella and her family now lived. The air was impossibly clear and sharp. She could see every detail of her dream-version of the house, which turned out to be far more baroque than the plain Edwardian lines she knew it to possess. The only point of similarity was the single rounded tower at the corner, where a yellow light shone out like a beacon.

"I'm not getting involved," she told her husband. "It's none of my business."

His face was reproachful.

"I know what this means," she said. "You're my conscience, whenever you turn up in my dreams you're the personification of my conscience. But I'm in control here. I choose not to take any notice of you. I'm sorry, but that's the way it has to be. I like my life the way it is."

Something fluttered by her feet, in among the heavy gas cylinders. She reached down for it and found she was holding a child's picture. A woman with long yellow hair lay in bed, while a smaller figure with yellow hair sat on the floor. Ella's mouth was a clownish downturned circle and fat blue droplets rolled down her cheeks.

"You're not fooling me with this." Despite its childish iconography and primary-colour palette, the drawing was of a far higher standard than Ella could ever have produced, with a depth of ominous expression and an emotional weight that only an adult imitating a child could create. "This is all in my head. I'm dreaming this. It's my brain talking to itself. And I'm not having it, do you hear? I'm in control here."

Her husband's mouth was moving, but there was no sound coming out. She let go of the oars, stood up in the boat and sat carefully down on the edge, her back to the frozen sea.

"I'm going into the water now," she said. "You can stay here if you like, but I'm going down there where it's quieter." She wore her usual outfit of thigh-high waders, thermal leggings under jeans, a t-shirt and a jumper, and all her air lay in tanks in the bottom of the boat, but she knew this wouldn't matter; she was dreaming after all, and in her dreams, she could do anything. "The water's turned back to liquid now," she said, and tipped herself backwards off the side of the boat, feeling the water welcoming her like an old friend, sinking down and down and down beneath the waves to the place where the fish darted among the weedy ruins of her favourite wreck-site and where no one, living or dead, would ever come to disturb her in her private meditations.

When the alarm sang out its little electronic song, she allowed herself the luxury of a single push of the snooze button, and lay in the morning darkness, savouring the warmth of her bed and the knowledge that the entire day before her was hers. She suspected very few people had the discipline required to live alone. For her, solitude was like the air she breathed or the water she swam through.

The alarm shrilled out once more, reminding her of the importance of self-discipline. She obeyed it immediately, rolling out of bed and commencing her morning routine with the same faint sense of pleasure that she brought to the start of each day. Standing by the open window over the kitchen sink, waiting for the kettle to boil, she looked at the sky and took a deep lungful of air and thought hopefully that perhaps she'd misremembered or even miscounted and there would, in fact, be enough cylinders left in her storage shed for her to spend this afternoon diving and not taking the boat around the coast to the marina to do a refill run.

She took her notebook out and checked, but she already knew what it would say. She had used all her supplies, and her refrigerator was almost empty, and her boat needed fuel.

"So that's that," she said briskly. Not moping was another important part of her self-discipline. The course of her day was set. She would have to speak to Derek at the marina and Sarah at the scuba club, but Derek was a shy hobbity creature whose dread of small talk would make their brief interaction a pleasure, and Sarah was always mysteriously and dramatically busy and could hardly finish a sentence before rushing off to the next task, and the supermarket by the marina had self-checkout tills, which Mrs Armitage considered to be the best idea anyone had had in years. A morning of busy effort, perhaps a brief stop in the little café for an elaborate sandwich and expensive lemonade, poured from a fiddly glass bottle. She dressed quickly and without thought, enjoying the freedom from choice that came from a wardrobe containing only the utterly functional. Her husband watched her from behind his sheet of glass.

"I'm not taking any notice of that dream," she said. Talking to herself was not allowed, but talking to her husband was permitted – surely no more foolish than women who spent all day yattering away to their cat. "Dream interpretation is for people who haven't heard of neuroscience." The best thing about talking to a dead man was that he couldn't talk back, couldn't argue, couldn't challenge, couldn't do anything but blandly reflect the echo of your own words. "I'm not changing my plans because you turned up in my sleep."

She locked her front door and dropped her keys into their place in her rucksack. A woman of her age was supposed to have graduated to something classic and expensive, a Mulberry perhaps, or maybe something by Dior or Chanel. Instead, she had her rucksack, that sat perfectly on her shoulders and had pockets for everything she needed from house-keys to tins of biscuits and wore its salt-stains and frayed straps with modest confidence. She enjoyed its utter and essential lack of beauty. She enjoyed knowing she would never own something tasteful and discreet in tooled brown alligator.

And when she turned left instead of right, taking the road through the village and towards the gravel track that ended at the house where Ella and her family lived, she did so knowing she was her own autonomous person, and had made her decision entirely of her own choice, free of any expectation from either the living or the dead.

The house wore its new occupants lightly. There were curtains at some of the windows, but the paint on the front door was the same slightly peeling red it had been for several years now. There was no car in the driveway, although at least one car was surely an essential tool for any family living in this place. (Of course, she herself had no car, but that was because she had her boat instead.) So her assumption must have been right, and the husband was at work. Would his wife be asleep, locked in her room like Sleeping Beauty? Would Ella come to the door when she knocked? The knocker was a brass lion with a thick fat ring in his mouth, faintly greened with salt. In the silence that followed the heavy thump of its falling weight, she found she was holding her breath.

Silence. Silence. Silence. A scuffle of movement. Another moment of silence, and then the door swung wide. Standing in the space was a woman so like Ella that even if she hadn't spied out her face, hadn't secretly listened to her voice from the tall cliffs, she would have instantly known her.

"Hello." The woman's smile was sweet but wary, as if she

was expecting enemies. Sensing the potential for disaster, Mrs Armitage rummaged hastily in her rucksack.

"I'm Mrs Armitage," she said. "If you go out of your garden and turn along the cliff-path, my house is the first one you come to." She held out the tin as if Maggie was a small animal she had to entice to eat from her hand. "I brought you some biscuits."

"That's so nice of you. Do I know you? I feel as if I know you." The woman's smile was unexpected and very lovely.

"I don't think we've met."

"Maybe we met in a former life or something. My name's Maggie, by the way. Have you got time to come in?"

"Thank you." She followed Maggie over the threshold. Ella's unicorn wellies sat side by side, a little apart from the litter of shoes that piled like puppies. The house was a little warmer than the November chill outside, but not by much. Despite this, Maggie's feet were bare, the soles rimmed with black. The sight ought to have been disgusting, but beautiful women were allowed to break the rules. In the kitchen, Ella sat at the table, bent over a printed worksheet. When she saw Mrs Armitage, her mouth made a perfect *oh* shape.

"This is my daughter," said Maggie. "Ella, this is our neighbour, Mrs Armitage."

They eyed each other warily, waiting to see if the other one would crack and give away their secret.

"This is my worksheet," Ella said at last. "I'm doing numeracy today."

"That's nice."

"She's home-schooled," said Maggie. "Ella, when you've finished that sheet you can go and play outside."

"Should I do some drawing?"

"No, you need some fresh air." She ruffled Ella's hair. "Fresh air and fresh hair. Just in case you meet a bear."

"Why do I need fresh hair to meet a bear?"

"So you taste good when he eats you, of course. All finished? Off you go."

"There aren't any bears here, though," said Ella, sounding as if she thought bears might be possible.

"No. No bears."

"Are you sure, Mummy?"

"I'm sure. Go on, off with you." Ella headed obediently for the door. "No, put your coat on first. And some shoes. No, the shoes by the door."

Ella sat down and tugged at the Velcro fastenings of her worn trainers. "Should I wear my wellies?"

"Your trainers are fine. Go on. Mrs Armitage and I are going to have a cup of tea and talk about grown-up things."

Mrs Armitage would have preferred Ella to stay. Now here she was, in a strange kitchen with a strange woman who was making them tea so they could talk about grown-up things. She reminded herself that there was only one person to blame for this, and sat down at the table to peek at Ella's worksheet. It was to do with multiplication tables. She had no idea whether this was appropriate for Ella's age or not.

"It's very quiet here," Maggie said, her words coming in short little bursts between tasks. "My husband –" she turned the tap hard so the water gushed out, turned it back to slow it again – "my husband chose it." A sharp movement to shut off the tap again. The washer must need changing. "He likes the quiet." The click of the kettle as it fitted onto its base. "For us, at least." The clink of china as she took two mugs from the cupboard. "He goes to work. And our son Jacob goes to school. And I look after Ella." The rattle of spoons in a drawer. "And that's us." She sat down at the table. "How about you?"

She'd forgotten she might have to trade some information in return. "I don't work. I live alone. My husband died in a boating accident." Her trio of conversation-stoppers. Maggie took the shock well, pausing only a moment in the making of tea and the arranging of the tin between them.

"Would Ella like a biscuit?" Mrs Armitage asked, as neutrally as possible. She'd chosen this box specifically because of its abundance of foil-wrapped and chocolate-coated extravagances.

"We'll save her some," said Maggie, her fingers fluttering over the selection. "She'll like the ones with wrappers on, I think. And maybe some of the chocolate ones." Her conspiratorial smile was frighteningly endearing. It took an effort to keep her own answering smile within bounds. "How many do you think I can give her before I'm officially a Bad Mother?"

"I wouldn't know. I don't have children." The final brick in her defensive wall. Now there would be no more questions about her, and Maggie would feel compelled to fill the silence between them with information of her own.

"Then you'll be the best judge of all. They don't let criminals become judges, do they?" She laid five biscuits aside, then chose one for herself, a wispy wafery thing that seemed more crumbs than anything else. "I think this will be a good place for the kids, don't you?"

Personally, Mrs Armitage couldn't think of anything worse for children than being dragged to a village at the end of the world with one shop and dubious public transport links, but she was here to discover, not to challenge. "Maybe. Do you feel settled here yet?"

"My husband – Richard, he's called Richard – he chose it." Maggie was crumbling her biscuit between her fingers. "I said that already, didn't I? I'm sorry, I'm out of practice with conversations." Her face was very vulnerable. "If I talk too much, tell me and I'll shut up. Richard says I talk too much sometimes."

Richard was sounding like more of an arse with every word Maggie spoke. "Have you been married long?"

"Since just before Ella was born. Jacob isn't my son, you see, Richard already had him when we met. He was a single dad." Maggie laughed. Her biscuit was entirely crumbs now, a heap of fragments on the table. "They're like unicorns, aren't they? You read about them in books but you never imagine you'll actually meet one." She reached for another biscuit, broke off a piece and lifted it to her mouth, but did not eat it. It was like watching an actress with a cigarette; the pose and the pantomime were perfect, but each time she stopped short. "Do you like to read?"

"Sometimes."

"I'd like to write. That's one of the reasons why we moved here. So I'd have a good environment to write. But if I'm any good, I should be able to write anywhere."

At Maggie's elbow was a stack of exercise books Mrs Armitage had assumed were for Ella. "Is that what you're working on? Is it fiction?"

"Yes, I suppose. Although it feels real to me when I'm writing it. I feel a bit trapped here, you see, and writing everything down is a good way to escape for a while. Richard's very stern with me."

"I hope you're stern back."

"We have the most amazing fights." Her smile was conspiratorial, as if she was sharing a private joke. "Sometimes I think we might bring the cliff down. Only when the children are in bed, of course. You shouldn't fight in front of them, should you?"

"I wouldn't know."

"I don't think anyone knows really. It's all made up in the end, isn't it? Maybe we're all just characters in a book somebody wrote and we don't realise it." Her laugh was thin and unconvincing. "I'm talking rubbish again, aren't I? If I'm not careful you'll put me out for the bin men. Would you like some more tea?"

"And you home-school Ella?"

"It's better for her. Apparently. I wonder sometimes. But I love her so much, I don't know if I could stand letting her go. That's really selfish, isn't it?"

"I couldn't really say," said Mrs Armitage, since Maggie seemed to be waiting for her to say something. They both reached for the same biscuit at the same moment. In the moment of awkwardness that followed, Mrs Armitage wondered what she was trying to achieve. She would drink the last inch of tea in her mug and then leave, and this peculiar family could carry on being as peculiar as they wished without her knowing any more about it.

"You know what I'd like to know," said Maggie thoughtfully.

"What's that?"

"The only things I know about you are that you live here, you don't work, you don't have children and your husband died in a boating accident. And asking *why* or *how* about that would be rude. But going on and on about myself is also rude. And I do want to know about you! I really do! So what I thought we might do is, I'm going to ask you some questions about your life, and if you don't want to answer you can reply by, I don't know, talking about the weather or lobbing a biscuit at me or something, and then we'll both know where we stand."

Mrs Armitage could do nothing but laugh.

"How did you meet your husband?" Maggie asked.

"We were at school together. Although we didn't know each other then. Then we met again when we were twenty-four and both joined a sailing club." She was surprised by how fresh and bright these memories were, how happy they made her. The crack of the sails and the plummy shouts of the instructors; the way the sea looked as it rushed past her nose when she hung out of the side of the boat, straining to counterbalance the weight of wind. Even then she'd daydreamed about how good it would feel to let go, finding the calm below the surface of the water, because really, how much wetter could they possibly be? And my goodness, how wet they'd always got! They came home soaked and shivering even when the weather was relatively kind and the sun shone. She remembered the cheerful warning of the man who ran the club – "Owning a boat is like standing in a cold shower throwing fifty pound notes out of the window."

"A sailing club!" Maggie's voice was warm and encouraging. *I like you. You're interesting. Your story is worth sharing*. "What did he look like? Was he handsome? Was it love at first sight?"

Perhaps not love for her, but something instant, something that mattered. Standing in the queue to pay, and making eye contact with the boy whose thick fair hair and well-cut face had already caught her attention. The moment of recognition as the name of their school rose in their minds like a fish, first inklings of a deeper recognition. Astonishing how she could recall all of this in the few seconds it took her to take yet another biscuit, snap it in half and then in quarters, and pop the first fragment into her mouth. "Yes, he was handsome. Very." What she thought might have been called *classic good looks*. Like a film star, but from the Golden age, when the men used to wear suits and brush their hair very neatly. Even when he came home from work sweaty and covered in oil and glue, he used to look as if he'd been made up by the props department to look like someone who'd done a hard day's work. "He used to tell people that he fell in love with me the moment he saw me. Although I don't know that I believed him." Astonishing to remember a time when his declaration, "I'm in love with you, you know. You're the only one for me" had prompted not a melting at the very core of her, but simply incredulous laughter.

"That's very romantic. Was he a romantic sort of person?"

"I – yes, I suppose he was. He believed in following his heart. That's how we ended up living here. He had some money from his parents and instead of training as a solicitor and buying a flat in London, we bought our little house and he found work at a boatyard."

"Did you mind? Would you have preferred London? Tell me to stop if you want, I'm not good at knowing when to shut up."

"If I minded I wouldn't be answering. I certainly would not have preferred London. I like to be near the sea." How long had it taken her to accept that this was her life, her actual life? That she had met a man who, against all probability, worshipped her, in all her awkwardness and all her strangeness, who was willing and even eager to indulge her reluctance to work and her passion for a life lived as much as possible in the water? That the cottage on the cliffs was theirs, that it would never be taken away from them? Of course there was the ever-present gnawing of the sea, but the cliff-edge had been much farther off then, so that even when she stood at the end of the garden and listened hard there was only the faintest sigh of water. *I live here,* she would remind herself every morning when she woke up. *This is my place. This is my man. This is my life.* The sense of undeserved perfection was so strong that when the disaster had come, it had felt like a relief.

"So how did he die?"

"He took the boat out one evening when it wasn't really safe. There was a storm warning, but he went anyway." For a moment it was difficult to breathe, then the feeling passed. "He liked taking risks. He said life wasn't worth living if you didn't. I wouldn't go with him, I said it was too dangerous, so he took his friend instead, and somehow they got into difficulties and the boat went down and they went down with it. It was a stupid accident."

"That's very sad."

"Yes." She pushed away the memory of how she had felt when she saw the men coming up the front path towards her front door. She'd known immediately what they were going to tell her. "But I got over it. I made a new life for myself."

"Sometimes I think life would be easier if I lived alone," said Maggie. "I mean, I love Richard. I do. But I wonder how much good love really does us. I was – I was with someone before Richard, you see, and I thought that was how love was meant to be. Then I met Richard and everything changed. And when he found out I was leaving him, he was so angry with me –" the tin of biscuits was earning its keep; Maggie's long fingers hovered over the diminishing selection and chose another victim to reduce to crumbs. "And we're back to me again. I need to work on my manners."

"Does your ex-husband ever try to get in touch with you?" Mrs Armitage asked, suddenly inspired.

The biscuit snapped between Maggie's fingers. "What? Why? Have you seen anyone? Was there anyone else outside?"

"There was no one but me outside," said Mrs Armitage. Then, because she disliked inaccuracy in any form, "or at least, no one else that I could see. I suppose there could have been someone lurking behind a tree or something. But I didn't see anything that seemed odd."

"He was so angry," Maggie said, as if she wasn't really listening to Mrs Armitage's reassurances. "He threatened Richard, and he threatened me. We've had to move so many times – I thought we'd be safe here, it's so far away from everywhere, but he keeps finding us and I'm never sure –" She looked at Mrs Armitage anxiously. "At least I think he keeps finding us. Sometimes I wonder if it's Richard making it happen so I'll do what he wants. I think I see him sometimes, but then I'm not sure. I mean, what if it's Richard who's trying to keep me trapped?"

"I really couldn't say," said Mrs Armitage cautiously.

"He says he wants to keep me safe. But sometimes I think he wants to keep me *in* a safe. I'm talking about myself again, I know I shouldn't. It's too much when we've only just met, isn't it? Too much, too young. We need to let our relationship grow up a bit." Her hands were shaking. "Have I convinced you that I'm not worth visiting yet? If not, I'll make some more tea."

While Maggie was occupied, Mrs Armitage lifted the cover of one of the exercise books and peered in, only to let it fall again when Maggie turned around.

"You can read it if you like," said Maggie, looking hopeful. "It's not finished, is the only thing."

How little could she get away with reading? At least if she was reading, she wouldn't be expected to talk. She read the first few pages to the swoosh of the boiling kettle. Then she read a few more. When she reached the end of the first exercise book, her tea had grown cold.

"You don't have to be nice about it if you don't like it," Maggie said, and laughed. "But I do wonder what you think."

"It's very interesting. Is it based on your life?"

Maggie shrugged. "Isn't all fiction based on people's lives?"

"You know," said Mrs Armitage, "if you're not happy, you could always leave your marriage."

"We're not really married," said Maggie unexpectedly. "I mean, we are but we aren't. I call him my husband and he calls me his wife but it was difficult enough getting away from that other one, so I never got around to getting divorced. So before Ella was born, we went to a jeweller's and he bought me two rings and we started telling people we were married, and that was that. I forget myself sometimes."

Mrs Armitage couldn't think of anything to say to that, so she kept silent. Against all probability, there really was a strange and dangerous man who stalked this family and threatened their safety. Or – an alternative explanation – a man whose demons were not outside the walls of his house, but inside the bones of his head, using the threat of a bogeyman to keep his family from putting down roots and growing strong and independent. In either case, there was something strange going on in this house. Of course, all families were peculiar if you looked closely enough.

"It's so nice of you to come here and listen to me and bring me biscuits," said Maggie. "I know I must sound absolutely mad. It's a bit disorienting, moving somewhere new. Sometimes I'm not sure if I'm even really here. And I've been so sleepy! It must be the sea air, mustn't it? They say the sea air makes you sleepy, don't they? And there's so much air here. I mean, I know there's the same amount of air everywhere but it does feel as if there's a little bit more than the average when you live right in the sky like this.

It's got to be good for us all. We'll be happy here. Don't you think?"

She wasn't even convincing herself, Mrs Armitage reflected. The knowledge was written in the silence behind Maggie's eyes, even as she tried to fill the spaces in between with words.

"I'm going home now," she said firmly. "I'll take the cliff-path back. It's quicker. If you would like to come and visit me, go to the end of your garden and turn along the path. It passes right by the bottom of my garden."

"Richard doesn't like me going out to visit people. He worries that – *he* – might see me and do something to hurt me."

But, thought Mrs Armitage, which *he* does he mean? Which do you?

"Goodbye, then," she said. Feeling the need for a formal gesture of parting, she held her hand out for Maggie to shake, only to be startled when Maggie took it between hers and held it for a moment as if it was something very fragile and precious.

"You're so kind. Thank you for listening to me and not laughing."

"None of it sounded like anything to laugh about," said Mrs Armitage. She freed her hand as gently as she could, and took the back door into the garden.

Beneath the apple tree, Ella was threading tall strands of brown, seedy grass into her coat-sleeves – one of those inexplicable games children seemed to create from nothing, with no visible component of joy and no logical end-point. As Mrs Armitage passed, she walked beside her to the end of the garden.

"I couldn't come yesterday or the day before that or the day before that because Mummy wasn't asleep," Ella said. "Are you cross with me? Did you come here to tell Mummy I forgot to come?"

Mrs Armitage kept her face neutral. It wasn't Ella's fault she had all the self-centred egoism of a small child, the belief that all the calamities of the world weighed solely on her narrow shoulders.

"I came to bring your mother some biscuits," she said. "As far as I'm concerned, she doesn't know you come to visit me, and if you're waiting for me to tell her, she never will know. Have you said anything to her?" Ella was tugging at the stalks gathered in her sleeves as if they were hurting her. "And why have you filled your sleeves with grass?"

"I'm going to be a scarecrow," said Ella. "For the next time I come to see you. But I'm a bit scared of the cliff. But, I'll be seven on the nineteenth of December, so then I'll be braver." Her face was anxious. "If you don't mind waiting, I mean. But, I can only come when Mummy's sleeping. Because I can't come when Mummy's awake."

For a moment, Mrs Armitage was back in her dream, with the sea set to a thick muddy soup and the light in Ella's house calling like a silent siren. A better woman would do more than she had done, would not rest until she had found the truth and put everything to rights. Her husband would have done exactly this; he always loved a good project, a good opportunity to prove himself. But she was not her husband. She would make her own choices.

"I don't mind waiting," she said. "You can come to me the next time she's asleep."

Chapter Nine
Now

When Jacob woke, the brightness of the sunshine made his eyes water. At some point during the night he must have opened the curtains. Groping back through the mists of sleep, he managed to summon a faint half-recollection of Ella appearing in his doorway, of him holding open the cover of the duvet for her to creep in beside him, of her going to the window and pulling open the curtains, of the startling chill of her feet against his calves and the tickle of her hair against his chin. Was that real? Had he really let a strange girl with his sister's face crawl into his bed in the early hours of the morning and sleep there? Surely not. He must have dreamed it and opened the curtains himself.

He glanced at his phone. It was early, not even six, but he felt a sense of bone-deep wellbeing, as if he'd slept for weeks and weeks and was now waking to a bright new day filled with promise and excitement. How long had it been since he'd had a night where he didn't have to spend hours patrolling the house with his father, searching the shadows for phantoms? With this much sleep he could hold up the cliffs on his shoulders.

One day on Mercury lasts approximately 1,400 hours
Or, as teachers call it, "Monday"
I am THE FUNNIEST PERSON YOU KNOW rite?
- D

Love it :-D
- J

He peered around the door of his father's room. His father was awake but quiet, standing by the window and looking emptily out into space. When he turned around, Jacob saw that the front of his pyjama bottoms was soaking wet.

"Hey, Dad. It's me."

"Course it's you, who else would it be? Morning, son." The cold damp fabric clinging to his thighs must be uncomfortable, but he seemed oblivious. Perhaps he genuinely hadn't noticed. Or perhaps he was embarrassed, and hoping he could pretend nothing was wrong.

"Shall I get some toast on, then?" he said, trying to keep his voice sounding casual. "And a pot of coffee? While you have a shower?"

"What's the rush?"

"I thought, you know, a nice way to wake up." He didn't care for himself but he minded for Ella. He wanted her to see their father clean and presentable, not smiling that peaceful idiot smile rendered terrible by his piss-soaked pyjamas. "Or how about a bath? I'll put it on for you, shall I?"

His father laughed. "I'm not having a bath first thing in the morning."

"Okay, a shower, then. Have a shower, Dad, you'll feel loads better."

His father's expression was suddenly very knowing.

"Want me presentable for the girlfriend?"

"Dad."

"Don't worry. I know she stayed the night. Heard her getting up this morning. Quiet as a little mouse she is. Very discreet. What do they call her again?"

"Ella, it's Ella, she's Ella." He waited, but there was no flicker of recognition, only that faint roguish oh-you-crazy-kids expression. "I'll see you downstairs, okay?"

"Make her a nice breakfast," his dad called after him.

How many times had he come down these stairs with Ella's ghost just ahead of him, one hand clutching the toy currently most in favour, muttering a song under her breath? He'd conjured her so often that the memory was almost more beloved than the reality, the reality of his almost-grown-up sister in the kitchen, and the faint homely clinks and chinks of plates and cutlery and the rising swish of the kettle coming to the boil. She'd come back to him, but as a stranger, and now his life, which had been anchored to one spot for so long, was sailing into the unknown. For a treacherous minute he wished he was still alone with his memories. What was he going to do? What were they going to do? What would happen when Ella had to leave? What would happen then?

Then he opened the door and Ella turned towards him and he saw, behind the warm smile, the same fear that was nipping at the backs of his knees, and felt the whole weight of his astounding good luck break over him like water, leaving him breathless and fully awake, eager for whatever the day was going to bring.

"I made a start on breakfast," Ella said, holding up the spatula as if it was something precious she'd borrowed without permission. "I heard your – I mean our – you know – moving around upstairs so I thought I should maybe get some bacon on. Do you still have bacon and eggs in the holidays?"

"You didn't need to do that." Jacob took the spatula from her hand. "You're the visitor, you're supposed to be getting the good service."

"I wanted to help."

As well as beginning breakfast, she'd opened the blinds and the window. No wonder he felt so filled with wellbeing. He wished fiercely that he could leave them as they were.

"Dad'll lose the plot if he sees these open," he said apologetically. "He can't cope with the idea of people being able to see in. He's – well, you probably noticed, he's a bit paranoid –" Above their heads, the ceiling creaked.

"Is that him? Is he upstairs?" Ella glanced towards the door.

"It's okay, he knows you stayed the night. He – um – oh, I'm really sorry about this, but he –" In spite of himself, he could feel himself blushing, not just his face and neck but his whole body tingling with heat, and he bent over the pan of bacon and hoped vainly she would think it was the heat of the stove – "he's still convinced you're my girlfriend. I know that's really gross and awful but he honestly can't help it, I think he's –" he managed to stop himself from saying *he's forgotten you*. "He's got confused."

What kind of reaction should he expect? An appalled giggle, perhaps, or an echoing of the deep embarrassment that trembled up his spine like a tuning-fork. A shy turning away. A flat refusal (*well we're going to have to tell him and tell him and tell him until he gets it because there's no way we can –*) Instead Ella nodded seriously, the face of someone committing important information to memory, medical instructions perhaps, or care advice for a potentially dangerous animal, and then said, "You've got a girlfriend? And he thinks I'm her?"

"No, it's not that. He's not sure who you are, so that's what he's come up with."

"And does he mind me being here? Is he going to be angry with me staying?"

"No. I – I think he thinks it's quite sweet. I know that's awful."

"He can't help it."

Did she really not mind? It was difficult to read her face. She looked as if she was trying to work something out in her head. He reached for the box of eggs. "I know it's really gross."

Instead of answering, Ella hesitated, then put a shy arm around his waist and leaned against him for a second. The way she used to hug him when she was small. He remembered the way her hair looked when he glanced down at her, the roughness of its unbrushed tangles against her scalp, waiting for the lick of their mother's hairbrush. Now she was old enough to brush her own hair, and tall enough for her head to rest against his shoulder. When she let go, the places where she'd touched him felt cold, as if she'd stolen the warmth from his body with her own.

"Morning, you two love-birds," said his father, cheery and bright and inappropriate from the kitchen door, and Ella jumped. "Glad to see Jacob's got things under control." His dad was in his dressing gown, looking clean and damp from the shower. "I'm sorry, pet, I've forgotten your name."

"I'm Ella."

"Course you are. Sleep well? I know, none of my business."

The wink his father gave Ella made Jacob want to slap him. When he cracked the first egg against the side of the frying pan, the shell shattered into fragments and had to be retrieved with a teaspoon. Ella poured tea from the pot, added milk and sugar, took the mug over to her father, barely flinching when he patted her arm. Jacob, watching as well as he could around the edges of the eggs, forced himself to stay calm. It wasn't his father's fault that grief and alcohol had drilled great holes in his memory. And, amazing miracle, he hadn't yet insisted on checking for break-ins. Perhaps this was the start of a new phase in their lives.

"Listen." The mug of tea slammed into the table; a great slop of beige spilled out over the side. "Did you hear that?"

"I didn't hear anything, Dad."

"Listen!" His father's hand was imperious. "Turn off that pan right now. I need to hear."

"Dad. There really isn't anything there."

"What the fuck would you know anyway?" His father glared at him. "You're a fucking idiot." Ella shrank noiselessly back against the counter. Of course she was terrified. How could she not be? His father pushed his chair away from the table. "Come on."

"I can't leave the eggs."

"Eggs!" His father was actually spitting with contempt. "There's someone trying to break into our house, you unbelievable idiot! Now bloody well man up and come with me."

131

He couldn't help the sudden rage. The day had begun with such beauty, and now his father was ruining it. His head insisted that arguing with a paranoid dementia sufferer was pointless, but he felt like a warrior on the battlefield, getting a dusty scroll of paper from some remote high commander: *this seems like a bad idea chaps, maybe back off for now*. He was going to win this one. Just this one.

"Dad! Will you listen to me! First of all, this is Ella, do you understand! And she's not my girlfriend, that's a disgusting thing to say, she's my little sister for God's sake, she's your daughter! There is nobody fucking there! There never is! Now sit down and drink your bloody tea and wait while I make your breakfast and shut up about people coming into the house before I fucking well make you!"

The roar of his voice echoed in his head. The eggs and bacon crackled quietly in their pans. The sunshine crept around the edges of the blinds. He braced himself for the blow he knew was coming, telling himself fiercely *I won't cry, whatever happens I won't bloody cry*, but there was nothing but that terrible sizzling stillness that pressed against his ears. The smell of food. The minute fractions of sunlight that his father would tolerate. And then, a new sound, something he was sure he should recognise but that was so far away from what he was expecting that, for a few moments, he was unable to process it. His father was weeping.

"Oh Dad," he said, sick and wretched.

"Don't you touch me!" His father hunched away as if he thought Jacob might strike him.

"I'm sorry," Jacob said. "We can go and look if it'll make you feel better."

"You're always against me," his father whispered. "You never believe me, never, you laugh at me when you think I'm not looking, but I see you…"

"Don't say that, it's not true. Please, Dad, I don't ever laugh at you."

"I don't have a daughter, do you understand? I've got you

and nobody else, it's just us two, but now you're against me. And you take things out of my room when I'm asleep, you hide things from me, I wake up and see you doing it –" his father was working himself into a frenzy now, the rage and panic that bubbled constantly beneath the surface looking for an outlet. *Here we go. Get ready for impact.*

"Mr Winter?" A soft female voice, and a hand resting on his father's forearm. "I've made you some breakfast. I hope you don't mind."

"What? Who are you?"

"I'm Ella, remember? I – I'm Jacob's – um – friend. You said I could stay, remember? So I've made breakfast to say thank you."

"I – um – oh, what was I – " his father's hands groped and fumbled at the air as if the words he wanted were visible before him, dangling out of reach. "I can't remember, there was something I had to –" The chink of china against wood distracted him. "Where's Jacob? I was looking for –"

"He's here." She put the knife and fork down beside the plate, letting them chink and clatter. "Would you like ketchup too?"

A moment of blankness, as his father groped for the correct social mode, the right bit of scripted dialogue to carry him forward into the future, and then – thank God, thank God – that indulgent roguish smile re-surfaced, and his father was shaking his head and chuckling once more.

"Jacob, you're a disgrace," he said. "Guests don't cook their own breakfast." His gaze turned to Ella. "I didn't raise him to behave this way."

"I know, Dad. What am I like?" Jacob sat down in his usual place, despising himself for letting himself get carried along by his father's tide of fantasy. His father tore at his bacon, then stabbed it greedily into the fat disc of yolk. As he watched, a plate arrived for Jacob, then one for Ella, and two mugs of tea, milky beige for Ella, the perfect burnt umber for him. The shock of eating a meal in his own house that he hadn't cooked was so sweet that it brought tears to his eyes. He forced himself to wait until Ella took her place at the table – not the place that had once been hers, Not the one that had been her mother's, but the seat beside him that he had mentally reserved years ago for the friends he once imagined would come home with him on the bus to visit after school.

"Right." His dad pushed himself away from the table. "Better get dressed. Don't you let my son talk you into helping with the washing-up."

"I thought he was going to hit you," said Ella, as soon as their father was safely out of the kitchen.

"He wouldn't do that." He forced himself not to tug down the sleeves of his t-shirt. "He just gets upset sometimes."

"When did it start?"

"More or less as soon as – you know. I think it was the shock." It wasn't the shock, it was the drinking, but that didn't alter the truth: if *she* hadn't left, his dad would never have got into this state.

"That soon? So he's been like this for years?" Her voice quivered.

"We've managed."

"But how do you manage? I mean, does he go to a day centre or something while you're at work?"

"He'd hate that, he doesn't like going out. He stays here." When he said the words out loud, his father's world sounded unbearably small.

"And you promise he doesn't hit you?"

"Ella, I swear, you're absolutely safe." It wasn't exactly the question she had asked, but it was the truth. He would make it the truth.

Throughout the tasks of the morning, he was haunted by a feeling of duality. The child Ella still hovered at his elbow, frozen in the moment of disappearance, never growing, never changing, with all the sweetness and the small annoyances that had become unbearably poignant in his memory. But now, her place was filled by the Ella who had come back to him, clever enough to guess what was needed and to help without needing guidance, clinging to him the way he wanted to cling to her, terrified that their lives would whirl onwards and drag them apart again. As his father dozed off in his chair and let the last inch of liquid in his mug seep into the carpet, he seemed to lose her for a while, and roamed the house for several anxious minutes before it occurred to him to look outside.

She was leaning against the wall by the kitchen door, her hand up to her mouth in a gesture he recognised but couldn't quite place. Then she turned towards him and he saw that she was holding a cigarette.

"Sorry," she said. "I thought you wouldn't want me doing this inside so I came out for a minute."

"It's okay."

She looked at him shyly. "Do you mind?"

"No, of course I don't." Did he mind? He wasn't sure. Another difference he hadn't prepared for. Another sign that she was a young woman, her own person. The scent of her was nostalgic, the faint tobacco tang on her hair and skin combining with the shampoo and deodorant and cosmetics that made up her fragrance, tickling against some lost sweetness buried in the back of his brain. "I didn't know you did, that's all."

"I don't, not really. It just reminds me of Mum, when I was little."

"Why? She never smoked."

"Yes, she did."

"No she didn't, of course she didn't, you're getting confused." Ella looked at him sideways, clearly convinced she was right but not wanting to argue. "Maybe she started after she left or something, and you assumed –"

"But I remember her doing it, I promise. Not in front of you and Dad, she used to wait until you were out, but she definitely did. It wasn't loads or anything," she added. "She didn't want you to know and you didn't, that's all."

"But there's no way –" realising that he was talking nonsense, he forced himself to stop. "Are you sure?"

"She had one every morning, as soon as you and Dad had gone. She'd see Dad off to work, and then see you on the bus, and then she'd tell me to go upstairs and get dressed or clean my teeth or something, and she'd come out here and have a cigarette. And then she'd have another one in the afternoon, about half an hour before you came home, and sometimes another one at lunchtime as well."

Jacob found himself laughing in shock.

"She used to hide the packet in that plant pot," Ella continued, and pressed her own cigarette hard against the wall to put it out.

The upturned plant pot had sat in its spot by the door for so long that he'd forgotten it might be capable of being moved. Gingerly, he reached out for the plant pot and lifted it. Underneath, a packet of Marlboros Lights sat on a brick.

"Oh," said Ella, a small quiver in her voice, and put her hand up to her mouth.

"Don't be upset," said Jacob. "It's just some cigarettes." Ella was fighting with her own body, trying to keep her shoulders straight, her mouth uncrumpled, her breath even. "What's the matter? Come on, you can tell me anything, you know you can." She was whispering something but he couldn't make it out. "Please, Ella, tell me what's happened."

"I said," Ella whispered, so quietly he had to strain to hear her, "Mum's gone."

"Gone? You mean like – dead?"

"No! No. She's just gone. I went out to the shops, she sent me out to buy some stuff we needed, and when I got home there was a note on the table and some money and your address and the note said something like, *Dear Ella, I've decided I need a holiday. I'm perfectly fine and you don't need to worry, but it's time for your father to take care of you for a while.* And the address of this place was underneath it."

The coldness of the message took his breath away.

"And you came straight here?" he asked at last.

"No, of course I bloody didn't, I waited for three days first to see if she'd come back! But she didn't."

He had no mental picture of the house Ella had come from, no idea if it was warm or cold, small or large, well-kept or shabby. But he could picture her terror and confusion, the creeping dread at the long minutes that stretched into hours and then days with no word.

"You're here with me now. I'll look after you."

"But where's Mum gone? Why would she do that? Leave a note on the kitchen table and then disappear?"

Because that's what she does. She leaves people. It was obvious to him but of course Ella wouldn't see it. It had taken him years to realise that it was possible for someone to be bright, attractive and beautiful, but without a gleam of goodness. He groped clumsily for the words that would make Ella feel better. "I know it's horrible but it's not you, it's not you at all, it's her, it's just how she is. And at least she told you where to come, didn't she? So that's good. And when she's ready to have you back again, she knows exactly where you are." *And then,* he thought grimly to himself, *then she'll have to see all the damage she's caused.*

"I don't want you to have to worry about me as well as Dad. I'm not crying, I promise."

"I know it's a really thoughtless thing for her to do but some people are like that. She loves you, of course she does." It was so much more than the woman deserved, but he couldn't bring himself to hurt Ella any more than she was already being hurt. She hadn't had the same time to think that he had.

She was looking at him as if she wanted him to say something more. "But how could she leave me?"

"I don't know," he said helplessly.

The tears were beginning to dissolve her mascara. "And how am I ever going to find her?"

"I don't know," he repeated. "But I swear, it's going to be okay. You've got me now. You're home. It's going to be fine."

137

And all the time he felt a glad and righteous rage filling him up like water in a cup, because once again his mother had broken someone he loved, and now he had one more reason to despise her.

The man has been following me for many years now, ever since I first made my escape from the prison he kept me in. Sometimes I glimpse him in the edges of my vision, and it always makes me want to move faster, to run and run, run rabbit run, until my legs grow longer and stretch out to the stars and I can leap up to the moon. A moon hare. Witches can turn into hares and sometimes I feel myself growing long and brown, my ears flat along my back, bare in the sunshine where my vest lets the sunlight in, in to my skin, and I'm thin, thin as a witch. A witch-hare. Hares have no homes and soon I will have no home too. He's hunted me from my home, not with the dogs of war but with the dogs that he keeps in his hands and his feet, the dogs that spring out from inside him when he begins to move.

He can transform himself into a dog, I think. I saw him do it the other day while I was out shopping, which is more like scavenging since almost everyone around me is dead and the world has grown empty. He was standing outside the shop disguised as a big dog, a black dog with a white collar, and I thought for a moment that he was a priest come to exorcise me because I am a witch and all witches end up on the pyre in the end. First the pyre and then the fire. But then I saw that it was not a dog and not a dog-collar, but the man himself, and I had to hide myself in the corner where they cover all the old food with yellow stickers to mark it as unclean, and when I came out again he had disappeared but that was worse because then I didn't know where he was, and I had to go home and let the girl who lives with me take care of everything for a while and then it was all over.

He never seems to appear to her. Is this because she's his daughter? Or because she isn't?

My head is so full of stuff today. I will write some more tomorrow.

Chapter Ten
Now

"Where are we going?" Ella waited outside his room with her trainers in her hand, obedient but puzzled. "Are you sure you don't want me to watch him? I can manage, I don't mind."

"No, you're coming too."

"But do I need to dress up? I only brought jeans and things."

"You'll be fine exactly as you are."

"But where *are* we going?"

"You'll see."

He knew he was being annoying, but he was too giddy to care. He couldn't get over his excitement. His feet skittered on the stairs as he ran down them. He kissed the top of his father's head as he nodded drowsily in his chair in the living-room.

"Are you ready?" Just the sight of her standing in the hallway was enough to spread the great foolish grin across his face.

"My jeans are a bit grubby."

"Doesn't matter, I promise. Come on, let's go."

"But what about – ?"

"Don't worry, Dad's asleep, he'll be asleep for a couple of hours."

She still seemed reluctant to leave the house, but he bulldozed joyously through her hesitation, shooing her out of the door, not bothering to lock it behind them. Who would bother to come here and try to break in? His dad was asleep; it would be fine.

He stole small glances at Ella as they walked side-by-side along the track down to the village. He felt shy, and then embarrassed for feeling shy, and then angry with himself for wasting a moment on either of these emotions when he was so happy. It was a strange and wondrous thing to have a dream come true. Did Ella feel the same? He had no idea how to ask. He glanced at her again, only to find that she was looking at him in the same shy, sideways manner, as if she too couldn't quite believe her luck. When their eyes met, she stumbled over a tussock of grass.

"I'm all right," she said, as he reached out a hand to help her up. "Sorry, I should have been looking where I was going – can you feel that?"

There was a faint vibration beneath their feet. He stood deathly still and listened, willing the breeze to stop whispering in his ears so he could concentrate.

"Tractor," said Jacob.

"Are you sure? It sounded like – no, I'm being silly."

"You're not being silly, but it's nothing to worry about." He was still holding her hand, and he could feel the tension in her muscles.

"I know you're right."

Her smile was sweet and brave and did nothing to disguise her terror; the look of the true phobic, knowing that what she feared was irrational but caught in its claws anyway. He remembered the first time he'd forced her out of the house and onto the cliff-edge, when she was too small to resist and he was too unthinking to realise what he was doing. He forced himself to keep up a stream of light chatter as they walked, pointing out gorse-bushes and rabbit-holes, village landmarks and hovering seabirds, then realised he was talking nonsense, and let the silence crowd in around them.

"It's so quiet here," Ella said suddenly. "How do you manage?"

"What? With the quiet? After a week teaching it's quite nice to be honest, you wouldn't believe how loud a classroom full of English students can be."

"No, I mean, with – Dad." She said the word as if she wasn't sure she was allowed to use it. "Is it really just you and him? What happens to him when you're at work?"

"I told you, he stays at home."

"And he doesn't go out at all?"

Was she judging him? The feeling of his defences going up was almost a physical one, as if he could armour himself with spikes to keep out her questions. "He goes out in the garden. He likes that. And sometimes we go for walks. He's not a prisoner or anything."

"And I suppose he could always go out by himself for a bit."

"I don't like him doing that," Jacob admitted. "I always worry he might wander off and get lost. I try not to let him."

"It's not your fault if he does. You can't be with him every minute of the day."

"No, but I do have help." They were nearly at Mrs Armitage's house now. It seemed strange to approach it from the land, as if the house was in disguise. Any minute now Ella would realise where he had brought her. He wished he had a cape to flourish. "That's – that's actually who we're going to see. Do you remember?"

She couldn't speak, but the look on her face was enough. He knocked on the door, feeling his heart banging in his chest.

"It's the holidays," Mrs Armitage said as soon as she opened the door. "I have plans. I can't babysit your father, so don't even bother asking."

"It's not that," he said, breathless. "I – um – I've got a visitor."

"So you have." Mrs Armitage turned her gaze on Ella. "Is

143

there a reason *I* have a visitor? I'm not your mother, Jacob, you don't need to bring your girlfriends to me for inspection."

"No, she's not my girlfriend." Now that he was here, he wasn't sure quite how to break it to her. Surely she could see? The sun was behind them: perhaps that was why.

"Then who – ? Young woman, I'm sorry Jacob's dragged you here to meet me. I'm not anyone important, I'm just a neighbour. So don't feel as though you have to try and impress me, it's not as if my opinion matters to –" As if the floor had lurched beneath her feet, she suddenly clutched the doorway. "Jacob, who is this? Who have you brought? Jacob, what on earth have you done?"

"It's…" he found he couldn't say her name.

"It's me," Ella whispered, through a dry throat. "I know it's been a really long time."

"I know you. How do I know you? I don't know anybody your age."

"It's Ella," she said, her voice quivering. "I'm – I'm Jacob's sister. I don't know if you remember me but I used to visit you sometimes –"

"Of course I remember! Do you think I'd ever forget you?" Before Ella could do anything to stop her, she was being folded in the other woman's arms, and held in a fierce tight hug. "My dear, my lovely girl, of course I'm pleased to see you. I've hoped so much that one day –"

And Jacob, standing uselessly by and watching all the wild clumsy affection Mrs Armitage bestowed on Ella, but that she'd never given to him, felt his heart thump with jealousy.

A flurry of activity, the three of them clustering in the doorway, the hallway, the living-room. Ella helplessly exclaiming over the things she recognised and the things she didn't, her fingers reaching for a familiar mug, a print of a wood filled with bluebells, a small china dog on a three-tiered wooden shelf in a corner of the hallway. (He'd never realised how often Ella must have visited. How had he not known?) After a few minutes, some kind of order imposed itself and they were correctly seated and organised, armed with cups of tea, a plate of biscuits marking out the No Man's Land between them. Jacob and Ella side by side on the sofa, Mrs Armitage in a chair, straight-backed and knees neatly together, her eyes bright with what could have been either excitement or unshed tears.

"So," Mrs Armitage said at last, and looked at them thoughtfully.

What would she ask first? *Where have you been? Has your life been good? Have you been happy? Why have you come back now? Where's your mother?* What was the right question to ask in these circumstances? Was there anything at all that could be said between the three of them that would not be strange? He waited to see what she would say, but instead Mrs Armitage simply sat and looked at him and then at Ella, her gaze thoughtful and slow, enigmatic and penetrating. He reached protectively for Ella's hand and took it between both of his.

"Did you learn to dive?" Mrs Armitage said.

"I did."

"You learned to dive?" Jacob thought of Ella's terror of the sea, and was astounded.

"Good girl. Open water?"

"No. Not yet. I got a job at a leisure centre, they paid me in scuba lessons instead of money. But it's a bit difficult to organise."

"You mean you're still afraid of the sea." Mrs Armitage's words were severe, but her expression was gentle. "You've done well. Don't stop trying."

"Do you still dive?"

"Of course I do." Mrs Armitage nodded towards the window where the truncated remains of her garden, uninhibited by any fence, led the viewer's eye out towards the churning brown water. Jacob felt Ella's hand tighten around his. "It's still waiting for me. And did your mother ever finish her book?"

"How did you know she was writing a book?" Ella looked as guilty and startled as if Mrs Armitage had accused her mother of selling herself.

"She showed me it once. So, did she?"

"I – yes, I think she finished it."

"I see." Mrs Armitage was studying them both intently, as unembarrassed as if they were a painting in a gallery. *The boy and his sister,* Jacob thought, then checked himself. Why would it be *boy and his sister* rather than *girl and her brother*, or even *brother and sister*? He could imagine the girls in his class correcting him with the cheerful scorn of young unafraid people, knowing they were the coming generation and would soon remake the world in their image.

"What was it about?" Jacob asked. His voice sounded too loud and too male. "Her book, I mean."

"It's hard to explain," Ella said.

"Why would you care?" Mrs Armitage asked, at almost the same time.

Of course she was right: he didn't really care about the damn book. He tried not to mind the feeling that they would both be happier without him there. He let go of Ella's hand and took a biscuit from the plate, not because he wanted to eat it – it was a Rich Tea, so dull it was barely a biscuit at all – but to give himself an excuse to move, and remind them both that he was still in the room.

"Wait here." Mrs Armitage stood up. "I have something to show you." She knelt in front of the cherry-brown sideboard and opened the door. Jacob watched apprehensively. Did Mrs Armitage have photographs of Ella? Surely she couldn't have kept them from him all these years. When she stood up and turned around, she was holding a lever-arch file.

"I kept all the drawings you did for me," she said. A brief moment of closeness and then somehow Mrs Armitage was on the sofa between him and Ella, and he was conscious once again of an entire relationship whose shape and dimensions he had never recognised before now. There was a lump in his throat like a stone. He tried hard to swallow it, and told himself that of course Mrs Armitage had liked Ella best. She'd been little and cute and had drawn her pictures, while he'd been a lanky needy teenager who'd begged her for help she had no obligation to give.

"We can't stay long," he said. "I left Dad on his own."

"Doesn't he sleep in the mornings?" Mrs Armitage's eyes were bright and shrewd. "It's not even ten o'clock yet. Sit back down, Jacob, your father will be fine."

Before he'd had a chance to argue, he found he'd done as he was told and was sitting on the sofa once more, trying to convince himself he was wanted. Ella and Mrs Armitage were turning over the contents of the file now, each page in its own protective plastic wallet, apparently organised by theme. Pictures of animals. Pictures of flowers. Pictures of unicorns. Pictures of himself and Ella, falling into the sea, and the boat that waited for them at the bottom of the water, with the crab that would walk over their skulls. Ella's fingers stumbled and faltered.

"I still have that dream," she said. He could hear the tremor in her voice.

"Yes, I thought you might."

The file slipped from Ella's knee. "And the sea's so much closer. Look, you can see it from your window now."

"I decided it wasn't worth trying to fence it off any more."

"Doesn't it frighten you to see it?"

"I'm not afraid of the sea, you know that. But you are, aren't you?"

"Yes." Ella sounded as if she was confessing a shameful secret.

"So why on earth did you come back here?"

"She came back here to see me," Jacob said very loudly, and stood up so suddenly he knocked two cushions onto the floor. "I know that must seem really odd to you, but not everyone thinks I'm a complete waste of space."

He was being dramatic, and he wanted a response that

was equally dramatic – Mrs Armitage shouting at him to stop being so rude, Ella bursting into tears. Instead they both stared at him with expressions of blank concern.

"Right," he said, feeling his face reddening. "I'm going home to check on Dad. Ella, you know your way home. See you when you're ready."

He slammed out of the back door and strode out along the cliff-top, daring himself to worry. The cliff had been closed since last autumn and the public footpath diverted through the village but Mrs Armitage took no notice, and today he would take no notice either. He needed to be alone for a while, and to walk fast and carelessly in a dangerous place, until he could shake off the pain of discovering how little Mrs Armitage really cared for him. He walked as quickly as he dared and reminded himself that he was being ridiculous, the woman owed him nothing, and what did it matter if she so clearly preferred his little sister? Maybe there was something wrong with him, and that was why *she* had left him too –

The shriek of terror was so piercing that he thought for a moment it might bring the cliff down with it. When he dared to turn around, he saw Ella, sprawled face-down on the grass.

"Ella!" He threw himself on the ground beside her.

Her fingers were clutching two handfuls of grass. "I tripped, I think I fell over my lace. I can't get up, if I get up the whole cliff's going to come down, I know it is."

"No it's not, I promise it's not. You're miles from the edge."

"I can hear it, I can hear it crumbling away, if we move it'll all go."

"You're imagining it, I promise." But what if she wasn't? What if her fall had disturbed the earth? "We're not far from home, we'll be back in a few minutes."

"I can't get up, I'll fall, we'll both fall and it'll be my fault."

"No, we won't. You don't have to get up. Lift your head and take a look." He put his hand on her back and stroked gently, feeling the slow slackening of tension in her shoulder blades as he petted her. "I promise I won't let anything bad happen to you."

A deep breath, and for a brief frightened second her face appeared from the grass.

"See? We're miles from the edge." She looked again, for longer this time. "Try sitting up."

"But what if –" she caught herself. "No. I know I'm being silly. The cliff's not going to fall, it's solid." As she talked to herself, she was pushing herself slowly up into a sitting position. "It's all right, it's all right, oh Jesus I can't do this. Yes, I can. I can. We're safe, aren't we?"

"Course we are."

"Okay, I'll get up now." She scrambled to her feet, but her knees wouldn't hold her and she stumbled against him and he had to catch her by the arms and waist. "I'm sorry. I'm being so stupid."

"No you're not. I'm sorry. I shouldn't have made you come out here."

"You didn't make me, it was my fault. I should have realised we'd been too long. I know we left him – Dad, I mean – on his own."

Her belief in his selflessness made him cringe.

"It wasn't that," he admitted. "It was just seeing Mrs Armitage being so nice to you. She's never that nice to me. I know that's pathetic, but it's the truth." He tried to laugh. "I suppose I've got mother issues." She was heavier than she looked; her weight pressed against him made him breathless. "Ella, I'm sorry but I've got to ask you – what happened that night? I woke up the next morning and you'd both disappeared…"

The words shocked him. He hadn't meant to speak them. They'd crept out beneath his guard. He wondered if he'd done something terrible.

"Okay," Ella whispered. "Can we sit down, though?"

"Of course we can."

Side by side, they sat on the tough tussocky grass and listened to the sound of their hearts banging in their ears.

"I remember Mum coming into my room," Ella said at last. "It was really late, I think. The storm had blown out but the rain was still pouring down. She was really wet, and she wasn't wearing her clothes."

"She was naked?"

"No, no! Just – not wearing her clothes. They were someone else's. They smelled different. I noticed it when she took me out of bed."

Somewhere nearby, a gull threw back its head and screamed, a long pure cry that broke into a series of *yark-yark-yarks* and then grumbled into silence.

"She carried me downstairs and into the car," Ella continued. "I had this idea we were going on holiday or something, like flying from an airport. I knew you have to get to airports really early. I tried to ask, but she put her hand over my mouth and told me we had to be really quiet in case we woke Dad."

"Were you scared?"

"I wasn't, not at first. I still thought it was some sort of nice surprise for everyone. I mean, I wasn't even properly awake, I kept falling asleep and then waking up again, so it's all in little pieces. Then we were in the car, and I thought you were in there too because there was something on your seat, but it wasn't you, it was a big heap of clothes. I was going to ask where you were, but Mum wrapped me up in a couple of coats, and it was so warm…"

He waited silently.

"When I woke up we were somewhere else. It was a house I didn't recognise. We had one room and everything else was shared."

"Were you scared then?"

"I don't really remember. I think I thought it was a holiday somehow, I kept waiting for you and Dad to come and join us. I know I was worried because I wasn't sure where you'd

150

sleep – there were only two single beds. But I thought maybe there'd be another room somewhere, and you and me might have the first one and Mum and Dad would have the other one. And I was hoping you'd bring me some of my books and toys and stuff. This is sounding really maudlin now."

"No it doesn't."

"Yes it does. I mean, I obviously wasn't in any danger or anything, I wasn't cold or hungry or on my own. I just wasn't sure what was going on." She took a deep breath. "So anyway, we lived there for a while. I don't really know how long. We went out quite a lot, I remember that, museums and libraries and things. We used to play this hiding game, where we had to get behind pillars and things and watch out for people following us. I mean, I thought it was a game at the time." She put her hand to her mouth and nipped at the skin beside her thumbnail. "Then one day Mum was really happy, and she packed all our stuff up into bags and said we were going somewhere new. She must have got rid of the car somehow, maybe she sold it or something, I'm not sure, so we got in a taxi with all our things. I was really excited because I thought we were coming back home. Then we stopped outside this new house, I mean, not a new house, it was old, but somewhere we hadn't been before, a little terrace with a front door that opened right out onto the street."

He could feel her trembling with the fierce will it took not to cry. He wasn't sure how to feel. Which of them had been hurt the most?

"And Mum said – she said –"

He wanted to shake the words out of her, or perhaps to hug her until she felt safe enough to speak. He forced himself to keep still and hold his silence. When a bee blundered into his face and then away again, he refused to flinch.

"I don't know if I should tell you this. I know you love him."

"Tell me."

"She said we had to leave our old home because it wasn't

151

safe," she whispered at last. "She said – I know this must be really horrible to listen to."

"Tell me. I don't mind, I promise."

"She said it was him. She said – well, that she wasn't safe around him any more, and she'd had to leave. And I wouldn't be able to see you any more and I'd have to get used to that, but she'd look after me."

"Are you saying it's *Dad's* fault she left? No. That's not right. He *loved* us. He was good to us. He never did anything to hurt us, he never would –"

"Not to us, not to you, but to Mum. She was scared a lot, I know she was. You didn't see it, but when she'd seen him off to work and you off to school she was like a different person. And you remember how they used to argue."

"And how was that Dad's fault? She used to shout as loudly as he did. Even if she wanted to leave him she didn't have to do it that way, sneaking off in the night and taking you with him and not letting either of us see you ever again." Ella was trying to speak, but he had to make her understand. "If she was so wonderful and he was so awful, why did she leave me with him? Why did she take you and not me? Actually, don't bother answering that because I already know. All that crap about us being a family was rubbish. I was never her son. She said that so Dad would like her enough to marry her. And as soon as she'd had enough of him, she cleared off and left him. And now she's done it to you as well."

"No, that's not true! She couldn't come back for you, she was so afraid, you've got no idea what it was like for her."

He was an adult. He should be old enough to handle the discovery that Ella saw everything differently. The adult thing to do would be to hug his sister and tell her he understood, that it wasn't her fault she was the chosen one, that it didn't matter and he loved her just the same.

Instead, he stood up and, keeping his face turned carefully away from her, strode off across the cliffs to the house where his father would be waking up.

Chapter Eleven
2008

The rain had fallen all evening and all night and on into the morning, and by the afternoon it was still tumbling down. Beneath her feet, the cliffs had that breathless feel that Mrs Armitage associated with an imminent fall. The storms took the biggest toll, tearing great chunks of earth from the base so that the tops had no choice but to follow; but sometimes the weight of water soaking slowly through the mud induced a series of small slides, creating seeming paths to lure the unwary downwards. This image, as so many did these days, made her think of Ella. Of course she wouldn't see her today; it was too cold and wet. Too cold and too wet and too dangerous. Better for them both to stay at home. The garden could do with weeding, but she disliked the thought of getting closer than she needed to nature, on a day when Nature herself seemed so definitively not at home to visitors.

Then she saw the familiar rattle and shake of the gate that told her Ella was on the other side, struggling with the latch as she always did, and felt her stomach leap with gladness.

If she was a more grandmotherly woman, she might run down the garden in anticipation of a warm hug and a juicy kiss. She could picture this as clearly as if she'd actually done it, with a child who was related to her and not simply a stray who had wandered in. Instead she disciplined herself to wait in the kitchen, feigning unawareness of her imminent visitor, until Ella knocked at the back door.

Today Ella had accessorised her flowery coat and unicorn wellies with an absurd clear plastic rain-bonnet, tied under her chin in a long chain of granny-knots and slipping raffishly down over one ear. Beneath it, her face looked determined and sweaty. When she opened the door, Mrs Armitage had to fight the urge to take the bonnet off and smooth out the crumpled hair beneath.

"Where did you find that hat?" she asked instead.

"It was in a boot."

"A car boot?"

Ella smiled tolerantly. "No, a foot boot. Like a boot for men to wear."

"This hat belongs to your father? And he put it inside his boot?"

"No, my dad doesn't have any boots. It was just a boot that's in our house. And I looked in it, and this hat was inside."

It was a typical Ella answer, charming and mysterious and completely devoid of useful content, prompting far more questions than it answered. (Why was a woman's rain hat hidden in a man's boot? Whose boot was it and what was it doing in their house? Why was Ella looking in the boot in the first place? Had any of these things even happened?) Ella was removing her own boots, balancing on the doormat so that no part of her grassy, muddy wellies would touch the floor. She hung her coat on the door knob, then began on the knots of her rain-bonnet, picking away with an almost unnatural patience. Another minute and Mrs Armitage would give in to the urge to assist, to nurture, to parent this strange little child.

"I'll make you some juice," she said instead. An acceptable compromise. By now there was a cup in the kitchen that was designated as Ella's, a plate that the biscuits were always arranged on. She put the plate down in the centre of the table and waited. After a minute, Ella, triumphantly free from her hat, climbed up into the chair. She was growing out of all of her clothes. Her sleeves were halfway up her forearms and the crotch of her tights sagged towards her knees. Before she could stop herself, Mrs Armitage pictured the clothing aisles that filled half the superstore she sometimes visited, and of herself returning on the bus with a whole secret wardrobe of rainbow colours. No. It wasn't her place to dress the child, and besides, she had better things to do with her money than spend it on clothes for other people.

"I thought you might not come today," she said.

"It's safe today," said Ella, looking honestly surprised. "There's no storm. Only rain."

Heavy rain could be as dangerous as storms. Someone ought to have told Ella this. But then, would she ever dare to walk along the cliffs at all? How could she get the child safely home again? Would she have to walk her home through the village?

"As long as you're careful," she said.

"I'll be careful," said Ella, her voice pure patient teenager, and brushed biscuit crumbs from her mouth.

"So what do you want to do?"

"Shall we do some gardening?"

Mrs Armitage thought of the heavy breathless weight of the soil and the water waiting below. "It's raining."

"I've got my new rain hat."

If it was sunny, she could suggest re-creosoting the garden furniture, but even Ella wouldn't believe it was possible to paint in this weather. They could work on the pots and containers, but that wasn't what Ella meant by *gardening*. She was thinking of the plug-packs of bedding plants that Mrs Armitage bought and bought and bought, even though it was too late in the season and there were already far more than the soil could support. She was thinking of the endless digging of neat little holes, of the slow inevitable progression from the safety of the borders near the house towards the empty places at the bottom of the fence. In a minute she would say –

"We could go and plant out some flowers at the end where there aren't any flowers yet. That would look pretty, wouldn't it?"

Don't do it, her bones sang. *Don't walk at the end of the garden today. It's going to fall again and you know it.* But how could she say this to the child? Ella's faith in the power of Mrs Armitage's fence was unquenchable and irrational.

"It would look pretty," she said slowly. "But... you know what I'd really like? I'd like you to draw me a picture."

"But there's no more room."

Ella was right. The door of the fridge was covered. When had that happened? She'd put each one of them there herself, looked at them many times each day. She recognised each individual drawing – the vase of flowers, Ella in the garden with the smile so huge it bled over her face, the strange slug of a creature Ella insisted was a seal – but somehow she'd never quite realised how many there were.

"I mean a special one," she said, desperate now. "One I can put next to my bed."

"But isn't that where you keep your husband?"

"I'll put your picture next to my photograph of him."

"So he can look at it?"

"He can't look at it," said Mrs Armitage firmly, "because he's dead, and the photograph by my bed is just a photograph. But I'll be able to look at it and it'll make me happy."

She could see the conflict in Ella's face: her desire to bore holes in the soil and fill them with lobelias and pansies, and her compulsive need to do what Mrs Armitage herself wanted. A kinder woman would feel bad about guilt tripping a child. A kinder woman would let her go out and dig in the dangerous places at the end of the garden. It was lucky for Ella that Mrs Armitage was not kind.

"What would you like a picture of?" Ella asked at last.

"I don't know, I don't know anything about drawing. It has to be special, that's all. What would be a really special thing to draw?"

Ella's bottom lip was beginning to protrude. "I don't know what you like."

"You ought to know by now, you've been coming here for long enough."

"You like the garden."

"There you go."

"But I've already drawn the garden. So I can't draw that."

Sensing mutiny, Mrs Armitage slapped the packet of felt-tipped pens down on the table in front of Ella and added a pad of paper.

"You'll think of something."

She turned away from Ella's tight little face to the relative safety of the sink, and began washing the few pots that waited in the bowl. The pouring of the water and the clatter of the pots was not quite enough to drown out the silence in the room.

After a minute she risked a brief glance behind her. Ella was sitting heroically still, a black felt-tipped pen clutched like a weapon. Her eyes were scrunched shut and her face was crumpled and red.

"What on earth is wrong with you?" Mrs Armitage demanded.

"Nothing," Ella whispered, without opening her eyes.

"Of course there's something wrong. You can't possibly be crying over a picture you haven't even drawn yet."

"I don't know what to draw!" The words came out in a strange howl, and with their release Ella's expression dissolved into wet-mouthed misery and she laid her head down on the table and sobbed.

"Oh, good Lord." Mrs Armitage sat down in the chair nearest to Ella, stretched out a hand to the slim little shoulders, then let it fall again. "Come on, let's not have all this nonsense. Stop it now." Ella's grief shuddered through her body. "Would you like another biscuit? Or some more juice?" More shudders, and a quiet hopeless moaning. "Stop making that awful noise, please, I can't stand it." And then, with the brilliance of desperation, "Would you like me to tell you a story?"

For a brief and blessed moment, the moaning stopped.

"Right." She squared her shoulders. Telling stories must be something she could manage. People did it all the time. "So, once upon a time..." She cast around her kitchen for inspiration, came back to rest on the sight of Ella. "Once upon a time, there was a little girl."

The hopeless shuddering sobs were subsiding. She felt slightly giddy with triumph.

"This little girl lived in a great big house by the sea," Mrs Armitage continued.

Ella's face, red and bleary, appeared for a moment over the top of her arm and whispered something.

"I can't hear you when you mumble, you'll have to tell me again."

"Did she have a mummy and a daddy and a brother?"

"No," said Mrs Armitage, firmly. "She lived by herself." Was that something Ella would accept? Apparently it was. "She had everything in the house exactly how she liked it, and nobody ever got to move her things around or buy pictures she thought were ugly or tell her when she had to get up or what she was going to have for dinner."

"But she must have been scared to be by herself," said Ella, and licked unselfconsciously at a drip of clear snot. Mrs Armitage shuddered and reached for the box of tissues.

"Wipe yourself up, and don't ever do that again. She wasn't scared. She liked being by herself. It made her happy."

"I wouldn't like it," Ella persisted.

"It's not a story about you, it's a story about the little girl."

"What was her name?"

"Araminta."

"That's a funny name."

"There's no point complaining, that's what she was called. And she liked having an unusual name, it reminded her that she was different. So she lived all by herself in her house

158

by the sea, and she never felt lonely or sad, not even for a minute, because she had everything she needed."

Ella's eyes were red and swollen and her face was streaky, but at least her nose was now clean.

"Did the sea try to steal her house too?" she asked.

"Sometimes," said Mrs Armitage, before she could stop herself. "So Araminta would stand with a bucket and catch the sea with it, and throw it back over the cliff."

"The whole sea? In her bucket?"

"It was a magic bucket."

"Oh. But what about night-time? Did she stay awake all night just in case?"

"No, she didn't. She went to bed in her little bedroom right at the top of the house like a sensible person, and hoped she'd wake up the next morning on the land and not underneath the water."

"Sometimes I don't want to go to sleep," said Ella.

"Then you'll be tired the next day. Anyway," Mrs Armitage said, "one morning, Araminta woke up and remembered something beautiful. Her best friend was coming for lunch."

"Was she frightened of the sea too?"

"Araminta wasn't frightened of the sea. And it wasn't a her, it was a him. They'd been friends since she was little –"

"She's little now, isn't she? You said she was a little girl."

"Fine, *even* littler. I'm old, everyone younger than me looks like a child. So when I said she was a little girl, well, you might say she was a bit older."

Ella looked puzzled. "Older like you?"

"No, not older like me – how old do you want her to be?" Ella shrugged. "Well, have a think and let me know, and we'll say she's that age. So, she woke up, and she cleaned her house, and she put on her best party frock, which was all floaty and white and pretty, and she picked some flowers from her garden and she put them on the table, and she made a cake. And then at four o'clock, her friend knocked on the door, and she went to let him in."

"Was he wearing party clothes too? What do boys wear to parties?"

"He was wearing an electric purple suit with a green shirt and a purple tie," said Mrs Armitage without pausing. "And he'd brought a friend with him."

"What was the friend wearing?"

"He was wearing jeans and a t-shirt, because he hadn't expected to be at the party. But he looked lovely anyway."

"Was there somewhere for him to sit?"

"Yes, there was an extra chair."

"And was there a plate for him?"

"She got another plate out of the cupboard."

"And was there enough cake –"

"There was enough of everything for everyone," said Mrs Armitage loudly. "It was a big house and she had plenty of food and there was enough for everyone and Uncle Roger."

Ella looked baffled. "Who's Uncle Roger?"

"Oh for goodness sakes. When I was a little girl, when we'd made too much food at dinner, we'd say we'd made enough for Uncle Roger if he called round. He's not a real person, it's only an expression." She could see Ella's mouth opening. "Forget about Uncle Roger, he's not in the story. So, the little girl let the two boys in, and they sat in the garden and talked. And after a while, the little girl started to realise that even though she'd been best friends with the first boy for years and years, she might like the other boy even more."

"But that would make the first boy sad."

"Yes, it would."

"It's not nice to make people sad," said Ella severely.

"Is it nice to make yourself sad? When you pretend your feelings aren't real, that makes you sad."

"But what if you're feeling scared because of a dream, and you don't want to feel scared, so you lie in bed and you pretend to yourself that you're not scared so after a while you'll stop being scared and then you can go back to sleep?"

"Is that what you do?"

"Yes," said Ella. "No. I'm supposed to. But really I go and get in Jacob's bed with him."

"Well there you go then. It doesn't even work. And pretending you don't feel something is the worst thing of all."

"Oh." Ella reached for her felt-tips. "Should I draw you a picture now?"

"If you like."

The next few minutes were blessedly silent. Ella reached for colour after colour, scribbling industriously. The rain had turned the air soft and sleepy. Mrs Armitage drank her tea and was glad she would not have to finish her story.

"There," said Ella, and pushed the paper across the table. "Do you like it?"

Mrs Armitage held herself very still. She would not gasp. She would not flinch.

"It's my nightmare," Ella confided. "I nightmare that I'm with Jacob, and then the sea comes and someone pushes us into the water and we sink down and down to the bottom. And there's a boat there, and we have to go onto it, then a crab comes and walks over our skulls."

"I see," said Mrs Armitage. Her voice was not as firm as she would have liked.

"You look frightened. Do you nightmare this too?"

"No. No, I don't. It's very powerful, Ella. Well done."

"It won't happen to you because you can breathe underwater. I'm learning to do that too, only I can't hold my breath for very long, not like you can –"

"I have scuba gear on," said Mrs Armitage. "I can breathe underwater because I wear scuba gear. I think you should learn to dive too, Ella, as soon as you're old enough. Then one day you can come diving with me."

"But you can breathe underwater, you told me so –"

About to interrupt with a sharp reminder that she knew exactly how underwater breathing worked, Mrs Armitage was herself interrupted by a rattling knock at the door. Someone

161

had come into her garden, uninvited and unwelcome, and left the gate open so the sea could peer in.

"Someone's knocking at the door," said Ella, when Mrs Armitage didn't move.

"I can hear them."

The knock came again, far sooner than was polite.

"Should we let them in?" Ella asked.

"I'll go and see who it is."

Her unknown guest knocked a third and longer time, as if sheer loud persistence might get them a quicker admission. Mrs Armitage reached for the key. The handle shuddered and jiggled impatiently. Mrs Armitage counted to ten before finally unlocking the door.

"Is Ella in there with you?" The man on the other side of the door was unremarkable in every way except for his rudeness. After a minute, she recognised him: this was Richard, Maggie's husband and the children's father. The man who liked quiet.

"Yes," said Mrs Armitage, because she disliked lying, and then, because she was annoyed, "and who are you?"

"Thank God for that – I'm her dad. I'll take her home right away."

He wasn't, exactly, trying to push his way in, but there was a definite expectation in the way he loomed forward into the doorway and into the kitchen. She wasn't, exactly, trying to keep him out, but there was a definite steeliness to the way she stood, as tall and broad as she could, refusing to give an inch.

"She's not causing any inconvenience," said Mrs Armitage, leaning slightly on the *she*. "She's quite welcome to stay."

"She's a little kid! She's not supposed to be out on her own!" Thwarted by Mrs Armitage, not quite at the point where he was willing to push aside a stranger, he resorted to coercion. "Ella, come here, darling, it's time to go home."

Ella's face was white, but she slipped obediently enough off the chair. "Are you going to shout at me?"

"No, of course I'm not going to – well, I'm not very impressed, okay? Going off on your own? Not telling your mother? Coming into someone else's house? That's" – a quick glance at Mrs Armitage, a deep breath – "that is not all right."

"Mummy was asleep," said Ella. "She sleeps a lot. She goes to bed when you've gone to work."

Another furtive glance in Mrs Armitage's direction, the instinctive reflex of someone who has much to hide.

"So," Ella continued, her face very innocent and sweet, "sometimes I come to see Mrs Armitage. I don't talk to strange people or anything. Why are you home now, Daddy? Don't you have to work today?"

"We'll talk about this when we get back."

"Don't mind me," said Mrs Armitage.

"Mrs Armitage is my friend," said Ella. "I like visiting her."

With a visible effort, he assembled a smile.

"I'm sorry my daughter's been bothering you," he began, in a voice that made Mrs Armitage yearn to poke him with a stick.

"She's not bothering me at all," she said, with a smile as false as his own. "She's very welcome."

"She can't be inviting herself here without even –"

"Ella," said Mrs Armitage, "did you say your mother sleeps all day?" It wasn't that she cared, she told herself, she was simply interested to see how much she could annoy this near-stranger, Richard. "Aren't you home-schooled? Who teaches you to read and write and so on?"

"Don't worry," said her father through gritted teeth. "I'm sorting everything out. You don't need to get involved."

"But is your wife ill?"

"She's fine."

"Why does she sleep all the time?"

"She's just – she's not really ill, nothing serious – thank you for looking after Ella. I'll make sure she doesn't bother you again."

"Is Mummy poorly?"

"Ella." His fingers flexed, then relaxed. "We talk about private things when we're on our own."

"But am I making Mummy poorly? I heard you shouting last night and Mummy said you didn't know what it was like being stuck at home with me every day and she wished she could go out more."

"It's rude to listen to other people's conversations."

"And then you shouted at her and told her to stop going on about things she couldn't have."

"This is private."

"And then Jacob said we could play the underwater breathing game, but I said you'd be mad if we did, and he said it didn't matter, and then I heard you tell Mummy that you'd had enough of her and then something fell over and she started crying."

"For God's sake! Stop talking!" She thought he was going to hit the child, found herself moving between them to keep her safe, but instead he pressed his hand over Ella's mouth, his fingers big and brown against the pink bow-lips and pale tender skin. When he saw Mrs Armitage looking, he flushed scarlet and let his hand fall.

"I only want to know." Ella's bottom lip trembled.

The pulse on his temple was bulging and blue. *Poke poke poke,* thought Mrs Armitage. Ella looked so small.

"Okay. We've taken up enough of this nice lady's time." His hand closed around Ella's upper arm and propelled her towards the back door. "Get your coat. And your wellies. And not a word out of you until they're on, do you understand? Not a word." Ella reached obediently for her boots. "And hurry up. Or – or you'll know about it."

The scurrying anxiety in Ella's motions as she hurried herself into her wellies and coat told a story Mrs Armitage didn't like. She'd never seen bruises on the child. But had she been looking closely enough?

"I apologise for my rude daughter." His words struggled

to escape past his frozen jaw. "And for my rude self. I'm Richard, Richard Winter. I'll make sure she doesn't bother you again."

"She's welcome to visit."

He glanced at the table, at the felt-tipped pens, the pad of paper, the pictures that covered the fridge door. "She's made herself at home."

"She's always welcome," Mrs Armitage repeated.

"She can't wander into strange people's houses! Just because you're not a murderer doesn't mean the next person won't be."

"You might want to supervise her better, then."

"Trust me, I'm working on it."

"And in the meantime, would you prefer her to stay at home with a woman who's asleep for most of the day, or visiting someone who's at least conscious and responsive? Ella, do you hear me? Come whenever you like."

"Forget what Ella said, kids exaggerate. My wife went for a nap, that's all – look, it's none of your business anyway. Ella, you're not to come here ever again. Understand?"

Ella looked from one to the other.

"Now I don't know what to do," she said wonderingly. "What should I do?"

"What I bloody well tell you," said her father.

"Whatever makes you happy," said Mrs Armitage.

Outside, there was a low rumbling roar. The floor shuddered and shook. Mrs Armitage steadied herself against the wall as the bones of her house quivered. Then there was the scent of earth and dust and a patch of sky where her garden fence had once been, and Ella's expression.

"What was that? Daddy, what was that? Mrs Armitage, what was that?"

"Don't worry. We're all still here." The sky was filled with swirls of dust and wheeling gulls and it was difficult to see clearly how much had fallen, but she could still glimpse the green of her lawn.

165

"But what was that? Is the sea coming to get us? Is it?"

"Of course not." There was no point in trying to hide the truth. "It's the cliff falling."

"The cliff? The cliff's fallen? Is our house safe? Is Mummy safe? Is Jacob safe?"

"Yes. I told you, mine will go first –"

"Now do you see why I don't want you wandering off on your own?" Richard pounced like a cat. "You might have been walking on that cliff when it fell. And then what? Hmm?" Perhaps the pallor of Ella's face, the panicky whoops of her breath, softened his heart, because after a minute he put his arms around Ella. "You weren't on the cliff. Nothing bad happened this time. It's all fine. Stop that noise now so we can go home."

As he patted and stroked at his daughter's heaving back, his eyes met Mrs Armitage's over Ella's head, and she read the words as clearly as if he'd spoken them: *I win.*

There was no point in complaining; it was a fair move. And besides, Ella really might have been on the cliff-top when it fell.

"How can we get home?" Ella managed between sobs. "We can't even go home. And now Mummy's all on her own and Jacob can't get home and they won't know where we are and –"

"Fortunately for all of us, we can get back through the village."

"I'm not allowed to walk next to the road."

"Not by yourself you're not, but you're with me. But you are absolutely not allowed to come here again, do you hear me? Not by the village because you're not allowed next to the road. And not along the cliff-top because now you know how dangerous it is. No more visits. Understand?" Ella nodded. "Right. Then that's that."

They set off together, Ella hiccupping with sobs, Richard stern and tall. Mrs Armitage watched them leave and tried to recall a phrase she had heard years ago. After a moment, she

166

had it: the banality of evil. The dreadful truth that most acts of wickedness were committed by people who were perfectly unremarkable. Perhaps she ought to speak to someone. But what would she say? And who would believe her?

Ella had left her rain-hat on the table. Mrs Armitage held it for a moment, then folded it carefully into a tiny triangle shape and put it in the back of a kitchen drawer.

Chapter Twelve
Now

At three in the morning, Jacob woke to the familiar and terrible sound of his father's door opening. Swearing quietly, he forced himself from his bed, his ears ringing with dizziness and his heartbeat slow and reluctant.

"Dad?" Jacob felt ridiculous knocking at the inside of his own door, but he knew it had to be done. "Dad. It's me."

"Everything's fine, son. Go back to bed."

If only he could. He opened his door. His father stood on the landing, peering into the darkness that pooled at the foot of the front staircase.

"It's all right, Dad." Jacob came to stand beside him.

"Go back to your room. I'll take care of this. Shh! Did you hear something?"

"No, there's nothing. Come on. Let's go back to bed."

"There! There it is again. There's someone trying the back door. Right, I'm not having this." His father drew himself together and began creeping down the stairs. "I'm going down to sort this out once and for all. Stay up here where you're safe. I don't want you getting involved."

"I'll come with you." Jacob began following his father down the stairs.

"No, you won't. Go back to your room. What kind of a father do you think I am?"

"But if there's two of us –" No, he wouldn't get drawn into his father's imaginings; it would only make him more convinced there was something to be afraid of. "How about I make you –" was it too soon to suggest milk or cocoa? "I don't want you wandering around in the dark on your own. I'm coming with you."

"You're such a good lad. I love you, Jacob. You know that, don't you?"

He was so tired, that was the trouble. "I know, Dad. I love you too." When he was this tired, he was helpless to stop the tears.

"Hey, don't cry." His father's arm went around his shoulders, and he had to clench his jaw to keep himself from howling. "What's the matter? Is something wrong at school? Wait. What was that? Did you hear that? There's someone upstairs."

They must have woken Ella. If she'd stay in her room, she'd be safe. His father never looked behind that door. But what if he did? "Dad, I know who it is." How could he have left her out there on the cliff? What was the matter with him? "It's Ella, she's staying here, remember?"

"Stay here and keep quiet. I'll go and see."

"Dad, please, it's Ella –"

His father shook him off with the strength that still took him by surprise, and strode ahead up the stairs, down the corridor towards Ella's room. Jacob scrambled after him, slipping on the stairs and whacking his shin painfully against the bare wood, stumbling to his feet just in time to hear his father's glad incredulous shout: "Jacob! Why didn't you tell me – ? You didn't say you had a girlfriend. Why didn't you say? I'm sorry, pet, my rude son didn't bother to let me know you were coming. Nice to meet you. I'm afraid I don't know your name yet."

Ella looked pale and confused. She had borrowed one of his hoodies as an improvised dressing gown. "I'm Ella."

"Nice to meet you, Ella. Are you staying for dinner? Jacob, you should have said she was coming round."

"Dad, it's the middle of the night – you're right, I should have asked first."

"Don't worry, I'm sure we can feed one extra. I'll see what we've got in." He bustled off down the hallway. "Wait here."

"Ella." He wanted to hug her tight, settled instead for tidying her, brushing her hair away from her face, straightening the hoodie on her shoulders. "Don't worry, everything's fine. I'll sort him out."

"Is it because I'm here? Did I wake him?"

"No, he does this most nights, it's not you, I promise. I'll get him settled in a minute. You go back to bed."

"Jacob?" His father loomed suddenly behind his shoulder. "Just looking for… I can't seem to… She's just… I saw her… Jacob, where's your mum got to?"

He felt dizzy. This was the one thing his father never asked.

"Dad." What could he say? "She's – she's not here."

"I can see that, thank you. I'm asking where she is?" His father's sense that there was something amiss with his world was beginning to bloom once more. "Where's she got to? I don't want her going out alone, do you hear? I'm not having it! All the trouble I've gone to getting us here in the first place, and what's the first thing she does?"

"She won't be long. She's probably gone out for a bit."

"Well, she shouldn't have! I don't want her going off by herself, I've told her and told her and *told* her. My God, all the times we've had this conversation – no, don't you try and stop me, Jacob, I'm going to find her – where are you? I know you're in here somewhere, come on!"

His father's voice was like a peal of bells clanging in his head. He could hardly look at Ella. That conversation – that argument, really – they'd had on the cliff-top. *I don't want her going off by herself.* But it was his father's illness speaking, not his memories; it had to be. There was no way Ella, at six, could have seen something he had missed at sixteen. If only his dad would shut up so he could explain this. If only he could get his father to go back to sleep.

"He really does this every night?" Ella looked shaken. "How do you stand it?"

"I'm used to it." Somewhere downstairs, there was the sound of crashing. "Go back to bed, I'll sort him out."

"No, let me help."

He took the stairs three at a time. His father was in the kitchen, knocking over the kitchen chairs so he could look under the table.

"Not down here," he said vaguely. "Must have dropped it somewhere."

"What are you looking for?"

"I don't know! I – something – I was looking for something –" His father's bewilderment hurt his heart.

"Never mind." Ella took his arm gently. "Don't worry about it now. We'll find it later."

"She's right, Dad, we'll sort it out later. Shall I make us all a drink?"

"Got no chance with you two on the case, have I?" His father smiled. "Okay. Quick drink before bed. Come on, pet, we'll go and wait in the living-room. Let Jacob do some work for a change."

Because I don't do enough round here already, thought Jacob, looking for the humour and finding only resentment.

He finally made it back to bed at half-past four, and fell into a heavy unrefreshing sleep. When he opened his eyes and reached for his phone, he was appalled to find it was almost nine o'clock. He flung himself into the day in a kind of sleepy panic, but his father's room was empty, and he could hear voices downstairs. Ella, bless her heart, must have got up with him. He couldn't believe he'd slept through. When he came downstairs, his father and sister were huddled in the kitchen like conspirators.

"And here he is," his father said, with a wink. "Finally crawled out from your pit. Behave yourselves, you two. I'm going to get dressed. Back in a few minutes."

His father was already dressed, but that wouldn't matter. He would soon forget what he'd left the room for.

"You didn't have to get up with him," he said guiltily, as he waited for his toast to brown.

"I don't mind. I was awake anyway."

"Sorry Dad woke you as well. If you ignore him another time, I'll sort him out."

"It wasn't that. I could hear the sea."

Would she ever get over that old fear? He had still not apologised to her for leaving her on the cliff-top. Or would it make everything worse to drag it up again? He needed coffee, and to clear his head. Ella sat silently with him as he ate his toast.

"Do you think," Ella said suddenly, as he stood up to put his plate in the sink, "he might sleep better if he got some fresh air?"

"I don't know. I suppose he might do. But he's not very keen on going outside."

"Who's not keen on going outside?" His father was back again. It was years since Jacob had seen him looking so purposeful. "Jacob, we both thought we should go for a walk."

"It's a lovely day," Ella agreed, "the sun's gorgeous."

"But – um – I mean, I suppose –"

"Come on," said their father, and patted Jacob on the back. "Get some clothes on, and let's get this show on the road."

Let's get this show on the road. A phrase from their childhoods, on the rare occasions when they went out for the day. The days themselves were usually disappointing, but the setting-off was always hopeful. *Let's get this show on the road.* It must be Ella's presence stirring the pot of his father's memories, even if he couldn't recognise her as his daughter. His father was struggling with his shoes, and Jacob wondered wildly if he'd outgrown them. Then he realised it was only that his father had worn nothing but slippers for months, and had forgotten the feel of rigid leather against his feet.

"These are a bit stiff," he said. "Be all right once I've worn them in."

"That's right, Dad." The shoes were scuffed and worn, the brown of the leather showing white and then grey at the toes. "Have a bit of a walk in them."

Outside, his father set off with the purposeful air of an eager explorer. Something else new: his father taking the lead. The few times Jacob had taken him out by himself, they'd simply meandered up and down the lane for five minutes, until his father suggested it was time to head back.

"Do you remember when we'd go on days out sometimes?" he asked Ella. "About three times a year we'd go. And it took so long to actually get it organised, it felt like we were going trekking in the Andes."

"Yes! And it was always to a ruined castle or an abbey or something. You used to read the boards out for me. There was always loads of stuff about the kitchens for some reason."

"And when we ran out of boards I used to make it up." Their father was striding off into the distance, head high and arms swinging. "Did I tell you once they picked the King and Queen by the colour of their hair?"

"Yes. And we couldn't have kings and queens in charge any more because somebody discovered hair dye."

"Shit, I did as well. You didn't believe me, did you?"

"I loved it, it was great. Anyway, you were trying to look after me. Keep me distracted."

"From all the boring ruins, you mean?"

"No, of course not. From Mum and Dad."

So they were going to have to talk about yesterday after all. "Ella, listen." He remembered how his father had looked last night, the despair and rage in his eyes. "I shouldn't have shouted at you yesterday, that was unforgiveable. But I promise you, what he said about her being missing – he says stuff like that to me too. He gets upset when I go out of the room. He can't help it." She was looking at him with an expression he remembered from their childhood: there was

173

something she wanted to say to him, but she wasn't sure if he'd let her say it. "What? Tell me."

"Do you remember that time we went out once, and we couldn't find Mum? He got us to look for her too. And he was trying to make it into a joke, but it wasn't really. He was really angry. And then she came back, she'd been to buy ice-creams, but he was furious and yelled at her. And then he looked around in case anyone could hear him and he got all quiet instead. And that was the last time we went anywhere."

"But that was once! Not all the time. He used to get angry with us sometimes too, and he wasn't cruel to us, was he?" What could he share to remind her of how good their lives had been before? "Remember how mad he used to get with us walking slowly?"

"With me walking slowly. You used to hang back and keep me company."

Jacob could still feel the boredom of those walks, the continual irritation of nobody's natural pace quite matching up with anyone else's. If he didn't walk with Ella he'd be shouted at for leaving her behind; if he slowed to her pace they were both told off for not keeping up. Trying to explain counted as "answering back". The bliss of being an ordinary family whose parents were ordinarily unreasonable… sometimes he used to take Ella's hand to help her catch up. His phone was buzzing in his pocket.

Why is 6 afraid of 7?
Because….7 8 9 :-D :-D :-D
- D

Hey it's nearly lunchtime and you
haven't read my Daily Joke yet.
You're not dead are you? – D

"Just a mate from work," he said, embarrassed. "Hang on."

Sorry but yes I am dead. That joke
killed me. – J
Seriously, sorry – I slept in.
Please don't stop sending them! – Jx

His phone buzzed again.

Only if you promise to keep
validating me by telling me how
funny I am – Dx

"Come on!" His dad turned back towards them, and with the light behind him he could have walked straight out of their childhoods. "You need to keep up!"

He was used to having to stand by his father's side and direct every step of their few and brief forays into the outside world, but today their dad led them unhesitatingly into the village, pointing out apparent landmarks as if he was trying to convince them both to move there. ("Watch this corner, people tear round it." "Postbox. Last pick-up five-thirty, except Saturdays when they collect at one." "See that field there? Normally has sheep in it this time of year. Must have gone to market early.") Was any of this true? Was his father remembering, or just making it up as he went along? Jacob had no way of knowing.

"Shop," said his father. "Has the basics." He yawned. "Bit of a trek though."

They'd walked for less than ten minutes. Jacob wasn't sure if the spasm in his throat was tears, or laughter.

"And there's the bus stop," his father added. "For all the good it does. Only two buses a week. You need your car round here. Did I – where did I –" he began patting his pockets. "Can't quite remember – my memory's like a sieve these days…"

"You were telling me about when you moved here," said Ella. "You said it was like going to the end of the world…"

"… and turning right. And it is as well. You need a car if you're going to live here. Couple of buses a week, but they're for the old biddies really. The ones who don't drive. Enough time to do their shopping and get back for tea. Not much good for people our age."

This time, Jacob had to smile.

"Was it quiet when you moved here too?"

"Oh yes, that's why we chose it. We were looking for somewhere a bit off the beaten track. We wanted to be quiet." He looked around anxiously. "Jacob, have you seen –"

"Hey, Dad," said Jacob. "Is that a buzzard over that field?"

"What? No, that's a seagull, you fool. What was I saying?"

"You were telling me about living here," said Ella. "You said you wanted somewhere quiet?"

"Yes, that's right actually. You need a car to get anywhere, though. Otherwise, once you're here, you're here. Jacob gets the bus to school, special service that is, goes through all the villages and rounds them all up, but you need a car if you're working." His eyes were still pointing towards Ella, but his concentration had turned inwards, that familiar searching look that came when he began to suspect there was something dreadfully wrong with his universe. His hands fumbled at his pockets. "We didn't drive here, did we?"

"No, Dad," said Jacob. "We walked. Remember?"

"Where are my car keys, though? I always have the keys in my pocket. I don't like leaving them around. I don't want her going off in the car, you see. She's not supposed to be – where the hell are my bloody car keys? Jacob, my car keys were here a minute ago. Have you been playing around with them?"

"We didn't drive here, Dad, we walked. Look at that crow, I think it's found a dead rabbit –"

"I always have the keys, though. I never leave my keys lying around. Jacob, you've taken my bloody keys."

"No, I haven't, Dad, I promise. We didn't drive here. We walked. You didn't need your keys because we walked."

"But I always have my keys with me! Always! Because if

176

I leave them around, she's liable to – and I'm not having – oh shit, where are they, fuck fuck fuck, where are they…" His eyes were wild. "She's going to leave me. She's going to find the keys and leave me."

"Dad, let's go home. Maybe you left them at home."

"Not without my keys!"

"What sort of car is it?" Ella asked. "Can you remember what it looks like?"

"What?" His father turned his face towards Ella. "I'm sorry, pet, do we know you?"

"I'm Ella."

"Of course you are. You're Jacob's young lady friend, I remember, it's your name I wasn't sure of. It's lovely to meet you. We're having a bit of a crisis here though, my stupid son has lost my car keys and –"

"They'll be at home, Dad. Shall we head off? Hey, and there's a buzzard round here apparently, we might see it on the way back."

His father glared at Jacob. "You shouldn't have touched my keys."

"Shall we walk back?" Ella asked. "You were telling me about what it's like to live here. When did you move here?"

"Maybe I left them on the kitchen table," he said. "Better get back and find them. Can't leave them lying around." He glared again at Jacob. "You need to start looking after things properly, do you hear me? So help me God, if those keys are lost…"

"We'll find them, Dad," said Jacob wearily.

"We'd better." He was already turning towards home. "Come on."

How could the day turn so bleak so quickly? The way back was a dark rewinding of the walk out; their father still in front, still urging them on, but with all the light gone from his expression. Within a few minutes, the idea of the lost keys slipped from his faulty grasp, leaving only the shattering sense of something precious that was gone now, and would never be recovered. Jacob had to kneel in the long grass and pat his father's back as he sobbed hopelessly into his hands.

"He can't help it," he said to Ella, over the top of their father's head.

"I know."

His father's whole body shuddered with grief. Jacob wrestled with his own self-pity. Why was he stuck in this life with this man who was long past being any sort of real parent? Why was he the one giving all the comfort?

"Come on, Dad," he said, his voice sharp despite his best intentions. "Stop it now. We need to get home." His father mumbled something and hunched further over into himself. "Never mind that now. Please get up. Oh, come on, please, this isn't fair. We don't want to sit here all day. Stop talking rubbish and get up!" He pulled at his father's arm, knowing it was useless. His dad's mind had gone but his body was still strong. He had more chance of pulling his arm out of its socket than he had of getting him to his feet when he didn't want to.

"Let me try." Suddenly Ella was between him and his father, her hair in his face and her scent in his mouth.

"It's okay, I'll get him up in the end, but sometimes he gets a bit –"

"Can you hear me?" She was patting gently at his hands, stroking them with the tips of her fingers. "It's Ella. What are you so upset about? Maybe we can fix it."

"It can't be fixed." Their father turned his face up towards them, stricken with tragedy. "Some things can't ever be fixed. I hurt her too much. I let her down. She took my car and she left me."

Jacob shivered.

"But where has she gone?" Ella coaxed. "What happened to her? Can you tell me? And maybe we can go and find her?"

"Ella, don't. Please don't. He doesn't know what he's saying."

"I don't know. There's something wrong with my memory. I can't remember things any more."

"Ella, please, leave him be, he doesn't know –"

She was completely focused on their father now, her hands holding the sides of his face.

"You can tell me," she whispered. "You won't be in trouble. I promise. Why did you move here? What were you scared of?"

"Ella, stop it!"

Her ferocious glare was so unexpected that he flinched. "Let him speak!"

The silence stretched out.

"I don't really get out much at the moment," their father said at last. "Bit busy with things at home. Jacob and I get on fine between us, but we don't have a lot of time for going out." He took Ella's hand and squeezed it, then let it go. "I'm afraid I've forgotten your name, pet, but I'm glad you're here to help Jacob out. Jacob, we should get back to it, shouldn't we?"

"You're right," said Jacob dully. "Let's get home, Dad."

He waited for his father to get a little ahead of them before speaking to Ella.

"What were you thinking?" he hissed furiously, as soon as he was sure their father would not hear. "Upsetting him like that, and for what? What's the point? What's the matter with you?"

"I'm sorry."

"Well, that's not good enough! He's not well and he can't help that. The last thing he needs is to be reminded. How could you be so cruel to him?"

"Please don't be angry. I just –"

"Forget it, I don't want to hear it." The little-girl misery on her face tore at his heart – this was *Ella*, for goodness sakes, his sister. Fighting off the urge to forgive her, he reached instead for a piece of long-forgotten adolescent cruelty: the banishment he'd imposed on her whenever her puppy-dog dependence grew too much. "I'm sick of you. Don't talk to me until I say. I don't want to be around you right now."

179

He made dinner for the three of them, revelling in his own righteousness. He was angry enough to break things, but he would do his duty. He put the plate down in front of Ella without looking at her, ate without acknowledging her presence. Then he took his father into the living-room and put on the DVD of *Die Hard*, the film his father constantly suggested and watched at least once a week. Ella could join them, or not; he didn't care. He watched from the corner of his eye as she perched on the edge of the sofa, waiting and hoping for acknowledgement. She looked so young and lost that he had to look away before he gave in to his impulse to beg her to forgive him. When he looked back again, she was gone.

Lost in his own thoughts, he forgot to watch the time or to look for the right moment to wrestle the older man up the stairs. By the time he thought to check, his dad had already fallen asleep. Now he'd have to try and wake him without waking him, wrestle him out of one sleeping-place and into another, and today had already been so long... Jacob realised he was on the verge of tears. He'd dreamed of this change in his life, and now he had it, what had really changed? He had wanted his sister to come home to him, so much, and now it was all turning to ashes.

And whose fault is that? What's the matter with you? Her mum's abandoned her and you yelled at her. Twice. You'll be lucky if she's even still here.

He left his father sleeping deeply and went upstairs. He'd been a bastard, but he could make it right. He'd make it right. He'd apologise. He knocked on the door of her room, waited, then opened it a crack.

It was empty. But then he heard the faint clicking of water in ancient plumbing and knew instantly where she was.

The bathroom was damp with years of disuse, a single forgotten towel curled over the cold iron radiator. Beneath the water, his sister lay flat and still, dressed in a navy swimming costume, her eyes closed, her skin blue-white. For the first time, he understood why his parents had hated them to play this game.

"Ella!" He plunged one arm into the water, groping frantically. Her eyes came open and he saw her exhale, but the panic didn't begin to subside until she sat up, gasping and shuddering, and rubbed the water from her face. "What the hell are you doing?" He reached for the towel, but it was set like a carapace.

"Stay here," he ordered her, and ran for the airing-cupboard.

All his towels were threadbare now. Why had he not replaced them? Why didn't he have something vast and fluffy to wrap his little sister in and keep her warm? He and his father were short of money but not that short. He could have found enough to buy something better than this thin faded greenish rag. Tomorrow he would drive into town and buy a whole bale of new ones. Back in the bathroom, Ella stood huddled in on herself, shivering.

"I'm okay," she said. "You don't need to look after me."

He wrapped her up as well as he could. "Get yourself dry before you freeze to death."

"I didn't mean to disturb you. I wanted to think."

"I was horrible earlier. I can't believe I said that to you. I – it was all I could think about sometimes. You coming back, I mean. And now I'm fucking it all up like an idiot."

"I should have told you properly. But I was afraid to. I didn't think you'd believe me. But I want to tell you now."

"Can we get you warm at least? Come on, it's cold in here."

"No, let me talk, please. Do you remember why we used to play the underwater breathing game?"

"Of course I do. You were frightened of the sea. You thought you could learn to breathe underwater."

"But we only played it when they argued. So we wouldn't have to hear them. But we heard them anyway. He used to shout about – "

"I know! I know. They used to argue. But that's all in the past now, there's no point trying to decide whose fault it was."

" – he used to shout about how hard he'd tried to keep us safe," Ella continued patiently. "And he never wanted Mum going off by herself. And now she's disappeared."

He took a handful of the towel draped around her shoulders and began to scrub at her arms, trying to get the blood flowing again. "But she hasn't *disappeared*. She's just gone off somewhere. That's what she said in her note, isn't it? She's fine. She's having some time to herself."

"But she hasn't, she wouldn't, she wouldn't leave me!" Was the brightness in her eyes rage, or tears? "I need to show you something."

He followed her into her bedroom and watched in perplexity as she knelt by the doll's house.

"Don't you think you should get dressed first? What are you doing?"

She lifted the doll's house and moved it carefully aside. In the clean patch of carpet left by the movement were three stacks of paper that she gathered carefully into a single pile and held out to him. The sight of the handwriting made him feel sick.

"What is this? Is it letters or something?"

"It's her book. She wrote a book, she worked on it sometimes during the day and she kept writing it after we –"

"She wrote it by *hand*? Not on a laptop? Why would she do that? Who does that?"

"Please read it. I need you to read it. And then you'll understand and you'll see what I mean."

He looked at the thick stack of paper, and swallowed. "Ella, it's a whole book, it'll take me hours." Every word on those pages had been written by the woman he had once called *Mother*. He didn't even want to touch it. "Can't you tell me what it's about?"

"It's hard to explain, it's a really strange story, but I think it's about a woman who's being stalked. She's trying to get away from her husband. Only he keeps following her, all the time he follows her. So eventually she makes a plan to run away, leaving everything she loves behind, even her –" Ella swallowed fiercely – "even her daughter. She's going to become someone else, so he'll never find her. And now she's disappeared. And she left me behind."

"Ella, it's a novel. Writers make stuff up, that's what writing is."

"But what if it isn't made up?"

He wasn't sure where to begin.

"After we left you," Ella continued, "we moved house all the time. Every six months or so we'd find somewhere new. It took me a long time to realise not everyone lived that way, she tried to make it seem normal, but in the end I realised. She was afraid of someone finding us."

"And you thought the person she was scared of was *Dad*?"

"At first I did. And I thought, well, if he'd found her all the other times, all the times we moved I mean, he must have some way of doing it. I thought if I came here and talked to him, maybe he could help me find her this time as well."

"But you know he can't have," said Jacob. "Don't you? I mean, even if he wanted to he couldn't. You've seen what he's like."

"But what if Mum was with someone else, before, and *he* was the one trying to find her? That would explain everything, wouldn't it? Why we had to move so often, not just afterwards but before, before we came here. Why we even moved here in the first place. And why – Dad – " the word sounded strange coming from her. He hadn't realised until now how reluctant she was to speak it. "Why he's so paranoid all the time about people breaking in. I know how this sounds, I do. But both of them, Jacob? *Both* of them convinced someone's trying to get them? That has to mean something, doesn't it?"

She really believed this, he realised. Was this what had happened to her, in those days when she'd been alone, trying to make sense of her abandonment, waiting for the woman who was never coming back? He'd never guessed how much was going on inside her head.

"Ella, I can see how you got to this. I can. But really – think about it for a minute."

"You don't believe me."

"I do get why you want this to be true. No, please, I really do. She left me too, remember? She left me too. I know how much it hurts."

"I want to find her," Ella said, her voice trembling. "That's all. I don't mind if she doesn't want to come back or anything. I want to know she's safe."

So she hadn't come back for him after all. He tried to swallow his hurt. What must it have been like for her? To come to this house she had hated, hoping to meet a man who she thought had hounded her mother for years, on the slender chance that he could help her?

"Were you scared? To come here, I mean?"

"A bit. Well, a lot. I know how stupid that sounds. You must think I'm insane."

"Of course you're not insane. You were on your own for days, anyone would start wondering."

"You know," said Ella hesitantly, "when I came here, I didn't know you'd be here too. I thought you'd have left years ago, and it would be Dad on his own. And then you came outside."

He could feel the warmth of her smile glowing like a burning coal in his chest. Impulsively, he put his arms around her. Her weight against him felt unfamiliar, and her skin was very cold. She clung to him for a minute, then suddenly pushed him away.

"I'm sorry." His heart was knocking against his ribs. "I didn't mean to – "

"It's not that. It's just I'm all wet." She scrubbed roughly at the ends of her hair with the towel.

"You'll freeze if you stay in that costume," he said.

"I'll get changed in a minute."

"You know I'm so, so glad you came back, right? Even if it was just to try and find her."

"Of course it wasn't just to find Mum! I was looking for you too."

He felt as if he'd been given a box of diamonds. He wanted to say *I love you*, but the words sounded alien in his mouth. How often did siblings tell each other that they loved each other? It would be as pointless as saying *We're both alive*. He would save this moment in his back pocket to examine later, when his work for the day was done.

"I'll see you in the morning," he said instead, and went downstairs to rouse his father from his awkward, slumped slumber in the chair and help him upstairs and into bed.

Chapter Thirteen
2008

"What are you doing?"

Ella had stood in the doorway to his bedroom for a few long minutes – so long he'd almost forgotten her again. He sat in a patch of sunlight, a Chemistry textbook open but ignored on his lap, making the most of the months where he could sit in here by himself without paying the price in bulky layers and frozen fingers. When autumn came, he'd have to make the trade-off between being warm and being alone, but for now, he revelled in the fierce yellow light and his own company. He'd played with Ella all morning, had got her breakfast while their parents murmured and shuffled overhead, made sure she got dressed and found her crayons and paper. He was sixteen years old and he had exams to prepare for. Surely he wasn't expected to entertain her all the time?

"Revising for my exams," he said, without looking up.

"Is it hard work?"

"Yes, very."

"I drew you a knight."

"That's nice. Aren't you doing lessons today?"

"But you're not at school," said Ella, surprised.

"But I'm still working. And you need to do your work too. Why don't you go and ask Mum what you're supposed to be doing?"

"She's asleep."

"Wake her up."

"I've tried. It didn't work."

It was nearly eleven o'clock. There was no way their mother was still asleep. It was Ella being Ella, and preferring to be with him. It was sweet in a way, but in a lot of other ways it was completely irritating.

"Well, why don't you take her a cup of tea or something?" He turned a page in his book, carefully not looking in the direction of the door. She'd give up in the end. She always did. After a minute, there was a flutter of paper, and then the sound of small footsteps. He risked a glance up. She'd put her picture on the floor inside his room, and left.

He returned to his book, but it was too warm to concentrate. He tried to let his thoughts drift, but he was sitting in the wrong position somehow, or the sunlight was now too bright. He got crossly to his feet and went to collect the picture Ella had left for him.

She'd drawn the two of them, as she always did. They stood on a brown cliff, himself very tall, and Ella very small and squashed up. He held an inverted cross that was presumably a sword, waving it towards the blue wave towering over their heads. Beneath it Ella had written:

Thank you for keping me sayfe

If he didn't look for her, she wouldn't bother him again. She understood when she'd been dismissed. He swore, put his book down, and went to find his little sister.

She was teetering on a chair in the kitchen, stretching for the teabags. Beneath her, the overfilled kettle wobbled and bubbled and sent up scalding plumes of steam. He grabbed her firmly under the armpits, put her on the floor and reached for the teabags himself, swallowing his mental image of what might have happened if he hadn't come in to stop her.

"I'm making a cup of tea for Mummy," Ella said.

"I can see that. You do know you're not supposed to

touch the kettle, don't you?" The boiling water spurted and slopped as he poured it cautiously out. Ella watched wide-eyed. "See that? It's too full to pour properly. That could have been your arm."

It was his fault for telling her to make their mother some tea, but of course she wouldn't say that; she never blamed him, even when he was wrong. Together they climbed the wide front staircase to their parents' room.

Their mother lay as serene and beautiful as an enchanted princess, lovely even with her eyes shut, because then you had the chance to appreciate the delicate fringe of her eyelashes, the perfect swoop of her brows, the curve of her cheekbones. Her hair sprayed out across the pillow. She must be the only woman in the world who could look utterly beautiful without any effort at all, without even the benefit of consciousness.

"Mum." He put the mug on the bedside table, and shook her shoulder gently. "Mum, it's nearly lunchtime. We brought you a cup of tea."

She sighed, and opened her eyes.

"Jacob." Her smile was unfocused and brilliant. "Hello, my lovely boy. How are you? It's a beautiful day."

"It's nearly lunchtime," he repeated.

"There's nothing more beautiful than sleeping in the daytime," she murmured. "It's like eating in bed, or stealing flowers from people's gardens. Do you think Adam and Eve stole flowers in Eden? Perhaps that's why God was angry."

"I'll make lunch," Jacob said. "What would you like?"

"I'll just have an apple," she said, and closed her eyes again. "In a little while."

"Mum." He shook her again, but she was gone, vanished beneath the surface, leaving only her lovely form behind. What was she thinking, sleeping so late? Was she ill? Stroking a strand of hair away from her face, he found a small ring of dull black bruises circling her wrist.

"Is Mummy hurt?" Ella reached out a finger. Her hands needed washing. "Is that why she's so tired?"

"She's fine," said Jacob.

"But –"

"I tell you what," he said. "Let's make a picnic and go and have an adventure."

When they left the house, it was with a furtive sense of running away. Nobody knew where they were going; nobody would miss them for hours. Their father was at work, their mother asleep. No neighbours were there to watch them go. They were completely free, just him and his sister, making her steps as long as she possibly could to try and keep up with him. He took her hand in his, slowing his pace so she wouldn't have to scurry, and knew without looking exactly how her smile would transform her face.

The best route to adventure was the cliff-top, but he didn't want today tainted with fear. They took the route through the village instead, passing thin rows of tall houses and pebble-dashed bungalows whose residents they'd never seen, and who they might live their whole lives without ever knowingly laying eyes on.

"Where are we going?" Ella asked, after a while.

"To the beach."

"I thought this road only went to the shop."

"No, silly. The road goes all the way through and out to the rest of the world. How do you not know that?" Ella shrugged. "Doesn't Mum ever take you?"

"We go to the shop sometimes. Not every day, though. Only when it's safe."

"The cliffs won't fall in this far inland. Look, you see at the end of the road there? Where the road goes left but the path goes right? That's where we're going."

"Will it be the beach we went to before? That time we went all together?"

"Yep. Come on, keep walking."

"But where do we go to if we keep walking down that road?" Ella asked.

"Along the coast."

"Are there more beaches? Or are there only our one, the one we got stuck on I mean, and the one we went to with Mum and Dad?"

He tried not to laugh. "No, there's loads."

"If we walk down the road, will we find another one?"

"I don't know. Maybe."

"So, should we do that? For an adventure?"

The further they walked, the further it would be to walk back, and Ella would grow tired, and she was getting too heavy to carry. He thought about his parents, and the expressions on their faces if Ella told them he'd taken her off like this, without telling anyone where they were going.

On the other hand, since no one knew where they were anyway –

He knelt down in front of her and looked into her face, making sure she knew he was being serious. "We can only do it if you promise not to tell anyone."

"I promise."

"Seriously. Not anyone. Not even Mum or Dad."

"Will they be cross with us?"

"Yes, they will. We're not supposed to go off by ourselves. But we can do it this once, if you promise not to tell them. And you have to do everything I say. And not ask to be carried."

"I promise."

It was insane to put his trust in the promise of a child. But the road was inviting and both the school bus and his father always took a different route, so he'd never been along it.

"Come on, then," he said, and took her hand again.

Within a few hundred yards there was no footpath, but the visibility was good, no fences or bushes to conceal oncoming traffic, so they walked on anyway, and climbed onto the scrubby grass verge whenever a car approached. They could smell the distinctive muddy scent of the sea, and he wondered if Ella realised how close it was, but she seemed oblivious, so he kept quiet. It was past twelve o'clock, time to eat the sandwiches he'd hastily flung together in the kitchen. But Ella didn't complain, so they kept going, with no destination in mind other than the next slight curve of the road or a single tree, sculpted by the wind, that drew them on like a sentinel.

"Look." At the top of what looked like a farm-track, Ella's feet stumbled against a long wooden post, laid out like a felled tree. "A sign-poster."

"Sign-post." He knelt beside her and looked at the carved letters. *To the beach.*

"That says beach," said Ella, after intense study.

"Well done."

"A different beach, though."

"Different from what?"

"From the other beaches. Maybe the sea will be farther away on that beach."

"It's nothing to do with that, it's the tide. If the tide's out then the sea's further away."

"Maybe the tide will be further out on that beach," said Ella, with the obedient air of someone correcting a small lexical mistake.

"Maybe it will," said Jacob, giving in.

"Should we go and look? And then should we have lunch? If the sea is – if the tide is far out?"

The felled sign might mean something. Maybe they weren't supposed to use this path – perhaps because the beach wasn't safe, perhaps even because it had been buried by a recent collapse. But the sun was so bright and the sense of freedom was so intoxicating and Ella was already stumping down the path. What could he do but follow? If it looked dodgy they could come back again. And if it was worth visiting, maybe they'd have it all to themselves.

The path kept up the illusion of being a farm-track for a while, then narrowed and became more sandy. Soon, they walked between tall pale dunes, insecurely anchored by thick woody strands of grass that grew strong and tough, in defiance of the poor soil and salty air. When Jacob tried to snap a piece off, the sharp edge cut his finger.

"Ow," he said, more surprised than hurt.

Ella's eyed widened. "You're bleeding. Your finger's bleeding."

"It's fine." Jacob put his finger in his mouth.

"But it must hurt. Have we got a plaster?"

"Why would we have a plaster? Don't worry, it'll stop bleeding in a minute."

"You've been wounded," said Ella. "Now you need a potion to fix your finger and make you as strong as twenty men."

"You can make me one on the beach," said Jacob. "Look, we're nearly there."

The beach, unexpectedly, was utterly beautiful. Perhaps not in the way Ella might have dreamed of, an expanse of golden sand and rich rock-pools and with the sea several miles in the distance, but with a remote and slightly difficult beauty that made Jacob think of the word *wilderness*, and then the word *wild*, and finally filled him with a deep satisfaction that they had it all to themselves. He and Ella sat down in the lee of a dune and ate their sandwiches. They were only white bread and cheap ham and cheese so vividly orange it looked as if it was meant for making hard hats, but the long walk and the fresh air transformed their food into a feast of savoury flavours and satisfying textures. With the sandwiches gone, Ella looked at him hopefully, confident he had even more wonderful tastes to offer.

As an afterthought, he'd crammed in a giant packet of dry-roasted peanuts. He offered them dubiously to Ella, who tasted one in astonishment, then took a large handful and ate them one by one, licking salt from her fingers. The water had warmed in the bottles and taken on a faint plasticky flavour, but they were too thirsty to mind. He reached out for Ella and rolled her into the sand and tickled her, because she was small, and fluffy-headed from the breeze, and it wouldn't be so long until she was too big to pull around like this, and

192

because he'd so nearly not done this with her, had so nearly stayed in his room and wasted the day. She squealed and kicked him in the stomach, so he pinioned her arms and legs until she stopped wriggling. Then they lay curled around each other and watched the few thin clouds scud across the bowl of the sky.

"This is our adventure," said Ella. "We're on a quest to find the best beach in the world. Is that what knights did on quests?"

"Sometimes they killed their enemies. Or saved people from dragons. Or rescued princesses. Oh, and they looked for the Grail. That was like a special cup that was the greatest treasure in the world."

"When I'm a knight," said Ella, "I'll do quests to find beautiful secret places. And I won't show them to anyone. Except you. And this is our first one. So, now I'm a knight."

"If you like."

"I need a sword, though. I can't be a knight without a sword. Can I?"

"Hang on." Glancing around, he spotted a long thin shard of stick poking from a dune. "See that stick? If you can get it out, that'll be your sword, and you'll be a proper knight."

Ella rolled away from him, and began heaving at the stick. She pulled and pulled, getting louder with each attempt, as if being more noisy would make her more strong. He wondered if the stick was growing in the sand, living even though it looked dead. Perhaps he'd set Ella an impossible challenge. He got up to help her, but then she pressed down on the stick with all her weight and it broke at the base, tumbling her to the ground.

"I got it!" She was scarlet in the face with triumph.

"You did." He took the stick and tapped her on the left shoulder, then on the right. "Arise, Sir Ella. Now you have to go off and kill a dragon."

"Should I catcher the dragon and make it be friendly?"

"Capture, not catcher. Well, I suppose."

193

"Is there a dragon in Mummy's book?"

"What, in *Vanity Fair*? I shouldn't think so."

"She says her book is only for grown-ups. So, I think I'll wait until I'm grown up and then I'll read it. I hope there's a dragon in it, though. Should I make a potion to make your finger better now?"

"If you like."

"There won't be any sea-water in this potion, though," she warned him. "Because the sea isn't our friend. And there won't be any shells." She looked around. "I could put some sand in the water – ?"

"No, don't do that, we'll want it to drink."

"So what should I put in it?"

"Maybe you could pretend the ingredients."

"All right." Ella began taking pinches of nothing from the air. She sprinkled the ingredients over the water bottle, muttering and making mystic passes. "That's it, I've made the potion now."

"That didn't take long."

"It was quite easy. Hold out your finger and I'll pour the potion."

He held his hand out, and watched as she carefully tipped the bottle, allowing only a few drops of water to escape.

"You're all better now," she told him.

"That's good."

"This is the best beach in the world."

Jacob took a handful of fine sand and let it trickle through his fingers. "It might be, actually."

"But we can't tell anyone about it. Because I promised."

"Maybe we could tell Mum and Dad."

Ella sat down on the sand and leaned heavily against him. He lifted his arm and let her rest her head on his lap.

"I don't think we should," she said. "The best bit about this beach is that only we know about it. So, we should hide the sign so nobody else reads it, and then only we'll know the way."

"Are you going to sleep?"

"No." She yawned. "I'm just shutting my eyes for a minute."

"You can if you want. But I want my book first."

"I'm not going to sleep." She yawned again. "But maybe you should get your book. Because I might need to shut my eyes for quite a long minute. And you can read while I have my eyes shut."

He stretched out, captured the loose dangling strap of his rucksack and pulled it towards him. The sun had warmed it right through, so his book felt friendly in his hands, like a living creature. "I can't read you this book, you won't like it."

"It won't matter because I won't be able to hear you because I'll have my eyes shut."

"You hear through your eyes?"

"Yes. And I see through my ears. And I don't go to sleep in the day any more, because otherwise Mummy and me would both be asleep and there'd be nobody to watch out in case someone bad came."

"You're obsessed with bad people."

"No I'm not. What's obsessed?"

"It means you think about it too much." When she opened her mouth to answer, he stuck his finger in it. She laughed and pulled away. "There aren't any bad people here. And I'm awake. So stop worrying."

"It's so warm," Ella murmured. Her head burrowed into the muscle of his thigh and her thumb crept towards her mouth. Trying to angle his book so it wouldn't cast a shadow across her, he cautiously turned the pages. Another minute, and Ella was asleep.

He was stuck here now, with his little sister growing heavier on his lap and the sand not quite as soft and welcoming as it had seemed, and the sun in exactly the wrong position for him to read comfortably. None of it mattered. Just as some alchemy of taste and heat and exercise had made his shoddy picnic mysteriously delicious, these unpromising elements (empty beach, hot day, nothing much to do except watch his sister sleep) had created a brief secret paradise. If he was given his choice of anywhere else in the world, he'd choose to remain here.

Filled with a sweet lazy bliss, he laid his book down on the sand and stared blankly at the horizon. Ella pressed her thumb harder into her mouth, muttered something, then fell silent.

Out on the water, a small dot of movement drew his eye. With nothing but water to measure it against, it was hard to judge the scale. It could be a sea-monster scudding across the horizon. A small gull floating inland to hunt for sand eels and scraps of sandwich. A seal, turning and turning on its own axis as it watched him with bright liquid eyes. A mermaid, calling him to his doom. His legs were going to sleep. He pushed gently at Ella's shoulders, trying to redistribute her weight.

When he looked up again, he saw something rising out of the sea, a slick black nightmare figure with terrible webbed feet and a dreadful smoothness to the head. As he watched, the figure bent double for a moment, pulled its own feet off and stood up again, and he realised he was looking at a woman in a wetsuit. It took a long time for her to make her way up the beach, long enough for him to feel awkward about staring, and reach for his book again as cover. Ella slumbered on, oblivious even to the breeze that ruffled her hair and tugged at the hem of her t-shirt. Was she warm enough? He rested his hand on the back of her neck as he had seen their mother do. She felt warm, but not too warm. When he looked up again, the woman in the wetsuit was someone he knew.

"You're a long way from home," Mrs Armitage said. She glanced at Ella. "No wonder she's tired."

"She wanted to have an adventure."

He hoped Mrs Armitage would leave them alone and walk on, but she sat down in the sand, a slow process made difficult by the wetsuit.

"I usually have this beach to myself," she said.

He tried to read her tone. There was no reproach in her voice, not even much surprise, just a bald statement of fact.

"The sign's fallen down," he said. "And the path looks like it goes to a field. That's probably why no one else comes."

"No one but you."

"It's not private, is it? I mean, does it belong to you?"

"No, it's not mine. It's a public beach. You're allowed to be here." She glanced at Ella and lowered her voice a fraction. "Isn't she too old for a nap?"

"She's seven. She walked a long way."

"I know how old she is. She comes to see me sometimes."

This seemed so unlikely that he couldn't think of a thing to say in reply. Instead he stroked Ella's hair, taking comfort in its familiar silky texture.

"You don't believe me," said Mrs Armitage, "but it's true. Making things up is a great waste of time and effort. Ella comes to see me in the afternoons, when your mother's asleep. She walks along the cliff-top to get to my house. Sometimes she draws me pictures. She often draws her house falling into the sea. You and she are holding hands as it falls."

The words soaked into his bones with a slow sense of astonishment.

"But she's terrified of the cliff-top," Jacob said.

"Yes, I know. But she comes anyway."

What was he supposed to do with this information? He sat and looked at the distant sea and became aware of the occasional soft hiss of the dunes as the top layer of sand slipped down to pool at the bottom. He tried to think of something appropriate to say. Mrs Armitage seemed strangely comfortable with silence.

"It's all right," said Mrs Armitage. "I don't expect you to do anything about it. If I minded I wouldn't let her in the house. I just thought you ought to know."

"Thanks."

"And the sign hasn't fallen down. I took it down. Because I didn't want to share this place with anyone else. You don't have to do anything about that, either. But I like to get things clear."

"Isn't that illegal?" He hated the weak sound of his voice, the bleating pathetic conformity of his words.

"Yes, I expect so, but nobody's going to catch me. I've been doing it for years. Every spring they install a new sign, and three days later I take it down again. This is a special place."

"It is," he agreed, surprising himself, and then being surprised all over again by the warmth in her eyes.

"Most people don't see it. That's why I don't like them coming. My husband died just within sight of here."

He thought he must have misheard.

"His boat sank," she said. "He was out with a friend and the boat went down. It was all very fast."

"I – that's – um –" Was his neighbour unbalanced in some way? How quickly could he get himself and Ella away if he had to? "I'm sorry for your loss." Was that what you were supposed to say?

"It was a long time ago. But I still come back to remember him. You and Ella are the only people I've seen here since his boat went down." She stood up and stretched. "I have to go now. It's a long swim back to my boat."

He stared out at the empty sea. "You came on your boat?"

"It's moored around the headland. The sea's too shallow to get closer."

"I thought that's what the rowing-boat was for."

"It is. But I always swim in."

"Why?"

She looked at him impassively. As if she'd planted it there, an image came to him; a man, half-dead but still breathing, dragging himself through the surf and collapsing thankfully onto the sand. An escapee. A survivor.

"You should wake her soon," said Mrs Armitage. "She likes to be home by three o'clock for when your mother wakes. Don't be jealous," she added, as if she could see straight through his t-shirt and into his heart, "she loves you best. But you're not always there, and she's only young."

He tried to find some suitable words in response, or perhaps even some unsuitable ones, but his mouth was empty.

"Goodbye," Mrs Armitage added, and got to her feet.

He watched her all the way back to the water, saw her re-fit her flippers to her feet and surge through the waves. She looked much more at home in the water than she did on the land. Within minutes she was once more an ambiguous dot, making steady progress around the headland. He waited until she was out of sight before waking Ella.

She awoke instantly and completely, smiling into his face as she stretched and sat up. They took turns peeing behind a clump of grass, then Jacob threaded his rucksack onto his shoulders.

"It's time to go," he said, regretful.

He was prepared for protests and sadness, but Ella followed him up the path without complaint. At the top of the dunes, she looked back.

"It's a secret place," she said. "You can only find it if you're on a quest."

"We can come here again one day, if you like."

"By our own, though. Not with Mummy and Daddy."

"On our own," he corrected her gently.

"I like my way better," she said, not arguing with him, just setting the facts in order, and slid her hand into his.

Sometimes when I look in the mirror, I see a woman who isn't quite me. She has my face, more or less, but she looks older and colder, and she comes from an older, colder world. The world we all came from in the beginning, when our blood was cold and we all swam through salt water. At first she was a long way away and I only glimpsed her occasionally, but now she is with me all the time. Soon she will come out of the mirror entirely and climb into my skin and then we will both be cold enough to do what needs to be done, and then we can both go home and no one will ever bother us any more.

I wish I could make her come to me quicker so all of this could be over. Sometimes when I look at the sea I think about letting all the blood out of my body and filling up my veins with sea-water instead. Perhaps that's how the woman in the mirror came to be so old and so cold.

The first time I saw her was at night, when I was the only one awake in the house and everyone else in the world might have been dead, dead in their beds, with all the red spilled out of them and the sea-water poured in to replace it. I was so sure they were all dead that I got up to look. First I looked out of the window to see if there was anyone dead outside, because if there were dead people outside that would be a sign that I could go to join them. But there was no one. And I was so cold that I thought I might get back into bed, but then there was a dead body there, the body of a man. A man without his skin. And then I saw that he wasn't dead at all, he was breathing, but he didn't have his skin on and I thought perhaps it would be better if I made him dead, because who wants to live without their skin on?

Only I must have made a noise moving around, because he heard me and woke up, and he reached beside the bed for the place where he'd left his skin and then I saw it was him after all, and he took me into his arms and poured all his warmth into me and I remembered that I still love him.

And then, just as I was falling asleep again, I caught a glimpse of the woman who lives in the mirror watching me, and I could tell straight away what she was thinking, because I was thinking it too. She was thinking, One day he won't be able to trap us both like this. One day we will be cold enough to leave him.

Chapter Fourteen
Now

Jacob was glad he was driving. The strange dizzying freedom of being somewhere else, somewhere new, at a time when he would normally be inside for the evening, was intoxication enough. The high street was buzzing with women in glittery dresses and men in skinny jeans. With years of teaching under his belt, he'd thought he knew all about coping with over-excited people in small spaces, but for a single wild minute he wondered what would happen if he turned around and drove home again.

("Is it that PPI again?" His dad, unexpectedly looming behind him as he read his joke of the day from Donna.

Who was King Arthur's roundest Knight?
Sir Cumference
He ate too much Pi
:-D :-D :-D
Dx

"Yes, Dad."

"They're like vultures. I hope you're not taking any notice of them."

"Don't worry, I won't." The same conversation they'd had a million times, made bearable today because he had someone to share the joke with. And a few minutes later he was standing outside the back door with Ella watching the frail blue smoke twine into the sky from the end of her cigarette, and she laughed politely at Donna's terrible Sir Cumference joke and then turned to him and said tentatively, "I can watch him while you go out for the evening if you like?")

The street was a gaudy buzz of bars and restaurants, each with their own vibe. In a different life, perhaps he would have known this place as well as Donna seemed to, flitting in and out of the bars and choosing a different restaurant each Saturday. Maybe this might be the life he could have now that Ella was home.

He parked his car behind an express supermarket, hoping it was late enough that no one would be watching to see if he went into the store. A man with an earpiece and a stern expression stood at the entrance. Jacob tried not to make eye contact as he went past. He was glad to find the bar they'd agreed on and to hurry past the gaze of the bouncers into the darkness inside.

Inside were thin tall stairs that led downwards to a room where an implausible number of people sat at high tables. Against all likelihood, there was no music in the background, and the clink of the glasses and the rattle of the cocktail shaker were clearly audible above the hum of conversation. Each little group of drinkers sat clustered around a flat board littered with plastic tokens, or casually guarded a stash of cards or a wad of bright game currency. Was he in the right place?

(His palms wet and sweaty as he typed, glad for the chance to re-compose his message over and over, until finally he had the tone he wanted:

Hey there! I was wondering –
I've actually got a free evening for once
Any chance you're free to come out tonight
with a complete loser who doesn't know

any good venues or have any ideas at all
about what we could do? – J

Her reply came quick and cheerful:

You any good at board games?
We're meeting in the Spinnaker on
Queen Street at about 8pm. – D

What more could he have hoped for? He texted back an instant acceptance before he could talk himself out of it, and tried not to mind the implications of the word *we*.)

"Hey." Donna gave him a friendly wave. "We're over here. We got you a drink."

The vacant spot put him between Donna and a woman he didn't recognise. He offered his smiling face to the group – three strangers, two men and the woman beside him, and Megan Hopley from the Languages team. He could do this. He could do this. He would not fail.

"You didn't believe me when I said we were meeting in a rum bar to play board games, did you?" Donna patted his arm in a friendly manner. "This is Ellie and Joe and Will." A murmur of *Hey mates* and *Hi theres*. "Everyone, this is Jacob, my mate from work. Right, we're playing *Settlers of Catan*, I know you won't have played it before because I know everything but you'll get the hang of it pretty quickly. Drink your drink and it'll all seem much more normal."

By his elbow there was a sweating glass of something dark with a slice of lime floating in it. He took a long swallow, tasted ginger and lime and spice, felt the burn of the alcohol going down and had to stop himself from choking.

"Sorry. I'm driving so I can't drink."

"Oh, shit, I should have thought. And I was going to get you raucously drunk as well. Never mind. Give that to me and I'll get you something else."

"I'm really sorry," Jacob repeated.

"For being a responsible driver? Don't be daft." A whirl of motion and Donna was at the bar, and he was alone with a colleague and three strangers, all staring in that friendly way that meant they were going to start asking him about himself.

"Do you know Donna from work?" asked Will.

"We were NQTs at the same time. She's way better than me though, she'll be a head teacher by the time she's thirty."

"She will actually," said Megan. "Unless she becomes an MP first."

This was his moment to ask something in return. He fumbled for a question. "Um – how do you all know her?"

"I'm her best mate." Ellie held up her hand. "Will's my partner. And Joe's Megan's partner."

Two couples, and Donna, and Jacob himself. Was he being presumptuous? He risked a glance towards the bar. She was chatting easily with the barman, her dark hair swinging as she laughed. He could see the long lovely stretch of her legs, the glimmer of her sparkly shoes. She was absolutely lovely and absolutely out of his league. And yet, here he was… then she was lifting the glass and bringing it back to him, and he could smell her perfume as she took her place beside him.

"Cherry Coketail," she told him. "You ready to play?"

"I'm ready," he said.

The game was relatively simple – dice rolls, resources to collect, a bad guy to strategically deploy to scupper his opponents. He finished the first round in last place, but enjoyed himself enough to try again, and finished fourth. The group showered him with praise, and mentioned that they met here most weeks if he felt like it. He hadn't known until then that he was being auditioned as a possible regular member. He realised with a tingle of excitement that accepting this offer was now possible.

("Dad?" He patted his father's shoulder. "I've made you a drink, look."

"You're a good lad."

"I'm going out for a bit, okay?"

"Aha. So this tea is a bribe?"

"Ella's going to stay here with you."

"Oh? Okay, no problem."

"So, um…" he wanted to say, *please don't hit her.* "See you in a bit, then.")

He tried to buy a round of drinks, but was shouted down by Joe and Megan ("you're the noob, you don't get to pay for anything"). He wasn't drinking, but the gradual relaxation of the group as the cocktails did their work helped him relax too, as if feeling comfortable was something he could absorb through his skin. On the third round, he finished fifth – still satisfying, since it was only the third game he had ever played.

The whole time, he was conscious of Donna beside him. He'd known she was beautiful, funny and bright for as long as he'd known her, but until tonight it had been like noticing a painting of a beautiful woman in a gallery. He took a long swallow of his drink (dark and fruity but with a slight edge of bitterness to tone down the syrup, adorned with an impossibly scarlet cherry) and told himself that she couldn't be interested. He'd asked her out, and this was what she'd invited him to. He was just another body round the table to even out the numbers. But then, the other four were two couples, so perhaps –

"So what's new for you?" Donna asked him, in the sweetly awkward moment when the game was over and the other two couples somehow vanished for a moment and they were alone at the table with no game to focus on.

"Um." What could he say? *My long-lost sister who you've never heard me mention came back home and my mother who I've possibly led you to believe is dead is still alive, but she's gone missing* was probably not what she was looking for. "Not much really. Having a bit of a rest."

"Okay, I'm going to ask, but if I'm being too nosey, tell me to shut up. You look after your dad, don't you?" He nodded. "So is he – well, is he getting better or something? Or have you got some help at last?"

("You've got my mobile number, haven't you?" A last

briefing in the kitchen with Ella, putting off the moment of departure. "He should be fine, but if anything happens –"

"We'll be fine. Have a nice time."

"If you make sure he has that drink, he'll be quiet for you."

"Stop worrying! We'll manage." He couldn't quite read her expression.)

"That's right," he said cautiously.

"I shouldn't have pried."

"No, it's fine, I don't mind."

"Yes, you do. You mind massively. My fault. I should have kept my mouth shut." The rest of the group were clumped at the bottom of the stairs, watching politely. "I think we're on the move." She hesitated. "Unless you fancy staying here for a quick game of Scrabble or something?"

"Shall we stay here?" His voice sounded surprisingly normal.

"Okay, yes, why not? Hang on, I'll let them know."

When Donna spoke to them, they smiled and glanced over at him, but in a friendly way, and disappeared up the stairs. Donna took a long box from the stack of games at the bar and sat down opposite him. Her knee jostled briefly against his beneath the table and his heart leapt like a rabbit. He stared blankly at his Scrabble tiles, trying to conjure something more inspiring than *car*. When he glanced at his watch, he saw it was only nine o'clock.

(What would Ella and his father be doing right now? His father would be asleep, lost in the velvet embrace of the Diazepam. Surely it would be enough. Surely he wouldn't be stumbling around the house, flailing like a drunkard, searching for someone who lurked in the shadows. Surely Ella wasn't cowering in a corner as his father, desperate and confused, took out his frustrations on her.)

"If you need to get back, I don't mind," said Donna gently.

"What?"

"You keep looking at your watch. Is it the first time you've left him in the evening?"

"I don't – I mean – I'm sorry," he said wretchedly. "You're right. It's the first time I've left him in the evening. I have care sorted for the day but going out socially is not really on the agenda at the moment."

"How long's the moment been going on?"

"Oh, God. I don't know. A while. Years." Gloomily he picked out four tiles from his letter-rack, turned his previous pathetic attempt of *skin* into *bearskin*, with a double-letter bonus for the *b*. "I don't want to think about it to be honest."

"And I keep asking. I know I shouldn't but I can't help it. I worry about you, mate. I've known you for years and I still feel like we've just met sometimes. Sometimes I think you're a weirdo and I should stay well away from you, but sometimes I wonder if you need a bit of looking after from a friend." She smiled. "I mean, I don't lie awake every night thinking about you. But you do cross my mind from time to time. Why'd you come out tonight?"

"Because –" he'd been about to be honest there, been about to say *because my little sister came back and she made me say yes*. What would happen if he tried to explain what his family was like? How weird would she think he was then? "You know what? The truth is, I really like board games."

He was relieved to hear her laughter. At least he hadn't offended her. She was so sweet. She'd always been so sweet. He'd been noticing how pretty she was since the first day they met in the staff-room, fellow NQTs about to embark on their first full day at work, but it had taken him a few weeks to realise she was also a lovely person. Since then, he'd been like a dog with its owner, grateful for odd scraps of affection, but never imagining he took up as much space in her head as she did in his. And now they were on their own, in a pub, with a game of Scrabble, and Donna was laying down what looked like a monster of a word, smiling to herself as she did so. *Jukebox*, with a Triple Word score. He was getting thoroughly beaten, but he didn't mind at all.

"Am I allowed to buy you a drink now?" he asked.

"I don't know, that depends. Can I trust you to buy me what I actually want, which is a plain Coke with a slice of lime? Or will you get it with a couple of shots in so I'll be completely drunk by the time we're ready to leave?"

"I've dealt with enough drunks in my life, thanks," he said, without realising what he was saying until it was too late. "Oh shit. I mean –"

"Is that what it is for your dad, then? Drink?"

"It's part of it."

"I wouldn't have suggested meeting in a bar if I'd known."

"It's not your fault, I've never said."

"Well, now you have. Maybe in about ten years you might want to tell me something really personal, like what your favourite food is or something. But that'll do for now. Are you happy hanging out here, or would you rather go for a walk? There's a really good creepy cemetery about five minutes away if you want some fresh air. Unless you're really committed to this game of Scrabble."

"Creepy cemetery or humiliation."

"It's a tough call, I know. I'm going to the Ladies, you can decide while I'm gone."

He felt dizzy with the shock of what he'd done. He had shared a tiny, tiny part of his life with another person, and she had not flinched. When she came back, he had tidied away the Scrabble board and put his coat on.

Out on the street, the atmosphere had turned wilder, more unpredictable. The women, who had preened self-consciously on stilt-like heels, shrieked with laughter and clutched each other for balance. Clusters of men hovered around them. A stream of taxis arrived and left, arrived and left, sliding past the drunks stumbling into the road, pounding on bonnets and yelling through the windows.

Was this normal? Donna seemed unconcerned, clattering along beside him in shoes that were pretty and glittery but seemingly fine to walk in. When she brushed her hair back from her face and behind her ear, her manicure gleamed beneath the street lights. (He thought of Ella's worn trainers and bitten nails. Was she safe? Was their father asleep?) Beside the busy main road, the cemetery loomed as a sudden void of greenish blackness. Donna stumbled over the edge of the path, and took his hand for a moment.

The shrubby overgrowth was threaded through with little paths. There was a special name for these paths, he knew, and after a moment it came to him: *lines of desire*. He thought about saying this to Donna, but the word *desire*, spoken in this place, felt too dangerous. He lost sight of her for a moment, then saw she was sitting on the edge of a greyish-white sarcophagus.

"This is Violetta Thomas," she said. "She died about a hundred and fifty years ago. She's very comfortable to sit on."

He perched gingerly beside her. "Doesn't she mind?"

"She doesn't seem to. The churchyard staff mind like hell, of course, but I don't think they work at night. Which is weird really, because you'd think that'd be the time when most people get up to mischief. She's a good listener as well."

"Do you – um – do you talk to her a lot?"

"I came here quite a lot when my mum died. Her and my dad live down in Chelmsford and I wanted her to be cremated so I could have some of her ashes to keep with me, but my dad really wanted a burial so that's what she had, and when I really missed her I used to drive out here sometimes and pretend this was my mum's grave so I could talk to her." Her eyes were very dark and beautiful. "If you laugh at me I might have to kill you."

"Of course I'm not going to laugh."

"No, I know you're not really. I wouldn't have brought you here otherwise."

"I didn't know your mum had died."

"I don't tell people because I don't want them thinking about me that way. Because if I tell them she's dead, people immediately want to know what she was like, what happened to her, all that stuff. And I don't want to share her. She's just for me."

He recognised the feeling. Ella had been like that for him. She was still like that now, even though she had come back to him... Donna's hands looked very pale and slender in the moonlight and her lips were dark and full. He reached clumsily out for her and turned her face towards him.

"Jacob," she said.

Why else had she brought him to the cemetery? It was so dark and private here. Violetta Thomas was no kind of a chaperone. What a strange thought to have; what a strange evening. At Ella's bidding, he had taken a risk and sent a text message and now they were here, in the cemetery, kissing. Was this what Ella had wanted for him? Was she coping, at home on her own with their sleeping father? Was he doing this kiss right? After few seconds, Donna pulled away.

"I haven't kissed anyone for years," he confessed. "You're beautiful. Is this okay?"

"Are you asking me or yourself?"

He kissed her again. Donna's lipstick tasted faintly of strawberries, or rather of a chemical approximation of what strawberries were meant to taste like. He could feel the chill seeping through his clothes from Violetta Thomas. Perhaps he should lay his coat out for Donna to lie on. Was Ella warm enough back at home? Would she find the extra blanket he'd left for her on the chair? The cemetery was damp and the wind was chilly, but after all the years he'd spent living in their house of draughts and sea-spray, he should be used to the cold. He let his hand slip cautiously from Donna's shoulder to her right breast, taking his time so she could push him away if she wanted to. When she didn't, he let the palm rest against the curve. The warmth of her skin was soaking through the fabric like water.

"Um," said Donna.

"I'm sorry." He let his hand fall.

"No, I didn't mean that. I just meant that's probably not doing much for either of us… Look, how about we start again?" She leaned forward and planted a delicate butterfly kiss on his lips.

He closed his eyes and tried to relax. He was acutely conscious of the presence of the dead, crumbling into dust and greenery along with their grave markers. If they could see what was happening, would they be sternly disapproving, or would they be cheering him on? Donna's hands were beneath his coat, and he realised he should probably reciprocate. He put his hands on her waist, but that felt too much like dancing. His fingers found the smooth serrated edge of a zip running the length of her spine. Should he try and unfasten it? The angle they were sitting at was growing uncomfortable. Perhaps it would be better if they lay down –

"Okay, enough," said Donna wearily, and pushed him away.

"What? What's the matter?"

"You! Kissing me like it's some sort of unpleasant job you've got to get done."

"Jesus."

"I'm sorry, that was rude – actually, you know what? I'm not sorry. That's exactly what it felt like. Like kissing me was something you ought to do. Like it was your homework."

Driven by the hot flush of humiliation, he reached out for her again. This time he forced himself to act, to move, to reach for the zipper, to force his hand beneath her buttocks and pull her closer to him. For a minute he thought he had cracked the code, that this was the way to win the girl, but then she was shoving him away with both hands, so hard that he banged his head on the tall cross that stood guard over Violetta Thomas, and even in the dim ambiguous light of the cemetery, he could see she was furious.

"What the fuck?" she demanded. "What the actual fuck do you think you're doing?"

"I – I just –"

"I already feel stupid enough, all right? I didn't even have any of this in mind when I said I'd meet you, I was sorry for you because you never seem to have any kind of life outside of work – but then we had a nice time and you seemed to like me, so I thought, well, why not? And then –" she was trying to keep herself together, but he could see she was nearly crying.

"I got carried away," he said. "It was really stupid."

"But you didn't, did you?" She looked at him straight on, not flinching. "You weren't carried away. You don't even like me. You're not interested in having sex with me, or even fooling around a bit to see if that's where we might end up going, which for the record, was all I was going to do. You don't want anything like that from me at all. But you kissed me anyway. Because you thought that was what you were supposed to do."

"That's not true! I – I've liked you for years. More than that. I think I'm in love with you."

"You're not," she said. "You want to pretend with me so you can hide from whatever it is you really want. I mean, what is it, Jacob? Is it boys? Is it kids? Because it's something you're not comfortable with, isn't it?"

"Of course I don't like boys! And certainly not bloody kids! How can you even say that? What kind of pervert do you think I bloody am?"

"I don't know," she said. "But I know I'm never going out with you again. Don't call me. And don't speak to me when we get back to work in September. Good night."

He watched Donna walk away through the trees, straight-backed and head held high, undaunted. He thought he might die of humiliation, because every word she'd said to him was right. He was trying to talk himself into liking her. He was trying to pretend he wanted a normal life. And he had only just realised it.

The drive back took all his concentration and energy. He'd barely made it half a mile from the bar before he was pulled over by a police car. The two men inside studied his driving licence and asked professionally friendly questions about his evening, then invited him to take a breathalyser test. He blew grimly into the tube. It didn't matter that he would pass; the point was that he'd been driving oddly enough to attract their attention. When the screen blinked green, he sensed their faint surprise and wondered whether he should tell them that their first instincts were right: he wasn't in a fit state to drive. What would happen if he told the truth? He could feel the words perched behind his teeth. *I had a row with a woman I work with because I kissed her but I didn't feel anything for her, nothing at all, I mean I couldn't even get it up for her, not a flicker, not a twitch, and yet she's gorgeous and I like her, so what the fuck's wrong with me?* Would they arrest him? Was it a crime to be driving while sexually confused?

Another few minutes while they checked his car's tax and insurance status, and they sent him on his way, with a reminder to drive carefully and the memory of their faintly puzzled expressions. He would be home soon, with long weeks to forget about tonight.

He was expecting to come home to a silent house, or at most to the sight of Ella curled up on the sofa, the television flickering in the corner. Instead, as he crept into the hall, he heard the sound of voices that were unmistakeably his father and sister. His father should have been asleep hours ago. Had Ella forgotten to give him the mug of warm milk? He flung open the door.

"Jacob!" His father looked up as he came in. He was alert and beaming, his face bright and engaged. "I was wondering where you'd got to. This young lady of yours –" he looked at Ella. "I'm afraid I've forgotten your name."

"It's Ella," Ella whispered. She looked miserably guilty, as if Jacob had caught her committing a crime. What was she so ashamed of? She'd done a good thing for him tonight, even if he had managed to screw it up completely.

Then he saw the litter of papers by her feet, and understood.

"She's been showing me this book she's written," his father said.

"Ella."

"Not sure I quite understand all of it, though. What was the part about the woman again? The one who's being hunted down by the bad guy?"

"Ella," said Jacob, "come and talk to me in the kitchen, please."

"It reminded me of something," said their father. "Something I was supposed to remember."

"Forget it, Dad. Ella, in the kitchen."

"What was it? Oh, God, what's wrong with me? I can't remember anything, I can't remember your name, I can't remember – who was the man? The man who was chasing her? Was I supposed to be keeping her safe? Is she safe now? Was it just a story?"

The mug of milk sat untouched on the table. Ella saw him looking.

"He didn't get round to drinking it," Ella said. "We were talking, that was all."

"Wait a minute, Dad, I'll sort it out. Ella, clear up that rubbish and put it away where he won't have to see it."

"That's no way to speak to your girlfriend," said their father reproachfully.

"For the last time, Dad, Ella is not my bloody girlfriend! I don't have a girlfriend. And in fact I don't think I ever will. Okay? Ella, do as I say and then you can explain whatever the hell you're doing."

His rage made him fifty feet tall. His hands as they opened the fridge seemed many miles away from his body. Nonetheless, they did not flinch or falter. The milk poured into the clean mug without a drop spilled. Without pausing, he took three giant steps to the pantry and found the box of tablets, admiring the smooth movements of his fingers as they popped the blisters. One. Two. Three. Was it bad enough

215

for four? Probably not, but best to be on the safe side. He needed his father to be properly asleep.

"Jacob." Ella's voice was unexpectedly close behind him. Startled out of their smooth mechanical progress, his fingers became clumsy. The little tablets slipped through the cracks and rolled away. He turned around and found she was standing in the centre of the kitchen, clutching their mother's manuscript. For a minute she was looking at his face, and then her eyes dropped and she was seeing the tablets, the litter of them on the floor, the mug of milk, and most of all the expression on his face, and he watched in helpless horror as understanding finally came to her.

Chapter Fifteen
2008

In the quiet evening freshness that came after the storm, Mrs Armitage stood at the end of her garden and inspected the latest alterations made to her land by the ocean. The buddleias that had begun to take root were gone, as was the hebe she'd spent an extravagant twenty-five pounds on last spring, as well as the ancient blackthorn bush that had once marked the halfway point of her garden. Holding her breath, she crept another few inches towards the edge, listening out for the sound of rattling earth and pebbles that might give her enough time to leap back if she had triggered another fall. The shrubs, along with the most recent incarnation of her garden fence, lay in a tumbled heap of earth on the stony strip of shoreline below.

The last time there had been a fall this severe, she'd taken her boat out, rowed around the headland and reclaimed the fence-panels. She'd set them a propitiatory yard-and-a-half back from the edge of the land, ceding more than she needed to in order to delay the final battle. The effort of loading the panels onto the back of the borrowed boatyard truck and then offloading them at the other end, of pounding in the fence-posts and hanging the battered panels and making good the damage done by the fall, had made her ache for long days afterwards, and she'd vowed to herself at the time, *no more*. The next time the ocean invaded her borders, she would give up the struggle, and face the onslaught with her eyes open.

"No more," she said out loud now to the waters that boiled and crashed below. "From now on, I'll be watching you when you come for me. Do you hear?" She tried hard not to talk to herself, but the ocean was a person in its own right, not human but still a conscious living creature, like the seals that occasionally poked slick heads out above the waves, turning around and around in the water like tops before slipping back into the murky calm beneath. Some people might think she was mad, but in her opinion, anyone who didn't understand the importance of staying on the good side of the life that surged at their feet was more likely to be the crazy one.

She wasn't particularly hungry, but it was time to eat, and keeping an order to her day was important to her. So she turned away from the ruin of what had once been a herbaceous border coming out of its difficult adolescence, and went inside to make herself some dinner.

The evening was still bright, but the walls were thick and the windows small, so she put on the light. Now the fence was gone, when she took the boat out, she would be able to see the kitchen window. If she left the light on before she went, she could enjoy the sight of the small yellow square of light, newly revealed.

Behind the door of the fridge lived the memory of her husband, hurrying up the path and coming in through the door, calling her by the nickname she allowed him and no one else – *Harry! Harry! I missed you so I've come home early* – with a bunch of daffodils clutched in his hand, and the glad thumping of her heart as she turned to greet him. She fought the memory off by thinking about being out on her boat, wondering if there would one day be a device that would allow her to be in two places at once, so she could spy on herself as she stood silhouetted against the yellow square of light – all the while taking milk and ham and margarine from the fridge shelves, hesitating over the eggs, then deciding to leave them for lunch tomorrow instead.

There were some sausages too, that needed eating soon. She had seen on the news that too much processed meat could cause cancer, but chose not to pay attention when the reporter explained exactly what "too much" was. She'd known for years it would be the ocean that took her in the end. If she was somehow wrong about this and she ended up dying of a surfeit of bacon and sausages, well, that would be one up to the landlubbers. She took a tin of soup from the cupboard and filled a saucepan, rinsing the tin with a little milk and then pouring it into the pan for extra richness. Soup and a sandwich was a perfect evening meal in this warm weather. She had long weeks yet before she could structure her entire day around the buying and preparing and eating of stewed meat and vegetables.

She peered into the cupboard where she kept her tea and coffee supplies. She had chosen coffee for lunchtime so would have tea this evening, and she would have some biscuits, too, a little sweetness to take the edge off the austerity of her day. Until Ella began her visits, she'd never bothered with biscuits, but when there was the possibility of someone else helping to eat them before they grew stale, the purchase became worthwhile. Whether you were pleased to see your visitors or not, it was rude not to have something to offer them. Some might say she was sentimentally attached to the doe-eyed little moppet who had once come hopping along the cliff to see her every two or three days, taking a secret pleasure in choosing the prettiest and most elaborate biscuits the shop could provide, but she herself knew better.

It was simply manners, that was all.

The soup bubbled thickly on the stove and she stirred it with a wooden spoon to stop it from splashing. She enjoyed arranging the thin slices of ham with their straight folded edges laid against the borders of the bread. She disliked seeing raggedy edges hanging out of the sides. She cut the sandwich into four neat triangles and poured her soup into its bowl. *You could eat it out of the saucepan,* she thought, *and save yourself some washing-up. No one would know. But you don't do that; you get a bowl and pour it in and eat from that instead. And that's how you know you still have self-respect.* Sitting upright at her kitchen table, her face towards her newly unfenced garden, she spooned the soup neatly into her mouth, taking care not to spill it on her chin. *You could dip the sandwich in the soup and save yourself a dirty spoon. But you don't do that either.* A little gull landed on the thick windowsill and tucked one slender scarlet leg up into its plumage. She would remember to mark it down later on the chart she kept all year round and sent once a year to the RSPB. Did she need to interrupt her dinner to do it now, in case she forgot later? No, she would remember. *You're doing fine, Araminta. You don't need to worry.*

As she stood at the sink and rinsed her bowl, considering whether she might want to walk down to the boathouse later and go out for an evening dive, the telephone shrilled out its imperious call. For a brief unforgivable moment, until she got control of herself again, she felt all her muscles lock tight and her throat catch with dryness. *Stop it,* she told herself sternly. *The dead don't make phone calls.* The phone's cradle sat guard over a small patch of clean wood. The rest of the table was blanketed in dust. *Dust is normal. Dust is nothing to worry about.* When she pressed the button to answer the call, her fingers were precise and did not fumble.

"Hello?"

But there was nothing on the other end of the line but the sound of the ocean as it filled her ears as she made the slow descent down through the water.

"Hello? Hello? This is Mrs Armitage, Mrs Araminta Armitage. If you can hear me, I can't hear you. So if you really need to speak to me, you'll have to call back and try again. I'm going to hang up the phone now."

And then, as if the woman who spoke was very frightened, perhaps as if she was trying not to be heard:

"Is he there? Is my son there?"

Was that the line still roaring in her ear, or was it the swirl of her blood as her heart squeezed tight and then let go again?

"Do you have him? You have to keep him safe for me –"

A pause, and a raggedy hitch of breath.

"Can you hear me? Can you hear me? You said you'd help me. I need you to promise me –"

"I'm afraid I can't hear you," Mrs Armitage repeated. "I'm going to have to hang up the phone now. Goodbye."

"No, please –"

She stood for a few moments in the golden evening light that flooded her living-room, listening to her breath and her heartbeat, checking for signs of disturbance. She lived alone. She had to be careful. But there was nothing to worry about, nothing at all. She could return the phone to its cradle and go back to the kitchen and finish the washing-up. The handset wouldn't fit back into the cradle, it jumped about like a live thing and threatened to throw itself onto the floor, but she gripped it with a firm hand and forced it to dock onto the little connectors and then it was fine. The world was going to behave itself. The sight of her own living-room, orderly and familiar and empty of everyone but herself, filled her with calm. With the fence gone, there was nothing to shut out the light or hide the sky. She would sit in here much more often in the evenings from now on.

She'd put the bowl in the drying-rack and reached for the saucepan when someone knocked at her front door. First the phone, and now the door. The universe had remembered her.

Don't be ridiculous, she told herself sternly, inside her head. She was pleased that she had the sense not to speak out loud. She had no idea who might be listening. *You can ignore it if you want. It's an invitation to answer, not a summons. Wait a minute and they'll go away again. You don't even need to stop washing up*. The saucepan looked clean after its rinsing but she dipped it into the sudsy water anyway. The knock came again. *I'm not answering that. I don't feel like it. They can't see me in here. So whoever it is can come back another time.*

A third round of knocking, and then the sound of her side-gate rattling open. Whoever it was must be coming to try again at the back door. Sensible people would take the lack of an answer as a sign that she was either not at home, or not at home to visitors. Therefore, the person who was making their way round the side of her house was not sensible. She wasn't frightened, just annoyed. She had things to do. She didn't have time to deal with non-sensible people.

She put the bowl carefully in the draining-rack, and then lay down on the floor. This was not because she was frightened; it was just quicker and more reliable than leaving the room to hide. Her living-room curtains were open, and if she tried to escape upstairs, there was a chance they would see her go past. A shadow passed across the kitchen window, paused. Her unwelcome guest must be peering in. Another sign that they were not someone she wanted to spend time talking to. Holding her breath, she rolled a little closer to the kitchen cabinets.

The knocking started again, this time on the back door. She was glad she'd chosen not to have glazing in it. If the door had glass in, the visitor would be able to see her lying on the floor, and while she didn't especially mind what they might think of her hiding from visitors, she very much minded the idea that they might think she had fallen and hurt herself, and that their help was required. One more round of knocking, and then something else, something wilder and lower down, making the door shudder in its frame. There was no question about it. The stranger outside had kicked her door. As she stared in disbelief, it happened again. Then a flurry of pounding, as if the stranger was trying to beat her door into submission, and finally silence.

Lying on the floor, she considered her options. She could take a chance on being seen, creep out of the kitchen and into the hall, make her way to the stairs and watch developments from her bedroom. She could stay here on the kitchen floor and listen out for the sound of the gate. She could make her way to the phone, perhaps abandoning all pretence at concealment, and call the police. Or she could let her righteous outrage guide her, and go to the door and fling it open, ready to tear strips off whoever the disgustingly rude person was who was waiting for her outside.

The person was leaning against the wall, forehead pressed against the rough white pebbledash surface. After a moment's perplexity (*he looks like a teenager but I don't know any teenagers why would a young lad be trying to beat my door down*) she recognised him.

"I saved your life once," she told him severely. "That doesn't give you the right to behave like a moron. If I don't answer the door it's because I don't want to talk to anybody."

Jacob turned his face towards hers. There were red marks on his forehead that could have been from the pebbledash or could simply be the usual teenage acne, and his hair had been ruffled out of its careful shape by the salty lick of the wind. Despite his sudden arrival and wild appearance, he looked like the kind of boy who would grow up to be entirely average, the Styrofoam peanut of the classroom, soon to become replaceable workplace fodder for a mid-sized company with no real prospects, lacking Ella's delicate prettiness and charm. It was only the expression in his eyes that made him stand out. It was familiar to her from the nights when she woke and sat up and then left the bed to peer into the mirror on her vanity table.

"Well, come on in then," she said, and held the door open.

He slouched inside without speaking, and took the chair she pulled out for him without making eye contact. His demeanour had the appearance of rudeness but she suspected it was more the timidity of a lost animal who had no idea

223

how to behave, and therefore took refuge in saying and doing nothing at all. Without speaking, she filled the kettle and took out the packet of biscuits. For his little sister she would arrange them prettily on a plate, alternating two different kinds so she could watch Ella pause and hesitate over which to choose first, but for Jacob she laid down the box and turned away to the kettle so he could eat unobserved. She listened for the sound of rustling and munching, but the only sound was the roiling of the water.

She poured hot water onto the teabags, stirred, squeezed, laid them to steam and cool on the teapot-shaped piece of china she had bought years ago in Scarborough for her own mother. Added milk and sugar to both mugs (for Ella she would elaborately consult on the exact volume and ratio of dilutable squash to cold water, but her brother could have tea, made the way she made it, and like it). When she sat down opposite him, Jacob was slumped sullenly inside his coat as if she'd forced him to be here, and for a moment she considered flinging open the back door and waiting for him to run for freedom; but then he looked at her again, that frantic desperate look that made her heart turn over, and instead she handed him the mug of tea and held his gaze, waiting for his defences to crumble and the words to pour out.

"Are you going to sit there like a bump on a log?" she said at last. "Or are you going to tell me what you're doing here?"

"Ella used to come here," Jacob muttered. "She said you gave her biscuits."

"You didn't come half a mile for a biscuit. But you can have one if you like." She pushed the packet towards him. This week she'd chosen Jammie Dodgers, a biscuit she despised but imagined Ella might enjoy. Jacob took one from the packet and shoved it mechanically into his mouth, a single greedy bite that engulfed the biscuit and let loose a stormcloud of crumbs. "Or two, if you're that hungry." He took another, chewed it, swallowed with what looked like an effort. His hands were trembling as they reached for his tea. "I lost another six feet of garden in the storm. How about you? Did you lose anything?"

She was only making conversation, but to her surprise these words seemed to unlock whatever force kept him still. He pushed the mug away, slopping tea out onto the wood, and stood up so violently his chair fell over. She wondered if he was going to hit her, but instead he turned and bent over the sink, as if he might be about to vomit. His shoulders shook and a thin high sound threaded out from between his lips.

"I can't understand what you're saying," she said. She thought about going over to him, putting a hand on his shoulder, patting him for comfort, but he seemed too strange and too savage, and besides, she hadn't asked to get involved with his problems. "If you want help, you'll have to talk a bit more clearly." The thin sound began to resolve itself into words. "That's better, but not good enough. Try again."

"I said," he finally got out, "my mum's left us."

Good, she thought.

"These things do happen, you know," she said out loud. "Especially these days. It's not really anything to come crying to a stranger about, is it?" His expression made him look very young. "I don't mind this time, but you have to admit it's an odd way to behave."

"Dad told me. He said she left three nights ago. In the middle of that storm."

"Some people like a bit of drama."

"And he's spent every minute since then drinking." The boy's face, unremarkable in repose, became strikingly ugly when he let the terror show through. "He's always drunk quite a lot but now he just goes on and on and I can't make him stop."

She'd known this too. It hadn't been her problem then and it still wasn't now.

"Give him time to get over it. He'll settle down. People always do." Jacob wasn't listening to her. He was eyeing the

225

biscuit packet like a hyaena. "You can have another biscuit if you like."

He ate it in a single bite, and licked the crumbs from his fingers. Then he sat back down at the table and buried his nose in the mug of tea she'd made for him. Clearly he wasn't going to leave any time soon. She sighed, and wondered what was the least amount of effort she could get away with making.

"I'm going upstairs to wash my hands," she told him. "You can make yourself a sandwich if you like. And there's soup in the cupboard. Make sure you rinse the tin before you put it in the recycling. And clean up after yourself."

His gratitude was so open and needy that she couldn't stand to be in the same room. When she had washed her hands, she sat in her bedroom and stared at the photograph of her husband that stared watchfully out at her from the bedside table.

"What should I do?" she asked it. Speaking to the photograph felt artificial and forced, as it always did. As the years went by it became increasingly hard to connect the man she had loved with the single frozen image who looked out at her, unchanged and un-aging, from within the gold-coloured frame. Nonetheless she felt obliged to try it from time to time. "There's an angry hungry teenage boy I hardly know, who says his mother's left and his father's drunk all the time, sitting downstairs in our kitchen. What am I supposed to do about him?"

She waited. Listened to the rattle of wings as a pigeon took off from the gutter, and the small click of floorboards settling. Nothing came to her but a sense of embarrassment at talking out loud to a piece of printed paper shut away behind a sheet of glass. Her husband was not there. He would never be there. He was where he'd been for the last thirty years, resting peacefully on the soft brown floor of the North Sea. She would have to work this one out on her own.

Back in the kitchen, Jacob was standing over a saucepan

of soup and devouring a sandwich loaded with what looked like half a pig's worth of ham. Crumbs rained into the soup as he stirred it, but at least he'd wiped the worktop down, washed the knife and laid it to rest on the draining-board. That was a good sign. From the sounds of things, he'd need to get good at domestic tasks rather quickly if he wanted to stay alive. How much did he know already about cooking and cleaning and shopping on a budget? She wondered who would teach him now.

"Would you like some too?" he asked. His eyes were pink and swollen and his smile was watery.

"No thank you. I've already had mine. But you can make me another cup of tea, with milk and one sugar. Mine's gone cold."

She watched him as he moved about her kitchen – rinsing away the cold tea and then wiping the stains from the sink, guessing quickly where she stored the teabags, filling the kettle without splashing and only halfway. It was only tea, but it suggested someone who wasn't completely clueless about how to behave in a domestic space. Perhaps the boy might survive after all. He added sugar to her mug but not to his own. She felt a glint of satisfaction that she had guessed wrong. She didn't want to know any more about Jacob than she'd already been forced to.

"Don't forget to stir the soup," she reminded him as he was squeezing out the teabags. She'd chosen her moment deliberately to test him, but he dealt with it well, shuttling quickly between the two tasks of tea-making and soup-stirring, wiping up drips and splashes without having to be told. Something in his life had opened him up to the softer, more feminine skills of caring for people and things as if their welfare mattered enough to spend time over. He was pouring the soup into a bowl now, tipping the saucepan slowly to avoid splashes. Before he sat down to eat, he sluiced the pan out at the sink and then re-filled it to soak. The phrase that came to her mind was *your mother's taught you well;* but she remembered the little she'd seen of Maggie, and wondered if the lesson had been learned not by copying his mother, but by compensating for her omissions. Or perhaps he'd learned from watching his father.

"So what do you actually want from me?" she asked, and picked up her mug of tea.

The question startled him; he stared at her for several seconds, a bead of soup gathering and threatening to spill.

"Nothing," he said at last, and licked the soup furtively from his lips.

"If you want someone to talk to, I don't mind listening just this once. But I don't do sympathy very well."

"She left me behind," he said.

"She left in the middle of the night. What did you expect? That she was going to come and wake you up and hang around while you packed all your stuff?"

"She didn't tell me she was going. She didn't even leave me a note. She left my dad to tell me about it. How could she do that to me?"

The pained disbelief in his face was hard to look at. How foolish human beings were when they faced the first big hurt of their lives, imagining this was the worst pain anyone had ever endured, that this was the most life would ever demand of them. It made her angry to see how much emotion he was willing to expend on something so trivial.

"She was probably in a hurry."

"But it's like she didn't even remember I existed." His voice was petulant now, the words of a much smaller child coming out incongruously from a young man's frame. "I mean, how could she do that? She's supposed to love me."

"Stop being so dramatic. There are far worse things that can happen than your parents splitting up."

"Not when you're my age there isn't."

"Yes, there is. She could be dead, for example. That would be much, much worse." She saw him wince, and felt guilty. When would she learn that people who hadn't yet been properly hurt had far less scar tissue to protect them? "For goodness sakes, Jacob, I didn't mean she actually is dead. It's just an example of how much worse things could be. Please don't wipe your nose on your hand, it's disgusting. Get a piece of kitchen roll to wipe it on. And wash your hands before you sit back down."

He did as she said with the mechanical obedience of exhaustion. There were dark shadows under his swollen eyes. She wondered if he would expect her to invite him to stay the night.

"Now listen to me." She thought about putting her hand over his, but decided she could get away without having to. "Your mother's left your father. That's a shame, but it happens. She probably wasn't thinking about you when she left, but why should she? You're not the centre of the universe. I'm sure she'll get in touch with you when she's ready."

"My dad says she won't be in touch ever. That's about all he does say. He repeats the same thing over and over –"

"Your dad's been drinking. People say things they don't mean when they're drinking."

"No they don't. People tell the truth when they've been drinking."

"What makes you think you know better than me? He's angry with your mum, that's all. But he'll get over it. And so will you. People can get over much worse things than that. And once that happens, you'll be fine again."

"She took Ella."

"What?"

"She took Ella. Not me. Just Ella. I woke up and they were both gone."

Ella, sitting in the spot where her older brother sat now, looking at her over the top of her glass of juice. That elfish face and soft hair. For a moment, before she reminded herself that this was nothing compared to the awful things that could have happened, she felt her heart toll in her chest like a bell.

"She didn't wake me to say goodbye. She took Ella out

229

of her bed in the middle of the night and left. Who even does that? Why did she take Ella and not me?"

A drop of water fell from the tap and struck the base of the sink with a hollow aluminium thud.

"There's not much point asking me," she said at last. "How would I know what was going through your mother's head? I suppose you're thinking it's because Ella's her favourite. Well, even if she has got a favourite, that doesn't mean she doesn't love you too. Be grateful for what you have."

"Dad keeps saying it's for the best. They used to argue a lot. I think he feels guilty."

"I imagine he does. His wife's left him. He can't have been all that much of a husband if she's done that."

"Don't you dare say that. It's not Dad's fault. If it's anyone's fault, it's hers. She's so selfish –"

"Stop that right now. You're tired and upset and you're talking nonsense. People who don't love each other don't have to stay married. She's entitled to leave him if she wants to."

"But what about me?" The lamb-bleat wail of the abandoned child, unattractive coming from a boy so close to manhood. "What if I never see them again? Dad says I won't ever see them again –"

"He doesn't know anything. He's talking nonsense too. What makes you think he's got all the answers? Don't listen to him. Go home and go to bed and let him sleep it off. Things will be better in the morning. They always are. And don't feel sorry for yourself. There's nothing worse than people who feel sorry for themselves."

Her utter lack of sympathy seemed to be what Jacob needed. The terror in his face was ebbing away. When he stood up he seemed stronger, more ready to brave the world outside. Or perhaps that was just the soup and the sandwich. She opened the door so he would know it was time to leave. On the doorstep, he hovered awkwardly.

"Thanks," he muttered, without looking at her.

She closed the door as soon as he turned away, but then

went upstairs to watch his progress from the tiny slit of a window in the end of her bedroom. The glass was warped and wavery, but she could see the dim shape of him slowly retreating along the diminished cliff towards his house.

Ella's gone too, she thought, and felt again that hollow ringing in her chest. But it was too late, too late, too late, and she should have known better than to let herself get close. This was the best way. Things would work themselves out, in time. Human beings were strong. They could survive far more pain than they wanted to believe.

Chapter Sixteen
Now

"You drug him," she said.

The shame was a physical thing, a shrinking burning crawling sensation that invaded every cell in his body. He could hardly bear to look at her. Was it possible to die from the way he felt? No, of course it wasn't; he would have to feel this way for ever, every second of his life, as punishment.

"I don't," he said, not knowing why he was bothering. She'd seen him with the milk, with the spoon, with the tablets. She'd seen the furtive guilty shuffle as he tried to hide the packet. She was holding the tablets. What was the point in lying? She was looking at the label.

"Take one tablet as required before bedtime," she said.

There were three tablets in the spoon. His hand gave a strange twitching leap as if he might hide them. There was nothing he could do, nothing he could say. He forced his hand back to his side.

"But you've got three," she said.

"He's built up a tolerance," he said, as if that was any defence.

"Is that how you knew? That he couldn't have been the one who Mum –" she swallowed hard, shut her eyes for a moment, then forced herself to hold her face in a neutral position – "who Mum ran away from?"

"I don't drug him," he said. "I just – it's just –"

"Tell me about it. I want to understand. Please."

Was she truly the first one to guess? The doctor, who wearily authorised the endless repeat prescriptions, perhaps guessing that this was the cheapest and easiest solution to a near-impossible problem? The pharmacist, who made up the prescriptions? The assistant who handed over the bag? Did they have time to stop and look at what they were doing? Were they complicit? Or were they simply too busy to notice?

"There's nothing to understand. Forget it. What do you want for dinner?"

"Don't shut me out. I want to help."

"Well, you can't help, okay? There's nothing you can do to help, there's nothing anybody can do, this is how it is and it's how it's going to be until he –" His voice was rising; if he wasn't careful his father would hear him and want to know what was going on. He forced himself to lower the volume. "I don't want to talk about it."

In the silence between them, he became aware of a faint rattling sound. It was the packet of pills in Ella's hand, trembling slightly. She put it hastily down on the counter.

"I shouldn't have shouted," he said. What would happen if she reported him? Perhaps they'd get him some help. But then what? Would they look at his father's life, his pathetic stitched-together care arrangements, this wildly unsuitable house, and say, *this man needs 24-hour care in a residential home*? Perhaps, but what kind of a care-home? He couldn't afford to pay; it would have to be whatever there was, and what there was could be horrifying. And how would his father cope in a place where nothing and nobody was familiar? What would happen to him then? "Please don't tell anyone."

"Does Mrs Armitage know?"

"I – " he had been about to say *no*, but he wasn't sure if that was the truth. Perhaps she knew. Perhaps she'd seen the faint residue in the bottom of the glasses, counted the empty packets in the bin. But even if she did, she would never, ever say. Her judgement on him would be cold and clear, untouched by compassion for either his father or himself. She would know he was simply doing what he had to, in order to survive. "I don't know. Maybe. She's never said."

The look on Ella's face reminded him of when she was very small, and wanted to tell him something she thought he might not approve of. He remembered, for what felt like the thousandth weary time, that the girl standing in his kitchen was his little sister.

"What?" Now it was his turn to try and coax her into reluctant speech. "What is it? You can tell me." She was worrying her lower lip with her teeth. "Come on, it's not as if I'm in any position to judge you, is it? Please, Ella, don't shut me out."

"Do you remember when you found out how to do it?"

"Do what?" For a dreadful moment, he thought this was going to be a conversation about sex. He remembered again the expression on Donna's face, as if she had just understood some fundamental deficiency in him that, once seen, could never again be overlooked. The expression of someone who feels they've been tricked, but who also pities the trickster.

Ella reached for the teaspoons, balanced them one on top of the other, then pushed down with a quick decisive movement, grinding the tablets into powder. "Do that."

"I – I don't really know. Maybe a drugs awareness thing, we have them all the time at school. It's not exactly rocket science, is it?"

"It was Dad," said Ella, very softly but very clearly.

"What are you talking about?"

"Dad. He used to do it to Mum."

The accusation was as absurd as if she'd said *Dad used to lock us up in cupboards at night*. "No he didn't." His denial was immediate and instinctive. "What on earth makes you think that?"

234

"Because I remember. And you ought to as well. You *do* remember, you just don't know you do. We used to see him sometimes. When they'd had a bad night. You know the kind of night I mean."

The times they cowered in the bathroom, sometimes for one night, sometimes for three or four in a row. The water filling his ears, almost drowning out the voices below. The sound of things breaking. Ella's steady, careful counting. Watching his little sister sink in her turn beneath the surface of the water, eyes closed, hair fanning out like Ophelia. They simply had to wait for the storm to pass. If they kept still enough and quiet enough, eventually the sun would shine again. And each time, the storm would pass. They would wake to their parents happy in each other's company, exhausted but ready to begin again. Except that each time a little more of the landscape of their marriage had been eroded, until at last there was no land left and their relationship had crumbled into the sea and everything had changed. It hadn't been an ideal childhood but it had been the way it was, and he could remember every part of it.

"I know," he said. "It was Dad's fault. He'd get drunk, she'd get upset, they'd have a massive argument. Then they'd be back in the honeymoon period and it would all go quiet for a while."

"But don't you remember how she used to sleep all day after they had a row?"

"Oh," he said, blushing. "Oh. I know what you –" In his memory, the sun was always shining, even though this couldn't possibly be the case. He remembered his mother's slow sleepy movements, floating and blissful. Their father, solicitous and loving, pouring their mother her glass of orange juice, her mug of peppermint tea, kissing her fingers when she reached dreamily up to caress his face. Both of them wrapped in that unmistakeable rosy haze that Ella had been far too young to recognise. "You're remembering..." Was she really going to make him say it? "It was the sex," he said, as impersonally as he could. "You know about the concept of make-up sex, right? When you've had a huge row and you're making up to each other afterwards and both parties' emotions are really heightened so the, um, the sexual experience is extremely intense?" *Both parties' emotions. The sexual experience is extremely intense.* No wonder Donna had pitied him. "That's why they were always so spacey and happy afterwards, okay?"

"She used to go to sleep straight after breakfast. He used to take her upstairs."

"And now you know why." Even as an adult, the memory still made him squirmy and uncomfortable. His father holding out his hand to their mother, his gaze and his attention so entirely on her that it felt as if he and Ella were hardly in the room at all. Her dreamy compliance. The creak of the stairs; the firm closing of the bedroom door. The breathless silence in the house as he strained every muscle not to hear anything or know anything; the way his father looked when he came back downstairs, both weary and satisfied, as if he'd accomplished something important. *Come on Jacob, you're going to miss your bus. Ella, you stay in the house, do you hear me? Don't disturb your mother, she's sleeping.* "Look, do we really have to talk about this?"

"Yes, we do." It was so strange to see Ella so insistent. "Sometimes we'd come down early and see him in the kitchen. You must remember, Jacob, you have to remember. We used to stand behind the door. We used to check before we went in, to see if we'd get shouted at for being up too early. We used to look through the crack."

He remembered this, too; it wasn't a new memory, there was no sense of revelation. No monster lurched up from the depths of his unconscious. Just the well-remembered feel of Ella's sleep-warm paw in his, the smell of her sweat, the unbrushed tangle of hair that caught the light over the crown of her skull. The cautious peek through the crack in the door, watching their father shamble about in his dressing gown, muttering as he filled the kettle. Ella beside him, trying hard not to breathe too loudly, because he'd once told her off for that and now she was paranoid about giving them away with her inconvenient need for oxygen.

"Of course I remember."

Knowing when it was dangerous was easier than knowing when it might be safe. If they saw him slam a cupboard door or swear wearily into the fridge, they would go back upstairs immediately. Sometimes they'd stand transfixed for several minutes, savouring this unauthorised glimpse of their father when he thought he was alone. Jacob remembered it all, the good and the bad, the mundane and the shameful. The secretive trips to the pantry; the scrape and twist of the bottle-top, and the faint clink of glass against glass. The way his father wiped at his mouth when he came out again, his look of furtive relief. He could remember it all, even the moment when his father would go to the cupboard, take down the mug, and –

"Oh my God," he said, his voice sounding not like his voice at all. "He did. He did. We saw him. We did. That's what we saw."

"You told me it was sweetener. For her tea. Because she didn't like to have too much sugar. And I asked you –"

"– why he had to crumble it up, and I said it was so it would dissolve properly. And then you wanted to know why he was putting sugar in as well, and I said that was because the sweetener didn't taste very nice so she had half and half. I think I even believed it. I must have believed it. But how could I have?"

"And when she came downstairs, he used to give her that mug of tea and she'd drink it," said Ella. "And then afterwards she'd be all spacey and sleepy, and they'd go upstairs and he'd put her to bed. She'd sleep all day sometimes. And when she woke up, she wasn't like herself at all."

"Ella. This is awful. Please don't say any more."

"It was like she was walking underwater. She was really

237

slow when she moved, and sometimes she'd talk slowly as well. She'd go into rooms and forget what she'd gone in there for, but it didn't bother her. She'd stand there staring at the wall or watching the trees move."

"But why would he do that? Why would he do that to her?"

"And she'd forget the words for things, or make things up. One time she forgot the word for feet. She wanted me to get my shoes on, but she couldn't quite get it, so she said, *you need to get your walk-things dressed*. Do you remember?"

(Ella's face when she greeted him by the door, her little legs like sticks above the trainers she must have taken from his room. "Look, Jacob," she'd whispered. "My walk-things are too small for your shoes. We have to call them walk-things now, that's their new name."

"You mean your feet. They're called your feet. And those are my trainers, and you got them out of my room."

"No, Jacob, they're my walk-things." The frailty of her little foot emerging from the cavern of his trainer. "We're going to call them walk-things now. Mummy says so."

He'd thought she was being manipulative, trying out the effects of an artificial cuteness so he'd forget she'd been in his room again. He'd thought he was being quite restrained by not yelling at her, but instead simply saying that *walk-things* was a bit of a babyish word, and he didn't want to talk to her if she was going to be babyish. He'd held onto this memory so he wouldn't fall into the trap of idolising her. *Sometimes she was annoying. Sometimes she was naughty. Your life before wasn't perfect.* How many other times had she made these oblique pleas for help, only for him to ignore her?)

"I thought you'd invented *walk-things* to be cute," he confessed. "I didn't know."

"It wasn't your fault. How were you supposed to know what to do?"

"But I watched him. We watched him. We saw him drug our mother. How could I forget that? How could I? And then I –" the shame had left him for a few minutes, but now here it

238

was again, the searing realisation of seeing what he had done through his sister's eyes. "I started doing exactly the same thing to him."

"Jacob."

"Yes."

"Do you believe me when I say I'm not judging you because you're my brother and I'll always love you no matter what?"

"Not really. But carry on."

"Why do you do it?" she asked. "I mean, I know he keeps repeating himself and he gets upset, but is that really so hard to deal with? He seems so gentle –"

"Gentle!" He laughed. "Is that what you think he is?" He could make eye contact with her now, suddenly back in a place where he could be the blameless hero. "Ella, trust me, he's a lot of things but he's not gentle." He tore off his jacket, threw it on the floor, fumbled angrily with the buttons of his shirt.

The bruise where his father had struck him with the fence-post was beginning to fade, but it was still impressively large, spreading out across his ribs like the paper chromatography experiments that decorated the walls outside the science labs ("*separating black ink into its component parts*"). He let her look for a moment in angry silence.

"He did that," Jacob explained. "He thought there was someone in the house. I was trying to calm him down and he went for me."

She took three steps towards him. Her fingers reached out towards the bruise.

"And look." He turned around to show her the more recent injury, less impressive but still worth sharing. "That's where he shoved me into a doorframe. Same reason. Some days it's all he thinks about. If I don't drug him up, he prowls around the house, looking for imaginary people who are coming to get us. He can go all night sometimes. And if I try to stop him, he gets so angry." He'd thought he was being dramatic, making more of a show of this than it really deserved in a pathetic effort to win his sister over to his side, but he found his voice was trembling.

"But during the day?" She looked guilty even as she spoke the words. "I just want to understand –"

"He pisses me off." The air was cold against his naked chest. "That's all it is. Some days I can't deal with him another minute, the same conversations, the same questions, always wondering what's going to trigger him off, if he's going to start crying and not stop for an hour, if he's going to hit me. It's easier to drug him up. I don't do it very often." Except he did, he knew he did. "It's only every now and then." Except it was every weekend, every Bank Holiday, every day he was forced to spend at home and not at work. He'd even laid in extra supplies to get them through the long six weeks of summer. "I even make myself sick. I'm disgusting."

"You're doing your best."

"My best is pathetic. I'm just like him, aren't I? He drugged our mother and drove her away and drank until he broke his brain. I drug our father on a regular basis and I can't even get a second date, not that I've got time for dating anyway, and I'd probably end up drugging them up to stop them leaving me –"

"Don't say that. You're lovely."

"No I'm not." In the half-light of the kitchen, it was harder to see the traces of the little girl she'd been. She could simply be any other girl of her age, pretty and sweet and with the most beautiful eyes he had ever seen. "But you are. You're lovely. You're so lovely. I still can't believe you came back. I love you so much and I missed you so much and then you came back and even though my life's a ridiculous mess I don't care, I'm happier than I've ever been in my life. Is that weird?"

Her hand reached out again for the separated-ink bruise on his chest. "This is awful."

His breath was short. "Forget it. I was just being dramatic."

"Does it hurt?"

"No. Yes. No." It didn't hurt, but he found himself shivering beneath her touch anyway. Her fingers were so gentle. The kitchen was cold and he was shivering, but his skin felt delicious. "I should be looking after you." Reaching out for her felt strange, as if he was crossing a boundary that should not be breached, but they were allowed to hug. He put his arms around her. She looked so small and soft, but then felt lithe and muscley, like a weasel. He kissed the top of her head.

"I'm so sorry she left you with him," she whispered.

"I'm so sorry she took you away," he whispered back. He could smell the scent he'd been noticing for days now, the faint sweet blend of cosmetics and body-spray and the lightest mist of tobacco.

Time to let go, his brain reminded him. His body refused to co-operate. Instead, he kissed the top of her head again. Her arms tightened around him. He could feel the press of her fingers splayed out against the skin of his back. Her hair was tickling him. He stroked it smooth. She turned her face up towards his and he brushed her cheek with the ball of his thumb. His heart drummed. Could she feel it too? There was a flutter in her neck where her pulse-point lay close to the surface of the skin. Her sweet, tender skin.

He was the older one. It was his job to stop this now. He was projecting something strange and dreadful onto this moment, imagining a tension that didn't exist, letting a dark secret impulse he didn't even want to name take over his body. This was nothing, nothing that could ever happen, it was something that belonged only in the darkest places in his head, even though it felt pure and strong and irresistible. He had to stop this now. He was the older one. He had to stop this. He lowered his head a moment. The shape of her mouth was so perfectly sculpted to fit against his. Her lips parted a little. That sweet electric feeling. Did she feel it too? Please let her feel it too. No, please let her not feel it too, let this just be him, because if she felt the same then how would they ever stop?

"Ella," he said.

241

"Yes."

"Ella." He could feel her fingers against the line of his spine, the short-bitten nails with their raggedy edges. When his hand slipped beneath the back of her t-shirt, the warmth of her skin was astonishing. "Tell me to stop. Tell me you want me to stop."

"It's not you. It's me as well."

"Tell both of us to stop, then. Say the word and we'll stop this right now." His body, rebellious, was ahead of him. Her t-shirt was up around her neck, the smooth curve of her belly pressed against his groin. "Oh God. Ella, we can't. I love you. I love you. I love you so much and that's why we're not going to do this. We have to stop now."

"I know. I know. I'm sorry."

"Don't be. It's –" he bit back the words *it's the most beautiful thing that's ever happened to me*. "I don't want to stop but we have to. We have to."

Moving slowly, he let her go and took a reluctant step back. Ella pulled her t-shirt back down. He reached for the jumper he'd discarded, not trusting his fingers with the buttons of his shirt. He could feel every place on his skin where she had touched him.

"It's all right," he said. "I know what this is. I've read about it. When close relatives are separated as children. There's a name for it, I think –"

"Does it go away?"

"Yes, of course." He had no idea how that could ever happen. How could this feeling disappear? This was why he'd made such a mess of his almost-date with Donna. His true love, his real love, was waiting for him in the dark. "I mean, I don't really know, I didn't pay that much attention, but it surely must, it just –" he was reaching for her again, taking her hand, letting his fingers stray over her wrist. He had to keep talking. If he stopped talking he would kiss her. "It must do. We won't always feel this way. We'll just have to wait until it passes and then –"

– and then the most perfect thing that had ever come into his life would be gone, and he would be alone again –

" – and then we can get back to normal."

"Okay. You're right."

He wasn't right. He was wrong, every part of him was wrong. Wrong for what he'd done. Wrong for what he felt. Wrong for denying it. Wrong, wrong, wrong. All he could do now was try for redemption.

"I'll take Dad his drink," he said, and left the kitchen.

They sat as far apart as the living-room would allow them to, Ella curled in one chair, Jacob at the furthest end of the sofa, their father in his own chair in the middle. Their father glanced between them and raised his eyebrows.

"You two had a row?" he asked.

"What the hell are you –" Dizzy and sick with longing, Jacob found it hard not to smack his father's face, with its knowing/not-knowing leer. What would he think if he knew? Thank God he would never, ever know. "What do you mean, Dad?"

"No need to sit in separate chairs. Curl up on the sofa if you want, I don't mind."

"We're fine where we are, thanks, Dad."

His father yawned. "I'll probably be asleep soon anyway. Can't seem to stay awake in the evenings these days. I must be getting old."

Of course he'd be asleep soon. Nobody could stay awake with the amount of Diazepam he'd swallowed. Another reminder of all the ways he was failing as a human being. He could hardly look in Ella's direction. His father flicked restlessly through the channels.

"Nothing on, is there?" He sighed and laid the remote down by his chair. "Shall we watch a film instead? Jacob, how about that *Die Hard* DVD we got the other day? If that's all right with you, of course," he added, smiling at Ella.

"That's fine, I love *Die Hard*."

"Sort it out, then, Jacob, will you?"

He had to pass Ella's chair to get to the television. He was grateful for his dad, unknowing chaperone to his un-remembered children. He knelt in front of the DVD player, going through the pantomime of taking the disc out and putting it back in again. His father became agitated if he thought they'd watched the movie recently. Back in his chair, he let the dialogue wash over him and waited for his father to begin to nod and twitch.

"I'll take Dad upstairs," he said, as the sounds of the terrorists storming the party echoed around the living-room.

"Can I help?"

It would be so much easier with Ella's help. But afterwards, they would be upstairs, alone. He could already picture how good it would feel, how treacherously right – "It's okay, I'll manage." His dad, yawning and beyond speech, was swaying in the doorway. "Look, I'll take him upstairs and get him ready in the front bathroom, so if you wouldn't mind using the one in the tower – I mean, I know it's early, but –"

He didn't want to say *but we can't be alone together in the same room,* but he knew he didn't have to. She nodded and gave him a crooked little half-smile that made his heart leap. He wanted to kiss her, to feel her kissing him back. Instead he put his arm gently around his father's shoulders.

He was almost hoping for a night where the tablets would fail him and his father would refuse to settle, shambling around in a drunken zombie state that would leave them both tattooed with bruises afterwards. Instead, his father went through the ritual of getting into his pyjamas, cleaning his teeth and using the toilet with the willingness of a tired child. He'd been so much better since Ella came. Had her presence somehow healed something for him? Or was it simply that Jacob himself was more patient, more gentle, because he was happier too? He stood for long minutes in the doorway, watching his father breathe because he didn't trust his own body. Ella must be out of the bathroom now, must be safely beneath the covers with the door closed. Now he had to do the same. Perhaps in the morning the madness would have passed. When he cleaned his teeth, he could hardly meet his own gaze in the mirror.

"Stop it," he said out loud. "Stop thinking about it, you're only making it worse. It's nothing, it'll pass."

Moving slowly and carefully, he crept past Ella's door to the bathroom in the tower and filled the bath with cold water. Then, still wearing his jeans and t-shirt, he climbed into the bath.

The water was so cold he thought his heart might stop, but he forced himself beneath the surface anyway. As the water filled his ears and took the warmth from his flesh, he felt everything in his mind settle into stillness, like silt on the sea-bed. All he could hear was the thrum of his pulse and the occasional drip of water and, from somewhere very far away, a memory of his sister counting: "Eleven... twelve... thirteen..."

He reached a count of two minutes and five seconds when he heard the faint creak of the back staircase. He erupted from the bath in a great wave of cold water and ran down the corridor.

"Dad. Are you there? Are you –"

But his father was fast asleep still, breathing slowly and steadily. It took him a moment to realise what he must have heard instead.

He knew before he opened the door that Ella's room would be empty, but he had to check anyway. The bed was still faintly warm.

Why had he got in the bath with all his clothes on? He lost precious minutes stripping himself bare and finding new clothes. Then he began his search, the same methodical route he had taken with his father over so many nights. Room after room after room, empty. The back door was closed, but unlocked. She'd gone out. But not long ago. He rummaged in a drawer for a torch, then ran out of the back door and frantically scoured the garden. But there was no sign of her.

Could she possibly be out on the cliff-top? Surely not. He made himself check anyway, not wanting to admit that she might have taken the other path, down into the village and away from him, where he couldn't follow because he couldn't leave his Dad.

He wasn't going to lose her. There had to be a way. He floundered furiously around the kitchen for a while. Could he risk waking his father up, forcing another tablet or two into him somehow? No, it was already too dangerous. If he could be sure where Ella might be – if he could somehow find her and make her come back...

"Dad." He was back upstairs, standing by his father's bed, shaking him gently by the shoulder. "Dad, it's Jacob. Can you hear me?"

His father half-opened one eye.

"Bad dream? S'all right. Get in w'me, son."

"No, it's not that. I'm going out for a little bit."

"Get in w'me," his father repeated, and patted Jacob's hand.

"Dad, please listen. I'm going out, but I'll be back soon." Was this true? He could only hope. "I won't be long. Promise."

The tide of sleep was too powerful. His father was gone again. He ran to his room, found a pen and paper, wrote a hasty note. The chances were tiny that his dad would read it, but at least he'd tried. When he left the house, he felt as if he was pressing forward against a powerful elastic restraint trying to pull him back again. Should he take the car? No, because she might hear him coming and hide. He would have to rely on his longer legs and hope he could catch up with her. If only he knew where she was going.

And then he knew exactly where she was going, and he broke free of the restraints that bound him to his father and ran through the dark to the place where his sister would be waiting for him.

The track down to the secret beach was just as he remembered, right down to the felled sign-post. Ella was sitting in the lee of the dunes, her face turned towards the ocean. The wind was beginning to rise, and the sand blew in tiny eddies along the tops of the dunes. Until he saw her, he was tired and sweaty with half-walking, half-running, but then she looked at him and he felt as if he could run for ever, as long as she waited for him at the finish. Over her t-shirt, she was wearing the shirt he had left in the kitchen. Her hair was damp at the ends and her mouth tasted of toothpaste.

"I don't know what you like," he confessed, somewhere among the frantic fumbling movements that took them from standing to sitting to lying in the sand, unwrapping each other in the moonlight. "I mean, I don't know what women like. I've never done this before, with anyone. I'm sorry if I'm hopeless."

"I don't know either," she said, "I just – I just –"

And when he kissed her, he could taste her tears.

Chapter Seventeen
2008

It was that time of year when the few tourists who were going to come would arrive, gathering in lost bewildered clumps on the thin sand that lay like a sheet over the pebbles. Sometimes the villagers themselves created a small celebration of the warmth – a potluck picnic on the sands, perhaps, or a "fun day" for the local children. But Mrs Armitage took no notice of these things, preferring to let the season pass in its own time, waiting for the North Sea to become entirely hers once more.

Before the last storm, secret plans had come to her in flashes as she went about her business. Ella's small confiding hand in hers as they picked their way down a path like a farm-track. A wicker pannier, lid lifted, improbably beautiful food within. Tiny bare feet seen through water. Now she told herself that she'd been no better than a broody hen sitting over a clutch of stones, and when she came across the pannier, lurking in the shed, she carried it straight through the house and through the hatch to the small loft space, cramming it into the darkness. It had been five weeks and three days since the storm and Ella's disappearance, and she was herself again – calm and unruffled, needing no one, making no connections and leaving no footprints. She had her house and she had her boat and she had the whole silent world beneath the water. She'd let herself be distracted for a while, but now that was over.

Everyone was allowed a year of foolishness at some time in their lives.

The air was hot and heavy and the grass pollen made her throat itch. She craved the feel of cold salt water seeping in through her wetsuit to lie against her skin like a lover, and the slow descent into the silty twilight where nobody else would be. Did she dare go out by herself with the tourists watching? Once she'd come to the surface to find a Zodiac lifeboat crammed with grim-faced men in orange slickers, and the water ruffled by the blades of the coastguard helicopter. *We had a report of someone going over the edge of a rowboat,* they told her, and then, when she explained, *but don't you have a diving buddy?* And when she told them she lived alone and had no friends and needed no one, thank you very much, the final humiliation: *okay, so how about next time you give us a little tinkle, post your plans with us so we know where you are and how long you're planning on being down there? And then give us another little tinkle when you get back? Just so we can keep an eye on you.*

I dive alone because I want to be alone, she told them coldly. *I know these waters better than any of you ever will, and since I'm a grown woman I don't need to give anyone a little tinkle to let them know what I'm doing.* Rowing back, she made a fierce vow that she would check for other boats before coming back up, that she would rather drain her air-tank and slowly suffocate than have a conversation like that again ever in her whole life. Since then, she'd been wary of diving during the times when strangers gathered on the beach.

It was a pity, because a dive down through the sea's molten copper as the sun dissolved into the water would have been an entirely excellent way to end the day. Instead she took her secateurs and viciously attacked her heap of pruning waste, reducing each long stem to a series of two-inch scraps.

The heap disappeared quickly; too quickly. She was still restless and unsettled. The water was calling, but she couldn't listen. She found herself watching the empty space where the gate used to be, listening for the tell-tale shiver and rattle that would announce Ella's arrival. The girl always struggled with the latch, but Mrs Armitage had never gone to help her. It was important for children of that age to realise the world wouldn't always co-operate.

The pollen was dreadful this year. There was water in the back of her throat and the corners of her eyes. She put the secateurs back on their hook and told herself that Ella was gone and that was that, and she'd barely known the girl anyway. She needed more time in the water. Everything would be better once the year had begun its slow turn back towards winter. As a substitute for the dive she really wanted, she would walk along the cliffs, tormenting herself with the sight of what she couldn't have.

With her fingers closed around the door-handle, she was startled to hear something panting. It sounded like a large dog. One of those dogs that looked like a tank, perhaps, chasing a rabbit or its own shadow, disconnected from its people and therefore frightened and therefore dangerous. It sounded as if it was right outside. It would be better not to look. A large frightened dog or a large excited dog could very easily become a large dangerous dog if a stranger emerged unexpectedly through a fence. She opened the gate a fraction and peered through.

"Oh," she said, feeling faintly disappointed. The boy Jacob was there, white-faced and sweaty and seemingly half-mad with some emotion too huge for him to contain. He looked less well-cared-for than last time – his skin dull, his hair greasy, his lanky frame perhaps a little lankier – but on the whole, he didn't seem as bad as he might have been. Perhaps his father had been shocked by his wife's disappearance into behaving more like a normal person? But she knew she was wrong. If Jacob's father had begun to behave more like a normal person, Jacob wouldn't be here. She was literally the last person he could come to.

"I passed my exams," Jacob blurted out, and waved a brown envelope. "Every single bloody one of them." As if this was the worst possible outcome, his legs folded beneath him and there he was, sitting at her feet as though he expected her to pick him up and comfort him. She gazed at the tight cluster of dandruff nested at the back of his head, and wondered why he thought she'd want to touch him.

"Well," she said, when she couldn't stand the sobbing any longer. "Congratulations. I suppose. Why are you so upset?"

"I went home," he said. "To tell my dad." The whiteness of his face made his spots blaze out like lights. "And he – he was in bed and he – I couldn't – he won't –"

How was this sentence going to end? She could think of a number of possibilities. She waited, quite patiently she thought, but he was beyond speech.

"Is he dead?" she asked at last. He shook his head. "Is he angry with you?" Another shake of the head. "Is he in there with someone else?" The sound that escaped Jacob was too high and frantic to be a laugh. "Right, that's three guesses and I've still not worked it out, so I'm stopping now. You need to explain what's going on."

Another silence. Mrs Armitage was good at waiting. The water looked very welcoming tonight. Perhaps she might go out later after all, once she was sure the beaches were empty of idiots who thought she might be rowing out to commit suicide.

"I got home and he was upstairs in bed," Jacob said at last, in a fierce hiccupy whisper. "I thought I'd go in to see him. I thought he'd be pleased because I've done really bloody well. I mean, I know he's upset, but he doesn't seem to remember that I've still got things going on, you know? I thought if I told him how well I'd done he might, you know, just be a little bit pleased, maybe enough to stop drinking for one bloody day and think about me for once, so I went in to see him, and he –"

If he didn't get it out this time, she thought to herself, she'd go back into her house and make herself a cup of tea and forget she ever had this conversation.

"He won't wake up," Jacob finished, and took a deep, shuddering breath as if these words had freed him from an almost intolerable weight.

"Well, he's probably drunk," said Mrs Armitage briskly. "Give him a few hours to sleep it off."

"That's what I thought. He was drunk when I went out, he took a bottle to bed with him, he thinks I don't notice but I bloody do. But it's different, he's not even drunk it, there's this whole bottle lying on the floor next to him and he won't wake up."

"So call an ambulance."

"Will they be able to help?"

"How should I know? I'm not a paramedic."

"Will they take him to the hospital?"

"If that's where he needs to be."

"And then what happens to me? Will they leave me on my own?"

"I don't know, how should I know?" Her feet were getting tired with standing. She'd often noticed that standing still tired her out far more quickly than moving. "Do you want them to leave you on your own?"

He looked at her blankly, and with a sinking feeling in her heart, she realised what he was really asking. *Please come and help me. I need you. You're my only choice.*

She wanted, very much indeed, to ignore this skinny grease-monkey of a boy and go back into her house and shut the door. If she waited for long enough, he would give up and wander off – perhaps back home, perhaps on into some unknown future that might end almost anywhere, while his father woke up or didn't wake up, died or didn't die, went on with his life or sank beneath the waves. That was what she wanted to do. The only problem was that if she did that, she would eventually have to go into her bedroom and turn off the light and know that in the darkness, the photograph of her husband would be watching her. She allowed herself this single superstition: that the dead watched over those they had loved in life, and passed judgement on their actions. Her husband would not condone her leaving Jacob alone.

"All right," she said, cross because the universe was once more demanding something of her that she didn't want to give. "I'll come and take a look at him. But I'm warning you, I don't know much."

He was too much the awkward teenage boy to thank her, but she saw the relief in his eyes. They walked in silence, she a few paces ahead of him because like hell would she follow in his wake like a skivvy. The evening air was deliciously warm. So few days turned out as perfect as this one. What a shame she was having to waste it on looking after a near-stranger. If it had been Ella who had come to her –

But it would never be Ella. Ella was gone. She had to accept that, just as she had to accept that she was now committed to helping Jacob. She would not mope. She'd simply do what she'd promised, and move on.

The garden, unsupervised even by Maggie's fitful attentions, had grown wild and menacing. Picking her way through, she trod on the end of a rake that leapt up and tried to smack her in the forehead. She caught it in time, and turned her gaze towards Jacob.

"Sorry," he muttered, as if this was the only way he'd imposed on her that evening. He took the rake from her grasp, but then ran out of impulsion, standing bewildered in the long grass and waiting to be told what to do.

"Lean it against the wall," she told him. "Not like that, it'll fall over again. Don't you have a garden shed?" He took hold of the rake once more. "No, not now, do it later when I've gone. I'm not standing around watching you tidy things up."

The kitchen was reasonably clean, not immaculate but certainly passable considering who had presumably been in charge of it for the last few weeks. Was she supposed to tell him this? She looked at Jacob and saw him standing dumbly in the centre of the room, far beyond hearing compliments or even insults, only able to process the simplest and most direct instructions.

"Where's your dad?" she asked. Jacob pointed vaguely towards the door that she presumed led to the hallway. "There's no point trying to tell me. Take me upstairs and show me."

The staircase was scarred but magnificent, and in any other house but this would command a premium of thousands – even in its current condition, bare of carpet and with dust and fluff collected around the base of the spindles and the wood cracking for lack of care. When the ocean finally came, the staircase would make a beautiful shape in the water. Fronds of weeds would cluster along the spindles, and fish would dart between them as if they were taking an agility course. At the top of the stairs, Jacob turned right and opened a door.

"Right," Mrs Armitage said, and looked in.

She looked cautiously at the man in the bed, wary in case he should suddenly wake. The last time they had met, they had not made friends. She could see again Richard's resemblance to Jacob. They had the same look of fundamental ordinariness, although Jacob had acquired character through the grease of his hair and the grief in his face, an effect his father had achieved through the liberal application of alcohol. His face was puffy and greyish, uneven stubble turning to patches of beard in the spots he'd persistently missed with the razor. He was lying half-across the bed with his head and arms hanging over the side facing the door. She'd wondered on her way up the stairs if she was coming to examine a corpse, but he was clearly still alive in some primitive way; his chest rose and fell in a slow rhythm and his fingers gave an occasional twitch.

"Well, at least he's tried to get up," she said.

"No," Jacob whispered. "I did that. When I – when I was trying to wake him up, I moved him."

His father was taller than he was, with all the weight of fat and muscle that came with late middle-age. When she looked more closely, she saw the red bloom of bruises on the pale shrivelly skin of Richard's arms. Who knew a boy his age and size could be so powerfully cruel?

"I didn't mean to hurt him," Jacob went on, not knowing he was contradicting himself with every word.

They stood side by side and watched the slow rise and fall of his father's chest. She thought about slapping the man's face, trying her own brand of violence in case she might have more success at bringing him back from whatever place he was wandering in. He was disgusting to look at, filthy and gross and with a smell that permeated the whole room. There would be a distinct pleasure in slapping him. Perhaps Jacob had felt the same impulse. A proper adult would reprimand him for the way he'd left his father – it was harder to breathe with your head stretched back like that, he could easily have suffocated. Then again, a proper adult would probably not have let Jacob get into such a position in the first place.

"Right," she said, when it became clear Jacob had no more to offer than the numb guilty misery of silence. "Let's get him back into bed properly. Then we'll phone the ambulance." Jacob reached listlessly for his father's arm. "No, don't do that, you'll pull his arm out. Get underneath him, under his shoulder, and lift. Lift! And roll him. Keep going. That's it. Now prop him with the pillows. Good." She arranged the covers over the man's chest, trying not to let her fingers touch his flesh. Now he looked human again, a person someone cared about rather than a lump of inanimate flesh. "Where's your phone?" Jacob fumbled a flat black rectangle from his back pocket. "Call the ambulance."

"What do I say?"

"Tell them your father won't wake up and you need help. I can't do it for you, I don't like mobile phones." The pleading in his gaze was hard to bear. "If you dial the number I'll talk to them, but this is the absolute last thing, do you hear? I'll stay until they're here, but no longer. I'm busy."

From the relief on his face as he handed the phone over to her, he hadn't heard a word beyond *I'll talk to them*. A single ring and she was speaking to the dispatcher, explaining the situation as well as she could. No, he wasn't responding at all. Yes, he'd been like that for quite some time. No, she couldn't say how long. Yes, he was still breathing. No, she couldn't tell them any more, she didn't live with them and his son wasn't up to talking right now. Yes, she would stay until the ambulance arrived.

A kinder person than she would find a way to comfort Jacob. They would put their arm around his shoulders, perhaps, and take him away from this terrible room and downstairs to safety. Sit him down in a chair and make him a drink of some sort, then sit down beside him and say words intended to make him feel better. *It's not your fault. You weren't to know. You've done your best. The ambulance will be here soon. They'll soon have him on his feet again. I'll look after you.*

Instead, she stood beside him and watched the slow movement of his father's breathing, up and down, up and down, as if someone was pumping a bellows in his chest, and waited for the crunch of gravel that would tell them the ambulance had arrived.

She'd expected an instant diagnosis of stroke, but the para-medics seemed to have other ideas. In between the brisk bright reassurances as they tried and failed to wake him, then loaded him into a contraption that got him down the stairs and into the ambulance, she heard fragments of more puzzled discussions, and a muttered conversation over the radio.

"So, about Jacob," said the man in the green jumpsuit, whose name she hadn't bothered to remember, knowing her part was nearly over and she wouldn't be speaking to him again. "He's welcome to come along with his dad if he wants to, but since his dad's not actually conscious and there might be quite a lot of hanging around, he might be better stopping here with you and calling the hospital later. Is he always this quiet? He's not saying very much."

"I think he's a bit shaken up," said Mrs Armitage cautiously.

"I can imagine. Well, like I say, he's welcome to come but he's probably better off here, unless he feels very strongly about it. You'll be keeping an eye on him?" She hesitated. "Are you a relative?"

"I know the family," she said cautiously.

"I was going to ask about that. Is Dad a drinker, would you say? That bottle in the bedroom?"

"Yes. Yes, he's definitely a drinker."

"Right, that's good to know. Any idea of quantities? Just a rough estimate?"

Against her will, she thought of Ella, and then of Maggie. *Enough to damage everyone in the family,* she thought.

"More than is good for him, I imagine," said Mrs Armitage in her best prissy voice.

"And is Mum on the scene at all? Anyone else who needs to know?"

This was the moment when she could keep the secret, or betray it. She ought to tell this man the truth – that Jacob had been essentially on his own for weeks now, doing his inadequate best to cope with the useless slab of flesh they had loaded into the ambulance. That Jacob had a stepmother, who must surely be out there somewhere, and who could possibly be induced to return now that her husband seemed so definitively cancelled from existence.

"No," she said, impressed by how natural she sounded. "It's just Jacob and his dad. His mother hasn't been around for a long time." Once she began lying, it became suddenly very easy, the words opening up in front of her like a broad highway. "I'll stay tonight. Do you want to give me the details so we can call later?" *We,* she thought to herself; that was a good word to include.

257

"Perfect. And he's how old? Fifteen? Sixteen?"

"Sixteen, I think."

"Right." The ambulance man nodded to himself. "So we might need to involve Social Services at some point, then, if his dad's going to be ill for a while."

"I'll see to all of that." She gave him the small nod and half-smile she knew he'd want to see, telling him he could hand off any responsibility for Jacob and get back to his patient. "To be perfectly honest, I've thought for a while now they might need some help."

"You're a proper good neighbour," the ambulance man said.

She resisted the urge to slap his face for being so patronising, and instead summoned a modest smile.

"Not at all," she murmured, through gritted teeth.

"Okay, we're ready to move, so we'll be off. If you call the hospital in about two hours, we should have some news."

"Two hours. I'll make sure we do that."

She could tell by the way he hesitated, by the irresolute movement of his arms and feet, that he wasn't completely convinced by her dependable-neighbour act. She gave him another smile, hiding her teeth behind her lips, and held his gaze, willing the thought from her head to his: *you can trust me. I'll look after the boy. Nobody's missing; there's nothing to see. Everything in this house is entirely normal.*

"Steve!" It was the other paramedic, calling to her partner from the ambulance. "Ready when you are, mate."

"We'll get off, then," said the man called Steve, and patted her arm. "Thanks for looking after the young lad."

"It's a pleasure," she lied, and took her place next to Jacob in the driveway as the ambulance turned towards the road. In a moment of inspiration, she put an arm around Jacob's shoulders.

"Keep still," she ordered Jacob when she felt him jump. "Do you want them to leave you alone or don't you?" He kept obediently still. "Right, they've gone. Now, let's go

258

inside and talk about what happens next." He stood passively on the driveway, like a small child woken from sleep, so she gave him a little push. "That's it. In we go."

Inside, he stumbled into the living-room and took his place on the sofa. Like the kitchen, it was grubby and untidy, but could have been worse. Nevertheless, she was physically unable to ignore the litter of plates, cups and glasses strewn around like confetti. Despising herself, she collected them into a precarious stack and took them into the kitchen. *I will not wash these,* she swore to herself, but found herself running a sinkful of hot water anyway, leaving it deliberately too hot for her hands as a punishment for being so weak.

As the water cooled, she grew cooler with it, wondering why she'd committed herself, however vaguely, to any part in the care of Jacob and his father. The task went on and on, glasses followed by plates followed by endless knives and forks lurking in the thick bath of suds. It had been years since she'd had so much to wash at one time. She gritted her teeth and told herself this was the first and last time.

When she returned to the living-room, Jacob was, predictably, asleep on the sofa. Some people found such sights quite charming, claiming that sleep returned the sleeper to a younger and more innocent state. She crashed around the living-room for a while, straightening cushions and swatting angrily at the dust on the mantelpiece, but Jacob did not stir.

He was safe. He was sleeping. He had water and food. He wasn't stranded in his own filth or wailing with hunger. She could wait for the prescribed two hours and call the hospital, write a note explaining what had been said, then creep out of the house and return to her own clean quiet home, where there were fresh sheets on the bed and everything was tidy. If it was Ella sleeping on the sofa, there was no way she would consider it. But Jacob was older and less appealing; leaving him would be far easier. If she thought about it for too long, she could become quite disheartened at how much of what human beings call *conscience* was dictated by the curve of a cheek or the pitch of a voice or the softness of freshly washed hair.

"All right then," she said crossly, and went upstairs to see which of the bedrooms would be the least unpleasant place to spend the night.

It was noon the next day when Jacob woke up. In the intervening hours, she'd watched him sleep, been all over the house and visited every one of its rooms, then telephoned the hospital and taken careful and extensive notes. She'd scrubbed the bathroom nearest the bedroom where they had found his father, changed the beds, cleaned and re-cleaned the kitchen, gone through the refrigerator for out-of-date food (surprisingly, there was none – either a very good sign, or a rather bad one). After considering each bed in turn, she rejected them all in favour of a night beneath the apple tree, cocooned in rugs and duvets that grew steadily colder and damper as the night deepened, then turned to morning.

At some time between midnight and dawn, she made her decision, and finally fell asleep for a brief uncomfortable interval. She dreamed of her husband, and took this to mean he approved of her plan. She made herself toast with the last of the bread, and then, growing impatient, noisily vacuumed the hallway until Jacob finally woke.

"I've called the hospital," she told him, as he stood blearily in the doorway and stared at her in bafflement.

"What did they say?"

"I'm not telling you yet, you're not awake properly and you won't take it in. Go and have a shower and make yourself presentable. And wash your hair, it's disgusting. I'll be out in the garden."

She was prepared for protests, but he nodded meekly and headed for the stairs. Perhaps she reminded him of his mother. She had none of Maggie's ethereal prettiness, but perhaps she too had been stern with her stepson. Of course, he would have known that Maggie's sternness was tempered with love.

The last twenty-four hours had contained more effort and human interaction than she'd experienced in years. Outside smelled beguilingly of salt and summer. It would be another beautiful day, and tonight she would ignore all other claims on her time, take her boat out and tip herself backwards into the water. A clump of thrift grew from a scrap of soil collected beneath a rock that might once have marked out a flowerbed. She would never understand people who bought gardens, then neglected them. She picked the bloom and began shredding it, enjoying the tough resistance of the stalk and the thin dry petals. Perhaps Jacob would forget her, and she would be able to escape without having to talk to him. Then she heard the back door shut and the rustle of someone coming towards her through the long grass, and sighed. A moment later and Jacob was beside her, carrying two mugs of tea.

"I made tea," he said.

"I should think so too. I've been here all night."

"I'm sorry."

"No you're not. You asked me to come so I came."

He was too young to know how to argue with someone older than him. He blinked miserably until she took pity on him and took the mug from his hands. The cliffs were closer than the last time she'd been here, and would grow closer still as the autumn gales took their toll.

"So," she said. "Your father has something called – actually, I can't remember what it's called, I wrote it down but I can't remember it. But it's caused by drinking. He's in a coma, but they think he'll come out of it."

Jacob nodded blankly.

"When he does, he'll probably have some brain damage," she continued. "He won't be able to look after you, or even himself. He'll be brain damaged for ever, but the rest of him could well be all right. So, as long as he's got someone making sure he eats and washes and doesn't burn the house down, he could live a long time."

Was he taking this in? She wasn't sure.

"So," she continued, "you need to decide what you want to do."

"What do you mean?"

"You had your exam results yesterday, yes? And you passed them all?"

"How did you know that?"

"You told me yourself, when you came to get me."

He looked mystified. "Did I?"

"How else would I know? So, is that right? You passed them all? You weren't making it up?"

"Yeah, I passed them."

"Good. So now you can do anything you like."

"I'm sixteen and now my dad's ill. What can I do?"

"Anything at all. You just need to decide."

She'd hoped he'd be clever enough to understand, but he stared at her with those big cow-eyes of his, waiting patiently for her to start making sense.

"Your father's in hospital," she said. "That's your window of opportunity. If you leave now and don't look back, they'll never track you down."

"Why would I want to do that?"

"Or you can call Social Services and tell them you're on your own without a carer. You'll end up with a foster family probably, I think that's what normally happens, and they'll look after you while you do your A-levels. That's a possibility too."

"But what about Dad?"

"Did you read the notes I left?"

He took a sheet of paper from his pocket. He'd folded it clumsily, the creases uneven across her lines of neat, careful handwriting. She forced herself to concentrate on the bigger picture.

"Did you read it?"

"Yes."

"Did you understand it?"

"Not really."

"Do you understand your father's never going to be the same person he was, ever again?" He swallowed and looked away. "Good. So, do you want to spend your whole life until he dies looking after him? Or do you want to get away? And you need to think about this right now because you won't have long. Have you heard of *holding the baby*? Right now the hospital have the baby. But if you let them ship him back home, he's your problem."

He was looking away from her and out towards the sea, but she could see from the tremble of his jawline that he was about to cry.

"This isn't fair," he said.

"No."

"Mum should have bloody been here. She shouldn't have left him. Why would she do that?"

"Because she didn't love him enough," said Mrs Armitage. "Your mother's left you, and your father's damaged his brain with drinking. None of that's fair. But it is what it is. Now what are you going to do about it?"

She was trying to light the fires of rage in him, so that in the simple directness of his anger he'd find the strength to walk away from his crumbling house and his crumbling father and his crumbling life, and start again somewhere new, in a large city far away from the sea. But instead she saw a swallowing-down of childish emotion and a straightening of the shoulders that told her he was going to do something entirely different. For a moment, she was reminded of her husband.

"I'm not leaving him," he said.

"You have to. What are you going to live on? Who's going to take care of him?"

"Won't he get money or something if he's not able to work? There isn't any mortgage. And won't he be able to have a nurse? While I'm at college?"

"A nurse?" She laughed scornfully. "An actual nurse? In your house? So you can take yourself off to college twenty miles away? You'll be lucky if you get twenty minutes a day from some untrained teenager. And you'll have to pay for that, I should think, so you'll have even less money than you're imagining."

"I don't know. But everyone else has left him. I'm not going to."

"Then you'll starve," she said calmly, and took a long drink of her tea.

They stood side by side and gazed out at the water. Mrs Armitage was comfortable with silence, but most people were not. Whoever spoke first, lost the battle. Eventually, Jacob would feel compelled to fill the void. If she kept quiet, she would force him to do what she told him, and find some other future in some other place. Then this house would be empty, and the cliff-top would be hers alone. She would never walk this way again, and she would be able to forget that small girl in unicorn wellington boots and a pink-and-blue flowery coat. Why wasn't he speaking? She was stronger than he was, she was older and wiser and more ruthless.

"Or else go mad," she said. This didn't count as her speaking first. She was simply finishing her sentence. She still had the upper hand. Seen in profile, Jacob resembled his father. She suspected she could see Jacob every day for the next ten years and never glimpse his sister. Not that she'd see him ever again after today, unless they met by chance in a shop somewhere and looked at each other for a minute, and then looked away. She still had the upper hand. My God, he looked like his father – to her irritation she realised she was repeating the same thoughts over and over.

"You can't look after him," she said at last. "What on earth makes you think you can? Why would you even want to? He's a dreadful parent and you don't owe him a thing. Why do that to yourself? Get rid of him and start a new life."

"What if they come back?"

"Your mother and Ella? They're not coming back."

"Ella might, one day when she's older. This is where she'll look. If I'm not here, how will she find me?"

"But –"

"She left him," Jacob said, and from the bitterness of that *she*, Mrs Armitage guessed he meant his stepmother. "But I won't."

Damn it, she thought to herself. Love was always the hardest enemy to conquer.

"The house won't last," she reminded him. A rear-guard action, but one with potential.

"Then I'll stay until it's gone."

"And what happens after that?"

"I'll worry about it when it happens. Until then, I've got to stay here."

"You'll only keep the house if you take on your dad. And if you're stuck with him, you'll have nothing else. No A-levels, no university, nothing. There aren't even any jobs around here for you to do."

"I'll manage."

"How? How will you actually manage, Jacob? You won't have time to earn money, and you won't have money to pay for anyone's time. If you can answer that, I'll leave you alone."

"Why do you care?"

"I –"

She wanted to say *I don't care*, but it stuck on the end of her tongue. She knew then that he'd won, and all that was left for her to do was to salvage as much as she could from the wreckage.

"All right," she said grimly, to the universe in general. "Here's what we'll do."

"You don't have to do anything, I'm not asking you for –"

"Be quiet, please, I'm talking. I'll help you with your father. No, don't start telling me I don't have to, clearly I do. But there are some conditions."

"You don't have to, I never asked you to –"

"Last night, Jacob, whose door did you knock on? Well, then. Now listen. I'll look after your father when you absolutely can't, and no more. That means I'll be there when

265

you're getting an education or earning a living. For everything else, he's your responsibility. Now, here are my conditions. I expect you to go to college and do your A-levels. I expect you to do well in them too. Understand?"

"Yes."

"Liar. Never mind. What do you want to do afterwards?"

"I. Um. I'd like to be a teacher, I think, I don't really know –"

"A teacher." Of course, he had to choose a career he could actually pursue while still living here. She'd been hoping for something less universally useful. "You'll have to do your degree living at home, but at least you'll have one. That's the second condition, by the way. I expect you to choose a goal and work towards it."

"What if I'm not good enough?"

"Then you'll have to choose something else. And the third condition. Each morning, you and I will come down here and you'll tell me one thing you remember about Ella."

"What? Why?"

"If you're going to live this ludicrous life, you're going to remind yourself each day why you're doing it. Maybe one day you'll realise how stupid you're being and stop. Until then, you'll confront it. Every morning, you understand? That's my price."

His eyes were wide.

"Yes, I know. It's going to hurt, isn't it? Memories always do. Well, that's your choice, Jacob. Do you accept, or not?"

She wanted him to argue, but of course he wasn't going to. He was built not to rebel, but to endure.

"Okay."

She looked at him mockingly.

"Thank you," he added, as helpless as a bleating sheep.

"Don't thank me. I'm not doing this for you."

"Then why are you doing it?"

"Because otherwise my husband will never forgive me," she said, and smiled to see the bewilderment on his face.

Chapter Eighteen
Now

The sand beneath their naked skin was cool and slightly damp. When the wind blew through the stiff grasses, they rustled and shook over their heads. They were alone, in their perfect place, and the peace that flowed through his body was almost enough to drown out the throb of horror in his head. Ella was turned slightly away from him. He could see the immaculate curve of her thigh, the slight movement of her shoulder blades as she breathed, the small feathering of silvery stretch marks over her hips. She was the most beautiful thing he'd ever seen. But –

"Jacob." Her voice was a sob.

"Ella." He laid his hand gently on her back. "Don't blame yourself." *Or me*, the cowardly voice in his gut whispered. *Don't blame me, don't be angry with me, this is the most wonderful, the most beautiful –*

"I should have said no. I should have told you no."

"I should have stopped too. I'm the older one, I'm supposed to –" the phrase *know better* didn't feel remotely adequate for the situation. *Knowing better* was for not drinking too much, not parking on the double-yellow lines, not letting Ella go close to the edge of the road. What was the correct phrase to describe what they'd just done? "I'm so sorry."

She turned to face him, and for a moment, before she

grabbed for her t-shirt and pulled it over her head, he saw the shape of her breasts, and felt sick with longing. Her eyes were brimming with tears. "Are you?"

No, his body whispered, *you're not and you never will be, that was the truest, rightest, most perfect experience of your life and all you want is to do it again.* "Of course I am. I've hurt you."

"You didn't hurt me." She wiped fiercely at her eyes. "It was – oh God." She shuddered. "It was so – but – I mean, is it like that with everyone? Is that what – what sex is like?"

"I don't know. You're the only person I've ever – done it with." The voice in his head was far more eloquent, the words unfurling behind his eyes like the rushes of a bad romantic movie. *You're the only person I want to be with. I want to do it all over again, right now, but slower and more carefully so I can remember every bit until I die. And then afterwards, I want to spend the rest of my life with you. I want to take us both far away from everything to live alone on an island where no one will ever know, no one will ever guess that you're secretly my* – even inside his head, he couldn't say the words. Did Ella feel the same? He was afraid to ask.

Without the wild magic of need and passion, he was cold. He shook his boxer shorts out of his jeans and pulled them on, then his jumper. It was still faintly warm. How had so much happened in such a small amount of time?

"It was just one time," he said, and reached for Ella's hand, telling himself that this was normal, this was within the bounds of what was acceptable. His fingers were traitors. They swirled over her palm, felt out the delicate shape of her wrist, threatened to creep up her forearm. "No one will ever know."

"No. We won't tell anyone. We won't – not ever again –"

Because she was so close to him, because they both knew it would never happen again, he risked a quick kiss. He was aiming for somewhere innocuous, her cheek or her forehead or the top of her hair, but somehow her mouth came up to meet his and they were kissing again, mouth to mouth, as if they would drown without each other, and his hands were on her again and her hands were on him and it felt as if they had found the keys to a dark kind of Heaven. There was no way this could be wrong. This was surely what the universe had meant for them both. She was so beautiful, so warm, and when she straddled his lap he thought he might die with how it felt.

He wouldn't think about it. He couldn't think about it. They would have this one night and then it would be over. Or perhaps it didn't have to be over, perhaps this one night could become the first in a precious string of thousands of nights, a secret they could keep between them until they died. This beach would keep their secrets, this magical place they had discovered when – when –

And then he remembered, and forced himself to stop, and he felt the same remembrance take hold of her at the same moment, and they broke apart, breathing hard, hands on each other's shoulders and foreheads pressed together for strength, as if they had done battle with a monster and barely survived.

"We can't," Ella said.

"I know."

She looked at him miserably. "But you do want to?"

"Of course I want to! Do you think I'm faking this? Do you think guys even *can* fake it? Every bit of me wants to. But we can't do this. I mean, I remember you being *born*. I used to get your breakfast in the mornings, I used to help bathe you. Oh God, I used to bathe you." He felt a lurch of vomit gathering in the back of his throat. "Ella, I promise – it wasn't – I mean, I never, ever, ever – it's only now, since you came back, that I've even –"

"In the bathroom the other night. When you found me under the water."

"I thought you were dead."

"I almost wanted to be dead. I'd been so sure he – Dad, I mean – I thought he was the one in her book. I thought he'd frightened her away. I was going to tell him what he'd done, make him confess so I could get him put in prison or something. Even when he didn't recognise me, I thought maybe he'd found her somehow and he was going to see her, during the day when you weren't there. I mean, it wouldn't have been his fault, but – only then I realised he couldn't possibly – he couldn't ever – and I wanted to die because I thought I'd never find her. I know that's awful but I did. But then you came in and I saw your face when you pulled me out of the water and I thought – I thought – I mean, I felt so – I wanted so much for you to – but then I remembered, and I felt so disgusting –"

"Don't say that," he begged. "You're not disgusting. It could have happened anyway, we might have just met and not known who we were. It must happen to people all the time, only they never realise. We could pretend we met when we were the age we are now." He risked a glance at her face. "No, course we can't pretend that, I'm being ridiculous."

"Please don't cry."

"I'm not. Well, not really." Her hand on his cheek was delicious. He would let it stay there. This much must be allowed. "I've waited my whole life to fall in love and now it's happened and it's you, and now there won't ever be anyone else, not ever. This is it for me." He heard the pitiful whine of his voice and was appalled. "Forget I said that. Oh, Ella, what are we going to do?" She was in his arms again, and he was helpless against his own desires. Had anyone else in the world ever felt like this? And once they'd found how good it felt, how did they ever do anything else? The sand dune came up to meet them, folding around them just as they folded around each other. He could taste her tears mingling with his own. He wouldn't think. He would not think. They would have this one night.

When he woke the next morning to the first thin fingers of sunlight and the terrible cold that had settled deep in his bones, he thought that second time was perhaps more unforgivable than that first frantic tumble into each other's arms. This time he knew what he was doing, knew exactly how good and how terrible it would feel. Knew he was the older one and he was supposed to be responsible. Did it anyway. Let her do it too, let her take charge, taking what she wanted, giving himself up to her as completely as he could. Didn't stop himself. Didn't stop her. Sitting in the sand, while Ella crept shivering behind a tuft of grass to relieve herself, he felt the full weight of his own sin and thought it might crush him. If he had any sort of courage, he'd walk into the sea. But then how could he punish himself for something that had felt so good, not just for him, but for both of them? How could it be wrong when –

He reached again for his clothes. His thoughts went round and round in his head like a train on a too-small circuit, through the tunnel and out again, round deadman's curve (*I should kill myself I'm not fit to live*), then into the valley with its artificial grass and artificial trees that looked so real you were almost fooled for a moment (*but it felt so good so right we could run away somewhere and no one would ever know*), and back to the tunnel (*we can forget it and never mention it again no one will ever find out*). Soon the train would come off the rails and he'd be nothing more than a bunch of fried circuitry. He could hear a strange gulping noise, but he was so lost in his own head that it took him a minute to realise it was Ella being sick.

She was naked, crouched over on all fours, her mouth wide open, a cat with a hairball. He knelt beside her and stroked her back, gathering her hair into a long ponytail.

"I'm all right," she gasped, between retches. "Don't look, I know it's disgusting, I'll be fine in a minute."

Even on her knees and vomiting, sweaty and pale and smelling of stomach acid, he still loved her more than anyone else in the world. Was that a sign that what he felt for her was real and pure? At last the spasms stopped, and she sat back on her knees, trying to get her breath back.

271

"It'll be okay," he said, without any idea how he could make this happen. "I know, I know. But it will be. We'll do something. We'll find a way." He stroked her back, made himself stop. "Put some clothes on, you're going to freeze."

"I'm all right."

"No you're not. Don't be ridiculous. You need to get your clothes back on."

She'd been the same when she was little; her response to the cold was to shrink down into herself in a kind of torpor, refusing any unprompted move to get herself warm. This was the terrible thing, the inescapable truth that would keep looming up like a shark's mouth from the bottom of the ocean, ready to swallow them both. He could still remember. He could still see. He would never be able to forget.

Her clothes were crammed into the top of her bag. Had he done that, or had she? As she pulled out the crumpled disorder of her jeans, she also set loose a handful of papers that he had to pounce on before they escaped.

"It's Mum's book," Ella said. "I thought if I brought it down here to read I might think of something useful. I know that's silly."

"No, it's not. Maybe you're right. I'll have a look. You get dressed and I'll start."

The first time he saw it, he hadn't even wanted to touch it. Now it was here in his hands, and he was glad of this chance to escape, to sit and do something relatively normal with Ella, or at least (since reading the unpublished manuscript of a novel written by his mother, which might or might not provide the clue to their childhoods) to do something that could set them temporarily free from the ebb and suck and demanding pull of desire. He tried not to see the perfect looping cursive and focus on the words. Why had she written it by hand? *I've been thinking lately about becoming someone else.*

At first it was just a way to avoid looking at Ella and thinking about what they had done, but gradually he found himself drawn in by the sheer strangeness of the manuscript.

Was this his mother's life, tamed by ink and made haunting by her imagination? Or was it entirely fiction? How could he, or Ella, or anyone at all, ever get a grip on such a slippery story? It was hard to say if it was brilliant or awful. He turned another page.

We met in a pub. Such an ordinary way to meet the love of your life and the nemesis who will haunt you until you die. A lovely pub with lovely grub, and within two hours we were grubbing away in the back seat of his car, which should have been disgusting and horrible but was in fact delicious. He seemed delicious too, so simple and so sweet. Perhaps it was the crème brûlée he ate before I took him by the hand and told him I thought we should go somewhere quieter. When he first put it inside me he looked at me as if he was afraid, and I thought perhaps I might swallow him whole and he would have to live there for always, like the mariners who lived in the stomachs of whales. Or maybe that was what he wanted, to climb right up inside me and fill me up like a

He turned the page hastily, and risked a glance at Ella. She had lit a cigarette, and was watching him as he read. *Reading is a way to escape into a different world.* He told his students that at the start of every year. But had any of them ever tried to escape something so strange and terrible?

When I first told him about the baby, I was afraid he would be angry, because the baby would take up room inside my body where he liked to be and inside my heart, where he liked to be. There had been just him and me, and now there would be one more. I was afraid he would be angry, but I wasn't afraid enough. His whole face changed in front of me and I saw inside of him and he was filled with black stuff like treacle, and all the treacle poured out of his mouth and spilled out onto the floor and he was yelling, yelling, yelling that I shouldn't have been so stupid and what was I thinking and we had promised each other that it would be only us, only us and nobody else. I was so frightened. Partly because I thought he might kill me, but also because I wasn't sure how I was ever going to get the treacle stuff out of the carpet. So I went upstairs and locked myself in the bathroom and climbed out of the window and ran away.

And I thought he might let me go, but of course he didn't, because he loved me. And I loved him. And now there was a baby.

Was this an episode earlier in the woman's life, or later? Was her pregnancy the cause of their first break-up? Or had it happened during one of their many reunions? Each time he thought he had a grip on the story, it slipped away from him again. Each episode flowed into the next with no clear sense of place or time. The heroine and her stalker moved in and out of each other's lives, coming together, then parting, then meeting again. At times she seemed unclear even what the man looked like; he could change shape or perhaps even bodies. Was this an attempt at magic realism? Or was it simply her way of saying that the man was able to hide his true nature beneath a veneer of charm?

"Here," said Ella, and held out a crushed sandwich.

"You brought food?"

"I was going to leave," she said. "I wanted to see this place one more time first."

"I'm so glad you didn't."

"Are you?"

They sat in silence and ate, watching the sea. They were both eager for the sun, but within a few minutes of rising it was already beginning to dim. The piled grey spear of a storm front crept across the sky, as if some elemental or other force had been made angry by what he and Ella had done last night. The belief that the weather could take on human emotions and moods was known as *pathetic fallacy*. As a student, he'd found this briefly hilarious.

274

"We need to get home," he said. "Look at the weather. It's going to rain soon."

"Okay." Her face quivered. "Would it be all right if you drove me into town and dropped me at the station?"

"Of course I'm not going to drop you at the bloody station. Where would you even go?"

"I can't stay here."

"Yes you can. Of course you can."

"But we're criminals now," she said to herself, as if she was trying out the idea. "We could go to jail for it, couldn't we?"

"No one will ever know."

"I think they will."

Perhaps she was right. Perhaps what they had done was written all over their faces. He could smell her on his skin when he moved. If anyone came near them, would they know what they'd been doing? Or would it seem too unnatural and outlandish to even imagine? He reached for her hand, stopped, then took it anyway. The hell with the world. No one was here to see them. She came to him willingly, and he pulled her close, wanting to keep her warm. Was what they had done so terrible? Who had they hurt? Who had they stolen from? And if they were both sick and miserable with guilt (he remembered Ella, naked, retching on the sand, remembered the convulsions of her muscles when he put his hand on her back), was that because what they'd done was wrong? Or was it because they'd been taught to think it was?

He didn't dare hold her any longer, and the rain would be here soon. He crumpled up the foil and stuffed it into the top of her rucksack. He might be a criminal but he wasn't going to pollute this place with litter.

"Jacob." Ella pointed towards the track. "Look."

"Oh shit."

He watched the remorseless march of the small sturdy figure coming down the track towards them. The last thing they needed now was the company of others, let alone this woman. Nonetheless, they stood side by side, waiting for her to arrive. She was like a wise woman in a fairy-tale and there was no point trying to escape, because she knew them both to the bone and there was no hiding anything from her.

"This storm is going to be a bad one," Mrs Armitage said to them, no greeting, no introduction or *fancy-meeting-you-here* or *you're up early* or *funny old place to spend the night*. She glanced at their clasped hands, nodded, and then looked away again. "I went to your house to warn you, but you weren't there. You should probably spend today somewhere inland."

"Dad," said Jacob, in horror.

"He's safe. I woke him up, although that was a lot harder than it ought to have been. How many did you give him this time, Jacob? Four? Five?"

"Four." He forced himself to meet her gaze. "But how did you – where did you – I mean, where is – is he at your house, or –"

"My house will fall before yours will," she said, calm and unemotional as always. "But I think this storm might take both of them. Listen to the wind."

They could hear it rising now, a high fading whistle that brought an intermittent terrible pressure, as if someone was leaning against them and then letting go, trying to push them into the sand and then to trick them into falling under their own counter-pressure.

"I borrowed your car," Mrs Armitage added. "I bundled him into the passenger seat and drove him into town and got him a room in a hotel and ordered him some room service and locked him in. It's not ideal but it's the best I could do at the time. You can pay me for the room later. And let's hope he doesn't try to wander."

"I didn't know you could drive," said Jacob.

"I can do a lot of things that I choose not to do. I suppose I could have stayed with him, but I thought I ought to come and find you two."

"But how – I mean –" The presumption of her actions was

276

so vast, the favour she had done for him so huge, he couldn't begin to speak of it. "How did you know we'd be here?"

"You're neither of you as mysterious as you like to think." She looked again at their hands. "So what are you going to do about all of this?"

"I – well, I suppose if the house falls – do you really think it will, though? Well, anyway, if it does, then we'll have to –"

"I don't mean about the house, you fool."

He could pretend he didn't know what she was talking about, could tell her she was a strange and filthy-minded old woman who was seeing things that weren't there. But what would be the point? They both knew she was right. Probably she'd seen it before they had. Perhaps that was why she had looked at them both so strangely, that morning when they'd gone to visit her. He held tight to Ella's hand, kept his head up and held her gaze.

"You think you're monsters," said Mrs Armitage, quite unexpectedly. "But that's not true." She looked at Ella. "And you think you're going to find your mother. That's probably not true either. What on earth made you think you could?"

"I read her book," said Ella.

"What book? That book she was writing all those years ago?"

"Yes, I think so. She finished it. Sort of. I found it in her room. And I read it and I think it's about her, it's like a clue to what happened to her."

"Your mother wrote a novel about a woman being stalked by a strange man and you think it's a clue?"

"You've read it too?" Ella looked baffled.

"An early version. A long time ago."

With a soft sighing swoosh, the rain began to shiver down. Far out over the sea, a jab of lightning earthed itself into the water. Jacob counted the beats until the faint rumble of thunder arrived. Ten miles away.

"You need to make a decision," said Mrs Armitage. "You can both stay here if you want, and see how long you last in the rain with no food and no shelter. Or you can go back home and wait to see if this is the storm that brings your house down. Or you can come with me."

"To your house?"

"No, of course not to my house. I told you time and time again, my house will fall before yours does. But I can take you somewhere we'll all be a lot better off." She pulled her hood over her close-cropped hair. "I have your car parked at the top of the track. Take a minute to decide, if you want. I'll wait a few minutes, but don't be too long."

They watched as Mrs Armitage stumped off through the rain.

"She knows," said Ella.

"But she'll never, ever tell."

"Does she think we're disgusting?"

"No. Actually I don't think she does."

"Do *you* think we're disgusting?"

"I don't know what I think," he said, because it was the truth.

Hand in hand, they stood and watched the sky do battle with the water. Out beyond the black wet streaks of seaweed, the waves were growing higher.

"We'd better go," said Ella at last. "She'll be waiting." She laughed. "I was telling myself we don't have to do what she says. But we do really, don't we? She was like that when I was little too. She'd tell me to do things, like to wash my hands before I sat down at the table, or to hang the garden tools up on the right hooks in the shed. She never let me make a mess or leave things in the wrong place. The funny thing was I quite liked it. It was nice having someone in charge."

He knew what she meant. Mrs Armitage had always told him what to do, too. *I don't care how tired you are, make sure you do your assignment before you go to bed. Take three painkillers and you'll be fine. Make a schedule for all your bills; I use a notebook, but I suppose a spreadsheet's fine too. Apply for this job.* He'd thought he was an independent adult, but in fact she was directing him the whole time. Why would she do that? Was it out of some strange need for control? Or was it a mysterious act of love?

Chapter Nineteen
2008

Standing in the inadequate shelter of shallow eaves and a leaking gutter, rain slapping at her face and body as it tried to drive past her and get into the house through the open sliding doors, Mrs Armitage thought that the storm tonight was full of greed.

In her life, she'd known several people (in her opinion, several idiots) who claimed to love the sound of the north-easterly storms tearing in like Vikings across the wild waters. *It's so exciting*, they declared, their eyes starry and unfocused, like people (like idiots) who had recently fallen in love. *I love lying in bed and listening to it. Or standing by the window to watch. So much power –*

Of course, what they loved was not the storm's power but their own immunity to it. The people who loved a North-East sea-storm had never lived close enough to the water's edge to know how dangerous it could be. And by the time you realised that the sea had no mind and no mercy, that it would grab whatever it could take and drag it under and come back for more and more and even more, until you had nothing left to give, it would be far too late to save yourself. She presumed many of the people (the *idiots*) she knew had fallen in love with the wrong partners for a very similar reason.

"I miss you," she said out loud, surprising herself. She

hadn't known until she said the words that her dead husband was tugging at her thoughts, but she could feel him there now, as if he'd crept into the room behind her and out onto the patio and was about to put his fingers against her throat and plant a kiss on the base of her neck. It had been so long now that she found it hard to remember his face without looking at his photograph, but sometimes her skin could still surprise her with its ingrained memory of his presence.

A woman who was losing a grip on reality might turn around to see if he was there, perhaps reach inside for the light-switch to send him away again. But she was not a woman losing her grip on her reality, so she continued to stand just outside, letting the rain soak her clothes and assault her skin, listening and waiting for what she knew must surely come soon: the rush and tremor that would announce the fall of another chunk of the shrinking patch of dry land she'd once believed belonged to her. She was glad her husband wasn't here to see. He'd believed the cottage would outlast them both. He'd also believed he and she would still be living here when they were old. If she chose, adding him to her list of idiots would be more than justified, but her loyalty was the last gift she could offer him.

A blinding sheet of light flashed across her eyeballs, followed a few moments later by a crack of splitting sky. The sudden brightness and the blind darkness that followed reminded her that Ella would be standing in the tower-room, watching for the light. Mrs Armitage had once liked to imagine the tower-room as a bedroom, remote and romantic with specially made furniture fitted into curving stonework, but Ella had told her that it was a bathroom, cold and draughty and banned from use for reasons Ella herself was unable to explain.

Had she left the light on? She couldn't be sure. She could go inside and check, or she could stand here in the rain for another minute and retrace her steps this evening until she was sure, and save herself the journey. Her days blended into one another sometimes. It was hard to keep track of the small differences that separated the undertakings of any particular Tuesday from those that came before or after. But with a little effort she would remember. It wasn't that she was reluctant to see the photograph of her husband that she kept by the bed. It was certainly not that she was remembering the night she had stood on the cliff and watched the rough surface empty of all vessels and known, even before the knock on her door, that the boat had gone down with all hands and he wouldn't be coming back. It was simply a good discipline to force herself to summon up, not the pale vague recollection of what she *would generally have been doing* at a certain time in the evening, but the small vivid details that would place her in that particular fragment of time.

She allowed herself to stir a little, to look at herself and see what evidence she could find. She was wearing the scarlet jumper that lived at the very back of her drawer and which she chose only rarely, because the colour didn't suit her but its warmth was unparalleled. That meant she must have been upstairs since the wind veered sharply around to the North-East and the clouds swallowed the sun like wolves. And now the lock turned in her mind and she had the whole memory; she'd gone upstairs to fetch an extra layer, turned on the light even though it was not really dark enough to need it yet, taken down the blue vase that lived on the sill of her side-window and pulled the curtains as wide as they would go. Ella, standing in her tower like a medieval prisoner, would see that Mrs Armitage's house was still standing. *Mrs Armitage*, she always called her, never *Araminta*, possibly because she had never invited Ella to call her Araminta. Thank God the child had never attempted *Auntie*.

In the part of her garden that had once been eleven feet from the cliff-edge and was now where she had re-installed her fence, the slice of panel that made a thin, barely-visible gate was shaking. There was a bolt along the top that, if she shot it home, would make her garden impregnable to walkers, but she chose not to bother. There was only one invader she feared, and a few centimetres of salt-rotted wood had no chance of keeping it out. Perhaps it was the wind, battering away at the weakest point of the barrier. She refused to give in to the fancy that it might be her husband, returned from the sea to reclaim his bride. What the sea took, it never gave back. She looked away again and stared steadily out into the storm and relished the numbness in her face and hands, the rain that dripped off her nose and darkened the concrete beneath her feet.

The gate flew open, then slammed shut once more. The wind must have got behind the panel, amused itself for a moment with trying to tear it from its hinges. If she was given to imagining things, she might imagine there was someone creeping up the garden, someone turned slick and smooth by the storm, their features soaked off their face and their hands blindly reaching out towards her. If she was given to imagining things, she would be frozen to the spot with terror –

But she was not given to imagining things, so she simply stood and stared and waited, and after a minute the ghoul resolved herself into a woman she recognised. Ella's mother, Maggie.

"I saw your light and I knew I had to come here," Maggie said, no greeting, no apology. They might have been meeting by appointment in a quiet hotel dining-room, dressed in expensive dresses and crimson lipstick and elegant white gloves. "I can't be in the house with Richard when there's a storm. Not even one in a teacup. Do you have teacups? Can I come inside and check? I'm a bit confused, I think it must be the weather we're having." Her laugh was high and uncertain. "Do you find that? Do you get confused by the weather we're having?"

"I don't understand what you're talking about."

"It's been a long day, I don't really know what I'm saying. Can I come in or will I get blood on your carpet?"

"I don't know. Are you bleeding?"

"I feel like I might be but I'm not sure. Can you see any blood? Or is it the rain? I'm very cold, is that a sign of blood loss do you think?"

The woman was babbling nonsense, swaying on her feet. How had she made it from her house to this one, with the wind tugging at her and the cliffs ready to crumble? Mrs Armitage toyed for a moment with the idea of going inside and slamming the patio doors shut and closing the curtains to shut out the blue eyes and blue flesh and pleading expression, but Maggie held her hands out in entreaty and Mrs Armitage, not liking to be touched, stood a step away from the doorway, then cursed under her breath as Maggie took this as an invitation to stumble over the threshold. Once inside, she stood apathetically, water pouring from her clothes in long silvery strands, eyes fixed on Mrs Armitage. Whatever blind force had driven her this far seemed to have burned itself out.

She could put Maggie back out into the rain and let the cliffs take her. She could march her through the house and send her out the front door towards the road. But then, both of these actions would make her complicit in whatever came next. There was no help for it. Maggie was in her house now. She had definitely become her responsibility. She sighed and squared her shoulders.

"Stay there and don't move. I'll get you a towel and some dry clothes."

She hurried around the tiny bedroom and tinier bathroom, assembling what she needed. Her whole house felt cramped and crammed with the knowledge that there was an extra person in it. Maggie was standing exactly where she had left her, frozen in place like a statue. When Mrs Armitage put her hand on her arm, Maggie leapt beneath her touch.

"Don't be ridiculous." In spite of herself, she softened her voice to make it gentler, less threatening. "I won't hurt you. You need to get undressed and dry yourself off and then put these things on."

Maggie was pitifully underdressed. Her thin long-sleeved

t-shirt was transparent with water and her jeans were plastered to her legs. When she pushed off her trainers, they squelched, exposing long slim feet, sockless and dyed blue and purple with cold, or perhaps with bruises. Her fingers scrabbled uselessly at the edges of her t-shirt.

"My hands won't work," she whispered. "I'm so cold. Is this my clothes? Or am I taking off my skin?"

"Fine, I'll help you. Put your arms up."

Mrs Armitage peeled the t-shirt off in one smooth slick movement. Maggie's skin was mauve and mottled, scratched and battered, the shape of her slender and lithe. A body so vulnerable in its bruised beauty that it seemed to invite the viewer to touch it roughly and damage it further. Mrs Armitage set her teeth and wrestled with the fastening of Maggie's jeans, tearing a fingernail on the zip but finally getting enough purchase to tug it down. Her fingers and nails left red tracks on the younger woman's flesh as she wrestled with the uncooperative fabric, trying and failing to leave the plain black cotton pants in place. Maggie stood like a martyr and let Mrs Armitage do what she liked. Her expression was frightened but compliant. Her ankles felt small and breakable in Mrs Armitage's hands.

"There," said Mrs Armitage. "Now dry yourself off." She held out the towel. Maggie took it and dabbed briefly at her skin. "No, rub hard. Get the blood moving. I'm not doing it for you, you're not a child. And then put those clothes on. And then come into the kitchen and I'll make you a cup of tea."

Maggie reached out and stroked Mrs Armitage's cheek. "You're wet too."

Mrs Armitage was too startled to push her away.

"We're the same, aren't we? We're both cold and we're both made wrong inside our heads. Did you know you're made wrong inside your head? Sometimes I know, but sometimes I forget. The strange thing is that when you remember that you're made wrong, somehow that helps you behave normally again. It's only when you forget who you are that you turn into your real self. That's why I had to come here. You know all the time who you are, don't you?"

"I'd like you to stop talking now. In fact, if you don't stop talking, I'm going to make you go back outside again."

"You should take your clothes off too," Maggie said, so calmly that Mrs Armitage wondered if she'd imagined the words coming out of her mouth. "We're both wearing the wrong skins for the weather. Is that the ocean coming for us?"

The ground shivered in distress. For a moment, the land outshouted the water.

"It's the cliff," said Mrs Armitage. "The cliff, that's all." She peered into the dark. "I think my fence has gone again."

Maggie smiled conspiratorially. "Maybe the octopus wants it for his garden."

"Maybe he does." They were both beginning to shiver now, Mrs Armitage because her wet clothes were sucking her body's heat from her skin, and Maggie because she was naked. "I'm going to get changed upstairs. You should put on the clothes I fetched for you, before you freeze."

"Ella says sometimes you put on another skin and then you turn into a seal. Did you know she believes that?"

"That's because Ella's a child. Children say a lot of silly things. She's thinking of my scuba gear."

"If you put your scuba gear on now and never take it off you'll always be ready when the water comes for your house," said Maggie, and the shiver that crept down Mrs Armitage's spine was not only from the cold.

She groped blindly for the bannister, her eyes still filled with the strange sight of Maggie's damaged beauty. Up in her bedroom, she turned the photograph of her husband to face the wall, not liking the feel of his eyes moving over her body, the body that had aged in all the ways his had not.

In the kitchen, Maggie sat and watched with eyes as wide and innocent as her daughter's as Mrs Armitage, newly armoured in fresh garments, put Maggie's clothes in the tumble-dryer and filled the kettle at the sink. The silence was awkward for a few moments, but Mrs Armitage refused to cover it over with idle conventional nonsense chatter. Instead the words she could have spoken (*I'll get the kettle on and we'll soon have a nice cuppa do you like milk sugar weak or strong biscuit no really you need the sugar*) jangled and clattered about her head for a while, then dissipated, leaving behind a different kind of silence that felt less like awkwardness and more like companionship. She filled two mugs with tea, thought about putting milk and sugar on the table but chose instead to make Maggie's mugful the identical twin of her own. The lack of words continued, the hum and turn and pause of the tumble-dryer slow and languorous like bees on a summer's day, a stark contrast to the cold chaos of the outside world. They sipped their tea and looked warily at one another, and Mrs Armitage tried not to mind that, even though the clothes she had lent Maggie fitted her dreadfully and should have looked ridiculous, the other woman was still beautiful.

"He gets so frightened," Maggie said at last.

Mrs Armitage waited for more.

"Frightened and angry. And when he's angry he doesn't know where to put it all." She sighed. "So he puts it inside me. Inside and outside and in my lady's chamber. You know how men are. He's not good with storms."

"You shouldn't let him if you don't like it. You don't have to."

"But I feel so guilty. It's all my fault, that's the thing. He gave up everything for me, for me and Jacob and Ella. He had a good life before he met me, and what does he have now?"

"How would I know? I don't know anything about him."

"He used to have a very normal life before he met me, you see. We met in a pub. I was running away from my husband, and he was running away too, but we both knew we'd have to go back home in the end. Only we met each other and decided not to. So we had to run away together. I'm not making any sense."

"Not really, no."

"You have to keep moving when someone's looking for you. But we thought we'd be safe here. Only then I saw him at the bus stop and I wasn't going to tell Richard, but he always knows when I'm keeping secrets, and he knew straight away, and he made me tell him and then he was frightened. Because we don't have anywhere else to go now, this is all we can ever have. We were the only ones in the world who wanted it and what happens if we don't want it? We spent all our money on the house and we'll never sell it because no one wants to buy it."

"Why do you need to sell the house to get away from him? I don't have any money to give you," she added, in case this was what Maggie was asking for.

"The thing is, when you're so close to something, you can't always see it properly. It's like I've got my face pressed right up against his chest and I can't see or feel anything but him."

Mrs Armitage could think of nothing to say, so she kept silent.

"Your silence is very beautiful," Maggie said. "Is that why Ella comes to see you? Does she sit here in silence and look at you?"

Mrs Armitage considered this. She was often silent when Ella visited, but that was because Ella herself filled the air with a rainbow hum of words, endlessly describing, speculating, wondering, until mere words were no longer enough and she was forced to reach for the felt-tips and paper that had appeared, like overnight mushrooms, in Mrs Armitage's kitchen one day. She could have made herself remember making the special and unwanted trip on the Tuesday bus into the nearest market town, the slow precarious choosing in the stationery aisle of the supermarket so vast it felt more like a cathedral than a place of business, the fumes that gathered like smoke in the interchange where everything had been improved and redeveloped and she had to look and look and look to find the right vehicle to take herself home again, the way the cold glass of the window felt and smelled against her cheek as they jolted back home to clean air and mud and silence, and when they finally got home she was so relieved she left her shopping bag on the bus and had to chase foolishly after it to flag the driver down and reclaim her prize.

She could have remembered all of this, but she chose not to. Some things were private. She didn't want Maggie reading her thoughts in her face. As it was, the other woman's eyes were darting slyly around the kitchen, alighting on first one thing, then another.

"Is that one of Ella's drawings? Can I look?" Mrs Armitage opened her mouth to say *no*, but Maggie was already out of her seat, reaching for the sheet of paper stuck neatly to the fridge door. Her hands were regaining their dexterity and her fingers did not tear the paper as she picked delicately at the Sellotape that held it in place.

You can look at it perfectly well where it is, Mrs Armitage thought, but did not say. It was too late to stop her anyway, the paper was already coming away from the door. Maggie smoothed it flat onto the table so she could examine it. *Why did you take it off the fridge door if you're only going to put it on another flat surface? What difference does ninety degrees make? Don't you think there's a reason art galleries hang the pictures on the walls?* Ella had drawn the image that, Mrs Armitage knew, haunted her dreams. The house she lived in crumbling into the ocean. She and her brother crumbling with it. The water reaching up to fill their mouths and ears and lungs. The boat below the water, where Ella had never been, but had somehow still conjured.

"Everything's falling," said Maggie. Her fingers rested on the figure that lay waiting in the water. "Is this a person? A person who's drowned?"

That's a seal. Or maybe I should say that's me with my true skin on. Ella drew me there because I told her my house would go first, so I'd be waiting in the water for her. That's

*how she comforts herself, that daughter of yours; with the
thought that a strange woman who goes around wearing the
wrong skin will be there to catch her when she falls.*

"And that's her," said Maggie, her finger resting on the
small falling figure with the long strands of yellow hair, "and
that's Jacob. She loves Jacob. If it wasn't for Jacob I don't
know what she'd do. She's frightened all the time. Do you
think she knows? Do you think she knows we're in danger,
all the time? Does she know that I'm frightened too?"

*She's frightened all the time because you brought a little
girl who's afraid of deep water to live in a house right next
to the North Sea.*

"You think it's my husband I'm frightened of," said
Maggie unexpectedly.

"Well, isn't it?" she asked, startled out of her silence.

"Sometimes. But it's not his fault. He's only doing his
best. Were you frightened of your husband too? Is that why
you invited me?"

"I didn't invite you, actually. You came here by yourself."

"You left a light on for me, I saw it from across the cliff. I
was running away from my husband, because I was afraid of
what he was going to do. Isn't that terrible? He loves me and
I love him but I'm still afraid of him. Is there a way you can
stop being afraid of someone you love? You'd think they'd
have invented something by now. Sometimes I think maybe
I've already invented it, but then I put the knife away and the
idea goes again." She wrapped her arms around herself. "I
used to be a whole person, but then I grew Ella and some of
me went into her and this is all that's left behind now. And I
don't think what's left behind is enough, not for me to stay
alive, properly alive. I'm like a zombie, but only Richard's
noticed, and he won't come outside when it's raining, he's
afraid of the cliffs. So then he tries to fill me back up, he's
trying to turn me back into a whole person, only sometimes
he tries too hard and it hurts and then I have to run away,
only it's always raining. I think it's been raining for years

now. Will the whole world flood? Perhaps we should build an ark."

She had been drinking, perhaps, or perhaps taking something or other, something legal or illegal, given to her by a doctor or bought from someone in a pub somewhere. Or perhaps she was frightened out of her mind. Mrs Armitage lifted her mug and took a long swallow. The tea was very sweet and good in her mouth.

"I used to make sense most of the time," Maggie added, as if this explained everything.

"Nothing ever makes sense," said Mrs Armitage, with sudden bitterness. "If there's any God at all, he's a madman with no plan or sense of purpose. I think you should leave your husband."

"Maybe you're right. Where should I leave him, though? I could take him into the forest and cover him with leaves. Maybe he'd turn into a bear and marry a princess. We all have two skins, did you know that? Ella told me that one day and I think it's true. I try sometimes to take my skin off and see who I am underneath but it hurts too much to peel. Where did you leave your husband?"

"On the bottom of the ocean."

"That's a good place to choose. Then when you go diving you can visit him and see how he's getting on without you. Is someone trying to come in? I can hear pebbles on the window."

"It's just the –"

"The rain's trying to come in," said Maggie, "but it's not allowed. Not yet. I got here first. It can't come in until I've gone. Only one visitor at a time, and only one biscuit, and no more than two riders to a car. If we didn't have rules, the world would all come apart at the seams."

"I think," said Mrs Armitage, speaking very slowly and clearly, "that you should leave your house and leave your husband and go and live somewhere else. It would be better for all of you."

"Maybe you're right. I used to be very good at running away. Then I met Richard and he climbed inside me and weighed me down. I thought I wanted to be stuck in one place. But what on earth would I pack? And what would happen if he saw me?"

"You should leave with only what you can carry. Don't take anything that doesn't belong to you. And go as far away as you can, and hide as well as you can. Get a job, everyone needs a job, and once you have a job you can start to build a new life for yourself. You'll never be normal again, and you'll never forget about him completely, but you'll be able to put him out of your mind for a while and get on with some sort of life."

"Is that what you did?"

"That's none of your business."

They looked at each other over the tops of their mugs of tea.

Chapter Twenty
Now

In the few minutes they'd spent climbing the track from the beach, the wind had gathered all its strength. When they broke through onto the road, Jacob felt Ella stagger under the weight of air. His car crouched impatiently, rocking slightly in the wind. Mrs Armitage was sitting cross-legged in the road, resting against the back bumper.

"Wait one minute," she said, holding up a hand. "We need to wait a minute longer."

Jacob was freezing and he wanted nothing more than to get himself and Ella into the shelter of the car, but they did as she asked. Alone on its own little headland, Mrs Armitage's house blazed with lights, pressed against the cold steel of the clouds with all its banners flying.

"What are we waiting for?" he asked at last, through chattering teeth.

"You'll see."

It took him a moment to recognise that the trembling in his flesh was not only because of the cold. Something apocalyptic was happening, something different from all the falls they'd experienced before. Then there was a terrible roaring rumble that outshouted the storm, and a distant rush of movement and a cloud of dust that rose in defiance of the rain, and the deceptive peace that came after felt almost like silence until their ears began to recover and they could once again hear the roaring of the wind and the sea, and see the new piece of sky where Mrs Armitage's house used to be.

"Well," said Mrs Armitage. "That's that. I thought it might be this year, but I wasn't sure. Ella, how are you doing?"

"I'm fine," Ella whispered.

"No you're not, you're terrified. But you shouldn't be. I always knew this was coming, and so did you. There's no point being frightened of something that's already here. Now all we have to think about is what comes next." She held open the back door of the car. "In you get, both of you."

"I can drive if you like," said Jacob.

"I don't like," said Mrs Armitage, and climbed into the driver's seat.

The journey was terrifying. It was the lift and tug of the wind at the car, as if a playful giant was considering turning it on its back to inspect the underneath. Or perhaps it was Mrs Armitage, muttering to herself as she peered sightlessly through thick sheets of rain. Where were they going? The car slowed, then stopped. The windscreen was misty with breath. She must have stopped to clear it. But why had she switched off the engine?

"Right," said Mrs Armitage. "Out you get."

"What? Why? Where are we going?"

"This is the marina. I have a boathouse down there."

"But –"

"If we stay here," Mrs Armitage said, with the patient air of one pointing out the obvious, "we'll soon be freezing. Down at the boathouse I have a stove, and also the boathouse is not in danger of blowing away."

"I thought we were driving into town. The hotel should have rooms. Or we can all cram in with my dad, I know it's not ideal but at least it's dry."

"It's not safe to drive."

"Then give me the keys and I'll drive, I don't mind, I'm used to this road –"

"My house just fell into the sea," said Mrs Armitage with great stateliness. "My boathouse is the only hospitality I'm able to offer you at this moment. I do have water down there as well. And soup, I think. And biscuits."

As he tried to decide what to do, Ella opened the door, then grabbed frantically at the handle as the wind tried to tear it off its hinges. Jacob scrambled to help her, and found himself suddenly outside the car and slamming the door shut. The wind was almost enough to blow them both over. Another moment, and Mrs Armitage followed.

The boathouse was dark and windowless, barely large enough to fit all of them. The walls were hung with wetsuits like flayed skins. Ella and Jacob crammed themselves in and tried not to shiver too obviously as Mrs Armitage put on the light and then lit the stove.

"You're both going to freeze," she said. "Take your clothes off at once."

"We're fine," said Jacob, through gritted teeth.

"Of course you're not fine. I can only offer you wetsuits, I'm afraid. Ella, take the one hanging on the hook behind you. It belonged to me when I was thinner. Jacob, you can borrow one of my husband's, which is the third one from the left."

"We're fine," Jacob repeated.

"Don't be so ridiculous. I'm not interested in seeing either of you with your clothes off. Let me know when you've done it and I can look around again."

Beside him, Ella was already peeling off her soaking outer layers. He waited another minute, then gave in to the inevitable and did as he'd been told. Ella's back gleamed with damp. Was there a towel he could dry her with? And would there ever be a time when he could see this gradual unwrapping of her flesh and not look for excuses to touch? Thank God for Mrs Armitage's chaperonage. He grabbed for the wetsuit and dragged it up over his legs, trying to suppress the feeling that he was putting on a dead man's skin. The harsh light of the lamp was dimming.

"Oh, for goodness sake." Mrs Armitage's hand reached for the lamp as its light sank down to a faint blue-white glow, then faded. "The batteries need changing. I have spares. Don't start crashing around in the dark, please, or you'll break things."

He stood as still as he could, but in the darkness it was difficult to hold his balance. He reached out for the wall to steady himself, and brushed against something warm and soft. For an intoxicating moment, Ella leaned against him and he felt her breath against his bare chest, the briefest caress of her lips against his shoulder. Was there any feeling more treacherously lovely than knowing the woman you longed for desired you too? They heard something being unwrapped, the click of metal and plastic, and the light blazed out once more, turning everything it caught as ugly as it could. Jacob pulled up his wetsuit, feeling it grip around his throat like a hand. Mrs Armitage turned around, gave a strangled shriek and dropped the lamp.

"What's the matter?" The lamp, miraculously, was not broken.

"Nothing. I just wasn't expecting – that wetsuit wasn't the one I thought you were going to wear. I said the third one from the left of the door."

"I'm sorry." Jacob looked blankly at the suits on the wall, then at the thick neoprene that held him like a cocoon. The one he'd failed to correctly choose had a tomato-red body and navy legs. The one he wore was plain black with a small white flash across the chest. What unspoken code of wetsuit borrowing had he failed to understand? "Um – was this your husband's best one or something?"

"It wasn't my husband's. It belonged to his friend. It doesn't matter." Mrs Armitage's voice was very steady, but her hands were trembling. "Ella, there are some chairs folded against the wall. Pass one to me, please, and then get one for you and one for Jacob and we can sit by the stove and get warm."

Jacob felt ridiculous in his wetsuit and the fabric was stiff and uncomfortable. He took his place next to Ella by the stove. His feet were like blocks of ice, but the rest of him was beginning to feel warm. Perhaps if he sat here for long enough, the storm might blow the roof off and he and Ella would be dragged up into the air and drift away into the stars.

"So what are you going to do about all of this?" Mrs Armitage asked, skinning back the lid of a can of soup. When she poured it into the saucepan, the contents looked like vomit.

"You can stay with us," said Ella.

"Sweet girl." Mrs Armitage shook her head. "Not that."

"I don't know what you mean," said Jacob. "We're not – we weren't –"

"I understand," said Mrs Armitage. "You didn't mean it to happen. Lovers never do."

Suddenly his skin inside the wetsuit was far too hot. He'd never felt so naked in his life.

"It's all right," said Mrs Armitage. "Ella, stop looking at me as if I'm going to throw you in jail. There are worse things you could have done, the two of you."

"No there aren't," said Ella.

"Of course there are. Have you destroyed a marriage? Hurt anyone? Killed anyone? No one's died, for goodness sakes. What? Speak up, Ella, I can't hear you properly."

"I said, maybe it might be better if we did die," Ella whispered.

"Don't be so ridiculous. Do you want to hear a story about the real damage love can do? I knew a woman once who killed two men because she couldn't choose between them, and she still hasn't paid the price for what she did."

Ella smiled faintly. "You don't need to make stuff up to make me feel better. I'm not six any more."

"I'm not making anything up. I never make anything up.

This story is the truth. The woman was married, very happily, to a man who gave her everything she wanted. But then she met the man's best friend, and she realised she wanted him as well. She could have looked away again. But she didn't. You're thinking none of that could possibly be as bad as falling in love with her own brother, but that's because you don't know the whole story yet. Ask me what happened."

"What happened?" Ella said obediently.

"She knew the other man would find it hard to betray his best friend, but she also knew he liked her. So she told him little stories about how their marriage was. She didn't lie, exactly, but she didn't tell the whole truth either. She made the other man believe that her husband was thoughtless and neglectful and cruel, and that she was trapped and desperately unhappy. And over time, she persuaded him into her bed." She lifted the saucepan from the stove. "Ella, put the kettle on instead, please, while I serve this."

Jacob took the tin bowl of soup Mrs Armitage offered. The warmth was comforting against his fingers.

"Of course," Mrs Armitage continued, "then he wanted to do the decent thing. He wanted them to both leave her husband, and make a new life somewhere else. But she didn't want that. She never had. She liked the life she had already. The only thing she'd been missing was a bit of fun on the side, and now she had that too so she was perfectly content. So she told her lover that her husband would never, ever let her go, that he was quite mad and very dangerous and often hurt her, and he would quite definitely kill her if he ever found out about what she'd been doing behind his back. And then she told her lover that they couldn't see each other for a while."

But at least they weren't brother and sister, Jacob thought wretchedly.

"She was quite clever, this woman," Mrs Armitage continued, "and she knew her lover would do as he was told. Not because he was afraid for himself, but for her. She thought everything would quieten down for a few weeks, and then she'd find a way for them both to be alone and everything would pick up where they'd left off. But she wasn't quite clever enough to realise how convincing she'd been. She didn't realise until the two men went out on a boat. It was a dangerous night, quite like this one, but they should have seen the storm coming and got back to land safely. Only they didn't. The boat sank. And the men drowned. And it was all her fault."

"How was it her fault?" asked Ella.

"Because," said Mrs Armitage, "I've been out to the wreck site, and the boat didn't sink. It was scuttled. He was so disgusted with what he'd done, with what he thought his best friend might do, that he killed them both."

"Oh my God."

"There is no God," said Mrs Armitage. "There's only us, and the terrible things we do for love."

Outside, the rain beat on the roof like an enemy.

"That's the worst thing I've ever done to someone I love," said Mrs Armitage into the electric silence. "Jacob, how about you?"

"No."

"Yes," said Mrs Armitage.

"I'm not discussing that with you."

"Please stop thinking I give a damn about what you and Ella choose to do together."

"Then please stop asking about it."

"I'm not. I'm asking you why you give your father sleeping tablets during the day."

"I – I don't –"

"Yes," said Mrs Armitage, "you do."

"It's not Jacob's fault." Jacob was startled and touched to hear the protective anger in Ella's voice. "Don't you dare judge him for that. You've got no idea what it's like."

"I take care of him every day while Jacob's at work."

"And does he hit you?" Ella was so angry she was trembling. "Are you covered in bruises from where he's gone

298

for you with anything he could get his hands on? No, Jacob, I'm not going to shut up, she needs to know."

"No!" Jacob shook his head in despair. "She's right, okay?" He made himself meet Mrs Armitage's gaze. "You're right. I should do better with him, I know I should. It's just – sometimes I'm afraid…"

"Of your father?" The kettle was beginning to sing. Mrs Armitage poured hot water into mugs.

"Yes."

"No," said Mrs Armitage, and offered him a mug of tea.

"Stop giving me things!" He took the mug anyway. "Would you please just leave me alone?"

"Be honest with me. Or I can't help you. Why do you drug him? No, Ella, don't answer for him. Jacob, tell us both."

"Okay, I give in! I'm afraid of myself, okay? What *I* might do. Because if I hit him back harder, or pushed him down the stairs – who would ever know? He's got no way of telling anyone. And so – and so, on the days when I know I can't face dealing with him, I – I mean, it's better than hitting him back, isn't it? At least if he's asleep he's not getting hurt, I know he's safe and looked after."

"So why do you keep him with you?" There was no passion in Mrs Armitage's voice, only a gentle relentless ruthlessness.

"Because I love him," Jacob said.

"Even though he hardly knows where he is most of the time? Even though he forgets how old you are and what he's doing with you and barely realises how much you do for him? Even when he hits you because he's frightened and he forgets you're on his side?"

"Yes."

"And even though you shout at him sometimes, and drug him when you need some space for yourself, you still love him?"

"Yes, I do! I chose to look after him, nobody made me. And I know I don't always do very well at it, I do know that, but – well, it's the best I could manage, okay?"

"Ella?" Mrs Armitage's voice was softer when she spoke to Ella, as if Ella merited special treatment, but this time he felt no jealousy. It had not been Mrs Armitage's affection he craved after all, but his sister's. "Do you know what terrible mistake you've made out of love?"

Ella raised her chin. "I thought you said it wasn't terrible."

"I mean your mother. You read her book, didn't you?"

"Is that so terrible? I thought it might be about her life. About her first husband, stalking her."

"A book where people change their skins and turn into animals and disappear? You thought that might help you find your mother?"

"Don't you laugh at her," said Jacob.

"I'm not laughing at her," said Mrs Armitage. "I'm trying to help her see. But since you ask, what do you think? Was your mother writing about her own life?"

"I suppose she might have been. I mean, magic realist writers often use fantasy elements to explore difficult themes –" He stopped himself, embarrassed. "I'm sounding like a teacher."

"So stop it! Think like a human being for once, not a reader. The man who stalked her, could he be real? Is it even possible?"

"Well, no, not exactly the way she wrote about him, I suppose, but –"

"But," said Ella, "it wasn't only Mum. Dad knew about the man too. He did! He talked about him! Didn't he?"

"Yes. He did!" Jacob heard the triumph in his voice. "They both saw him. That's why we moved so often – because he was looking for them, and they couldn't let him find them. They used to talk about it sometimes – well, they used to argue really – after we were in bed."

"And does that seem likely to you? That a man would hunt your family for years, stalking your mother? Did you never wonder why your parents didn't go to the police?"

"Well, because – because – I mean, I suppose –" There had to be a flaw in this somewhere that he wasn't seeing. Mrs

Armitage was right. Going to the police was the logical thing to do. Why had that never happened?

"Because Dad was making it all up," said Ella. "I know you don't like me saying this, Jacob, but it's the truth." She raised her hand to her mouth, caught hold of a loose peeling of skin next to her nail and tugged sharply with her teeth. A bead of blood bloomed in the wound. "Maybe the man was real once, but not by the end."

"Dad saw him."

"He *said* he saw him."

"And why would he do that?" Mrs Armitage was watching them intently, willing them both to see something that remained beyond Jacob's grasp.

"Because he thought the man was real," said Jacob stubbornly. "He wouldn't deliberately upset her, not ever. He loved her."

"Because he wanted to make Mum afraid," said Ella. "He was afraid she was going to leave him. And whenever he thought she was getting restless or making plans, he used to tell her he'd seen the man again, and she'd be so frightened –"

"He was trying to keep her safe!"

"How was he keeping her safe?" It was a shock to see Ella angry. "By giving her stuff to make her sleep all the time and telling her someone was coming to get her? He damaged her. She never got over it. Even after she'd left him she was terrified he'd come after her."

"The problem with you, Jacob," said Mrs Armitage, "is that you put too much faith in your father. And you – " she nodded at Ella – "have too much faith in your mother. Imagine this story wasn't written down. Imagine it was someone sitting here, talking to you. Imagine a woman, sitting here, telling you that she was being pursued everywhere by a man who could change his face and that sometimes she thought he swapped places with her husband. What would you think these things mean?"

Jacob shrugged. "I don't know."

"That's because you're not imagining it. Do as I'm telling you, Jacob. Imagine that exact moment I described. Close your eyes if it helps."

He closed his eyes, then opened them again. It had been so long since he'd seen his mother that her image had been replaced with the single picture he'd kept. She had never been a real woman at all, only ever an image in a photograph of his sister, frozen in that one moment of laughter. Mrs Armitage's gaze never left his face.

"I don't know why you're asking me this," he said, exasperated. "I mean, it's *not* someone telling me the story, it's something that's been written down. And writing's different, the rules are different. Of course none of it could happen in real life. You'd have to be mad to think it could."

Mrs Armitage's eyes glittered. "Say that again."

"You'd have to be mad to think it could happen? Well, of course you would, but –"

"Yes. You would. You would have to be very, very mad indeed. Your stepmother is mad, Jacob, and she always has been. Didn't you realise, either of you? Didn't you ever suspect?"

The stove clicked and bubbled. The rain rattled against the roof. A draught of wind crept around the back of Jacob's neck and raised the little hairs there.

"She isn't," said Ella.

"Of course she is. There never was a man stalking her. Not while she was with your father. Not after she left him. It was all in her mind."

"No."

"Yes. You know that's the truth, my dear, you just haven't been ready to face it yet."

"But she saw him! She did! I wasn't even allowed to have my photograph taken at school –"

"And did anyone else ever see him? Did anyone come to the door? When your mother said people were following you, did you ever see the same person twice?"

"But she looked after me. She took me to school. She had jobs. She organised places for us to live. She can't possibly have been –"

"She did her very, very best for you, Ella. She wasn't perfect, but she loved you very much. She looked after you as well as she could, for as long as she could. And then, as soon as she thought you were old enough to manage by yourself, she left you alone."

"Stop talking about her as if she's dead! She's not dead."

"Maybe you're right. Maybe she'll come back to you when she can. Or maybe she thinks you're better off without her now. But I promise you, living or dead, your mother is in no danger from the man she wrote about. He never existed outside of her head. And your father knew it. But he loved her anyway. He was trying to keep her safe, but from herself."

"But why didn't he get some help for her? Surely she would have been better being looked after in a hospital?"

"Because he loved her," said Jacob. "And he thought he was the only one who could look after her properly."

In the silence that followed, Jacob reached for Ella's hand, telling himself it was a brotherly gesture of solidarity. The shape of her bones was so perfect beneath the skin. Her bitten nails, the chirpy beetle-blue nail polish that had flaked off in patches, were so poignant they hurt his heart. He'd found his soulmate, but there was no future for them. How could they ever get married? What would they do if they wanted children? How were they going to live? How could anyone live with the dreadful beauty of what had grown between them? She was thinking the same as he was: he could feel it through her skin. There was no hope for either of them. He felt Mrs Armitage's gaze on him, and looked up at her defiantly.

"It's time," she said.

"What?" Jacob's head was spinning. "Where are we going?"

"You're both wearing wetsuits. Where do you think you're going?"

"But isn't that because we were soaking wet? I thought we were going to wait here until the storm passed over?"

"She's going to take us out in the boat," said Ella. "Aren't you?"

"What?" Jacob laughed. "No, of course she's not going to take us out in the –"

"Yes, I am."

"You are bloody well not. What are you thinking?"

"Why not?"

"Because – because – well, look at the state of the weather!"

Mrs Armitage's expression was almost eerily calm, as if Jacob was the peculiar one for objecting. "I know. The storm. It's dangerous. But this is the only way I can help you."

"We don't need your help!"

"Of course you do. You'd both have stayed on that beach until you died of cold if I hadn't made you leave. I can show you a way to solve everything. But you have to trust me. Unless you want to leave now? You're not prisoners, you're free to go."

Ella's hand was warm and real in his. Perhaps falling in love with her was the only real thing that had ever happened to him. If they drowned, at least they'd be together for ever. When he looked at Ella, he saw his own thought written on her face.

"Fine," he said. "Let's go."

As they slithered through the rain to the pontoons that writhed and shuddered and tried to throw them off, Jacob heard another deep rumble. Was that thunder? Or was it the sea, taking his house for its own?

Even in the shelter of the marina, the boats were like restless sleepers. Out in the bay, Mrs Armitage's motor-launch rode the swell like a seagull. Sick and terrified, Jacob and Ella clung together in the wheelhouse where Mrs Armitage stood.

"Where are we going?" Ella asked. Her throat was hoarse.

"To see my husband."

"But – he's – isn't he dead?"

"Yes. Drowned on the bottom of the sea. Along with his best friend. When the world turns stormy, there's no better place to be. Put those BCDs on."

Jacob stared at the diving gear lashed against the wheel-house wall. "How does it go on?"

"The way you'd think it goes on. Ella, you've done this before, help him. I need to watch the GPS and keep us afloat. You're reasonably bright children, you'll work it out."

He thought about arguing. But why bother? They'd come this far. Why not follow this madness through to its end? He kept as still as he could while she helped him, wincing when a tip of the boat sent her shuffling across the deck. The weight against his shoulders was immense and unexpected. How did Ella stand it?

"Is this right?" he asked.

Mrs Armitage glanced at them indifferently. Despite the pitching of the waves and the sickening sensation that the boat was about to spill over, she balanced effortlessly, seemingly a part of the boat she was steering. "Close enough. You'll need weight belts as well. In that crate. One each."

"I can't. I'm too heavy. The boat's moving too much."

"You can and you will. Ella, take that torch."

Feeling as if he was carrying an extra person on his back, he wrestled with the crate. The weight belts dragged at his hips. "What about you?"

"Now your flippers. No, not that way, the other way. Spit in your mask, it's fogging up. Watch Ella, she'll show you." Holding tight to the ropes strung along the edge of the boat, Mrs Armitage made her way over to them and fumbled at the tanks on their backs. "Gloves on. That's right. The valves are open. Get ready. We're nearly there."

"But aren't you coming with us? Aren't we supposed to go down and come up at a certain rate? How long do we have? How do we breathe? What if we get lost?"

Her smile was bright and dreadful, and he realised with a

305

shock that Mrs Armitage was, in her own way, as mad as she claimed his mother was.

"I won't need diving equipment. I don't think we'll meet again, so I'll say this – it's been interesting getting to know you both. By the way, Ella, here's one last thing you need to know: you look absolutely nothing like your father."

"But –"

"Regulators in," said Mrs Armitage, and jammed a rigid plastic plug against Jacob's teeth. "Breathe out as you go down. You'll have about an hour, but the deeper you go and the faster you breathe, the sooner the air will run out. If you decide to come back, do it slowly. At least two minutes from the bottom to the top. I'm sorry I can't do any better, but we're simply out of time. Say hello to my husband and my lover for me."

Then a hard hand pushed at the centre of his chest, and Jacob was falling backwards, over the side of the boat and down into the water.

I try to sew together the edges of my life, but it keeps tearing apart again. I think maybe it's the bits of my skin that aren't strong enough any more, because if you keep picking and unpicking at the places where you've sewn yourself back together then eventually the fabric unravels and you're left in pieces on the floor. There's something sharp and true hidden in all this mess, like a needle in a haystack. We had sex in a haystack once, when I was still running and he was still keeping me hidden and we couldn't let anyone see us, in the days before we were married. I remember the way the straw scratched the back of my neck like needles.

Soon I'll be the woman in the mirror, that older colder woman who nobody loves, walking through the fields with her gloves on so nothing can touch her skin. I need to set everything in my life free first, leave behind all the things I thought I loved so I can go back to my home, like the woman in the fairy-tale I heard once but never really understood. Her husband tried to keep her skin from her but she found it in the chest. I tried to open up my chest once, but it hurt too much and I couldn't find the key.

He tried so hard to keep hold of her, to keep her locked away, but her veins were full of sea-water and she was always bound to get away from him in the end. You can't keep hold of water, it slips through your fingers. He was always the shapeshifter but now it's my turn. I've been writing this book for so long I thought I would never finish it, but I think this is the end at last. I've written all the words I have in me. So now, all I have to do is to draw a picture of a woman who is nothing like me, and then the picture will come to life and she will stay behind and take care of my life while I slip away to somewhere nobody will ever find me.

Chapter Twenty-one
Now

At first there was nothing but shock and blackness, and the gasp of his lungs as the water slapped him in the back and then drew him under. He felt himself sinking, began to panic, realised he was holding his breath, and fumbled for what Mrs Armitage had told him before pushing him over the side. *Breathe out as you go down.* But what if there was nothing else to breathe in? He shut his eyes and forced himself to exhale, then sucked frantically at his regulator. Air filled his lungs. He exhaled again and let the weight take him down.

The chop of the water vanished almost immediately. To his surprise, he realised he felt safer and more secure below the surface of the waves than above it. He'd been here before, after all; they both had. All those nights in the bathtub with the water filling their ears, trying to be as still as possible, as quiet as possible, listening out for the slow steady count in the corner of the room. *One and fifteen. One and sixteen. One and seventeen.* When he closed his eyes he could imagine he was there once more. When he opened them, Ella floated in front of him in a bubble of torchlight, her hair drifting like seaweed.

He blinked inside his mask, tried to make himself understand that this was real, it was really happening. Above their heads, the storm raged, and their house might fall into the sea, but they were safe below the water, for as long as their breath could last.

Where should they go? He had some idea they were supposed to descend slowly to avoid bubbles of gas getting trapped in their blood; or was that only on the way back up? If only they could stay forever.

Ella pointed the beam of light down towards the bottom. The water was soupy and silty, stirred up by the storm, but perhaps it would be clearer further down. A minute later she was slipping slowly through the water, propelled by the slow flick of her flippered feet. He hesitated a moment longer, then followed her.

The feeling was extraordinary. He'd been set free from his two-dimensional crawl across the earth's surface. He wanted to laugh, but wasn't sure if it was safe. A large silver-brown fish cruised across his vision, hesitated as if surprised to see him, then swam on. When he came to rest beside Ella, he could make out the dim raggedy shape of something that looked unmistakeably man-made, resting on its side, half-sunk into the mud.

As they grew closer to the wreck, they could see the out-lines more clearly. The boat was in a shape that Jacob vaguely thought of as denoting a fishing boat, with an enclosed wheelhouse and a long deck. It wore a fringe of weeds and shells, and fat clumps of anemones put out delicate tendrils. If they stayed here beneath the sea, they'd have their own garden. They could live in the wheelhouse, spear fish as they passed. They swam on, Ella slightly ahead of him, a stream of bubbles rising up behind her. Then she came to a slow halt, paddling frantically to try and slow her momentum, the light wavering over the surface of the boat.

The wreck was already occupied. Two tumbled collections of bones, browned with algae and stirred by the movement of water and the nosings of curious fish, so long in the water they could be mistaken for the first slow beginnings of coral, for the curved branches of seaweed. But there was no mistaking the smooth round dome of the skulls with the black caves of the eye sockets turned upwards towards them. *And there were all little fishes swimming in and out of our eyes, and crabs crawling over our heads.* The nightmare she'd described so many times to him, the terror that had haunted her childhood.

But it was not them, not yet. They were still alive, still breathing. These bones were the bones of the two men who, Mrs Armitage believed, were dead because of what she'd done. Why had she risked all their deaths and the safety of her boat to send him down here with his sister to look at this? If she'd wanted to keep them safe, she would have let them stay on land. Instead she'd forced them out into the storm and into the deceptive peace of this alien place where they were almost certainly the only two humans for hundreds of miles. No one knew they were here. No one would come looking for them. If they stayed here, they would never be found.

It was a replaying of his own fantasy. *If only we could be alone somewhere no one would ever find us. If only we could leave the world behind.* And the darker thought that had come to him as they set off into the storm. *If we die now, at least we'll be together forever.*

That was what Mrs Armitage had done, the help she was offering them. She'd sent them down here so they could die.

Was this what they wanted? What was there left for them back on dry land? His father, locked in his hotel room and awaiting discovery by the housekeeper. His job, which he had never loved, and which would only become less lovable with time. His house, which might be already gone. A life without love.

He looked at the boat and wondered which man was which. If he stayed here too, there would be three men here who had died for love. Did they think it was worth it for that brief mad ecstasy? If he swam down to join them, Ella would never follow. That was the way, he realised; he would stay here, and Ella would return to the surface. She was stronger than him. She would find a life without him.

311

He tried to swim down towards the deck, but Ella had hold of his arm. He tried to make her let go, but she shook her head. He pointed to her, then upwards towards the surface of the water. She shook her head again. With some effort, he prised her fingers off his arm, then tried to give her a final hug, but she simply floated out of his reach, her gaze steady within the constrictive seal of her face-mask.

He was going to have to leave her without that final comfort, then. She was right. No good could come of pro-longing it. As soon as he began to descend to the wreck she would understand.

He could feel the temperature dropping as he descended, but soon that wouldn't matter any more. It shouldn't take long, this dying business. What was it Mrs Armitage had said, about the air running out quicker the farther down you went? He had no idea how long they'd been here, and no idea how to read the gauges that hung at his side. He only knew that death would come, as inevitable as the tide. The boat was nearly upon him now; his flippers grazed the slime of the deck. He was surprised to find he could still see. Ella must be pointing the torch downwards to guide him.

He looked up to give her a final acknowledgement, a last glimpse of her to take with him into the dark, and found she was almost on top of him, and then beside him, the stream of bubbles growing stronger as she took deep panicky breaths, but still she came, letting her feet touch the deck with barely a shudder. She turned her face towards the place where the remains of the two men lay, forcing herself to confront them. A crab tiptoed delicately across the deck towards her flippered foot. He saw the moment when she realised, saw the heave of terror in her chest and the thick plume of bubbles rising. Then she closed her eyes and put her hand over her belly, willing herself back to a place of calm, and then she opened her eyes again and sat down on the deck.

He shook his head. She folded her arms. He pointed again at the surface, willing her to understand. He was the older

312

one. He was responsible for her. He was supposed to keep her safe. He'd failed in every way he thought a person could fail, but he would succeed this time. He fastened his fingers around her arms and pushed her away, taking deep greedy draughts of air, knowing this would drain his tank even more quickly and glad to know it. If he could only get her away from the boat, she would never dare the descent a second time. But the moment he let her go, she was back with him again. Her meaning was unmistakable. *I'm staying with you.*

He wanted to take out his regulator and yell at her, but what would be the point? His words would dissolve in the water. And what could he say? He wanted to tell her, *I'm staying here so you can be free,* but what if she didn't believe him? He was so tired. Even buoyed up by the water, he could feel the tremble of fatigue in the muscles of his legs. He took another breath. It felt strangely difficult this time, as if someone had narrowed the hose. Perhaps it was the pressure of the water. He exhaled, watching the stream of bubbles rise. He took another breath, felt the same strange resistance. What was happening?

The answer came to him on the third breath: he must be running out of air. This was it, then. He was here, on the bottom of the sea, among the dead where he belonged.

Now his only remaining task was to convince Ella to leave him behind. Another deep, difficult breath, as if he was sucking something thick from the bottom of a glass. He was beginning to feel dizzy. He pushed weakly at Ella, pointing again to the surface. Ella looked at his gauge, and then pointed imperiously up towards the surface.

He shook his head. *No.* She pointed again, her gestures frantic. Again he refused. She took him by the shoulders and shook him, then spread her arms wide. *Why are you doing this?* He made the shape of a heart with his hands. *Because I love you.* His hands felt clumsy. Was that the gloves? Or was it the lack of oxygen? He let his hands fall apart. *And my heart is broken.*

He tried for one more breath. The edges of his vision were

beginning to dim. In another moment Ella would leave him. This was how it had to be. This was the right and proper end for everything he had done and not done: to let it all be washed away by the North Sea and buried in the mud. He could go into the darkness knowing he had done one good thing, one pure and beautiful deed to make up for all the ways he'd failed. His body hurt and his chest hurt and there was a terrible pressure building in his lungs, but soon that would all stop. Soon the fish would pick his ribcage naked and swim between it with clean little flicks of their bodies. He would be free. And so would Ella. He closed his eyes. Would it hurt to die? Or would he be drawn into a quiet dark tunnel and on into endless peace? his lungs were convulsing, painfully dragging the last few ounces of air, but there was a bright light around him now, and he felt as if he was floating.

Then someone tugged at his regulator, and even though it was now near useless he felt in some primitive way that he needed to keep hold of it. He clamped his teeth around it, but then it was gone, and he tasted salt for a moment before something else was jammed in there, and before he could stop himself he took a long deep breath, easy and painless this time, and he felt life rushing back into his resisting body. When he opened his eyes he slowly realised what had happened: Ella had taken out her own regulator and forced it into his mouth, and she now hovered in front of him in the water, floating in the column of light that came up from the torch, abandoned on the deck of the boat.

Hadn't he made himself clear? Life wasn't what he wanted. He snatched the regulator from his mouth, nodded in satisfaction as Ella took it back and drew her own deep breath. Then she offered it to him once more.

He shook his head. He'd tried so hard to do the right thing. All he wanted was to set her free. He could still do it. All he had to do was get past his primitive terror and open his mouth and let the water flood into his lungs.

She floated in front of him, beautiful in the dim torchlight.

The regulator floated between them. Was she ever going to take it? He tried to read her expression. Using her teeth, she took off one glove, then put her hand gently against his face.

You won't need to be afraid, ever, because we'll be together.

She was going to make him keep his promise. He took the regulator between his teeth and took a deep, blessed gulp of air. Only then did Ella take it back from him and do the same.

Holding tight to each other, ascending as slowly as they dared, they rose through the peaceful depths and back towards the turbulent surface.

He had no idea how long the journey back to the air took them. He only knew that he was sick with exhaustion and his body felt as if it weighed a thousand tons. He was alive only through the force of Ella's will, as she dragged him up through the thick weight of water and forced him to draw air from her tank.

He knew they had reached the surface when the air hit him round the face and forced him to open his eyes. The storm was subsiding, leaving behind a choppy sea and a relentless mizzling rain. He tried to tread water, but the weight of the equipment was like trying to hold up the earth on his shoulders. Ella was shouting something, but he couldn't hear her over the roaring of the water against his ears. He felt her fumble around his waist, and then the release as the weights dropped from his hips. Her hands were on the front of his chest, unfastening the clips that held his tank to his back. A quick shrug of his shoulders and the whole useless lot of it was making its way towards the bottom of the sea.

Ella shed her own equipment, then grabbed for his arm and pointed towards the spot where something loomed inter-mittently between the sheets of rain. It was Mrs Armitage's boat, not drowned and not set adrift, but waiting for them like an obedient dog. The boat looked almost impossibly tall and he had no idea how they would ever scale its sleek sides, but as they grew nearer they saw there was a rope ladder dangling near the stern.

"Come on!" Ella was at him again, almost slapping him, forcing him to stay with her. "Climb up!"

"I can't. I'm sorry. I just can't."

"You have to." She had thrown away her mask along with her tank and belt. The rubber seal had left red indents in her skin. "We have to get out of the water."

He took hold of the first rung, but his limbs were as limp and boneless as seaweed. "I just feel so tired."

She was close enough to kiss him. Another moment, and she was kissing him. He thought her tongue must be the last warm thing left in this world. "You can do it. You can do anything."

And because he would do anything to please her, he found that he could do it, and somehow he was struggling up the rope ladder and onto the smooth wet wood of the deck, and he could finally rest.

He lay flat for what felt like a long time, long enough to drift into a half-dream where he was back in his own bed and the house was filling with water and his bed was floating away. The sea was soaking into his covers and making him cold. No, it wasn't, he was cold because he was out in the rain on Mrs Armitage's boat, sprawled on the deck as if he'd been harpooned. The roaring in his ears had subsided, and he could hear water smacking against wood. Was Mrs Armitage waiting for him to wake up, with words of sharp comfort and difficult questions about what had happened to her scuba gear? He imagined her expression and cringed.

But then again, he could have been dead right now. His flesh could have already begun to bloat and swell in the gloom of the wreck. At least he was alive. Whatever came next, for now he was alive. He slowly sat up and looked around, but saw only Ella, propped against the side, as pale as her own ghost.

"Mrs Armitage? Mrs Armitage?" Was there a part of the boat he hadn't seen? Some below-decks space, perhaps? The boat was tiny, there was no way she could be hiding from them, but he stumbled around anyway, convinced that he must have missed the sight of her.

"She's not here," said Ella.

"She must be. She wouldn't leave her boat."

"She's gone. She said she was going and now she has. She's left us, Jacob. She's gone back home."

"How can she possibly have –" Exhaustion was making him stupid. He felt his eyes prickle with tears. "She's gone into the water, hasn't she? She's drowned."

"Maybe she hasn't drowned. Remember when we first met her and we thought she was a seal? Maybe she put on her other skin and went back home to her people."

"Do you really believe that?"

She looked straight at him. "Don't you?"

He was too tired to know what he believed. He only knew his oldest and kindest friend was gone, and his house might well be gone too, and his father and mother were both lost, and he was out on the ocean in a boat he didn't know how to pilot and the future was a blank to him. He let the tears fall for a while, leaning against Ella for comfort, knowing from the way her chest heaved and the small hurt sounds that crept out from her that she was weeping too.

"Why did you save me?" he asked at last, when their tears began to dry up along with the rain, and a watery shaft of sunshine shot from the grey sky and into the water, then disappeared again. "I was willing to stay down there. And you could have had your whole life without me. That was what Mrs Armitage wanted, wasn't it? For me to set you free."

"No," said Ella, with conviction. "That wasn't it. She sent us down there so we wouldn't drown trying to save her."

"But then why bring us out here at all? She knew about – us – remember? She knew what I did. And she knew the only way for me to fix it was to leave you for ever."

"It wasn't what you did," said Ella. "It was what *we* did, both of us together. And I know what you were trying to do,

317

but I couldn't leave you down there, I couldn't! If it was going to be either of us, it should have been me."

"No! Don't you dare say that, Ella, don't ever ever say that, please –"

"Yes, it should. Whatever happened to Mum – seeing things, imagining people following her – what if it happens to me too? It can be inherited, can't it? It might be in me right now. I mean, there's got to be something wrong with me, hasn't there, for me to fall in love with –" Even now, she couldn't make herself say the words.

"I don't care. I love you, I'll always love you, no matter what happens to you. Nothing's ever going to change that."

"I bet Dad thought that once too. He must have realised what was wrong and thought he could cope. But he didn't, did he? It destroyed them both in the end. I don't want that to happen to us. And even if it didn't – we'd still be looking over our shoulders every day, wondering if someone was going to realise. We couldn't have children, God only knows what they might end up with. I ought to have stayed down there on the wreck. I did think about it. But your air was running out and I knew you'd never get back to the surface on your own and I was too afraid –"

And there it was again, that helpless, irresistible tug that drew them together even as they knew it was doomed and hopeless. She was soaked and scruffy, her face and hair speckled with grains of seaweed and streaked with tears, but she was the love of his heart and she always would be. He put his arms around her. There was no one to see them, out here in the sliver of space between the grey sea and the grey sky. And besides, who was there left in the world that would care?

"She was the last one who knew," he said wonderingly. "She was the only one who knows you're my sister. And now she's gone too." He kissed the top of Ella's head. "What did she say to you again? Before she pushed us in, I mean?"

"Oh." Ella shrugged. "She said I look absolutely nothing like Dad."

They sat in silence for a while, feeling the boat rock beneath them.

"What do you think she meant?" Jacob asked.

"Just that I don't look like Dad, I suppose. I mean, I don't, do I? You look more like Dad and I look more like Mum."

"But she must have had a reason to say that to you. She knew we'd never see her again. Ella, have you ever seen your birth certificate?"

"Maybe. I don't really remember."

"Was Dad's name on it?"

"I don't know." She turned around in Jacob's arms so she could look at his face. "Why?"

"There were two men in her book, weren't there? She left the first one to be with Dad. But we don't know when it happened, because they never told us. All I remember is Dad bringing her home to meet me, and then a few months after that, you were born. But Mrs Armitage was right. You don't look anything like Dad. I know I do, I see him in me all the time, but you don't. And you never have."

Ella's eyes were huge and brimming with tears.

"But then –"

"Is it possible, do you think? Is that what she meant?"

"But you're my brother," she said. "Whatever happens, you *are*. Even if we're not related, we grew up together. We're brother and sister." She held his hand against her cheek. "Aren't we?"

"I don't know," he said, and kissed her. "I don't know anything any more. But it will be okay. It will."

When he looked again at the sky, he saw that it was clearing, and a thin shadow of land was beginning to appear through the rain. At the end of the boat, a thick rope hung from a winch and over the side. That must be the anchor. They would have to haul it in, and then they would have to work out how to start the engine, and somehow find their way back to land; to land, and to whatever would come next in their lives.

Acknowledgements

The first and most important thank you belongs to my amazing editor Lauren Parsons, and everyone else on the Legend team. Thank you for inviting and encouraging me to write *Underwater Breathing*, and for all you do to support us all in becoming Legendary authors.

A special thank you to my lovely friend Krista Wood for advice on police procedures, to Shirley Gubb for advice on nursing and medicine, and to everyone who joined in my Facebook thread speculating on the dissolution properties of various prescription tablets in warm drinks. Like most writers, I have a Google history that makes me look like an uncaught serial criminal, but your brilliant (and almost alarmingly non-judgey!) advice saved me from looking even more arrestable than usual.

Thank you to Louise Beech, Vicky Foster, Michelle Dee, Linda Harrison and Julie Corbett. You are truly the Sisterly of Hull, and I'm honoured every day to be one of you.

Thank you to my daughter Becky for making sure I remember to leave the house at least once a day, and to my son Ben for asking such brilliant questions at my book launches. You're the most amazing support team a writer could ask for.

Most of all, to my husband Tony – none of this would be possible without you, but for *Underwater Breathing*, I owe you even more than usual. Thank you.